The Happy Hour Choir

The Happy Hour Choir

Sally Kilpatrick

KENSINGTON BOOKS
www.kensingtonbooks.com

This book is a work of fiction. Names, characters, places, and incidents either are products of the author's imagination or are used fictitiously. Any resemblance to actual persons, living or dead, events, or locales is entirely coincidental.

KENSINGTON BOOKS are published by

Kensington Publishing Corp.
119 West 40th Street
New York, NY 10018

All Kensington titles, imprints, and distributed lines are available at special quantity discounts for bulk purchases for sales promotion, premiums, fund-raising, educational, or institutional use.

Special book excerpts or customized printings can also be created to fit specific needs. For details, write or phone the office of the Kensington Sales Manager: Kensington Publishing Corp., 119 West 40th Street, New York, NY 10018. Attn. Sales Department. Phone: 1-800-221-2647.

Kensington and the K logo Reg. U.S. Pat. & TM Off.

eISBN-13: 978-1-61773-569-1
eISBN-10: 1-61773-569-8
First Kensington Electronic Edition: May 2015

ISBN-13: 978-1-61773-568-4
ISBN-10: 1-61773-568-X
First Kensington Trade Paperback Printing: May 2015

10 9 8 7 6 5 4 3 2

Printed in the United States of America

For Ryan with love—
you're the best man I know

ACKNOWLEDGMENTS

Writing these thanks is even scarier than writing the book because I'm terrified I'll forget someone in the six years and three laptops that it's taken to get this novel published. Hopefully, in the tradition of the novel, I will be able to buy your forgiveness with beer.

First, to my mother who always told me to shoot for the moon—the stars are lovely, Mom—and to my father, who's always kept my feet on the ground. Thanks for a spectacularly normal childhood. And to my in-laws, aka bonus mom and dad, for their love, encouragement, and possible novel fodder.

It took more than a village to bring this novel to fruition—more like a metropolitan area. Thanks to Nikki and Peter, in particular, and Kensington, in general, for not only taking a chance on my quirky story but for also putting up with me. A gold star in each of your crowns!

Thanks to Tanya Michaels, the Statler to my Waldorf, and to Anna Steffl, my conference wife. Thanks also to Jenni McQuiston and Romily Bernard who "recruited" me to be a critique partner with them, and I am all the better for it. (See! Stalking really works!) Thanks to Nicki Salcedo [booty smack] and to Kim Brock of the Gumbo.

Thanks to Stephanie Bond, who gave such an encouraging Gin Ellis Critique and has taken the time to answer so many business questions. You rock, ma'am!

Thanks to Robin Hillyer-Miles, who wanted to read this story based on a contest submission and was one of the first to read it, and to Pam Mantovani, who gave some excellent thoughts—I'm still waiting for that Maggie mojo to kick in!

Thanks to all of the members of Melanie Sumner's women's fiction class where this baby was born and to Dianna Love and Mary Buckham in whose Break Into Fiction workshop I found the spark. I'm not forgetting you, Tony Grooms. Sorry about all that Persephone, but hopefully you'll see some of those lessons learned in this novel.

Thanks to all of these folks who beta read: Raymond Atkins, Jennifer Burress, Tamara LeBlanc, Debbie Kaufman, Marilyn

Estes, Tammy Brothers, Linsey Lanier, Aurora McBride-Moore, Cindy Koenemann-Warren, Katie Mae Poore, Gretchen Swales, Tonya Byrd, Denise Jordan Lane, Ashley Phillips, and Kimberly Knight, the self-proclaimed president of my fan club. Special thanks to Janette Gay, who's read almost all of my words since the very beginning.

Folks on the PRO Loop who helped me with the details of Ginger's cancer, thank you. Any mistakes there are mine and mine alone. Thanks to Bryan Black for our discussion of the Cokesbury and for putting up with me in the choir. Thanks to Sophie Kimble and all of my former teacher workmates; in a way you inspired this version of, ahem, choir practice. Oh, and Kari? Ask and ye shall receive.

To all of my Georgia Romance Writer peeps, thank you. I wouldn't have made it this far without all of the knowledge you dispense or the encouragement you give. I can't forget my current church home, First United Methodist, in Marietta, or my old church home, Pinson United Methodist. Thank you, Cyndi McDonald, for keeping me straight on all things Methodist—all errors are mine alone. Oh, and sorry you had to wait so long, Miss Wanda, but here it is.

When I finally found my voice, I discovered one important thing: community. I wouldn't be who I am without each person who has touched my life. Whether we met in high school or college or somewhere here in Georgia, you are all a part of me, and I thank you. If I listed you each by name, that'd be a separate book. Just know that I thought of you as I was writing this. Yes, you!

A million thanks to The Hobbit and Her Majesty, who've often had to forage for lunch or wear mismatched clothing of questionable cleanliness while Mommy wrote. I love you two more than words, which is something because I'm a writer.

Finally, thank you to Ryan, who gave me grad school as a gift just as I was ready to give up this crazy writer dream. Grad school trumps paper products, and I love you for everything that was, for everything that is, and everything still to come.

The Happy Hour Choir

Sally Kilpatrick

KENSINGTON BOOKS
www.kensingtonbooks.com

This book is a work of fiction. Names, characters, places, and incidents either are products of the author's imagination or are used fictitiously. Any resemblance to actual persons, living or dead, events, or locales is entirely coincidental.

KENSINGTON BOOKS are published by

Kensington Publishing Corp.
119 West 40th Street
New York, NY 10018

All Kensington titles, imprints, and distributed lines are available at special quantity discounts for bulk purchases for sales promotion, premiums, fund-raising, educational, or institutional use.

Special book excerpts or customized printings can also be created to fit specific needs. For details, write or phone the office of the Kensington Sales Manager: Kensington Publishing Corp., 119 West 40th Street, New York, NY 10018. Attn. Sales Department. Phone: 1-800-221-2647.

eISBN-13: 978-1-61773-569-1
eISBN-10: 1-61773-569-8
First Kensington Electronic Edition: May 2015

ISBN-13: 978-1-61773-568-4
ISBN-10: 1-61773-568-X
First Kensington Trade Paperback Printing: May 2015

10 9 8 7 6 5 4 3 2

Printed in the United States of America

Chapter 1

"Time to raise some hell and make some bank," I muttered to myself that night as I slammed the door to my ancient Toyota hatchback. The gravel parking lot of The Fountain was still empty, but soon it would fill up with old trucks and loud rednecks.

Unease skittered down my spine. I looked around, but everything seemed normal. The sun sank over the Graingers' pasture in front of me. County Line Methodist still sat across the road behind me. To my right, the cinder-block exterior of The Fountain hadn't changed since the fifties, but the parsonage across the parking lot had a light on.

Ah, someone was moving in. Probably another loudmouthed, double-chinned, potbellied, red-faced hypocrite like my father. To that I said, Let the games begin. No preacher had managed to stay longer than two years since one minister declared war on The Fountain back in the eighties. He hadn't counted on people's affection for Bill. Or for beer, for that matter.

"Ho there, Beulah," Bill said as I walked in. He scrubbed furiously at a wooden counter several generations older than I was. The counter was a holdover from when The Fountain had been the County Line Store, a respectable establishment where old men sat on five-gallon buckets to play checkers while drinking Cokes from glass bottles with peanuts in the bottom.

When the old men went the way of the dinosaurs, Bill made a startling discovery: His store actually sat in the neighboring county, a not-quite-as-dry county. The County Line Store was reborn as a place to buy your beer and even relax and knock one back with the boys. Entertainment in the boondocks was scarce, and that's why I eventually entered the picture.

"I got you something new to try." Bill stopped his scrubbing to reach into the huge ice-filled stainless-steel trough behind him. He was always buying a six-pack of something different because he knew better than most how I didn't like to follow the crowd. Never more than a six-pack, though, because he also knew the majority of The Fountain's patrons preferred the same old same old.

He popped off the top and placed a longneck in front of me. "This here's a Stella something or other. I tried one when me and Marsha went up to the Budweiser plant in St. Louis. It's another one of them foreign beers you like."

I kept my smile in check. Bill believed in buying American beer, specifically Budweiser, and American cars, specifically Chevrolet. I didn't have the heart to tell him the Germans had bought the former and every country but America was producing parts for the latter. Instead, I took a long pull of the beer and appreciated how it went down smooth. "This is a good beer, Bill. Thank you."

"I'm glad you like it." He grinned widely and hitched each thumb behind his suspenders. Bill was old enough to be my grandfather, but I liked him a lot better than Grandpa Floyd. He handed me beers instead of stale chocolate-covered cherries accompanied by backhanded compliments.

I looked over at my piano, an old upright that had seen two world wars come and go. I wasn't ready to weave my way through the cluster of café tables and chairs then hop up on the risers. No, I'd stay put with my Stella for a little while longer.

"Hey, y'all." Tiffany Davis walked in, letting the screen door slap behind her. She leaned on the counter beside me, and Bill reached underneath for her apron. As usual, she had poured herself into a tight, low-cut tank top and a pair of shorty shorts. She also wore a UT baseball cap with a ponytail down her back—that was not usual.

"Hey, Tiff, I guess you've decided where you're going?" Bill asked. He drew out a cola of some sort and slid it toward her.

"I'm going to Knoxville." Tiffany beamed as she pointed to her obnoxiously orange hat. "In a few months I will officially be a freshman at the University of Tennessee."

"Well, I hate to lose you," Bill said, "but it's good to see someone go off and show those college girls how we play ball around here."

Jealousy squeezed my chest. I'd had my chance to get out of town and blown it. That was no reason to be mad at Tiffany. I forced goodwill into the smile I gave her. "You're going to knock 'em dead, I know it."

Blushing, she looked down at the wooden floor. "Thanks, Beulah. Maybe I ought to sweep up before folks start getting here."

She went off to find a broom before we could remind her sweeping wouldn't do a lick of good since everyone and his brother would track in dust and grime from the parking lot.

"That girl reminds me a lot of you," Bill mused.

My eyes snapped to where Tiffany stood in the midst of the café chairs, broom in hand. She reminded him of me? She, who had decided to emulate Daisy Duke after watching one too many *Dukes of Hazzard* marathons on CMT? I looked down at what I was wearing: a low-slung black blouse that showed off my cleavage, the one Ginger claimed had to be on backward because it was cut down to my navel.

The last light of day seeped through the tiny windows at the top of the wall and caught Tiffany's ponytail. I gulped. She'd dyed her beautiful blond hair my shade of red, a color that clashed something awful with her orange cap. That girl and I needed to have a serious heart-to-heart about a few things. She had a future. I didn't.

I'd taken two steps in her direction when Bill hollered, "Hey, Beulah, it's time."

Talking with Tiffany would have to wait.

I took my seat at the piano and played a series of scales. Bill shook his head. He could never understand why I didn't just sit down and start playing. Of course, after taking piano lessons with Ginger for over half my life, I had to start with scales. It was as though my fingers couldn't find the keys if I didn't follow the ritual.

The Gates brothers rolled in as I launched into Hank Junior's "Family Tradition." As always, they were happy to sing along, and Bill nodded in approval as he sold them a couple of beers. Next, Old Man MacGregor shuffled in. He settled at one of the café tables closest to me. I refused to look at his beady eyes or unkempt gray beard. He didn't scare me, but I knew only too well he wasn't quite right in the head.

Other patrons trickled in—most I knew, a few I didn't know but still recognized—and I went from jazz to country and back to jazz again. I was playing one of my favorites from Ginger's old New Orleans records when *he* walked in.

I had eyes. I could appreciate a superb male specimen just as well as the next person, but this guy was not your garden variety Fountain patron. In his polo and khakis, he stood out like Dom Pérignon and caviar at a Yessum County High School football game. He also stood about a foot taller than everyone else in the place.

Despite *my* superior powers of observation—and that while playing piano—the guys and gals never noticed but went on playing poker and pool, laughing and clapping. Old Man MacGregor took another drag of his cigarette, and Pete Gates picked up his brother Greg by the collar, indicating they were ready for their first fight of the evening. Bill, of course, would serve a bull moose without batting an eyelash as long as said moose had cash. He passed the new guy a beer.

Then Mr. Dom Pérignon looked my way, and he did one of those subtle double takes that never gets old. His eyes didn't leave mine as he reached for the beer Bill offered him. I missed a note as I took in his broad shoulders and how his bicep flexed when he reached for the bottle. A new guy in town could be just what I needed to liven up the summer.

I was halfway through one of my favorite ragtime songs when I gathered the courage to look at him again. He seemed to know what I was playing. Bill, meanwhile, gave me the "wrap it up" twirl of the finger, a sign that he felt the patrons were getting bored and restless. I didn't care.

I didn't realize I'd been staring at Mr. Dom Pérignon until he gave me a lopsided smile. I grinned back in spite of myself, but then the cuckoo clock sang out the nine o'clock hour. I beat out a premature ending to the song.

Bill gave a shrill whistle and everyone looked over to where he stood behind his beloved counter. "Ladies and gents, I want to thank you for coming out tonight and I hope you're having a good time."

The Gates brothers quit elbowing each other long enough to catcall and clap. The stranger lifted his beer.

"As you well know, something special happened when the old jukebox in the corner died. We found someone even better, the lovely and talented Beulah Land."

I ran the heel of my hand down the keys to enhance the drama. *Let's see how the new guy in town likes the old song that gave me my name.* Slowly, I began to sing. *"Far away the noise and strife upon my ear is falling."*

I winked at the stranger, but he frowned. He looked at patrons around him, stunned they'd all started singing along. A bad feeling settled in the pit of my stomach.

"Then I know the sins of man beset on every hand."

"Damn straight," cackled Old Man MacGregor.

"Doubt and fear and things of earth in vain to me are calling. None of these shall move me from Beulah Land."

I paused again for dramatic effect and chanced another glance at the new guy. He sat perfectly still, his beer stuck midway up. He was not amused.

"I'm living on the mountain underneath a cloudless sky."

"Praise God!" shouted the Gates brothers over everyone else.

"I'm drinking at the fountain that never shall run dry."

Tiffany ducked under two beer bottles clinking. Guffaws, cheers, and clinks always drowned out the next few words: *"Oh, yes, I'm feasting on the manna from a bountiful supply, for I am . . ."*

The whole bar, minus one, joined me with a raucous *". . . dwelling in Beulah Land."*

"You wish, boys," I drawled as I segued into a jazzed-up instrumental instead. The stranger finally lifted the beer to his lips, but he put it down without taking a drink. He put the half-empty bottle down on the ledge where he'd been sitting and headed for the door. My heart sank with an irrational disappointment. When I started singing the chorus again, though, he pivoted and walked toward me instead.

While I added a little something extra to the last verse, he took a seat at the table closest to me, patiently waiting. Man, I'd always been a sucker for baby blues, especially when paired with such dark hair. And for smoothly shaven cheeks that showed no signs of a wad of tobacco. Despite my disdain for the reddest of necks, I had a rule about not getting mixed up with rich men or preppies. Of course, rules were meant to be broken.

I sat there for a moment, my fingers still hovering over the keys, and the bar came to life around me. They knew the drill. My intermission was the time to yell across the room to one another. In fifteen minutes we'd start all over again, only everyone would be a little bit drunker and a whole lot rowdier.

"May I have a word?"

I didn't expect the calm, low tone of his voice—nor the even gravel. He stepped closer, and a crisp scent floated over me: sandalwood.

"Sure. It's my break," I heard myself say.

"Maybe we could step outside where it's a little quieter," he suggested.

I looked him over, searching for signs he might be a serial killer. I didn't think so, but one couldn't be too sure. "Bill, I'm stepping outside," I shouted, my eyes never leaving the stranger's.

On the other side of the security light were several good spots to steal a kiss or three, but we stopped short in the triangular beam of light that splashed across the parking lot. Even with the door closed, I could hear the ruckus inside. The parsonage was only a few yards away, and I tried to imagine how any preacher there had to feel living so close to a party to which he hadn't been invited.

"So, what word did you want to tell me?" I asked. "Or was that an excuse to get me outside and kiss me?"

His blue eyes widened ever so slightly, but he quickly composed himself. "I couldn't leave without telling you how I felt about the song you played."

My mouth went dry. How could I have been so stupid? Of course he wasn't interested in me. He'd rolled into town from the college, and he'd been offended. "I've been playing that song for five years now, and I've never had one single complaint before tonight."

"Five years?" He looked me over thoroughly as though he'd misjudged me. Based on the slight laugh lines at the corners of his eyes, I'd misjudged him, too. He wasn't a college student, but he couldn't be too much older than me.

"I was twenty at the time. Not that it's any of your business."

"Five years or not, it's rude to sing a song like that and then stick sexual innuendo on the end."

Great. New Guy was tall, dark, and handsome. Now, if only he had a mute button. "What are you? Some kind of preacher?"

"Fully ordained."

Of course you are. "I'm sorry. I couldn't tell since you were drinking a *beer*."

He studied me carefully. "I vowed self-control, not abstinence. Besides, it'd be more impolite for me to sit around and not buy something."

Damned, if that didn't make sense. Still, he had to want something. "Are you here to 'save' me?"

"Not tonight."

I snorted. *Quick-witted sonuvabitch.* "I don't need to be saved, so you can stuff it."

I could tell it was on the tip of his tongue to say something trite about how everyone needs to be saved. Instead, he exercised his vaunted self-control to stare me down. I had to admit some grudging admiration. No one stared me down except Ginger, and they all knew better than to try in The Fountain. New Guy didn't know he was supposed to get mad, lose his temper, and call me names. Instead, he faced my anger with reason. "All right. I'm familiar with these vendettas. You play whatever you want to play, but stop and think about the other people in that bar. Do you really want to drag them down into sacrilege with you?"

"Sacrilege?" Something snapped behind my eyes. "You want to waltz into *my* workplace and talk to me about sacrilege. It's a free damned country. If you don't like the songs I sing, then you can leave."

"Free country or fascist state, I wasn't going to leave without telling you that singing hymns like a sexpot isn't appropriate." He still hadn't looked away. "No matter who you are."

"Appropriate? Who gives two shits about being appropriate?" I stood up straighter and crossed my arms, which had the unintended but fortunate effect of pushing my breasts up and out. *Good. Let him take a look at what he isn't going to touch. Ever.* "I'll do what I need to do to put food on the table. If I'm going to be saddled with this ridiculous name, then I might as well make the most of it."

He arched an eyebrow. "Are you making the most of what you've been given?"

More preacher-speak. As if I hadn't heard all of this mess about gifts and talents from my father a long time before. It was my business if I wanted to stay put in tiny Yessum County instead of driving up to Nashville to see if I could get a better job.

I turned to go. "You know what? Screw you. You don't know the first thing about me."

He grabbed my arm. "You have real talent. You shouldn't be wasting it here."

We both looked down to where his warm hand lightly circled my arm. He quickly released me, almost as though he couldn't believe he'd reached out to touch me.

"I'll do as I damned well please." *And I could've done you, but that ain't happening now that I know you're a sanctimonious asshole.* "These people took care of me when I needed help, so my talents aren't 'wasted' here. You can mind your own business, Preacher Man."

He winced at my nickname for him, but he didn't stop me when I made for the door. Instead, he shoved his hands in his pockets as though making sure he wouldn't reach for me a second time. "Maybe you don't know that much about me, either."

"I know you're a holier-than-thou jerk." The screen door slammed between us for emphasis.

I bellied up to the bar and motioned for a beer. Bill handed me one as Tiffany stopped to load her tray. "Who was that guy?"

"Don't know. Don't care."

"I care," she said with an appreciative growl before carrying her wares across the room.

Bill looked from me to the half-full beer on the ledge. "C'mon, Beulah. Please tell me you're not running off new customers."

"Trust me when I tell you he's not our type." I chugged the rest of my beer. Time to get back to work.

I sat down at the piano a full seven minutes early, and perversely launched into another hymn. I wondered if my friend Preacher Man was still in the parking lot. Could he even hear me being more sacrilegious than usual? Probably not. I didn't need to waste another thought on him, but the warm circle around my upper arm reminded me it'd been a long time since I'd been touched like that.

I hoped he was still out there fuming. When I hit a verse about the many dangers, toils, and snares, my heart squeezed. *Is this actually guilt?* No way was I going to feel guilty for offending some

Holy Roller who should've known better than to come into a bar in the first place.

Of course, if I'd known what was going to happen next, I might've thought twice about playing hymns to piss off the Preacher Man.

Chapter 2

At the first whiff of French toast, I knew my day was headed straight to hell in a handbasket. I stumbled into a pair of shorts and made the executive decision to ignore my smoky, matted hair. Playing piano until three in the morning didn't exactly inspire good hygiene. Besides, Ginger had seen worse.

I stopped in the hallway, my toes squishing into shag carpet far older than my twenty-five years. There at the end of the hall sat the one room in the house I refused to enter, the nursery. On a morning not quite ten years ago, Ginger had served French toast. That was the worst morning of my life, so I didn't have high hopes for this one. "Beulah Lou! Get down here and eat before it gets cold!"

I jumped out of my skin and headed for the stairs. At the bottom, I almost tripped, grabbing the newel ball from the post to steady myself. Instead it popped off into my hands and I bumbled into the wall. If Ginger was worried about my well-being after the thud, she didn't say anything. I put the newel ball back gently. House maintenance wasn't my specialty, and what Ginger didn't know wouldn't hurt her.

"Took you long enough." She turned and smiled as I padded across the well-worn linoleum. She stood with her hands on her hips, holding the spatula in her right hand so it poked from her body at a weird angle. It shook with the palsy that had robbed her of the ability to play piano anywhere but church. These days, even while playing hymns she'd played a hundred times before, she still missed notes, but I doubted anyone at County Line Methodist would ever say anything. That sorry bunch had their own assorted problems.

"Well, don't just stand there," she said. "Get you a plate."

I took the spatula from her and opened the cupboard. "I'll get breakfast for us. It's the least I can do since you cooked."

"Ah, but you'll be doing dishes." She winked as she eased into a metal chair with a vinyl seat. When she sat over the slash of duct tape that held the vinyl together, you could almost believe the chair was brand-new. Almost.

I slid a plate of French toast in front of her and turned to the coffeepot. Taking two mugs, I doctored the coffee: cream and three sugars for me, black with one sugar for her. My stomach flopped as I sat in my own scarred vinyl chair.

"Eat! Eat! You have to eat it while it's hot!" She cut a generous hunk of toast and dipped it into the pool of syrup on her plate.

"How're you feeling this morning, Ginger?" I already knew the answer because she was still wearing her pink terry-cloth robe with the threadbare elbows.

"Oh, I'm plodding along." She smiled, but she wasn't wearing lipstick. Ginger always wore lipstick. Without that telltale slash of red, she looked washed-out and faded, just like the gingham curtains behind her. Even her hair was a dull grayish blond from where she hadn't been to the beauty shop to get it dyed. At least she had her eyebrows penciled in. And they were fairly straight considering she always shaved them off before attempting to re-create them with pencil in shaking hand.

I put my fork down, the first bite of my toast still dangling from the tines. "Go ahead and tell me how yesterday's trip to the doctor went. I'm too old to be softened up by French toast."

She studied her plate. "I'm not doing chemo this time."

"It's back? But—"

"No buts! Dr. Bowman told me he could only promise me two years with chemo, six months to a year without. I'll keep my hair and take the six months, thank you very much."

Tears stung my eyes. "Ginger, please—"

Her hand snaked across the table, her skin almost transparent except for the brown spots that did nothing to hide sinew and blue veins underneath. I would've thought it a skeleton's hand if it hadn't still been strong and warm.

"Beulah, we talked about this the first time. I can't stay here forever. I'm pretty sure I've already outstayed my welcome."

Tears blurred my vision, and I willed them back. Ginger patted my hand. "Don't you worry about me. When I meet the good Lord, we're going to stick our tongues out at you, and I'm going to convince Him to send thunderstorms when you misbehave just because you fuss about getting your hair wet. You think about that every time it rains!"

I laughed a nervous hiccup-laugh. My throat burned.

Her bleary brown eyes searched past their cataracts to find me. "All you have to do is remember what I told you about my funeral. If you let Anderson's Funeral Home have an open-casket visitation so everybody and their momma can gawk at me and talk about how my shriveled-up corpse looks just like me, so help me God, I will haunt you every day for the rest of your life."

I couldn't help laughing again, but my throat cramped, choking the laugh into a grunt.

She looked absently out the breakfast room window at a fat cardinal perched on the birdhouse. "Now, I do have one last favor to ask of you."

You took me in when I had nowhere else to go. "Anything."

She chuckled, and her bleary eyes returned to lock with mine. "You might want to hear what the favor is before you answer so quickly."

"Anything, Ginger. You've done so much for me. Without you . . ."

"I want you to take my place."

"Take your place?" What did that mean? How could I ever begin to take Ginger Belmont's place? I didn't really have the disposition for teaching piano lessons to the neighborhood kids. Was I supposed to troll the town looking for unwed teen mothers? Could it be as simple as ladling out soup at the Jefferson Homeless Shelter every Tuesday? Or would it be defending the need to shelve Harry Potter books at the local Friends of the Library committee meeting?

"I want you to take my place at County Line."

I felt the color drain from my face. Anything, *anything* but that. I owed my life to Ginger Belmont. But I didn't owe one damned thing to God, and I wasn't about to play piano for Him.

"Ginger." I fought back nausea.

"It's my dying wish. Would you deny me my dying wish?"

"That's not fair, and you know it," I croaked.

She squeezed my hand. Hard. "Life's not fair, sweetie, and, oh, how we both know it."

"But I can't stop playing at The Fountain. Bill needs me," I said.

"I didn't say you had to stop playing at The Fountain."

"Well, I can't play at The Fountain *and* at church!"

"Why not?"

Ginger knew very well why not. Last night's stranger wasn't the only one who didn't approve of my song selections.

Her eyes shifted to the floor. "Well, you could always find a new song to sing."

I crossed my arms and settled in for a fight. "Bill renamed the place because of that song. I'm not changing it now."

"Beulah, you can't stay ticked off at God forever."

I slammed my fists down on the table and stood. The metal legs of the table shrieked, but my voice came out low: "Watch me."

Ginger's penciled-in eyebrow arched to unnatural heights, telling me I needed to take it down a notch and have a seat. "Beulah Lou, you keep punishing yourself. You—"

"How am I punishing myself with *your* cancer? Can you tell me that?"

"Rejoice when a person dies and . . ." Ginger paused, but forced herself to forge ahead. ". . . mourn when a child is born."

Her words stabbed me at my most vulnerable spot. "I don't know how you can quote that religious bullshit to me," I whispered.

"Because it's the truth," she said grimly. "I know you don't see it that way, but it's the truth. Now sit down and eat."

"I'm not hungry."

"Sit down. And eat."

I couldn't argue with her or her penciled-in eyebrow, so I picked up my fork. My stomach pitched at the thought of food. For a moment, I felt sixteen again, and I tried to brush it aside. That was a year I hated to remember, much less relive.

Even with only a kiss of syrup, the sweet, sweet toast gagged me. The bacon didn't look burnt, but it tasted like ashes.

I consoled myself with the idea that the preacher would probably fire me the minute he realized I was the woman from The Fountain. Then, Ginger wouldn't be able to blame me for not fulfilling her dying wish.

Ginger's hand shook as she tried to meet her mouth with a piece of French toast. My smile faded. No amount of thumbing my nose at the new preacher would keep Ginger with me.

And no amount of her well-intentioned roadblocks would save me from the path I'd started down years before.

Chapter 3

Ginger wasted no time calling in her favor. The next morning she knocked on my door at eight, once again too early for someone who played piano in a honky-tonk to all hours. "Beulah Lou, get on up and take a shower. We've got a nine o'clock appointment with Reverend Daniels to talk about how you're taking my place."

"This couldn't wait?"

"Doc says I could drop dead at any minute, so no. Time is of the essence."

At least I knew she was feeling chipper since she'd used "Lou," her made-up middle name for me. As if being named Beulah Land wasn't bad enough, I also bore my maternal grandmother's name: Gertrude. When she took me in, Ginger quickly decided Beulah Gertrude didn't roll off the tongue.

I went through my morning routine in record time, even putting on makeup minus the eyeliner. I hopped down the steps in a sundress and sandals with barely enough time left to get out the door and to our appointment on time.

Ginger did something she hadn't done since I was a teenager. She assessed my ensemble with a long head-to-toe look and pointed upstairs. "Try again."

"What?" I looked down at my sundress. So, yes, it was cut a little low, but it wasn't *that* bad.

"Go, or I'll wrap one of my shawls around you." She crossed her arms over her chest and tried to raise her eyebrow. That's when I noticed she hadn't penciled in her eyebrows, which she only neglected to do when her fingers shook their worst. I took a deep breath and swallowed any more arguments before I raced upstairs.

I pawed through my closet until I found a more modest sundress and exchanged outfits with a minimal amount of cursing. I stopped at the foot of the stairs to give a twirl and a mock curtsy.

"Much better." Her frown didn't match her words, but, before I could question her, she added, "You're driving."

She placed the keys in my hand, and my mouth fell open. I had never been allowed to drive the Caddy. Even when Ginger had gone through chemo, she had ridden in my antique Toyota hatchback rather than let me drive her Cadillac.

"C'mon," she said from where she stood at the front door. "And close your mouth before you swallow a fly."

Walking out into the hazy heat was like walking into an invisible wall of humidity. Ginger shuffled around the Caddy, and I had no choice but to move forward.

After helping her inside, I rounded the car and slid over the slick worn-leather interior of the Caddy. I couldn't help but marvel at the reversal of fortune. At sixteen, I had been newly homeless and pregnant when I crawled in the passenger seat of the Caddy, concentrating on keeping my lunch down. Back then Ginger had been in the driver's seat. She had worn her hair high, never letting the gray show.

"For Pete's sake, start this car and get the AC going!" Ginger jarred me back to the present, and I looked at where she sat in the passenger seat, slumped and with her hair cut short. She had attempted lipstick, but the burgundy color had escaped the natural boundaries of her lips, further betraying her shaky hands.

"Get your head out of the clouds," she harrumphed. "Most

people have the good sense not to leave a dog closed up in a car on a day like this, much less a person."

I turned the key, and the engine rolled over with a solid, satisfying rumble. Was driving the Caddy some sort of consolation prize for agreeing to take her place at the County Line piano, or was this the first in a long line of things and traditions that would come to me and only me?

We eased through town and out into the country, the Caddy's V-8 purring. After the anemic engine in my Toyota, I felt I could conquer the world with Ginger's classic Cadillac.

"For heaven's sake, Beulah, air her out."

I grinned and pressed the accelerator almost to the floor.

"Oh, but watch out for that Barney Fife sheriff of ours. He likes to sit there by the pond at the beginning of the swamp. Thinks he's running a regular sting operation."

I practically stomped on the brakes. We crawled past the pond and into the long, flat stretch of bridges that crossed Harlowe Bottom.

"We're not in a school zone," she muttered. I sped up again. The Caddy went from a purr to a roar, and I watched the speedometer hit sixty, seventy, eighty. The crooked cypress trees on either side of the car waved in a blurry, macabre dance.

"But look out for deer. And the big curve where people like to take their half down the middle."

I hit the brakes harder than I meant to, and we both jerked against our seat belts. "Ginger, would you like for me to pull over so you can drive?"

"Don't sass me, Beulah Lou. You are not too big to spank."

At a quarter of a century old, I was pretty sure I was, but I wasn't about to argue. She would probably hurt herself trying to prove me wrong. I stifled a grin at the thought of Ginger trying to catch me long enough to spank me. Something really was up with her. She wasn't normally *this* crabby.

"Ginger, you doing okay this morning?"

"Some days are better than others." She sighed as she leaned back into the passenger seat. "This is definitely one of the others."

She rested like that until we reached the church and the Caddy's tires crunched gravel. Now, I had to face the Reverend Daniels. After the last go-round at County Line Methodist, I had told myself I would never darken another church door. I had reasoned I could even be married by the justice of the peace, if it came to that. Of course, I hadn't counted on Ginger and all of the stupid things I would do for her.

My clammy hand hesitated over the key. If I took it out of the ignition, I wouldn't have a quick getaway. If I left it in the ignition, one of the Gates brothers would probably steal the car for beer money.

"Quit piddling around, Beulah." She heaved open the heavy door with a grunt. "I'm sure Reverend Daniels has other things he would like to do today."

I sucked in a breath and grabbed the key. My sandals wobbled over the uneven gravel as we approached County Line Methodist. I stopped at the bottom of the steps of the small clapboard building. There was probably some imaginary line that, when crossed by a heathen like me, would cause alarms and bells to sound. "Are you sure he can't step outside for this conversation?"

Ginger had already climbed the stairs, an indicator that I was, indeed, dawdling. "In this heat? Heavens, child, I wouldn't do that to my worst enemy." She turned and hobbled into the building.

I took one step then another. No alarms sounded. No lightning came down from the sky. I sprinted up the stairs and landed on the small portico. No angels appeared to block my entrance.

Ginger had left the door open, and cool air rushed past me. Familiar mahogany-stained pews with red velvet cushions sucked the light from the interior. Even the stained glass windows were dark and held out more light than they let in. I reached my toe across the threshold just to see.

"Beulah Land, get in here this instant. The church cannot afford to cool the whole outside."

I jumped across the threshold and shut the door behind me, then chastised myself for acting like a seven-year-old girl. I blinked several times, waiting for my eyes to adjust to the cave-like interior. Ginger stood to the left of the altar, and there the preacher stood beside her with his hands in his pockets.

In khakis and a crisp button-down shirt.

My Preacher Man really was *the* Reverend Daniels. *Of course, you idiot. What other preacher would walk into The Fountain other than the one who couldn't sleep for all the noise?*

Looking ready for a country club picnic, he was most assuredly neither potbellied nor double-chinned. My life would've been so much easier if he had been. Instead, he had to look like a *GQ* model who'd taken a wrong turn and ended up in church school.

At that moment his eyes widened as he recognized me.

He had to be wondering if he'd met my evil twin a couple of nights ago. At The Fountain I never clipped my curly red hair back in a barrette, choosing instead to let it fly free. I also never wore subdued makeup or demure and neatly pressed dresses. Ginger was trying to sell him a wolf in sheep's clothing, and he knew it.

"Why don't we come into my office where we can have a seat and where there's a little more light?" His voice came out more pleasantly than I'd expected, and I had to give him brownie points for not losing his temper and yelling me out of the place.

We followed him through the large all-purpose room behind the sanctuary. My eyes struggled to adjust to windows full of sunlight winking over the metal chairs against the wall, but the good Reverend Daniels didn't share my aversion to the light.

On the other side of the room sat his office, a tiny hole that wasn't anywhere as tidy as I would've expected from his appearance. Thick books stood in knee-deep stacks around the room, and the filing cabinet was open with overstuffed manila folders leaning precariously on top. Behind his desk he had tacked a poster of the Beatles crossing Abbey Road.

"Have a seat." He took an armful of books from the metal

folding chairs that faced his desk. "Sorry about the mess, but I'm still moving in. I hope to get some comfortable chairs soon."

"That's quite all right." Ginger eased into a chair and held her leather Aigner purse primly over her knees. "We won't keep you long. I'm sure you're busy."

"Never too busy for you. It's Miss Ginger, isn't it?" he asked with a smile. His accent didn't hang on the "r" like that of most West Tennesseans, but he obviously knew how to play the respect-your-elders game. "Did you come for next Sunday's hymn numbers?"

"Actually, I've come to tell you I won't be playing piano anymore, but I have Beulah here ready to take my place. Beulah Land, Luke. Luke, Beulah Land."

We shook hands then stared, each one daring the other to crack first.

"Beulah Land. Like the hymn, huh?"

I swallowed hard. Even after I'd bitched him out, he'd still managed to say my name softly and not at all the way my father used to bellow it. "Yes. Like the hymn."

He nodded, and I felt unreasonably grateful he hadn't told Ginger any of the things I'd said to him. Of course, he still could.

"Good. That's settled then." Ginger reached for the edge of his desk to stand up. "You give me those numbers, and I'll get her started Sunday morning."

"Ah, Miss Ginger, it's not that easy. Playing the piano is a paid position." Luke's level gaze never left mine and told me he hadn't forgotten a word of what I'd said to him. "Paid positions have to be advertised to everyone."

I snorted. The "position" paid twenty bucks a week, hardly worth all of the preparation that went into playing each Sunday.

Luke's eyes cut to mine, his glare pinning me to the chair even as his words came out crisply polite. "You know, the Equal Opportunity Act."

Oh, well played, Preacher Man.

Ginger stared him down. I had seen that look before and was more than happy to not be on the receiving end. "Young man, we can do it your way, but I guarantee you won't find anyone who plays better than Beulah. She's a prodigy, you know."

I sat up straight. Ginger had never given me such high praise before.

"While we're here, Beulah can audition for you," she continued as she used the edge of his desk to pull herself to her feet. "Give her a number, and she'll play it. You tell her a style, and she can do it. There's no one in this town—no one in this state—who plays better than she does."

I blushed and studied the hole in the carpet to the side of the desk leg.

"I don't doubt her talent. There are . . . other considerations."

Ginger didn't get mad often. Even worse, she didn't scream and cuss like normal people even when she did. No, she got dangerously calm. "Beulah, you go on out there and turn on the lights. Warm up a little. We'll be out in a minute."

I jumped up and leaped out the door. To this day, I have no idea what Ginger told Luke to make him change his mind. All I know is he wasn't so interested in the Equal Opportunity Act when the two of them came into the sanctuary to hear me play.

She stood beside him, gripping his arm a little too hard. "Pick a number, Reverend."

"This really isn't necessary at this point," he said, shaking his head as though still puzzling out how she'd talked him into it.

"Beulah, play two-forty-five. Play it straight."

I opened a familiar and worn brown hymnal to "Whispering Hope." Not one of these songs was difficult because Ginger taught me to play them when I was only a girl; playing it without embellishment was going to be the hard part. Technically, I put each note in the right place at the right time, but there wasn't a lot of heart and not even a whisper of hope.

"You taught her how to play using the Cokesbury Hymnal, didn't you?" He marveled. Now he knew how an infidel like me had known about a golden oldie like "Dwelling in Beulah Land."

"But that's not all," she said to him before turning back to me. "How about some Bach?"

I launched into the opening of the Toccata and Fugue in D Minor. The solemn, menacing notes rang hollow in the little sanctuary, but my eyes cut to the organ to my right. *That* could liven things up, and I'd always wanted to learn to play the organ.

"Beulah, one-twenty-seven." A flush of revelation ran cold then hot on my cheeks: Ginger Belmont had been grooming me for this moment from the day we met.

I shook off the epiphany and played another hymn with the same cold precision I had used to play the classics.

"Jazz 'er up," she commanded.

My shoulders relaxed, and I leaned toward the piano as our trip to "Higher Ground" took on a winding Dixieland route.

"That's lovely," Luke said calmly. "Now, could you please play number eighty-nine from the blue hymnal?"

The blue hymnal? The last time I'd been at church, those bad boys had done nothing more than gather dust.

Luke cleared his throat. "There's a stack on top of the piano."

I took one of the books in question, sucking in a deep breath. I could sight-read music—no problem there—but just the thought of something unexpected gave me another chill. I flipped to Luke's request and scanned the hymn, reading all the way to the bottom. Beethoven?

My fingers started slowly, fumbling only once before I recognized the melody as having come from Beethoven's Ninth. By the second verse I was confident enough to add my own syncopation and ornamentation.

"That's enough." Luke's firm voice echoed through the sanctuary. "I would prefer you play all songs exactly as written."

"Play it straight, Beulah." Ginger spoke so softly, I almost didn't hear her. Still, I sat up tall and played as though the Mormon Tabernacle Choir planned to join in at any minute.

"Thank you," Luke said with something that sounded oddly like victory. "I'll get you the bulletin for this Sunday, but I'm afraid you can't jazz it up. You may be talented, but that's not why you're here. I don't want people to get confused and lose their place while they're trying to sing."

I slumped the minute he disappeared. *No jazz?* I could think of no worse punishment than having to play high church hymns every Sunday for the rest of my life. My stomach roiled.

"C'mon, Beulah Lou, it's not the end of the world." But Ginger's tone of voice told me she knew he'd just sucked the life out of me.

I stepped down from the choir loft where the piano sat, and she gripped my hand. "You did a great job. I feel so much better knowing you'll be taking care of County Line."

"Ginger, I still don't think this is a good idea. Maybe County Line doesn't want me to take care of them."

Luke appeared and handed me a copy of the bulletin as well as pressing one of the blue hymnals into my arms. "I'm sure Miss Ginger can show you everything you need to know. But remember what I said about ad-libbing. This job isn't all about you."

His barb stung, but I couldn't keep from looking up to meet his gaze. Was he making this demand because he knew about my piano playing at The Fountain, or did he have another agenda?

I wanted to ask him if the job was all about him, but I couldn't embarrass Ginger like that. Instead, I bit my tongue so hard I tasted blood. We walked down the center aisle, our shoes sinking into deep burgundy carpet that felt as though someone had put new carpet over the old instead of taking the time to rip up the worn-out bottom layer. Disapproval radiated from Ginger's stiff carriage, and I looked over to see her lips pursed. She herself had never been above embellishing the songs on the written page, particularly between verses.

Once outside, Ginger extended her hand for the keys. I hadn't proven myself worthy after all. I hesitated only a moment before placing them gently in her palm and reasserting the natural order of things. I eased around the hood and plopped back into the passenger seat, my seat. She lowered herself into the Caddy with a grunt, then sat as tall and straight as her osteoporosis-humped spine would allow. She threw out sharp elbows as she moved the gear shift on the side of the massive steering wheel. Something about the determination in her profile reminded me of the day she rescued me from my mother. Today, she had tossed me into the lion's den.

I crossed my arms over my modest sundress. Why hadn't he said no? He knew who I really was and still he'd gone along with Ginger. It made absolutely no sense.

Because you expected him to judge you based on what he saw the other night or at the very least to call you out.

But he didn't.

No, Luke Daniels wasn't a man to call out your sins in front of the whole congregation. I shivered at the realization that he might be waiting for another time to resume our argument.

Oh, well. I'd agreed to take the job. He'd be the one to decide if I kept it, and I'd seen a man with buttons to push underneath that unflappable exterior.

Chapter 4

Of course I waited until Saturday afternoon to look at the hymns Luke wanted me to play. I dutifully plunked through each of them until I came to the last one, the invitation.

"Hey, Ginger, could you take a look at this?"

She hobbled into the room and leaned over my shoulder, squinting to read the hymn, as the familiar scent of Emeraude washed over me. "Never heard of it."

"There are familiar songs in the book, and he comes up with this?"

"And it's in three-two time. That's going to be fun. Good luck." She hobbled toward the kitchen before I could ask for guidance.

"Some piano teacher you are!" I yelled.

"The student has surpassed the master!" she hollered back.

"Surpassed the master, my ass. The teacher doesn't know how to play this song," I muttered.

"Quit grumbling and get to playing! And quit cussing!"

I played through the crazy three-two song until I felt ready, but I had a feeling it was going to be a train wreck. What was that man up to and why couldn't he have been like every other preacher I'd ever known and tossed me out on my ear?

"Beulah, supper!"

I sat at the piano, my hands levitating above the keys. I had forgotten all about supper. I padded into the kitchen to see two boxes of pizza. Apparently, I had missed the doorbell ringing, too. "I like the way you cook, Ginger Belmont."

"I learned from the best," she said with a grin.

"Hey, that's my line!" I went to give her a playful slug on the arm, but my fist stopped short. Ginger was so fragile, I was afraid even the smallest touch might bruise her.

We took a seat at the metal-and-Formica table. Air whooshed from my chair.

"Beulah!" Ginger said as she waved one hand in front of her nose. I had to grin because she had to be feeling better to crack a crude joke like that. She passed me a paper plate, then the two-liter soda. "So, are you ready for tomorrow?"

"Not really," I said between bites of pizza. "That man has no sense of an invitation—that's where he put that crazy three-two song."

"Oh ho, and I suppose you're the invitational expert, considering you haven't been to church in"—Ginger put down her piece of pizza to count fingers—"nine years."

"My daddy was a Baptist preacher." I took a huge bite of pepperoni pizza, savoring sauce underneath melted cheese. "I almost starved to death on more than one occasion waiting for him to wrap things up."

"I know that's right." Ginger smiled. "Granny Reynolds was a Missionary Baptist, and sometimes I would go to church with her. They would always keep singing the invitation until someone came down the aisle. If they sang all five verses and no one had been moved by the spirit, they started repeating them. A couple of times I rededicated my life to Jesus just to get to the fried chicken."

"Ginger!"

"That righteous indignation is rich coming from you! Nothing wrong with trying to be a better person, and being nicer was going to be a whole lot easier with a full stomach. Besides, you gotta admire people who are dedicated enough to sing all of the verses. Nothing lonelier than the third verse of a Methodist hymn."

I nodded my head. "You know, maybe I should put to use all those Sundays spent on the first pew in black patent shoes and frilly anklets. Maybe Mr. Daniels needs to get a little Baptist in his invitation."

"Beulah Land, I didn't get you to play the piano so you could cause trouble."

"I'm not causing trouble," I said as I stood up from the table and started putting leftover pizza in an oversize freezer bag. "I'm just helping him along. You know as well as I do that the whole congregation is going to balk at singing a bunch of new songs. You told me they can't even handle sitting in a different seat."

"True," Ginger said with a nod. "But you don't need to take your vendetta out on that man. He's not the one you have a beef with."

She had a point. Luke couldn't be held personally responsible for all the things that had happened to me. He hadn't been the one to point and stare at me when I was a preacher's pregnant daughter or, worse yet, blatantly ignore me. He hadn't been the one to patronize me or make me feel like a second-class citizen in my own hometown.

But he had condescended that night at The Fountain. And he had forbidden jazz in his church, so I wasn't the only one with a vendetta.

Shrugging away any thoughts of the preacher man, I got a trash bag for the pizza boxes. Ginger preferred they leave the premises immediately because older houses harbor nooks and crannies that invite bugs, rodents, and other unsavory guests. "Hey, I'm headed to The Fountain. Do you need anything?"

"For you to behave yourself," Ginger muttered as she crossed her arms over her chest.

I leaned over to give her wrinkled cheek a kiss. "Aw, Ginger, I always do."

* * *

Sunday dawned quicker than I had hoped. Having run out of "respectable" dresses, I had surrendered to Ginger's safety pin even if I was afraid she was going to accidentally stab me in the boob as she closed the gap that showed my cleavage. Far better to risk a prick than to wear one of her shawls from the fifties.

We rode in silence to the church. She insisted on driving again. I didn't want to admit I was nervous, and she, blessedly, didn't feel the need to ask me. She patted my hand before we got out of the car. "You're going to do fine, Beulah. Just fine."

It sounded like she was trying to convince herself.

I took my seat on the first pew, and Luke nodded at me before making his rounds. County Line only ran six pews deep so it didn't take him long to shake palsied hands and kiss wrinkled cheeks. Most everyone in the place was over the age of sixty.

At fifteen till, I took my spot at the piano in the choir loft. I looked over for Ms. Lola, but she wasn't playing the organ as she always had with Ginger. Instead, she sat on the second row with her arms crossed to indicate she wasn't joining me in the choir loft any time soon. I looked at Luke, and he nodded.

County Line didn't usually have a formal choir, so I waited for the spirit to move the usual suspects to come forward and climb the steps to join me in the loft. No one came. I played another hymn just to be on the safe side and realized the church piano was more out of tune than the one at The Fountain. As warped notes bounced off the walls, I reminded myself to get John the Baptist to tune them both as soon as he got back from Guatemala.

Playing the music as written, I ignored the itch to embellish, the desire to cover up the stark humanity of simple out-of-tune notes. As suspected, the congregation mumbled through the first song. I didn't hear Lottie Miller's distinctive rough-hewn soprano, so I chanced a glance over my shoulder. She sat beside her twin sister, Lola, with her arms also crossed and lips firmly closed. I told myself I didn't care what Ms. Lola and Ms. Lottie did, but my stomach flipped over in betrayal.

I narrowly resisted a nervous tic as I played a spiritual without being able to jazz it up. Luke looked back at me as we finished the song with a whimper, definitely not a bang. I glared at him for the injustice done to "Soon and Very Soon." He arched an eyebrow that said, "My church, my rules."

I eased into one of the choir seats next to the piano, immediately realizing the mistake of not going back downstairs to join everyone else. The eyes of the sparse congregation, some curious and some hostile, bore through me, so I studied the perfect crown on the back of Luke's head. He read that judge-not-lest-ye-be-judged passage, and I rolled my eyes. Please. Obviously, I was going to have to think of something, anything, other than what he was saying.

From my vantage point, I couldn't see his feet. Was he even wearing pants? What did he wear under those robes? I had a vision of him taking off his robe to reveal only a faux shirt collar and the old-fashioned sock garters and black socks with his dress shoes. Of course, he had to wear tighty whities. How could anyone as obsessed with rules and propriety not wear briefs?

I smothered a snicker into a cough, but he didn't miss a beat. Looking for something else to keep my mind off what Luke was saying, I almost reached for a Bible to thumb through it.

Yeah, no.

Next week I'd sneak a couple of magazines up to the choir loft. Maybe I'd see if I could read about *Cosmopolitan*'s new sex positions while holding a properly pious look on my face.

"When my wife left me, it was easy to blame her."

I sat up straighter. *Luke was married?*

"It was too easy to hold myself blameless, to not see that God was leading us both to a better place. I had to take a look at myself, not just her."

Intriguing. *I wonder what he saw.*

What would it be like to have Luke look at you with affection crinkling those beautiful blue eyes? He'd given me a similarly friendly smile when he first walked into The Fountain. I frowned as I realized he hadn't been as judgmental then as I'd thought. After all, he'd walked in and ordered a beer. He'd enjoyed the music, even looked at me with respectful admiration, not like I was a slab of meat.

And you played that song and winked at him like a world-class flirt.

No. I wasn't going to feel guilty about that. I hadn't known who he was. Even if I had known, I would've still played the song.

So I probably would've skipped the winking part. Maybe the double entendre at the end. But I still would've played the song.

He looked to his left again, and I studied his profile. Why would any woman leave him? Sure, he was too uptight for my tastes, but there was an undeniable integrity about him. Or was it his decency that had ultimately repulsed her? Lots of women went after bad boys, but I could testify that bad boys were overrated. Still, I'd never survive a relationship with someone like Luke. He was too *good* and too *perfect,* the sort of man who would always emphasize how I fell short.

The congregation bowed their heads for the closing prayer, but I looked straight ahead. I might have fallen from grace so far as those people were concerned, but no way was some freaky off-kilter hymn going to wrap up *this* sermon. Luke said his amen, and I scribbled a number on a sheet of paper and passed it over the choir loft railing to the song leader who sat below me. Jason Utley looked at me like I had lost my mind. I pointed to the paper, and he shrugged his shoulders. Best I could tell, there wasn't a song leader alive who could resist "Just as I Am."

Jason stood, and I turned to face the piano. He announced the change of hymn, and I could feel daggers in the back of my head, courtesy of one Luke Daniels. They were daggers of Christian love and fellowship, but they were daggers nonetheless. Jason's tenor warbled through all six verses of the song, and I struggled not to add one flourish, my concession for changing his song. I wrapped up the last verse and chanced to turn around. There stood a new family, three of only seven new faces, and they wanted to join the church. The daggers, I noticed, had subsided.

When I finally finished, Ginger clapped. Her lips twisted in that way that suggested she was somewhere between pleased and perturbed. "You played spectacularly. You even found a little heart there in those last numbers."

"Thanks, Ginger." I came down from the loft and gave her a hug. "Mexican?"

"Of course," she said as I wrapped an arm around her shoulders. "It's a Sunday, isn't it?"

"Perhaps I could join you?"

I looked up to see Luke still standing at the front door from where he had shaken the last hand. My gut twisted. *How would you feel if someone changed your songs?*

Luke rocked on the balls of his feet, waiting for an answer. I wondered if he got nervous energy like musicians after a concert or athletes after a big game. This was his big performance of the week. And, of course, thinking of rock stars reminded me of Luke in nothing but tighty whities underneath his robe. I managed to convert that giggle into a cough as I looked at the floor and was irrationally disappointed to see sharply creased trousers hanging underneath.

For the love, Beulah. The man just admitted his first wife left him.

"I think we might need to speak about my expectations."

All of my goodwill dissipated. He wasn't keyed up or lonely; he wanted to ream me out for having the audacity to change his hymns.

"You have to understand, Beulah and I don't talk any kind of business at Sunday lunch," Ginger said, despite my glare.

His blue eyes bored through us. "What if lunch is on me?"

Ginger and I looked at each other in surprise at this unexpected boon. Neither one of us was exactly rolling in money, but Sunday lunch was a tradition so deeply ensconced that we would often eat peanut butter and jelly during the week to keep our Sunday tradition.

"And no business?" Ginger said.

"No business."

"Can't beat it with a stick," she said. "You're welcome to join us at Las Palmas."

He nodded stoically, those lips still pressed together tightly to keep all of the things he really wanted to say from spilling out. When we reached the parking lot, I couldn't help but look over my shoulder. He shrugged out of his robe slowly and draped it over one arm, keeping it balanced so it wouldn't touch the ground. Beneath he wore a crisp white shirt and mercilessly pressed pants. I expected to be disappointed by this last revelation but instead found myself admiring how well he filled out his pants.

Why did he have to be a preacher? Why not a plumber, a used-car salesman, or even a telemarketer? It seemed so unfair that a man that good looking would have to be a preacher.

He turned then as if he could feel my scrutiny, and I thought I saw a shadow of the man beneath the minister.

No, I would not worry about the preacher man, I would not. I wouldn't wonder about what happened with his wife or how he came to be stuck with what had to be a less-than-plum assignment in the hinterlands of West Tennessee. I would not marvel at how he could express such raw emotion and compassion in one moment and then want to chew me a new one in the next.

And I certainly would not dwell one moment more on how, for a single traitorous second, I'd wanted to kiss his cheek and tell him it'd all be okay.

Chapter 5

When Luke ordered cheese enchiladas I did a double take.

"The burly man is ordering cheese enchiladas?"

"Vegetarian." He flashed a wolfish grin before taking a savage bite of a chip.

"Oh, you really don't want to fit in around here, do you?"

"Fitting in is overrated," he said as he scooped another chip into the salsa. How many times had I told myself that same thing? But the preacher man lived it. I hid on the fringes where it didn't matter.

"Afraid of hurting the wittle animals' feelings?" I taunted.

"Nope. Gave up meat for Lent one year, and I really didn't miss it."

Having seen on the first night the guns he kept hidden under that dress shirt, I couldn't argue with his diet plan.

Then he had to ruin the moment by changing the subject.

"Beulah, I appreciate how your song may have inspired someone to join the church today, but you can't deviate from the bulletin."

"Now, Reverend—" Ginger started.

"I thought I told you to call me Luke," he said with a winning smile. That was an invitation he might want to rescind. After all, she had almost worn my name out.

"Luke," Ginger began as she sat up as straight as she could. "I believe I told you we wouldn't discuss business at the lunch table."

I put one hand on her arm. "We'll waive it for now. Go on."

"Look, a lot of work went into picking out that song. You can't just waltz into my church and tell me—"

"How to do your job?"

I let that nugget sink in. Would he apologize? Doing so would require him to tell Ginger about our argument outside The Fountain, and he didn't want to do that, for some reason. His eyes narrowed, and for a minute I thought he'd tell all anyway.

As he shifted uncomfortably, his knee brushed against mine. I moved my leg to rest against his on purpose.

His eyes widened for the merest of seconds before his mask was back in place. "Fine. You choose your songs, but I have final approval."

Not as magnanimous as I might have hoped, but it was probably the closest thing to an apology I was going to get. Of course, I wasn't above gently rubbing knees with a preacher while I did it. "And I'm sorry for most of those things I said."

"Most?" he scoffed.

"What are you two carrying on about?" Ginger said as we all leaned back for the waiter to slide our plates in front of us.

"Luke doesn't care for my signature song," I said.

"The song or how you play it?" she asked.

Great. A double dirty look.

"Well, it's a better song than that mess *he* picked out today."

His fork bore down into his enchilada, and cheese oozed out. "And what's that supposed to mean?"

"It means the last time I checked—which was admittedly about nine years ago—County Line was an old church set in its ways. They happen to like the little brown books full of golden oldies." And why was I discussing hymnals with this man?

Ginger took a bite of burrito and leaned against the wall. She'd decided to take in lunch and a show.

"And your little brown book of golden oldies is actually the young upstart from the twenties," Luke said. "The songs I chose go back to the seventeen hundreds. It's my job to take County Line back to its roots."

Heat flooded my face. Damn if I didn't hate to be wrong.

When I shifted in my seat, his leg pushed solidly against mine. I looked up to see steely eyes and his lips quirked upward as if to say, "Turnabout is fair play."

"County Line may be an old church set in its ways." He looked at Ginger. "No offense, Miss Ginger."

"None taken," she said with a shrug. "Always been a fan of calling a spade a spade."

"But the superintendent has told me that if we don't increase attendance the conference will close County Line and send members to the newer building at Deep Gap. We need a fresh start."

"By switching books?" My nachos weren't as appetizing as I'd thought they would be. Either that or I was losing yet another religious argument, which brought nothing but nausea from the memory of a hundred Sunday dinner arguments with my father. At least I didn't have to worry about Luke making me repeatedly copy Bible verses as punishment.

"By getting back to the basics."

I leaned over the table. "And yet you bagged a new family this morning with the song I chose."

He winced at the word *bagged* but nodded in concession. "Yes, this morning. But are they going to keep coming if we don't have more of the programs and music most families like? Overall attendance was down by ten today—that's twenty percent less than the past six-month average."

"And you seriously think a bunch of stuffy forgotten songs are going to do the trick?"

"This is ridiculous." Luke pushed his plate away. "How can someone who loves music as much as you do not see the need for both traditional and contemporary songs?"

By now both sets of knees pushed against each other under the table, thanks to how he had to fold his tall frame into the tiny booth as well as from our argument.

"Well, if you see the need for"—and I broke out my air quotes—" 'contemporary songs,' then why can't I jazz up what I play? What we did to 'Soon and Very Soon' was a disgrace!"

"Why is an artist like you so vehemently opposed to learning something new?"

Did he just call me an artist?

"And by new, I really mean only new to you. I thought only the older folks resisted change."

Ginger crunched loudly on a chip.

"Uh, no offense, Miss Ginger."

"Oh, none taken, Luke. We old people are notoriously crotchety and set in our ways. It's common knowledge."

"Nobody likes change," I murmured. The words rolled off my tongue of their own accord, but I realized I'd spent the past nine years of my life in a rut. It hadn't been an unpleasant rut, but a rut nonetheless.

"Well, change has to happen. Without it, County Line will shrivel up and die."

The idle chatter around us chose that moment to lull. The Powers family looked up from their booth across the restaurant to see who was going to die and what all the fuss was about. I held my eyes on Luke's. I was not going to think about anything or anyone shriveling up and dying.

"And that is why we don't talk business at Sunday lunch," Ginger said with a sigh. "You'll be happy to know we also don't allow sermon dissection until suppertime. That gives us ample time to properly digest the message."

Luke and I stared at each other, neither one of us willing to look away first.

Ginger put her napkin down on the table. "Come on, you two, that's enough fussing for one day. Let's walk on outside and let poor Jorge turn over his table."

Luke snatched the bill and went ahead to the counter while I helped Ginger slide out of the booth. Even mad, he was a man of his word. For a moment I thought he would walk out the door and not look back, but he waited at the door and held it open for us.

Once outside, Ginger pointed a palsied finger first at him then at me. "You. And you. Sit."

We both sat, next to each other, on a bench.

"Beulah, you are going to have to follow Luke's rules because he is, for now, your boss."

"But—"

"No buts. Luke, you need to get together with Beulah and talk about hymns because she's right. You can preach like crazy, but you don't know jack about music."

"But—"

"No buts from you, either, young man. Now, the only thing that's going to shrivel up and die around here is me, so you can just get it out of your head that the whole church is going to—to Hades in a handbasket if you don't 'save' it. Besides, I have some news for both of you."

She paused dramatically, daring either one of us to stop her.

"Beulah, Luke is right. The little brown book isn't full of old hymns. It's full of hymns that were new back when I was knee-high to a grasshopper. I simply prefer the songs of my youth," she concluded with a sniff.

I looked over at Luke, who was entirely too smug.

"And you, young man, should realize that many of the songs in that book are popular because they're powerful. No need to ignore them completely and throw the baby out with the bathwater. And Beulah's right about the 'Soon and Very Soon' massacre. I cringed."

That wiped the smirk off his face.

"Now, it's not really about what songs you sing," Ginger continued. "You had a nice new family join this morning, and they joined because your words spoke to them. So did Beulah's music. Imagine what would happen if the two of you ever learned to work together."

Luke and I looked at each other, two kids who'd been called to the side of the playground for fighting. I didn't want to work with him, and he sure as heck hadn't asked to work with me. I was about to tell Ginger that, but Luke spoke first.

"All right, Miss Ginger, what do you propose?"

On the one hand, I liked the fact that he was willing to listen to Ginger. He certainly didn't have to. He draped an arm over the bench behind him, clearly relaxed. He wasn't going to do a thing he didn't want to, but he also didn't see the need to tick off an old lady.

Her mouth turned upward a hair, and I felt a twinge of jealousy for how quickly he'd wormed himself into her good graces. "I'd say Wednesday would be a good day to compare notes with Beulah, don't you? You do have your sermons done by Wednesday, don't you, Luke?"

"Yes, ma'am." The look in his eye said he was no stranger to procrastination, but he wasn't about to admit it.

"Beulah, think you can hop on over and see the good Reverend Daniels since The Fountain is closed on Wednesday?"

I had trouble forcing out the words. I reminded myself I was twenty-five, for crying out loud. "Yes, ma'am."

"I'm sorry, I couldn't hear you."

"Yes, ma'am!"

"Good. Now, Beulah Lou, take me home. It's time for my nap."

I stood, but turned to Luke first. "Thank you for lunch."

Luke stood and shuffled from one foot to the other. "You're quite welcome."

Interesting. A vegetarian with muscles, a generous man not used to gratitude, and a squeaky-clean minister who hadn't been afraid to press his legs against mine. Obviously, there was more to Luke Daniels than I'd thought.

I kicked at rocks in the church parking lot for a good ten minutes the next Wednesday. I'd already proven I wouldn't catch fire upon entering the church, but that didn't mean I wanted to go inside. Of course, the afternoon sun and several persistent gnats made the idea much more appealing.

Once inside, I waited for the cool air to hit me, but the sanctuary was too hot for anything holy. Walking through the church back to Luke's office felt like pushing my way through invisible blankets, damp with steaming heat.

"Have mercy, Preacher Man, why is it so hot in here?"

He looked up from his desk, and I sucked in a breath. There he sat in one of those sleeveless undershirts, the last thing I would have expected to see him wearing. Stubble had taken over his jaw, and he wore a pair of glasses. He looked both domestic and dangerous in a soap-opera hero sort of way. "Beulah, I'm sorry. I lost track of time. I'm almost finished. Have a seat."

There were so many questions I wanted to ask him. What was going on with the heat? Did he really need glasses? Where *did* he get those muscles? Nope. I wasn't going to think about Luke doing push-ups so I looked to the wall. A poster of the *Sgt. Pepper's Lonely Hearts Club Band* had joined Abbey Road as well as a framed sketch of a pretty woman.

"Beatles fan?" he asked.

"Yeah," I said, wondering who the woman in the sketch could be. "I don't play them much, but I like to listen."

He grinned. "Good. If you'd told me you preferred the Stones, I would have had to fire you."

"I prefer the Stones."

"Nice try," he said pointedly before looking down at his desk to finish writing notes in the margin of the typed page in front of him. It was easy to forget Luke was a minister when he looked like this, rough around the edges with an easy smile.

"So, why is it such an inferno in here? It wasn't this hot last week." I swiped at the sweat that had beaded up on my forehead and leaned away from him.

"Oh, yesterday I got our new budget, and I had to crunch some numbers. Excess air-conditioning had to go." He capped the pen he'd been using and took off his glasses.

"*Excess* air-conditioning? But you work here during the week."

"Well, it's either this or let Joleen go because the conference didn't bother to tell me about a shortage of funds until *after* I had ordered handbells." His eyes met mine to see what I'd make of that.

Ginger once told me Joleen had been contracted to clean the church at some point before the civil rights movement. I averted my eyes. Curse him for making it so hard to dislike him. Wait, handbells?

"Then why don't you send the handbells back?"

"Handbells are a great way to get people involved in the church, and one of our members generously funded half the purchase." He leaned back in his chair and ran his fingers over the stubble on his chin, daring me to contradict him. "Besides, I'll be able to include AC again in a couple of months."

I blinked twice. Handbells seemed like a ridiculous waste of money to me. We already had a piano and an organ, but I didn't need to waste my time or what little breath I could catch arguing the point with him. Let him roast all summer if they meant that much to him. "Suit yourself."

"I'm going to need some songs on grace. Want to read the sermon to see what I'm talking about?"

No, I want to know what your exercise regimen is and if I can come watch. "No, thanks. Let's see, grace . . ."

A bead of sweat fell from his forehead onto an envelope he was about to open, and he hastily brushed it away. When my fingers twitched to help him out with that, I decided I didn't need to be in a room alone with him.

"I think it's actually cooler outside. Want to move this conversation to the oak tree out front?"

"You go ahead, and I'll be there in a minute." He frowned at the letter he held in his hands.

Once outside I could breathe easier, which said a lot for the sad state of the church. Didn't Luke realize he was never going to get the building cool enough in time for Sunday? Whatever. That was his problem. And it gave me a good excuse to wear my favorite spaghetti-strap sundress to church, too.

Underneath the oak, I sat at one of three old picnic tables to think about grace.

Grace was the girl's name I'd picked out.

For a brief moment I remembered New Orleans and pressing a hand to my rounded belly while standing shoulder to shoulder at Preservation Hall. That was about a month after Ginger had taken me in, and she was sick and tired of the bad attitude and the stomping around. She'd put me in the car, and we didn't say a word other than "I have to pee" until we reached the outskirts of New Orleans.

"What's all this about?" I'd asked in a surly teenage tone that Ginger didn't in the least deserve.

"Something I think you need to see," she finally said as we pulled up to the curb of an aging but elegant hotel that overlooked the streetcar line. Ginger passed the valet her keys, and I gawked. I'd never seen a real life valet before. She even let another uniformed man get the bags out of the trunk, as though letting someone else handle her luggage was the most natural thing in the world.

"What could there possibly be here that I couldn't see at home?" My question trailed off as I looked all around me at the faded opulence. Once upon a time, this hotel had really been something.

"We both need an attitude adjustment," Ginger had said primly as she took the key and led me to the elevator.

After a nap, she took me outside to catch the streetcar, and we rocked and clanked our way to Bourbon Street. Warm jazz and raucous laughter oozed out of dingy buildings into the street as day faded into night. Ginger took my hand and pulled me to the middle of the street as I gaped at a swing with fake legs above a doorway. Everywhere people laughed, danced, and drank.

Up until that point, I'd only known Ginger as the prim and proper lady who sat beside me for years of piano lessons. The faraway expression she'd once worn was gone, and her eyes twinkled as she led me through unbridled revelry.

We waited in a long line, and my lower back began to hurt. I didn't want to say anything, though, because I wanted to know more about this Ginger who nonchalantly tipped valets and waltzed down Bourbon Street like she knew exactly where she was going.

Finally, we shuffled inside. At first I was disappointed. The room had no air-conditioning, no decoration, and precious few seats. The grizzled musicians appeared with the air that *they* were doing *us* the favor despite the fact we'd paid them.

When they began to play, I realized they were.

They played "Just a Closer Walk with Thee" in a way I'd never heard it before. Clarinet, trumpet, trombone, and banjo played over, under, and around each other in a beautiful chaos, then gave way to a solo from each player. The pianist plunked keys with steady confidence, helping the drummer keep time. We listened to a handful of New Orleans classics, then filed out and came back in for more.

Ginger made a request, again flashing cash. *Who is this woman?* I wondered. At the end of that set, they played "Amazing Grace," and it all clicked for the Baptist preacher's girl that there was a whole world beyond what I'd always known. For that one moment in time, I could believe in a world where good and bad lived side by side. For that moment, I believed we could all tamp down the bad a little more and let the good rise to the top. For that moment, I was ready to try again, to try things Ginger's way.

We never talked about what happened that weekend in New Orleans, but Ginger fed me well and I came home a new person. On the long car ride home, I decided I'd name my baby Grace if she was a girl.

"Any luck?"

I jumped out of my skin as Luke's question brought me back to the present. "Didn't your mama tell you not to sneak up on people?"

He took a seat beside me and held out a glass of sweet tea. "Nope. She didn't have time to teach me much of anything before she passed away."

Sweat dripped from the glass and plinked on my leg. "I'm sorry."

"Don't be. It happened a long time ago." He took a gulp of his tea and eased onto the seat across from me.

"But still—"

"Wound's healed, Beulah. She's in a better place."

I gritted my teeth against the memory of a ridiculously small white casket—no way would I ever talk so easily about his death. How were we supposed to know for sure our loved ones were in a better place? "So, I was thinking about a few hymns you could put here."

Luke's eyes bored through me as if he knew why I was changing the subject. "Who did you lose?"

I could tell him. I could tell him about how I called my baby Grace right up until the moment I popped out a baby boy and named him Hunter. I could tell him about how scary and awful it had been and how I wasn't old enough to take care of myself much less a baby. I could tell him how much it hurt to lose that child just when I felt I might make it after all, but I hadn't said anything to anyone about my baby for so long that the words were rusty, unable to move out of my throat and into my mouth. It hit me. I'd allowed myself to think about my sweet, sweet baby boy by name for the first time in years, and I couldn't think his name twice in one day.

I choked out different words. "You could use 'Love, Mercy and Grace' here or stick with an oldie but goodie, 'Amazing Grace'—"

Trying to change the subject again gave me a reason to ignore how he gazed patiently, relentlessly. I didn't know it then, but Luke was an expert at excavating secrets. "Beulah, we don't always understand why someone has to die, but—"

A sob escaped in spite of my best efforts, but I wasn't about to let him see me cry. "Do you really think I haven't heard all of this hogwash before? You don't know. You. Do. Not. Know."

I stood, ready to run, but he was there with his hands on my shoulders holding me in place.

"I'm sorry. I didn't mean to make you cry," he said.

I swiped at both cheeks and cleared my throat. "Well, you did. The heathen has a heart. There? You happy?"

"Not really." From the way he studied me, I thought he might kiss me. Just when I'd decided I'd let him, something, some deeply buried secret of his own, made him release my arms and step back. " 'Love, Mercy and Grace,' huh?"

I nodded, reaching for the tea. If I could swallow the tea, then I could swallow a lump of sadness. For a minute I thought I was going to make it. Now he sat on the other side of the picnic table holding his own tea and waiting patiently for me to talk hymns or lost babies.

When the moment came to speak, I walked to the car instead.

Chapter 6

The next night I should have known immediately something was wrong with Tiffany. She looked a little green around the gills, as my aunt Edith would have said. And she kept bolting for the bathroom. But I didn't notice those things at first.

Instead, I was still in my funk about Luke and his questions, wanting to think about Hunter and not wanting to think about him all at the same time. I was on my third slow song with "baby" in the title when Bill leaned over to whisper, "Think you can play something a little peppier? The boys are getting kinda down."

I nodded and vowed to play something up-tempo next. "The boys are getting kinda down" was Bill-speak for "You're making folks so sad they'd rather go home to their miserable lives than hang out here, which means we won't make any money." I humored everyone with classics like "There's a Tear in My Beer" and with some audience participation in "You Never Even Called Me by My Name." By the time nine rolled around, I was ready to sing my song with my usual gusto. After a particularly rowdy version, I snagged a beer and stepped outside for my break.

There was Tiffany at the side of the building retching her fool head off. Then I knew, but I was the one who felt dizzy. "Tiffany, you okay?"

"Hell, no. I want to go home and lie down."

"What's wrong?" My heart was beating so loudly in my ears I wondered if I would be able to hear her answer. *Please, please let me be wrong.*

She turned to face me, wiping her mouth on her forearm. "I don't know. I swear I thought it was some bad shrimp I got from Seafood Sam's, but I should have been over that by now. And I'm so damned tired. All I want to do is go home and take a nap."

She didn't know. Bless her heart. She didn't know.

"Think you might be pregnant?"

Her brown eyes widened in horror.

"Maybe you ought to ask Bill for the night off." I patted her on the shoulder and turned to go back in. It wasn't any of my business, and I shouldn't have said anything. From behind me, Tiffany made a horrible choking, mewing sound. I told myself I didn't want any part of it. I didn't want to get involved with her growing belly. I didn't want to see her healthy baby boy, a baby she would think she didn't want. And I hoped to goodness she wouldn't have to find out how much she did, indeed, want that baby.

Not like I did.

"Beulah, please."

At that, I turned around, and she fell into my arms before I could stop her. I wanted to shove her away and to yell at her for being so stupid. How could she throw away that scholarship for some asshole guy? What had she been thinking?

And I remembered how plenty of people, particularly my parents, had yelled those questions and accusations at me. I wouldn't do that to Tiffany. No one deserved to be skewered for mistakes that couldn't be erased. No one.

I drew her closer and rubbed her shoulder with my free hand. "It's going to be okay. Promise."

Total bullshit, but she didn't have to know that yet.

Bill poked his head out the door. "Beulah, you gonna play tonight? Tiff, you gonna pass out beers? You two having some kind of Summer's Eve moment out here?"

"Just a minute, Bill. Keep your pants on," I said.

He let the screen door slam behind him.

"I gotta go play," I said. "Why don't you go on home and rest? You can get a test in the morning to be sure. Maybe it's bad shrimp after all."

She nodded but then followed me in and finished out her shift with a grim determination I couldn't help but admire. But I made sure I didn't sing any more songs with the word *baby*.

Just after the eleven o'clock rendition of my song, Luke walked in and sat down beside me at the bar.

"I didn't expect to see you here," I said as I motioned to Bill. "Hey, get a beer for the preacher man, would you?"

"I'm not staying long," he said. "I only wanted to see if you were okay after this afternoon."

"Just peachy," I said as I took a swig from my foreign beer of the week, a Hoegaarden. My pulse beat double time. Luke had come back into The Fountain to check on me. "But thanks for asking."

He gave me that half smile I was growing to like in spite of myself. For a second or two, I caught a glimpse of Luke the man as he sat on a stool and drank a beer.

"I gotta get back to work," I whispered.

"Take any requests? Maybe a Beatles song?" he asked.

"Only for a tip," I said with a grin.

He fished around in his wallet for a single and held it out to me.

"That's only good for 'Yellow Submarine.' Just so you know," I said.

This time he came back with a five. "How about this?"

I whistled. "For that kind of money, you get to pick."

He closed my fingers around Abe Lincoln. "Surprise me."

I sat down to sing about how I could get by with a little help from my friends, but then I hit the line about believing in love at first sight, and I couldn't stop the furious blush at the edge of my cheeks. Damn him! No one made me blush. No one but the Beatles-loving preacher man!

I just need somebody to love.

Nope. Not going there.

Blessedly, the song ended. Luke saluted me with his beer bottle and quietly left. While watching him go, I broke a cardinal rule by sitting silently. Leaving any amount of dead air meant that someone from the pool table would have the opportunity to shout, "Play some Skynyrd!"

I sighed deeply. "That one's going to cost you!"

They came up with the necessary twenty bucks, and I had to play "Sweet Home Alabama." In my heart, though, I was still humming the Beatles.

That Sunday, with the help of one of Ginger's hideous shawls I had no intention of wearing past the car, I managed to slip out of the house in my favorite sundress and cowboy boots. Since we were already running late, Ginger looked at me and shook her head.

Running late was part of the plan, too, because it meant I could sneak past Luke and into the choir loft without having to speak to him. Between breaking down into tears and accidentally playing a song about needing someone to love, I didn't really want to chance saying something else stupid.

We went through the motions just fine. Luke had smiled at my song choices, even if he wasn't happy about a return to the little brown book. I smiled, too, until I looked over at the empty choir loft. Were the members all absent or still boycotting me? If so, then so much for last week's whole judge-not spiel.

From my perch in the choir loft, I looked for the usual suspects. All I could remember from nine years ago were the twins. There Miss Lottie and Miss Lola sat side by side. Counting the other heads was no problem since the pews were more empty than not. Even so, I saw Lester "Goat Cheese" Ledbetter on the back row, twisting his fingers one over the other as if he'd prefer to be smoking a cigarette. No doubt he'd come out of curiosity, since the only person more in the know about community doings had to be Miss Georgette. I looked behind me at the dusty wooden sign with cardboard numbers, the one that proclaimed attendance and weekly offering. Twenty-two present that day. The sign declared record attendance to be six, but that was only because County Line had long ago lost the other six that used to hang in front of it.

I remembered the day we set that record, too. It was my second day in church with Ginger, and I sat beside her in the most hideous blue paisley maternity dress. Tom Dickens had come by and chucked me under the chin, thanking me for being number sixty-six.

I missed Tom Dickens.

I realized the sanctuary of today was eerily quiet, and the whole bunch of them looked at me expectantly. Song leader Jason Utley needed a song. I whispered a number then took my place at the piano while everyone thumbed through their books.

After church, I skipped down the choir loft steps and leaped into the mix of cliques that gathered to exchange well wishes for the week. I rushed for the only choir member I remembered. "Miss Lottie?"

She had her back to me, and she stiffened, steeling herself to turn and answer me. "Beulah."

"I can't help but notice you haven't been in the choir the past two Sundays. Everything okay?"

She gathered herself tall, pulling in as much of her ample bosom as she could muster. In her rust-colored suit with her double chin and regal bearing, she reminded me of a Rhode Island Red preparing to scratch around the chicken coop. "We feel you should not be playing the piano here if you're going to continue to play at The Fountain."

My smile stayed in place. "I don't really see what one has to do with the other."

"Good Christian people don't go *there.* And they certainly

don't make fun of hymns and drink and carouse while they do it."

"And how would you know all that if good Christian people don't go there?" I batted my eyelashes. I couldn't help myself.

"I hear things," she sputtered.

"Maybe you shouldn't believe everything you hear." I leaned forward.

"Tell me I'm wrong," she said, leaning forward to meet me.

"You're wrong." After all, I didn't drink and carouse *while* I played. "I would think you could help me out since I'm only doing this as a favor to Ginger."

"Yes, yes. That Ginger is a remarkable woman." The unspoken "but" hung heavy in the air. I was the blemish on Ginger's record, the one stain she couldn't explain to others. I'm sure Charlotte Miller wouldn't have dreamed of taking me in, and she would have kicked me out the minute I started playing piano at what was then known as Bill's Tavern.

Miss Lottie stood up taller, suddenly sporting a smile. "I'll tell you what. You get out of that honky-tonk, and we'll go right back to singing in the choir," she said in an unnaturally loud voice. She pinched my cheek then gave it a rougher-than-usual pat. "We all know a good girl still lives in there somewhere."

At that moment I wouldn't have quit playing at The Fountain for a million dollars. "Funny how people there are a whole helluva lot nicer to me than people here."

I wheeled around to make my escape and came nose to chest with Luke. The last part of Miss Lottie's speech had been for him. When I looked up, I saw his flashing eyes and clenched jaw. He was going to bless me out for cussing in front of an old biddy in church.

Instead, his stare was for her. When he looked down at me, he asked, "You okay, Beulah?"

"You're asking if she's okay?" huffed Miss Lottie. "I think it's time Mr. Dartmouth and I had another chat about how things are being run around here!"

Luke winced at her comment, but his eyes didn't leave mine.

"Fine," I murmured. I needed to move, but I was drawn to him even though a good four inches separated us.

"Beulah? Ready to go?"

Dammit, Ginger.

Luke took one step back and then two.

"Yeah, I'm ready." It was so stupid to be leaning toward Luke Daniels. Especially in the middle of a church with an audience.

Ginger tugged on my arm and pulled me back in the direction of the choir loft and out of the earshot of exiting church members. "Now why'd you have to do that?"

"I wanted to know why no one was in the choir."

"No, you didn't." Ginger shook her head. "I should have thought about how petty people could be. Maybe this wasn't such a good idea. Maybe I should have left well enough alone and found someone else to play the piano."

"Oh, *now* you decide that," I muttered. It was irrational to feel she was disappointed in me when she was so clearly disappointed in her fellow church members, but I felt tiny. "No, Ginger. I promised you I would play for you, and I'm going to do it. If Miss Lottie and her friends want to pretend we're in junior high, that's their problem."

Ginger squeezed my hand. "That's my Beulah. Let's go get some lunch."

The sanctuary was empty except for the two of us and Luke. He looked out at the parking lot, his face sad and pinched. Ginger dropped her purse, and his head snapped toward the two of us and he summoned a smile. "Just had to get me alone, didn't you?"

"Oh, you know us, we're a couple of wanton hussies," Ginger said as I stooped to get her purse. "I was hoping you might squire us to lunch again—with me paying this time. It's the least I can do now that Lottie's going to sic Dartmouth on you."

My eyes cut to Ginger. "Who's Dartmouth?"

* * *

I had to wait until after we'd ordered at Las Palmas before I could get the answer to my question.

"Thomas Dartmouth is the district superintendent. He was planning to come sometime in the next three weeks, depending on his schedule." Luke dipped his chip into salsa and took a huge bite.

"And?" I couldn't help but notice Luke was being very sure not to brush knees with me.

"And I need to show County Line in the best light possible," Luke said. "Remember what I said about increasing attendance to keep both churches going? As long as County Line has at least fifty members and shows signs of growing, I don't think there's a problem. But I have a bit of a complication."

"A complication?" I thought everything had gone well. Except for the part where I'd cussed Miss Lottie.

He looked away. "Miss Lottie has complained to the superintendent that she doesn't feel comfortable singing in the choir as long as you are playing piano. Now I have no one in the choir and the church's overall attendance is down."

"What?" I looked at his eyes for some sort of confirmation or denial that he saw me as a problem. I found neither. "Well, I guess that settles it. I quit."

About thirty seconds into staring at the little cast-iron bowl of salsa, I realized I wanted him to tell me no. I wanted Ginger to say no. I wanted both of them to tell me how much they needed me and that everyone else needed to get over themselves. Instead, Luke was looking at Ginger with an "I told you so" glance. She, then, looked at me.

"But if you quit now, then they win," she said.

"Let them win," I spat, but my words tasted bitter.

"Oh, no. You're not quitting now," Luke said. "I've already sent an e-mail to Dartmouth outlining my reasons for hiring you and telling him how well you play. I'm *not* getting moved to another church because of petty infighting. We go on, business as usual."

"Excuse me? What if I don't want to go on, 'business as usual'?"

"We've started this, and we're going to finish it." His chin jerked up as Jorge slid plates in front of us.

"*I* didn't start this, and *I* don't have any desire to finish it."

"You know, I didn't take you for a quitter," Luke said.

The imaginary smoke coming from my ears matched the smoke patterns rising from my fajitas. I imagined tiny Indians with blankets standing on the pile of meat, onions, and peppers sending signals in the pattern of an SOS on my behalf. "It doesn't matter what I want."

"What do you mean?" His eyes narrowed, and his fork stopped midair.

"Miss Lottie doesn't want to share the choir loft with a honky-tonk harlot. The choir is protesting, as you so eloquently put it, me." I glared at him.

"Then we find another choir. A younger choir, a fresher choir." He took one bite of salad then another. The restaurant was so empty I could hear the crunch of his lettuce over the Tejano music.

"What's this 'we' stuff, kemosabe?"

He leaned back. "You're right. Not we. You. You're going to find the choir for me."

"Me?"

"Yes, you. The choir left because you started playing, so I think it only fair that you convince some new members to sing in the choir. You know, people who want to sing with you."

I looked to Ginger for support, but she shrugged her shoulders as if to say she didn't have a better answer.

"Luke, seriously, why do I even care if you have a choir? Especially not since I quit, and I won't be coming back." I stabbed a hunk of meat with my fork and considered waving it in his face.

"You care because I'm asking you as a favor to me." He took an equally big forkful of lettuce and pointed it at me before shoving it in his mouth.

I snorted. *Wait, he's asking me for a favor?*

"And you care because you promised Miss Ginger, and you don't want to let her down."

Ginger frowned into her best impersonation of the tragedy mask and nodded her head, only half mocking me.

Very well. He had found my Kryptonite. Suddenly, I saw a vision, an almost holy vision. Or an unholy vision, as the case might be.

"Uh-oh. Beulah Land, what are you up to?" I hadn't realized I was grinning, but it was a look Ginger had seen before.

"Oh, you'll see. Let's just say I was struck with inspiration."

Chapter 7

The next night, I was a woman on a mission. Maybe your average choir director would think of ways to appeal to the goodness of people. I surveyed the crowd at The Fountain, searching for people I could easily blackmail or flirt into joining my choir. The greater their transgressions, the better. Either I'd have the satisfaction of knowing Lottie Miller was sharing a building with people she despised or Luke would be exasperated enough by such tactics to finally fire me. It was win-win, really.

My eyes locked on Old Man MacGregor, and I knew I had my first member. One night two years ago I'd gone outside for a breath of fresh air. He'd jumped from around the corner and flashed me. He'd been hoping to shock me. Willing my face to keep its earlier bored expression, I'd asked him if I could bum a cigarette. I'd quit by then, but I needed a smoke after the sight of his shriveled junk. He'd sheepishly closed his raincoat and fished through his coat pocket for a pack of cigarettes, and that was the last time he'd tried such a trick on me.

These days he wasn't wearing that nasty old raincoat, so I supposed he was limiting himself to improper tipping. As if inspired by my thoughts, he tried to ram a fiver down Tiffany's shirt.

Oh, it's on, old man.

I jumped down from the risers the minute I finished my song

and took a seat across from MacGregor. "Next time you want to tip Tiffany—and I highly recommend you continue that practice—you can leave it on the table."

He grinned sheepishly. "I'm sorry, Beulah. I don't know why I do that."

"I don't either. Maybe you need a new hobby."

In his surprise he swallowed air with his beer then coughed to recover. "Say what?"

"I need to put together a choir for the church over there. Seems to me you know how to read music from your stint as a trombone player in the navy."

"It was a short one," he muttered as he studied his feet.

I puzzled over my first choir member. Shoulders slumped, salt-and-pepper hair hanging to his shoulders, Old Man MacGregor was a lonely old man who spent entirely too much time at The Fountain or with the adult-only channels of his satellite dish. "Long enough to read notes."

"Beulah, I don't know. I don't have much time for—"

"You're retired."

"I don't like to get in front of crowds."

I raised an eyebrow, refusing to look away. He must've remembered the night I couldn't forget because his ears turned red.

"I think we both know that isn't entirely true," I said softly.

"You wouldn't!"

"Oh, but I would. Wednesday night. Be here at seven."

I slapped my hand on the table and went back to the piano, not giving him a chance to argue. About halfway through my rendition of "Flashdance," he got up and left, but I knew I had him.

As luck would have it, Julian McElroy and his bestest buddy, Ben Little, strolled in. Julian was easy on the eyes with his blond hair and farm-boy strut. Ben grinned at something his friend said, white teeth flashing against dark skin. So pretty to look at, the both of them, and I knew they could sing from back when we had a karaoke machine.

Julian had destroyed the karaoke machine, mind you, but there wasn't much he could smash up in the choir loft. At my first break I sidled over to their table, pulling my shirt a little lower along the way. I dragged a chair over, turning the back to the table and straddling it so the back of the chair helped elevate the girls. What else could I do?

"How are my favorite karaoke singers tonight?"

Julian's smile faded into the somber expression I was more familiar with. "Thought you were still mad at me about that machine. I've almost saved up enough money to replace it—promise."

I waved away his concerns and batted my eyelashes a little. "Oh, let's let bygones be bygones. But funny you should mention singing—"

"Actually, *you* mentioned singing," Ben said as he took a long pull from his beer. Damn lawyers.

"So I did." This wasn't going well. They looked at my cleavage, though I'd heard both men were attached at the moment, but I would've been sorely offended if they hadn't at least *looked.* Might as well be straight. "I need some singers for a choir."

"What kind of choir?" asked Julian with a frown.

"Um, a church choir? Across the street at County Line?"

They had the audacity to laugh.

"No can do," Julian said.

"Come on, please?" *Am I really begging? Not cool.* "Ben, tell him. It'll be fun."

Ben had frozen and was looking at me as if I'd sprouted an extra head. "Let me get this straight. You, Beulah Land, are asking us to join a church choir."

"Yes." I reached across the table to grab a hand of each and leaned forward conspiratorially. "To tell you the truth, it's kinda a big deal. I could really use your help."

"Well, my presence is required at Zion Baptist each Sunday morning, so I'm afraid I can't help you out," Ben said.

I turned to Julian.

"Oh, no. If I go to church, it's going to be over at Grace Baptist."

"Come on, guys, can you help a girl out?"

"Sorry," Ben said with a shrug.

Julian looked away, a sure sign my presence was not wanted.

"Well, thank you anyway." I put my chair back and headed up the risers.

So much for being nice.

The next night I finished the nine o'clock singing of "Dwelling in Beulah Land" and turned my sights on the Gates brothers. There they stood at the pool table, both baritones, best I could tell. Not for the first time I wondered how these two could be brothers. Greg was blond and pale, freckled from years of farmwork out in the sun. Pete stood a foot taller with creamy caramel skin and wavy reddish-brown hair—he was my next victim.

Not that I felt too good about what I was about to do.

"Hey, Pete, come outside a sec. I wanna ask you a question." I headed for the door, knowing he would follow because those were the same words he'd said to me six years ago. His question had been a very succinct "Wanna screw?" My answer wasn't one I was proud of, but, in my defense, I was suffering from losing Hunter, trying to take care of Ginger, and trying to figure out why people ever bothered with this sex business anyway.

Needless to say, Pete and I didn't have any answers for each other.

By the time he rounded the corner, he had fear in his eyes, something the Gates brothers inspired but rarely experienced. "What's this all about?"

"I need a little favor from you and your brother," I said sweetly.

"What?" he asked warily.

"Oh, only a little bit of your time on Wednesdays and Sundays to sing in the church choir."

He took three steps back as if I'd scalded him. "Nuh-uh. No way."

"Pete, Pete," I said. "Surely you'd like for me to keep your secret, wouldn't you?"

He swallowed hard. "You wouldn't."

I twirled a strand of hair around my finger because it seemed like a femme fatale thing to do. "I wouldn't like it, but I'll do what I've got to do."

He ran a hand through his closely cropped hair. "What the hell? Why would you go around telling everyone about us and—"

"Whoa." I shook my head. "What kind of person do you think I am? I was going to tell everybody how you really chipped your tooth over there in the parking lot that night you got drunk and fell."

"Aw, Beulah."

I smiled. Pete scraped together a living with his Walmart job, a smattering of farming, and a pet project: his animal removal business. His business had finally taken off when he spun the tale of how he got kicked in the mouth by one of his horses after a nest of copperheads hatched outside the barn. I was the only person who'd witnessed what really happened with his tooth.

He cursed under his breath, knowing he was had. "What am I supposed to tell my brother?"

"I'm sure you'll think of something," I said.

He swore loudly and profusely. "Why would you do a thing like that?"

"I need a choir. You can sing. It won't be that bad. Promise."

He turned to face me and grinned, giving me a hint of his chipped front tooth. "You could have asked nicely."

"I could have," I answered sweetly, "but that's not my style, and you would've said no."

"Dammit, Beulah!"

"If I had a dollar for every time I've heard that."

"I mean dammit."

Greg leaned out the door. "It's your shot, dumbass."

That was my cue. "Wednesday at seven. Don't forget your brother."

A few minutes later, I took my seat behind the piano, relieved by my progress but less than happy about how I'd achieved it.

One go-through of Jimmy Buffett's "Why Don't We Get Drunk," and Pete Gates was shooting daggers at me from the other side of the pool table. Just when I thought I'd overplayed my hand, he turned to Greg and whispered something in his ear. Based on Greg's expression, I was back in the game.

My mind whirled with possibilities. Ginger would have to be in the choir because she'd gotten me into this mess, but a soprano would be hard to find. Romy was an old karaoke regular, but I hadn't seen her in forever. I also might have ticked her off the last time I saw her. I could sing soprano sometimes, but I was really more of an alto.

Tiffany had a pretty voice and could even hold it steady while she walked, but for some reason it felt worse to ask her for help than to blackmail either of the guys.

Because you don't like to be beholden to anyone. With them, you'll be square.

Be that as it may, it was time to swallow my pride and ask a favor.

I motioned for Tiffany to come over. She leaned forward, her cleavage almost meeting mine in a way that stopped several conversations. "Tiff, can you send a couple of Bud Lights over to the Gates brothers, compliments of me?"

"Sure," she said, but she was looking at me like I'd lost my mind.

And maybe I had. I'd recruited a flasher and two barroom brawlers, one of whom was gay, to sing in a church choir that objected to me on the grounds of an unwed teen pregnancy and generally loose behavior.

Speaking of a teen pregnancy . . .

As I watched Tiffany hand a beer to each of the bewildered Gates brothers, I knew I had to ask her. We would bring misfit to a whole new level. Pete looked at me quizzically, and I nodded my compliments. Then he raised his longneck in mock salute.

I hadn't been forgiven, but I might be on the path.

* * *

That night at closing, I caught Tiffany as she was going out the door. "Hey, Tiffany, how would you like to maybe sing in a church choir?"

She looked me up and down, her features suddenly cynical. "Is this some kind of joke?"

"No, I wish it were. Ginger's got me playing piano across the street—"

"I'd heard that."

"And I kinda ran off the choir and need a new one. Something about Luke getting a visit from his boss and—"

"Reverend Daniels who lives across the parking lot?"

Well, that certainly perked her up. "Yes. One and the same."

"I'd be singing where *he* could hear me?" Her cheeks brightened.

"Yes," I said slowly. "He does preach there."

"I'll do it."

That was easy. Too easy.

Now I only needed a bass. Maybe I should put Luke and Ginger up to praying for one since I couldn't remember hearing a good bass in The Fountain in years.

Wednesday afternoon rolled around, and I still didn't have a bass. I surveyed the little group of people sitting at the foot of the risers. Ginger wasn't there, but she would be my alto. Tiffany was going to sing soprano—as long as she didn't toss her cookies trying. Old Man MacGregor sang a high, thin tenor, but he sang surprisingly on key . . . when sober. Both of the Gates boys sang in the middle range—they just couldn't read notes well enough to pick tenor or bass . . . yet.

"Well, I wanted to thank you for coming out here."

Most of the gang grumbled. They weren't there because they wanted to be.

"And thanks to Bill for letting us use The Fountain on his night off." The crowd, most of whom held a drink courtesy of yours truly, cheered for Bill, who held his own beer up in salute.

"All right, we're going to get in and get out—"

"That's what she said," snickered Pete Gates.

I leveled him with a stare.

He cleared his throat. "Sorry, what were you saying?"

"I was saying let's make it quick, and—"

"Ha! That's what *she* said to you," Greg said as he elbowed his brother.

Now that one hit too close to the mark, so I raised an eyebrow at Pete, who immediately smacked his brother upside the head with a "Shut up, man. I told you to be serious."

Taking in a deep breath, I forced myself to continue instead of telling them all to go to hell. "I'm going to try this one more time. The next person who interrupts me has to hand me his beer."

That did the trick.

"We are going to sing number two-thirty-three, "Love Lifted Me." We're going to sing it in unison, and we're going to like it."

"Sorry I'm late."

At the impossibly deep voice, I looked up to see a tall, lanky man who looked like a cross between an older Rick Astley and Grizzly Adams. It took me a minute to recognize him without his trucker hat, but it was Carl Davis, Tiffany's father.

I had never once heard Carl sing along with my songs, but if his speaking voice was any indication, he had the range I was looking for. "Can you sing bass?"

"Only thing I can sing," he said, his gaze going to Tiffany.

I looked at Tiffany. She shrugged with a weak smile.

"Okay, then. Welcome to the choir, Carl." Someone helped Carl find the proper page in the hymnal, and I played a gorgeous introduction. My choir gave me a lackluster effort.

"That wasn't half bad," Bill said, probably as much to smooth my ruffled feathers as anything else.

"You think so?" asked Tiffany, her cheeks pink. Had she taken the test? Was she glowing with relief or motherhood?

"Okay. Let's try that again with harmony. We'll just see how it goes."

The song's natural tempo picked them up, but they were

also gaining confidence. I had them sing a couple more songs before we returned to the harmony on "Love Lifted Me." First, I played individual parts. Greg took the higher tenor notes with Old Man MacGregor. Pete took the lower notes but couldn't sing quite as low as Carl, whose voice had been ravaged by cigarettes but was otherwise surprisingly in tune. Then we put it all together.

When we finished, we all sat there and let the song linger in silence. They didn't sing perfectly, but they sang well. Moments of pure harmony had jumped out at me, a promise of potential. And by the last verse? As Ginger would say, they all had even put a little heart into it.

"Good job," I murmured, still amazed that my plan had worked to this point.

All of the components were there but the polish. Of course, I knew Ginger would sing alto with me any time she could. The Gates brothers and Carl needed to practice their line, but the song had spoken to us.

I felt it, deep in my bones. These were people who knew what it was like to sink, constantly bobbing, coughing, and sputtering through life. They weren't bad people; they were people with bad problems. They, like me, wanted to be lifted out of the angry waves just like the song promised.

Unlike Lottie Miller, who sang to hear herself sing, my little ragtag choir sang because they had to or just to help me out. They had bewildered me with how seriously they'd taken practice. The music had reeled them in from those angry waves, and the room was all smiles.

As folks stacked my contraband hymnals and finished their beers, Bill sat somberly in the corner. "I was going to joke and say y'all were just a happy hour choir, but you sang good. Real good."

"Thank you," Tiffany said, genuinely smiling for the first time in a week.

"The Happy Hour Choir?" Old Man MacGregor laughed his

crazy cackle. "I like it. What do you say there, Beulah? Do we look like a Happy Hour Choir to you? I think we'd need a round of beers for that."

"You heard the man, Bill, another round of beers on me for the Happy Hour Choir." I grinned at them, marveling at the puff of pride in my chest. I'd thought making a choir would be like pulling teeth, but I was proud of them, so proud of all of them.

"Hey, Beulah," Old Man MacGregor asked timidly. "Think we could play 'In the Sweet By and By' sometime? That was always my mother's favorite."

"That's a great idea, Mac." And with that sentence I started a second tradition. Old Man MacGregor was no more. He became Mac. Just that night he started sitting up a little straighter and drinking a little less. "I'll see y'all tomorrow," I said as I gathered the hymnals.

"Where're you going, Beulah?" Tiffany's wide eyes blinked at me.

"I'm going home," I said. "I have a date with a lumpy couch and a persnickety old lady."

I couldn't make it out the door, because Tiffany blocked my way. I stepped to the side, still weighed down by my stack of books. "Beulah, you were right. What am I going to do?"

"Why in the hell are you asking me?" I whispered.

"Because, you know . . ." She shifted from one foot to the other, her hands in her back pockets. We both knew she was asking me because I was one of the most famous unwed teen mothers in Yessum County history. "Baptist Preacher's Daughter Falls Spectacularly from Grace. Father Dies of a Broken Heart." Those weren't actual newspaper headings, but they might as well have been.

My throat closed up. "I can't. I—"

"Please, Beulah. I can't tell Daddy." She looked at Carl, the only person who'd willingly agreed to join the choir. "He's gonna blow a gasket because I'm sure to lose my scholarship when I tell the university."

I closed my eyes and inhaled in search of an answer. Tiffany's softball scholarship. She had been poised to be the first Davis in the family to make it to college. Until now. I wanted to rant and rail and call her stupid, but I had walked at least half a mile in her shoes and couldn't toss stones at that particular glass house.

"What about your momma?" I asked, as if having a mother somehow made the situation better instead of worse. It hadn't for me.

"I don't know where she is," Tiffany said softly. "South Carolina with some truck driver, last I heard."

"Well, you don't have to keep the baby," I said. On paper it seemed the logical choice, but I hadn't been able to do it.

She shook her head no. "I don't think I can do that."

I wanted to brush past Tiffany, but she blocked my path.

"Tiffany, I don't know what to tell you. I wish I did." I knew I should help her, but I couldn't. I certainly didn't know how to do teen pregnancy right.

I turned to go before she could stop me, and I ran smack into Luke just outside the door. The screen door slapped shut, and I almost came out of my shoes trying not to bowl him over.

Luke's hands landed on either side of my waist, their heat burning through my jeans. "Whoa, Beulah, what's the rush?"

Then I made the mistake of looking up into those blue eyes of his, eyes the color of the crashing, angry waves we had been singing about earlier. Not only was I especially susceptible to those eyes, but the grim set of his mouth suggested he had seen and/or heard the exchange between me and Tiffany.

"I've got to pick up supper for Ginger, and I'm already running late."

"That's fine. It was a rhetorical question, so no need to explain." He moved his hands to my shoulders and backed me up to take a look at what had been poking him in the chest. "Were you planning to sell those on the black market?"

I shifted the stack of hymnals to one hip. "No, just putting together your choir."

"My choir, huh?" He stroked his chin, and I could hear rather than see the hint of stubble. "Let me help you with those."

When he reached for the books, I flinched. He gently took them from me anyway.

"So why are you here, Preacher Man? If you keep crossing the parking lot, tongues are going to wag sure enough."

"I'm going to see if any of your choir members are interested in starting a Bible study."

I laughed out loud. "You're kidding me, right? I had to bribe and blackmail almost every one of those folks to do some singing, and you think you're going to walk in there and start a Bible study."

He tossed the books in the car and slammed the door. "Not a joke. Quite a few unconventional Bible studies have cropped up all over the country in bars and taverns."

"And you think this is going to work?"

"Maybe."

That had to be one of his favorite words: *maybe*.

"So, you're going straight to the sinners to tell them about the saints? Sip some beer with tax collectors? Maybe hang out with the social lepers for a while?"

He folded his arms and leaned back against the car. The old junker had never looked so good. "You put together the choir. Maybe I'm taking a page from the Book of Beulah."

Was that a compliment?

I crammed my hands in my pockets because they needed something to do other than test the feel of the stubble on his chin. "What are you going to call this Bible study? Suds and Scripture? Longneck Theology? No, wait. I like what I said before." I cleared my throat for dramatic effect. "You can call it the Sinners to Saints Bible Study: Everything You Always Wanted to Know About the Bible but Were Afraid to Ask."

His eyes flashed. "Jesus didn't just preach in the synagogues, you know."

"And you're not Jesus."

The words came out before I could stop them, and they hung

in the air, killing the moment. There'd been something sizzling between us, and I'd ruined it with my big mouth.

"Never claimed I was," he said with a sad smile as he pushed away from my car. "You could join us, you know."

Bible study was taking this whole thing too far. It was one thing for me to walk into the church each Sunday. I didn't need the church following me into my bar every Wednesday.

"No thanks. You have fun making saints out of those sinners." With at least two self-avowed delinquents, a soon-to-be unwed mother, and an assortment of old men drinking beer, it was sure to be a barrel of laughs. He turned at the door and gave me a wry smile. "It'd be more fun if you were with me, but I'll see what I can do."

"You don't need me for entertainment."

"Come in if you change your mind," he said before the door slapped behind him.

I stood in the parking lot, arms crossed, with a smug grin. They'd run him out of there on a rail. He wouldn't last ten minutes with that crowd. Fountain patrons had been proudly scaring off ministers for years. Those unsuspecting souls would be lured in by the promise of a tidy parsonage but ready to leave after the first truly rowdy Friday night.

Laughter floated through the screen door. I uncrossed my arms and leaned against the hood of my old Toyota. They had him on the ropes now. Any minute and he'd bust out of that door.

Any minute now . . .

More laughter, and this time I could've sworn he had joined in. They were traitors, and, even worse, Luke had managed to win them over in a quarter of the time it had taken me. Surely, he hadn't managed a truce between The Fountain and the church when no one had been able to do so in thirty years or more.

Sudden and eerie silence.

Praying? Really?

I crept to the screen door. Sure enough, each person had

bowed his or her head except Carl. He stared at Tiffany in a way that made me uneasy. I backed away from the door slowly.

If Preacher Man had people praying in a bar, then I didn't want to hear any whining over choir practice. Next he'd have church members in The Fountain drinking beer.

Yeah, right.

Chapter 8

That Sunday, the superintendent had the gall to show up a week early, a surprise visit no doubt moved up thanks to Miss Lottie's letters. Luke appeared quite calm on the outside, but he also wasn't looking at me. I knew I'd been out of line on Wednesday, but it was better for him to be mad at me. I'd felt sparks between us more than once, so I needed to pour a bucket of water on that fire before it started. Nothing good ever came of getting involved with me.

The Happy Hour Choir sat to the right of the piano in the choir loft. Tiffany's ample cleavage spilled forward, and Ginger frowned beside her as she toyed with the fringe on her shawl. If Ginger made it through the whole service without draping her shawl over Tiffany's chest, it was going to be heralded as a modern-day miracle.

The Gates brothers had shaved for the occasion, but they were wearing Western shirts and jeans—another source of contention with Ginger. She stood beside Mac, whose gray hair was still wet and plastered to his head even though his bushy beard stuck out. On the other side of Mac, Carl Davis stood tall. His hair and beard were both trimmed close to his face and head, but he wore his usual mournful expression complete with dark circles under his eyes. In his dress shirt with crumpled tie he reminded me of one of the presidents whose picture used to grace the American History classroom at Ellery High. Bill slouched in the corner and leaned against the unused organ, his red suspenders spanning his bloated belly. He wasn't singing but he had declared himself an unofficial mascot.

Superintendent Dartmouth, a short, wrinkled man with beady black eyes, stared through my ragtag singers as though they reflected poorly on the minister he had come to see. Luke pulled at his tie again, and his eyes darted to Lottie Miller. Her handbells hadn't arrived yet, and I'd heard she was having more trouble coming up with enough people to play them than I had had filling the choir loft. She sat on the second row, puffed up like an angry hen because she had missed her chance to show off.

"Our opening hymn is 'Love Lifted Me,' " Jason Utley managed. I turned around to face the piano and almost said a silent prayer before I caught myself. My hands had a mind of their own, playing a jazzy introduction before I could rein them in. I tended to get ornamental when nervous, which, based on the holes in my back, was something I should have warned Luke about.

Then the Happy Hour Choir started to sing.

They sang as I had instructed, braving the new harmonies I'd taught them. We breezed through the first verse and were halfway through the second when the last part of the verse grabbed me: *"Love so mighty and so true merits my soul's best songs. . . ."*

Half-exhilarated and half-terrified, I realized I was giving my soul's best songs. My fingers guided the Happy Hour Choir through the rest of the song as my mind worked over words that promised love.

God's love. Romantic love. Love for neighbors.

Love. Love. Love. "All You Need Is Love."

I narrowly stopped myself from segueing into the Beatles just as the Happy Hour Choir took the last time through the chorus a cappella. I turned to see their profiles, this motley crew of haggard faces with angelic voices. Sure, someone missed a note every now and again—especially the Gates brothers, who were trying to navigate the middle harmony—but their rough edges lent credence to the song.

Silence swallowed the memory of the last note. I turned to see the congregation, and the creak of the piano stool brought everyone to life. Miss Lola dabbed at the corners of her eyes with a handkerchief, but Miss Lottie looked away rather than meet my gaze.

Luke cleared his throat to stop the buzz and hiss of whispered voices then smoothly transitioned into joys and concerns, neither of which were very popular with a stranger present. I played a jazzy version of "Just a Closer Walk with Thee" as the ushers took the plate around the sanctuary. In for a penny, in for a pound, I figured. No doubt Luke was getting the urge to have one of his little chats with me. Maybe he would say the word *maybe* at least ten more times.

Only the knowledge that Superintendent Dartmouth was watching me kept me from groaning when Luke started reading the story of the prodigal son. He started with the older brother's perspective. The congregation nodded with his points; they followed all of the rules, after all. Lottie Miller's head lolled steadily over her double chin. She would never do something as stupid as taking her inheritance and blowing it on wild living. Thomas Dartmouth nodded, but his eyes fluttered. He wasn't much younger than Ginger and probably shared her opinion on how it wouldn't matter much to miss a sermon or two on the back end of his life.

I shifted in my little seat by the piano. I had been trying to daydream about something other than the sermon, but I couldn't help but think of that younger son. Maybe he hadn't meant to go live a life of dissolution. Maybe he'd planned to start his own business to make his daddy proud. Maybe he'd fallen into the party lifestyle completely by accident because his mother was entirely too strict with him and he was searching for meaning somewhere. Oh, wait, that was me.

I shivered. I knew what it was like to have disapproval weigh heavily on you. You wanted to shake it off, to be free. Sometimes in the process of breaking free, you accidentally broke something else, and more disapproval landed heavy.

"Beulah?" Jason Utley's hissed whisper brought me back to reality where the entire church, the Happy Hour Choir, and the superintendent all looked to me to start the last hymn. I jumped to the piano so quickly I turned over the stool. A collective gasp went up from the crowd, and my embarrassment burned hot on my cheeks. *Inhale and exhale,* Ginger had taught me. *Close your eyes and feel the music.*

I righted the seat and dug deep for some belated grace before sitting. Then I nodded to the Happy Hour Choir. They turned to the page for the invitation, a page I had marked for each and every one of them ahead of time with a tiny hot-pink sticky note.

"*Softly and tenderly, Jesus is calling.*" Tiffany's delicate soprano wafted over the sanctuary alone for the entire first verse, then the harmony of the Happy Hour Choir bowled over even me.

No one in the sanctuary moved. Thomas Dartmouth started to clap. Everyone looked at him as if he'd lost his ever-loving mind because County Line Methodist didn't do anything as rowdy as applaud. After a moment's hesitation, one person joined his applause. Then another and another.

I looked at my choir, and they all blushed. Every last one of them had a hint of color in his or her cheeks, including Bill, who hadn't done any singing. Then I looked behind me at the attendance board. Only thirty-two people had been in church for that beautiful moment, nowhere near enough to keep County Line open.

But it was ten more than the week before.

I was still humming while gathering up my contraband hymnals when Tiffany snuck up on me.

"Beulah, I really need to talk to you," she whispered.

I turned around to see a trickle of blood coming from one corner of her lip and a pink puffiness around her left eye that was going to become quite the shiner.

"What in the blue hell happened to you?"

Tiffany started blubbering before I could get the story out of her. "Daddy was in such a good mood, and we were standing behind the church. So I told him about, you know."

As if not calling a pregnancy a pregnancy would somehow undo it.

"And he hit me upside the head. He told me smart girls were more careful about that sort of thing and what were the neighbors going to think and—"

I wrapped my arms around her, tamping down panic. I needed to get away from her because she reminded me of my own panic the day I finally admitted I wasn't suffering from food poisoning after all. I gently pushed her out to arm's length. "Okay. You're going to call the police—"

"No!"

"What do you mean, no?"

"Please, I can't call them. I can't. I don't have any girlfriends. All my aunts are in Texas, and Momma is who knows where. What am I going to do?"

"You're going to come home with us. That's what you're going to do."

Both Tiffany's head and mine snapped to where Ginger stood at the foot of the stairs that led to the choir loft.

"And I guess we're going to need someone else to sing bass," she muttered under her breath as she hobbled toward the front door.

I scrambled out of the loft and ran after Ginger, not caring much that I'd left Tiffany alone in the loft. "You can't mean that."

By this time we were outside in the empty gravel parking lot, so she shielded her eyes to answer me. "Well, I'm sure not going to let a guy who hits pregnant women, let alone his own daughter, sing in *my* choir."

My breath came out in a whoosh. "No, I mean the part about Tiffany."

"What are you trying to say, Beulah Gertrude Land?"

I gritted my teeth at the sound of the name my mother gave me. "I can't live with Tiffany. She's going to be, you know, and—"

Ginger held up one hand and looked out at the cemetery but closed her eyes as she did. "And where would you be if I had said I didn't want to be reminded of my miscarriage?"

My mouth hung open, and the world spun around me. She'd never told me about wanting children or about losing children. She hadn't mentioned being married, either, so . . .

"So, you too?" I took a seat on the last few steps and Ginger joined me. Up in the choir loft Tiffany stood frozen, waiting.

Ginger heaved a ragged sigh. "We went down to Corinth for a quickie wedding before he shipped off to the Pacific. He didn't come home."

How could I have lived with her for all this time and not known this story? *Because you were so busy keeping Ginger out of your business that you didn't think to ask about hers.*

"After I lost the baby I was sad, but I told myself John and I could try again." Here she grabbed my hand. "We didn't get that chance."

I couldn't find the words to tell her how sorry I was for being a hateful little brat all those weeks before our New Orleans trip and then again after I lost my little Hunter.

"It was hard for me to watch you get bigger every day then deliver your child, all pink and rosy. It was even harder to lose him when I'd already told myself we'd made it through the hard part, the part I hadn't been able to make it through."

Goose bumps covered every square inch of my flesh despite the hot June sun. She'd hidden all of these feelings from me. She had tamped down her panic while I carried Hunter to term. She'd squashed down her own grief to make sure I came out of mine alive.

I looked at Tiffany. She stood at the altar, wanting to come to us but no doubt worrying about what we were saying about her. And of the three of us, I was the coward. Ginger had endured her miscarriage and lost husband with grace. Tiffany followed me doggedly, doing what she felt she needed to do to keep her baby safe, even though that baby had cost her more than one dream.

The time had come to quit wallowing in self-pity and pay it forward. There was only one question left to ask:

"But are you sure *you* want to go through all of this again?"

Ginger shrugged. "Third time's a charm? Besides, I'm due to kick the bucket either way."

I cringed at her words, but I didn't have it in me to have that discussion, not when my knees still wobbled from her earlier bombshell.

"C'mon, Tiffany, let's get some lunch," I called over the pews.

She stood taller with hope and trotted over to join us. Just as she reached me, Luke appeared from the back of the church. "Headed out to lunch? I thought we might celebrate our little bump in attendance."

Tiffany froze in place, keeping the back of her head to Luke. Her eyes widened in fear that he would come over and see what had happened. Now that she was directly in front of me I could see how much more her left eye had swollen. Her lip pouted unnaturally, too.

"I'm thinking this may be a day to eat in," I said.

"Oh. In that case, you ladies have fun."

I winced. *It's for the best. You need to be at least five hundred feet from that man at all times.*

Besides, Tiffany clearly didn't need to be out in public at the moment.

"Come on, let's get you some lunch," I said as I led her outside.

When we got to the Caddy, I had the weirdest sense of déjà vu as she slid into the backseat. From the driver's seat, Ginger took a look at her through the rearview mirror, and her eyes widened at the sight of both swollen eye and swollen lip. "Why don't we call for a pizza today?"

"Pizza going to work for you, Tiffany?"

She nodded yes, but her complexion turned gray and her hand went to her mouth.

"Don't worry," I heard myself say. "We can find you something else if that turns your stomach."

She nodded, closed her eyes, and laid her head back against the seat. I knew what she was thinking, praying, even: *Please don't let me throw up on this leather upholstery.*

After all, I had been there once before.

That evening I'd finally confessed to my mother. At first I thought she was taking the news really well. Then she turned on me with the wooden spoon she'd been using to stir spaghetti sauce for supper.

"You are a disgrace! I raised you better than this!" She aimed for my butt, but I spun to get out of her reach. My efforts only meant more slashes of spaghetti sauce on my favorite low-rise jeans. Damn things were barely held closed by a rubber band through the buttonhole, so it didn't matter anyway.

"Momma. I need to tell you what happened."

"I know *what happened. It was you and that Vandiver boy. Your Aunt Lucy told me you didn't go to the movies. Kari saw you two drive off in the other direction."*

She lunged for me, but I backed out of the galley kitchen, into the foyer, and out the door.

"Beulah Gertrude Land, you get back in here! Have you thought for one moment what this might do to your father? He could be kicked out of the church."

It always came back to Daddy and what other people would think of us, didn't it?

I turned my back on the house, not wanting to face her but knowing I'd have to eventually. Gravel crunched on the driveway, and I looked at Miss Ginger Belmont's brand-new Cadillac. Usually I went to Ginger, but I'd missed three piano lessons in a row, so maybe she was coming to check on one of her sources of income. I looked from the car to the door as Mama busted out, her curly black hair flying from her head like an amateur Medusa.

The car seemed the better choice.

Down the driveway I ran, hoping Miss Ginger wouldn't lock the doors on me. Blessedly the door opened, and I slid into the front seat, my stomach churning from the excitement and from the general feeling of carrying a baby.

"Could you please take me to the Greyhound station?" I asked.

Ginger looked through the windshield at how my mother stalked toward the car. As always she sat up ridiculously straight and smelled of Emeraude. Her pursed lips bled tiny lines of lipstick into the wrinkles around her mouth. For a minute I thought she would turn me over to my mother.

Instead she threw the car into reverse and squealed down the driveway as my mother yelled, "If you leave now, don't even think about coming back!"

I closed my eyes and concentrated on not throwing up in Ginger's car—it still had the new car smell, for crying out loud! When I dared open my eyes, I was looking at a white clapboard Victorian house, not the bus station.

"But—"

"I'm not taking you to a bus station with only the clothes on your back," Ginger announced. "You come inside until you and your mother can patch things over."

But I never moved home.

My mother had been true to her word. Fortunately, so had Ginger.

Chapter 9

"Beulah, show Tiffany where she can sleep," Ginger said as she started arranging containers on the table. I took Tiffany upstairs to show her the guest room, a yellow monstrosity. I showed her the bathroom and where the washcloths were so she could clean up the tiny bit of blood at the corner of her mouth.

"What's that room?" she asked, pointing down the hall.

"It was going to be the nursery." I cleared my throat, surprised I'd choked the words out.

"Oh," said Tiffany. "Oh."

Once downstairs I passed Tiffany a bag from the freezer to hold over her eye during lunch. At first we ate in silence, but then Ginger said, "If you tell us who the father is, we might be able to get him to help you out."

Tiffany choked on her bite of the sub sandwich we'd decided on. I whacked her on the back. Soon it became clear she wasn't going to tell us even when she wasn't choking. No matter how hard Ginger and I tried, we couldn't get Tiffany to tell us who the father of her baby was.

"Tiffany, he has a right to know and a responsibility to help." I purposely didn't look at Ginger while I took the bag of English peas Tiffany had been holding over her eye and handed her a different bag from the freezer. Good thing for her I didn't like English peas, and Ginger hadn't felt like cooking them. Otherwise Tiffany wouldn't have had anything to hold over the bruise.

"It doesn't matter, Beulah. He wouldn't be any help anyway." She leaned back against the chair and closed her eyes. She was wearing my Bon Jovi tee because she had nothing else to wear but her church clothes. Sooner rather than later, we'd have to make a field trip to the Davis trailer to get her things. I sure as hell wasn't looking forward to that.

"But what are you going to do about food?" Ginger asked as she took one of Tiffany's strong hands in her skeletal ones. "You're not going to be able to keep working as a waitress at The Fountain for much longer, you know. Breathing all that smoke and standing on your feet's not good for you."

"I know," Tiffany moaned. "But I don't know what else to do."

She sat up straighter. "Maybe I could help out around here to earn my keep. Clean up a bit, cook?"

My eyes locked with Ginger's. *Help the cancer-ridden woman go through her last days as comfortably as possible?* No, no need to tell Tiffany about Ginger until we absolutely had to.

I started pacing. "First things first, we're not going to mention this to anyone. That way, you can apply for jobs and not tell them you're pregnant."

"Beulah, that's sneaky," Ginger objected.

"It's a dog-eat-dog world. You know that. Tiffany's never going to get hired around here if people know she's pregnant and unmarried—trust me on that one. No, it would be much better for her to get a job and then 'discover' her pregnancy."

Tiffany sat up in the recliner. "Do you really think I'm going to be able to pull that off?" She'd thrown up three times since we got home.

"I think you should give it a try." I stopped pacing.

"What are you going to tell Luke about Carl?"

I inhaled deeply. "I'm not telling him anything. What does it matter to him?"

Ginger frowned. "Don't you think Luke needs to know these things in case Carl decides to show up uninvited?"

We both looked at Tiffany. If a man would hit his daughter, who could predict what else he might do?

"Fine. I'll tell Luke. Then the next time Carl comes into The Fountain I'll let him know his services are no longer needed."

Ginger stared through me. "You should probably ask Luke to be there with you for that, too."

The next morning I drove over to County Line Methodist to give Luke one of our old box fans and to tell him what had happened. I wondered how his impromptu Bible study had gone. Knowing The Fountain regulars, they'd converted him to a life of beer and laziness instead.

And I should probably apologize for that "you're not Jesus" comment, but I wasn't going to. Nope. I needed to say my piece and get away from him as soon as possible.

I rolled into the parking lot blasting classic rock with the windows rolled down because my air-conditioning had long ago ceased to function. Turning off the engine and stepping into the parking lot during morning hours was like stepping into a different world. Birds chirped to one another as crickets and frogs sang their last songs of the morning. Sunlight caught each spiderweb and every sprinkle of dew, and the air around me sparkled with a haze that promised a hot day ahead. Even the cemetery looked cheerful with the bright sunlight and the sound track of the birds. And it was fortunate I looked over at the cemetery because Luke was there with a sketch pad, sitting on someone's tombstone.

I took a deep breath. Time to tell him about the sordid exploits of the Happy Hour Choir and hope he didn't give me too much grief for being an ass a few days before. I crunched across the gravel, then hiked through the dewy grass of the cemetery, my nose crinkling at the distasteful sensation of wet grass clippings clinging to my feet and ankles.

"Hey, Luke, whatcha doing there?"

He jerked around. "Beulah, I didn't expect you this morning, but I'm glad you're here because there's something I need to tell you."

"That makes two of us." I stuffed my hands into the pockets of my cutoffs. "I need to talk to you, too."

"All right, you first." His eyes opened wide and bright, a complement to the sky above him. He thought I was coming to share my secrets, but that wasn't going to happen. I wrestled with the desire to talk to him about Hunter, but I pinned down that unruly urge and brought up the real reason I was there. "I'm going to need to ask Carl to leave the choir, and Ginger seems to think this is something I should discuss with you."

He put down the sketch pad and slid around on the marker to face me. I took a seat on the nearby Smith memorial. I didn't figure they'd mind that much.

"You like to express your opinions in the framework of what Miss Ginger likes, but, as I recall, she is quite good at expressing her own opinions."

A lump of coal formed in my stomach and started to glow. "You don't know the first thing about Ginger Belmont, so you can take that tone back."

We glared at each other for a moment. "I'm sorry. That was out of line, but I do wonder why someone as headstrong as you kowtows to an elderly lady."

That lump of coal cooled but moved up to my throat. "She was there for me when no one else was. The least I can do is return the favor."

Luke leaned back and studied me. He picked up the sketch pad and turned a sheet over to a new page before taking up his pencil. "She took you in when you had nowhere else to go?"

"I don't think that's any of your business, and I don't need a shrink." I crossed my arms and stared through him with my best mean look, but it didn't faze him.

"Did she help you the way you're helping Tiffany?" He looked up from the sketch pad, one eyebrow raised as if he already knew the answer.

No matter how many times I swallowed I couldn't get rid of that lump. There was no reason in this world I should have been ashamed to tell Luke my story. After all, Daddy always said a minister is certain to have heard worse. But I couldn't form the words to explain it all, so I settled on a simple, "Yes."

He nodded and looked down at his drawing. His lips pursed as his hand flew over the page in a flurry of strokes. I cursed him for his intuition. And for being so darn handsome there in the morning light with his sketch pad.

"So, how does all this add up to Carl leaving the choir?"

I exhaled with relief, more than happy to be back in familiar territory. "Carl smacked Tiffany around. As far as I'm concerned, he can go to . . . He can move all the way to Timbuktu for all I care."

"I'm assuming she's in good hands, though, since I saw her leave with you and Miss Ginger."

"Define 'good hands.' "

He chuckled and looked up at me with a half smile and his eyes twinkling in a way that made me melt. "I think your hands are better than you think they are."

"I'm sorry for what I said the other night. I didn't mean it."

Dammit. Where had that come from?

He looked back at the pad where he was sketching. "No need to apologize for speaking the truth."

"Even if I spoke the truth with a smart-alecky tone of voice?"

"Even then."

He continued drawing, and I thought of the sketch of the beautiful woman in his office. She was probably his girlfriend, and I'd do well to remember it. "So the sketch in your office is yours?"

"Sure is."

"Who is she?"

"My ex-wife."

I swallowed hard. Of course he was still in love with his ex-wife. He would do what was right even if she didn't hold up her end of the bargain. "Still in love with her, huh?"

He looked up from his book again to study my face. "No, I

keep her there to remind me I can't fix everything and everyone. Some people don't want to be rescued. Apparently, some people want to marry carpet salesmen and move to Georgia."

"I'm sorry," I said.

"Don't be. It's for the best, let me assure you."

"Well, she's an idiot."

"Thanks. I think that might be your first compliment to me." He studied me with such intensity I was glad to have a row of graves between us.

I shifted around on the top of the granite marker. Those rough, rounded edges were definitely not made for sitting. "So which church is this for you?"

"It's my third church and second denomination. I'm hoping for that 'charm' adage to come true because the first two didn't end well."

I snorted before I could stop myself. "Because you couldn't pick out an invitation to save your soul."

"Very funny."

"Wait, your second denomination?" I fidgeted as he repeatedly looked up at me and down at the paper while his hand flew over the page.

"The Southern Baptists frown upon divorced pastors. Even if divorce wasn't the pastor's idea."

He *was* still in love with her.

"Dad did for me what he could, but, in the end, the rules are the rules. Besides, I needed to go in a different direction." He shrugged, but I could see an inner war there, an admiration for his father combined with the overwhelming desire to do certain things in a completely different way. No matter what he might tell himself or others, Luke secretly wanted to be like his father, and, based on his pained expression, he felt as though he wasn't even close. I could understand that.

"When did you start preaching?"

"Twenty-two," he said. "I was going to be a star."

Twenty-two? I was still busy doing really stupid things at twenty-two, making up for lost teenaged years, I suppose. I tried to imagine being married and in charge of an entire congregation at such a young age. Nothing I had ever experienced could possibly compare with that kind of pressure.

"A bit young, weren't you?"

He looked up. "Ever heard of the Reverend Barnabas Daniels?"

I frowned as I racked my brain on that one. "No . . . Oh, Reverend Daniels, who used to have the show on Sunday mornings out of Nashville?"

Luke nodded solemnly. "That's my dad. I was a bit of a prodigy, they said. I settled down in the outskirts of Nashville and prepared to take over my father's empire."

"But it didn't happen that way, did it?"

"Of course not," he said with a bitter smile. "But it all turned out for the best. Quid pro quo, Miss Land," he said before looking back to his sketch pad.

Having a minister quote Hannibal Lecter was disturbing on many levels, so I felt it best to change the subject. "I guess I'll tell Carl tonight we won't be needing his services."

Luke's head snapped up. "Nice try. My turn for questions."

Oh, he'd told me all sorts of things about himself so he could find out more about me. Sneaky bastard. "I don't want to play your game."

"I'm not playing games, and I still don't take you for a coward."

"Fine," I huffed. "I've lived here my entire life. My parents sheltered me. I made some mistakes. I live with Ginger, my old piano teacher. That's all there is to know."

"What kind of mistakes?"

"A Tiffany mistake." *Among others that I won't tell you even if you start prying off my fingernails with pliers.*

"And that's who you lost, isn't it? The baby?"

"Yeah." *And my father. And my mother's love. And I'm going to lose Ginger someday, too.*

"I'm sorry," he said.

"Me too. And on that cheery note, I have some errands to run for Ginger. Just wanted to let you know about Carl before I told him to get lost tonight."

Luke frowned. "Maybe I ought to be there, too."

"I think I can handle a drunken redneck, Preacher Man."

He straightened. "I'll come anyway."

"That's not necessary," I said through gritted teeth.

"Free country, as you've so eloquently pointed out. Besides, I'm feeling a little thirsty."

I stood and looked over the edge of his pad. The sketch was still rough, but it was me. Only, I was beautiful in that sketch, so beautiful I sucked in a breath. "Wow, you're really good. Or really bad, since you drew me to look like a mischievous fairy."

"Just draw 'em like I see 'em, Beulah. The question is, how do you see yourself?"

"Not like this." And thank God he couldn't see the way I pictured him. I'd rather learn how to play handbells from Lottie Miller than admit how often I'd thought about his lopsided smile.

He ripped the page out of the book and handed it to me. "I have to get to work, but I'll be there tonight when you talk to Carl."

He got four steps away before I remembered something important. "You might want to wear jeans tonight," I hollered across the cemetery. "The Fountain isn't exactly a khakis-and-polo sort of crowd."

"I'll keep that in mind," he muttered drily.

"Oh, and we don't want you to keel over from heatstroke so I brought you a fan we had lying around. You can get it out of the backseat."

"Thank you," he said with a flash of dimples.

I watched him get the fan out of the car then walk around the church to the back door. I believed him when he said he would be there that night, and it was an unfamiliar feeling. For the longest time I'd only been able to count on Ginger. I looked at the church then back to his drawing of me and back to the church again. How could he so easily make something beautiful out of someone who was not?

At first I wanted to crumple the page and leave it behind with the Smiths, but I couldn't bring myself to fold it, much less crinkle it. Instead, I held it against my chest to shield it from the breeze while I walked back to the car.

No two ways about it, I had a serious crush on the preacher man.

Chapter 10

I should have seen it coming. You can't let someone live with you and expect to keep all of your secrets. Still, I wasn't prepared for the afternoon when Tiffany asked me, "Beulah, why don't you ever go into the nursery?"

"Do you see a baby?" I asked her in a tone far harsher than I should have. I closed my eyes and took a deep breath, willing my tone to soften. "No baby, no need to go into the nursery."

And she had to know that. Everyone knew about the preacher's daughter who got knocked up and then lost the baby. Or they thought they did. One asshole had even preached an entire sermon on "God's will" and used me and Hunter as his example. I quit going to church after that, and the preacher moved a few months later. I always suspected Ginger had a hand in his not being reappointed to County Line.

"But everything is ready for a baby. Well, except for the wipes that have dried up and the diaper rash cream that's expired," Tiffany said. "Don't you think that's a bit creepy?"

I stood and pushed my chair away from the table. "No, I think it's convenient for you because you have a nursery ready and waiting for you."

That might have been a bit harsh, Beulah.

I got all the way to the doorway before Tiffany spoke. "That's kinda what I wanted to ask you about. Miss Ginger told me to make myself at home and think about what I want to do in the nursery. Do you think I could decorate the nursery with different colors? Kinda do some things myself?"

Buttercream. That was the color I painted the nursery. I had thrown open all of the windows and painted the walls myself because we didn't know to worry about paint fumes and whatnot. Ginger and I had laughed at the huge smudge of beige paint on my belly, but I hadn't realized I was brushing the wall until I pressed hard enough for Hunter to kick me.

I willed my lungs to keep bringing in air and sending it back out. "Tiffany, you do whatever you want to do with the nursery. You can paint it black and go for a goth theme with bats hanging from the ceiling, but pigs will fly before I set foot in that nursery."

"Could you take a look at it, please?"

Her need for my approval took my breath away. I climbed the stairs slow and steady, but tears stung my eyes long before I reached the top. The nursery door was cracked, and broken spiderwebs hung from that corner where the door hadn't been opened in so long. I took one step down the hall and then another.

Ginger had survived losing both husband and child. Luke had lost his mother.

I can do this.

I pushed open the door. Sunlight poured into the room and lingered, thanks to the buttery walls. In one corner the airplane border had come loose, showing the pink gingham I'd originally put there because I'd been convinced I was having a girl. Leave it to me to make a snap decision and then get my comeuppance in the form of an ultrasound. Finally, I forced myself to look at the hand-me-down crib in the opposite corner. I'd been humming "Hush little baby, don't say a word" when I walked across the room and looked over the edge of the crib.

The world spun at the memory of his too-still body, and I

grabbed the door facing. I ran down the hall and slammed my door behind me. I shook worse than Ginger, and the words came to mind before I could stop them:

Lord, please take better care of Tiffany's baby than You took care of mine.

I was spoiling for a fight by the time I made it to The Fountain. I scanned the small room looking for Carl Davis, but he had yet to arrive. I couldn't know for certain he would come, but it was a safe bet. He couldn't have missed more than two nights since Tiffany had started waitressing.

After four songs, Luke walked through the door. My first thought was, *Thank goodness he took my advice about the khakis.* After studying Luke's jeans a little too closely, my second thought was, *Good heavens, I was better off when he was wearing the khakis.*

His jeans looked good on him—too good—as did his cowboy boots, an unexpected twist. His button-down shirt, a subdued blue plaid, almost fit in with the western shirts the Gates brothers wore. Luke Daniels was learning how to fit in and, as such, was a dangerous combination of the best of Yessum County along with the best of being from just about anywhere else.

He bought a beer and listened as I played. First, I played a rag as an inside Joplin joke for the two of us, then a little "Yellow Submarine" for him. He grinned at me then joined in on the chorus with the rest of The Fountain's patrons. By that time, I had to play a little Patsy Cline to keep the natives from getting restless. As I wrapped up "Crazy," the cuckoo clock signaled the nine o'clock hour. Luke stood, his lips pressed thinly together. He looked at me, obviously wavering between his desire to not be in the bar when I got all sacrilegious and his desire to stay and keep an eye on me. He checked the room for Carl then stepped outside, probably to go back to the parsonage, shove his fingers in his ears, and say, "La-la-la" as loudly as he could.

As luck would have it, Carl Davis walked in not long after Luke walked out. I played every verse of "Dwelling in Beulah

Land" that I could think of, then added an instrumental solo to give Luke time to come back in, but he didn't show.

Finally, I decided I would handle the situation myself. After all, I'd been dealing with half-drunk men without Luke for years. I hopped down from the risers and made a beeline for Carl. He sat at the little bar against the wall, nursing a Bud Light.

"Carl, I need to have a word with you," I said.

He glared at me over the top of his beer bottle. It appeared he was itching for a fight as well.

"I have a feeling I know what you're going to say, so I think we might oughta step outside." He eased off the stool.

"Fine by me." He might not know it, but I had no objections to a groin shot should the situation call for it.

He pushed past me to the door and let the screen door fly behind him—so much for ladies first. I stepped back and blinked as it almost hit me in the face.

Outside, he stood around the corner where Tiffany had been tossing her cookies a few days before. He cradled the brown beer bottle in the crook of his arm as he lit a cigarette. Once he'd put the lighter back in his pocket, he transferred the beer to one hand and the cigarette to the other. I felt better that both of his hands were busy.

"Look, I really appreciate all of the work you've done, but I'm going to have to ask you to leave the choir."

His eyes narrowed, and he sucked down about a third of his cigarette. "Seems to me that ain't very Christian-like."

"C'mon, Carl. Neither is beating up on people." I crossed my arms over my chest.

"Oh, so my little slut daughter has been bending your ear with her sob stories. Little shit had it coming." He took another long drag on the cigarette. He didn't plan to have both hands occupied for long.

"Tiffany's pregnant." I paused there because it was ridiculous to state the obvious. Fortunately, Ginger's words had lodged themselves somewhere deep in the back of my mind, ready for a moment such as this. "It may not be the best of circumstances, but that little baby deserves a chance to come into this world healthy."

"What about what I deserve? Don't I deserve a daughter who's loyal to me?" He sucked down the rest of his cigarette and flicked it at the ground. He stomped out the embers.

"I bet she won't even tell you who the daddy is." He stepped forward to challenge me. If he thought I cared who the father was, he was sadly mistaken. "I bet she doesn't even know."

Yeah, that wasn't going to bother me, either.

He took another step forward, and I took another step back. My instincts told me Tiffany *did* know who the father was. If not, then why not say she didn't know instead of hedging the question as Ginger and I pleaded? Unease tunneled its way into my belly. The screen door to the parsonage behind me slammed shut. Luke was going to make it just in time.

"Well, Carl. Let me help you separate yourself from your daughter. I'll be looking for someone else to sing bass." I turned to go, but he took me by the shoulder and threw me against the cinder-block wall in the shadows. His nose was less than an inch from mine, and the tobacco-beer scent of his breath turned my stomach.

His eyes glowed yellow. "You can't take her away from me."

I swallowed hard. Were those his hands on my waist? My mind snapped back to another night, another set of hands, and overgrown crepe myrtle branches scratching against wood. My breaths came too shallow and too fast. Panic seeped in from the edges. "I'm not taking Tiffany away from you, but I will call the police if you so much as lay a finger on her. Or me."

He laughed. "Don't look to me like you're in much of a position to be making threats."

"Hey!" Luke yelled from behind Carl. He had to have been running to get there so quickly.

Carl's eyes turned dark. Just when I thought he was going to let me go, he slammed my head into the wall behind me instead. My head smashed against the bricks, and I tasted blood, my blood.

And then he was gone.

I flailed as I fell, finally knowing how Wile E. Coyote felt when all those stars circled his head after one of his Acme misadventures. Above me I heard a punch and a groan, and I tried to stand up to help Luke.

Halfway to upright, the world tilted dangerously and I felt myself crumple, but strong hands caught me. I sighed in relief, then realized it could be Carl and fought to stand alone.

"Beulah, it's me."

I desperately tried to focus. I'd been hearing that voice of velvet gravel every Sunday for almost a month now. And Luke hadn't needed *my* help. It had to have been one of his punches that had knocked Carl Davis to the ground. My eyes closed in relief. I leaned into Luke, but then the nausea hit me. I turned and puked.

All over Carl Davis.

He hopped to his feet. "Look here, you little—"

"Mr. Davis, it's time for you to go home."

"Dammit, I will see both of you in hell. Bitch threw up on me." I could see two Carls, and both of them wiped blood from the corners of their mouths with the backs of their hands then clenched those hands into fists. Luke drew me closer, seemingly oblivious to any vomit I might still have on me.

"Well, if you hadn't given her a concussion, then she wouldn't have thrown up on you. Seems like poetic justice to me, and the least of your worries once Beulah calls the police."

"I'm not calling the police." My words sounded slurred to me, but Luke understood them even if he didn't get the reasoning behind them. He drew me out to arm's length, and that made the world spin all over again.

"But, Beulah . . ."

"No police." I shook my head, which was another mistake.

Both Carls slumped forward and let their hands relax. They pushed past me in a weird double vision and headed to the old Chevy pickup that one of the Carls drove. He left the parking lot with a spray of gravel and the squeal of tires.

"Beulah, you need to call for an ambulance, and the police are going to come when they find out what happened."

"No ambulance then." I couldn't call the police. All Bill needed was for the police to come, and the community would mobilize against The Fountain. On the other side of the county a waitress at the Five-Gallon Bucket had called the police; that tavern had been shut down over a bogus health violation within the week. Not that they'd pressed charges against the man who hit the waitress—they'd told her she'd got what she had coming, which is what they'd probably tell me, too. No, Bill ran a tight ship, and he deserved better than that. Besides, where would I work without The Fountain?

"Beulah?"

"I said no, Luke!" He was the last person in the world I should have snapped at, but by that point my head throbbed and felt entirely too big for my shoulders.

He studied me carefully. "Pupils are the same size, speech isn't slurred. Feel like you're going to throw up again?"

"Don't think so."

"Neck pain? Body pain?"

"Just my damn head. What are you, a *Grey's Anatomy* reject?"

He ignored me. "Come on, Beulah, let me get you a new shirt, then I'm going to take you to the doctor." He took my arm gently and led me in the direction of the parsonage.

"I don't need to go to the doctor. I need to go to sleep."

"No." He gently patted my cheeks. "No, you really don't need to go to sleep right now."

"Just a little nap?"

"Absolutely not." He supported me as we walked across the parking lot. He led me through the house and to his bedroom. He took off my stained shirt and tossed it on the tile floor in the master bathroom. I fell over and burrowed into his pillow. It was like drowning in a soft sea that smelled of him.

"Don't you dare go to sleep!" He pulled me to sitting position a little too quickly, which caused me to say, "Ow."

"Sorry, but you have to stay awake." He cupped my face with

his thumbs resting on my cheekbones. His eyes studied mine—no doubt looking at the pupils of my eyes—but then they strayed lower.

"Why, Reverend Daniels, were you looking at my cleavage?"

"No comment," he said brusquely as he pulled a T-shirt over my head and helped me get my arms through it. The T-shirt smelled of detergent, but it also smelled like sandalwood and . . . him.

Forget the headache; I wanted to burrow back under his sheets and sleep in the arms of someone who would take care of things for me. I didn't want to look after Tiffany. I didn't want to scrutinize Ginger, wondering if the cancer eating her innards was ready to wreak the ultimate havoc. I didn't even want to take care of myself. I was so, so tired.

"I'll have to wear red lace more often."

He grunted something and lifted me to my feet.

"With a matching thong," I added as he guided me down the hall.

"Beulah Land, you are a very frustrating woman," he said as he let go of me long enough to open the door. He was saying something else to me when I started falling backward again.

Chapter 11

I only lost a second before I came to in Luke's BMW Roadster. He was muttering under his breath about how he should've called 911 whether I liked it or not.

"Tell me, how does a small-town preacher afford a car like this?"

"It was a gift from my father *before* we had our falling-out," he said through gritted teeth.

When I almost nodded off, he patted my cheeks. "Hey, keep talking to me."

"Some would say your sports car is a classic example of penis compensation," I slurred.

He laughed out loud.

"What, no comment on that either?"

"None needed."

He turned right and I saw he had the good sense not to bother with the doctor's office in Ellery—it would certainly be closed—but he did get lost in the side streets of Jefferson. When he drove the wrong way down a one-way street, he muttered something under his breath that almost sounded like the tiniest of curse words.

I giggled. "Preacher Man, I am shocked. Shocked, I say."

"Hush, Beulah. I'm only human."

That sobered me up. Until then I hadn't really thought of him as mortal; he somehow seemed above so much of what went on around him. And that detachment had to explain why he was so lonely.

He found the emergency room and rushed around to help me out the door.

"I don't have my purse," I said as he put me in a corner seat by a trash can.

"I'll pay for it," he said. "This is serious." He walked to the reception desk and pointed back at me. I eyed the trash can, willing myself not to throw up again. I'd had enough of that.

"Been hit on the head before," I muttered under my breath when he returned with a clipboard.

"Yeah, well, that doesn't mean you should have been." He put the clipboard in the seat beside me. "I've got to move the car, but I'll fill this out when I get back. Since you aren't bleeding, I'm afraid this is going to take a while."

Apparently, Luke called Ginger to let her know where we were when he went to move the car. He told her not to come, but she had Tiffany drive her to the hospital anyway. The moment she arrived she hobbled over to the reception desk to see if she could spot any friendly faces to, as she put it, "hurry this process up a little bit."

Meanwhile Luke made a valiant effort to keep me awake, but I fell asleep against his shoulder while watching Ginger gesticulate wildly at the nurses at the desk. Either her hissy fit didn't do any good or my nap was shorter than I thought because she was sitting in a chair across from me when my eyes flickered open.

And Luke was holding my hand.

I quickly closed my eyes to avoid her shrewd gaze and to let the moment linger. When was the last time a boy had held my hand? So long ago that it was definitely a boy and not a man—that much I knew. Luke's hand was warm and not in the least clammy. His palm had a hint of calluses, which surprised me. Then again, Luke had probably tried out carpentry just to see what it'd been like for Jesus.

"Did you have any luck?" he asked softly.

"I might've asked for a certain nurse who knows me well," Ginger said.

Beyond me I heard canned laughter from the waiting room televisions.

"Beulah Land?" A nurse with a wheelchair struggled with my name, pronouncing it "Be-you-la."

"She's right here," Luke said. He nudged me and gently helped me into the chair. Tiffany offered a hand to Ginger, and we all walked to the nurse.

"I'm sorry, but we don't have enough room for all y'all back there. One of you can come with her."

Luke stepped back to let Ginger have the honor. She wavered for a second then pushed him forward. "You'd better go, Luke. Neither one of us could pick her up off the floor if she fainted and fell out of the chair."

He nodded to her solemnly. Tiffany slipped her arm under Ginger's and led her back to the seating area. I felt much better knowing Tiffany was there with Ginger.

I floated down the hall, Luke beside me as long as the corridor would allow. Guilt radiated from him, and I suddenly thought of a fist hitting a jaw. "Luke, you punched Carl, didn't you?"

"Twice."

"Not so 'turn the other cheek,' eh?"

"Extenuating circumstances," he said with a grunt as he hoisted me up on the exam table in a truly tiny room.

The nurse checked all my vitals, then the doctor came in to look at my eyeballs and feel around my head. "Well, you're going to have quite the bruise back there, but at least it's poking out instead of in. I still think you need an MRI."

"And how much is that going to cost?" I sounded drunk and felt hungover. Luke's warm hand reached for mine and squeezed reassurance.

"Well," the doctor said as he continued to scribble notes, "it depends. Your insurance should pay for it."

I slid from the table. "No can do. I don't have insurance."

"Now, Miss . . . Land." He flipped back a page on his chart. "A concussion is serious business, and—"

"I said I can't pay for it." I turned to Luke for help.

"She'll have the MRI," the traitor said.

"Luke, this is ridiculous. One of those things probably costs thousands of dollars."

"I said I'm paying for it. The most important thing is to make sure you're all right." His hand traveled to my cheek, and his thumb massaged my temple. I lost myself in the feeling of being precious to someone.

"You need to listen to your boyfriend," the doctor said as he pushed his glasses up his nose. "I'll send a nurse to take you back for your MRI."

He left the room, and I looked up at my "boyfriend," instinctively leaning my aching head farther into the hand that cupped my cheek. I suppose he did look like a boyfriend to someone who didn't know how impossible that would be.

"Beulah—" He couldn't form the words. Maybe it was because I had been bumped on the head, but I didn't want him to break the spell. For one moment I wanted to pretend I had found a man who cared enough about me to insist on a test neither one of us could pay for, to stick with me even when I puked, and to hold my hand while I waited in the emergency room.

"Miss Land? We're ready for you now."

A wish temporarily granted.

The nurse who both broke the spell of the moment and helped sustain it led us down a hall to an MRI machine. "Now you're going to have to lie down perfectly still." She helped me into the bed and stepped behind the machine.

"Sir, I'm going to have to ask you to step outside," she said as she started flipping switches.

He moved into the hallway, and I missed him. Being told I had to be still made me fidgety. My nose developed an unexpected itch; my toes started to cramp. My hand prickled with emptiness from not being held for the first time in over an hour.

Finally, finally, she let me get up and led us back to the exam room. Luke attempted to pace in the six-by-six room made even smaller by the hospital bed, sink, and his presence. He ran his hand through his hair.

"Hey, calm down. I feel better already." And I did, more or less. The nausea and dizziness had subsided into an immense throbbing ache.

He stopped and took both of my hands. "I am so sorry."

"Sorry for what? You've agreed to pay this crazy hospital bill that's going to have me working twelve jobs just to pay you back." If holding one hand was good, holding two was better.

"I shouldn't have left you alone for a minute. I should've been there to stop Carl from throwing your head against the wall." His hands tightened their grip as though he could somehow squeeze the concussion from me. "It was my pride that kept me from wanting to hear your song. I thought as long as he wasn't there yet, I'd still have time to—"

"Luke, don't blame yourself for that. I never should have stepped outside with the man. I knew he'd hit Tiffany; I just didn't realize he was *that* bat-shit crazy."

"I should have been there." His gaze locked with mine. He leaned closer, and I thought, for only a moment, he was going to kiss me. I leaned up to meet his lips, but instead he planted a kiss on my forehead. As I exhaled with a mixture of relief and regret, he cupped my face and pressed his lips on mine gently, so gently, and yet that slight touch sent shock waves through my body. He nipped at my bottom lip—

When the doctor knocked, Luke jerked away from me as if he'd been doing something wrong. Cool air rushed to fill the space where his warm body had been.

"Okay, Miss Beulah Land, you do, indeed, have a concussion," the doctor said as he consulted my chart. "Fortunately for you, it's a mild one. A few days of rest and no strenuous activity should be enough."

He put the chart back and took his prescription pad from his coat pocket. "I'm going to write you a prescription for something a little stronger for the first day or so. And remember: only acetaminophen, no aspirin."

The doctor clapped Luke on the arm. "Keep a close eye on her, son, but I think she's out of the woods."

"I'll do that. Thank you, sir."

He walked out of the room before either of us could betray our secret of not being boyfriend and girlfriend—not that either of us seemed particularly inclined to do so.

"Let's get you home."

"That sounds like a wonderful idea."

He pushed me down the hall and back to Ginger. He ran down the prognosis with her while I ran my fingers over my tingling lips. "Miss Ginger, if you and Tiffany will take her home, I'll settle up here."

Ginger nodded, and Luke helped me from the chair before he walked back to the desk. Tiffany got on my other side. The past, the present, and the woman bearing the future all walked through automatic doors to the parking lot beyond.

Chapter 12

I slept most of the night and into the next day, but I was cranky because either Ginger or Tiffany woke me up every two hours. It was supposed to be every two to three hours. When I pointed out the discrepancy to Ginger, she informed me she wanted to be on the safe side and that I was lucky she hadn't decided to wake me up every hour on the hour.

"I don't know why you two are fussing over me so much," I said while I fidgeted. They had me sitting in the recliner. Hovering like benevolent hummingbirds, they brought magazines and Cokes instead of sipping nectar and transferring pollen.

Ginger took my pillow and fluffed it before putting it back behind my head.

"Really, guys, the doctor said I'm perfectly fine. When he said you needed to watch me, I don't think he intended for you to hover."

"Hey, remember to wake her up every two to three hours if she goes to sleep." Ginger gave Tiffany the penciled-in eyebrow of doom.

"Ginger, I'm right here, and I can hear you."

She ignored me. "And don't let her do anything strenuous. Oh, and call Bill and tell him she needs a night or two off."

"Miss Ginger, you should really let me go instead." If Tiffany kept wringing her hands like that, she was going to end up with nubs, which would be rather problematic when it came time to change a diaper.

"Nonsense," Ginger said as she put on a rain bonnet to face the drizzle that pattered outside. "Luke and I need to run an errand or two. He'll be here any minute, and I don't want to keep him waiting."

"Chill out, you two. I'm sitting right here. I can get up when I need an Advil or two."

She turned on me, and I got the eyebrow. "No Advil, no aspirin, nothing in the aspirin family. You can have Tylenol and nothing else unless you want to have some kind of brain hemorrhage."

I couldn't sink myself into the recliner any more. "Sorry."

She pointed a bony finger at me. "And that's why you need people to look after you. Never been one to look after yourself, but you're going to have to fix that before—"

"Don't."

She scowled, shook her finger at me, then picked up her beige Aigner pocketbook, circa 1978, and headed for the door. "You watch that stubborn heifer, Tiffany."

Tiffany's eyes bugged out, but I managed not to snicker until the door closed with force. Not slammed, Ginger would say, just closed with force.

"She called you a heifer." Tiffany put her hands on her hips. "I can't believe Miss Ginger called you a heifer."

"Yes, yes, she did." I couldn't help but grin. In my first few weeks with Ginger she'd called me a heifer so many times it would've made a great drinking game. I'd gladly take the comparison to a stubborn maiden cow if it meant Ginger was feeling better than usual.

Tiffany took a seat on the sofa then popped up and looked to make sure Ginger was really gone before slumping back down. "I hate cows. Jesse Crawford's cows get out every other day and make an unholy mess of the garden in our backyard. Once they even knocked the clothes down from the line and trampled them so bad I couldn't get the stains out."

Tiffany's story twisted my gut. I had known she was poor in an abstract sort of way. I knew Carl got by on disability and wasted most of the money on booze and cigarettes. I knew they lived in the dingiest trailer park on the other side of Harlowe Bottom, but I hadn't thought about what that meant. Tiffany grew her own vegetables—probably out of necessity. She also had no dryer, at least not a dryer that worked.

"I know. I'm poor white trash."

I snapped my head toward her so fast I got dizzy and felt a stabbing pain behind my left eye. "People can be poor and any number of colors, but not having money doesn't mean you're trash. No person is trash."

Tiffany looked down at her nails, pushing each cuticle back with one of her other fingernails. "That's not what Daddy says."

"Your daddy is far closer to trash than you'll ever be," I muttered.

We sat in silence for a few minutes, and I wondered if I'd said too much yet again. I'd read enough subtitles on daytime TV to know all the experts talked about how you can't insult an abuser to the abusee. Montel once spent an hour on something like a milder form of Stockholm syndrome. Apparently, you had to remember Carl was still Tiffany's daddy even if he was a class-A jerk for hitting his own daughter.

"Tiffany, I'm sorry I said that—"

"Don't be. I think I want a sandwich." She hopped to her feet but stopped and turned at the doorway. "Are you ready to eat anything?"

"No, but you're not feeling sick?"

She thought about it for a moment. Her eyes rolled to the ceiling as she did an interior check for nausea. She looked back at me with an ear-to-ear grin. "No, I'm not sick. I'm not sick!"

"There's a twenty in the desk drawer if you want to order something," I said with a yawn.

Her eyes lit up. "In fact, I think I want a pizza. Do you want a pizza? No, wait, maybe I'll order Chinese. I've never had Chinese before. Do you think you would be okay if I ran over to Burger Paradise? Or maybe . . ."

I chuckled while she thought. Maybe Ginger and I had created a monster by introducing the poor child to the glory of takeout. We certainly weren't setting the best fiscal example.

"Tiffany," I said. "Let's stick with the pizza for now. If your nausea isn't completely gone then it has to be on the way out. You can make a list of what you want to eat while we wait for the pizza, then we'll check off each item one by one."

"Great idea! I'll order a pizza and go look for a pen."

She left with rosy cheeks, and I smiled after her before I realized what I was doing. Obviously, the hit to the head had damaged the common sense area of my brain. I couldn't afford this swell of pride because she had made it past morning sickness. I couldn't allow myself to get excited about Tiffany's baby. After all, I had said good-bye to morning sickness and then made a list of things to eat before diligently checking off each item. I had done everything the doctor said to do—even made those nasty applesauce cookies instead of eating the Oreos I wanted—but I still lost Hunter.

But what good would it do to tell Tiffany that? What good would it do to make her miserable and paranoid for the rest of her pregnancy? I closed my eyes. *Please help her not to do whatever it was that I did wrong. Please—*

Tiffany shook my shoulders.

"Beulah, are you awake?"

My face blanched. I had prayed. No, wait. I hadn't prayed. I addressed no one. It was just sending good vibes out into the universe. Then why did I feel like a kid with her hand in the cookie jar? "I am now."

"Good. The pizza's going to be here in thirty minutes, and I'm ready to start on my list."

That girl talked about barbecue, steaks, Chinese food, burgers, and catfish from over at Lacy's. I was so, so happy to hear

Ginger and Luke arrive. I couldn't hear what Luke said as they came in the front door—it was a low rumble that matched the distant thunder. My pulse raced and I had a hard time getting enough oxygen to my injured brain. I hadn't seen him since he'd kissed me. Was I stupid to want something more? Would he act like nothing had happened?

For the next few minutes, he moved things around while Ginger and Tiffany directed traffic and I battled the urge to get out of the chair and demand to know his intentions. Just when I reached for the lever that would put the footrest down he appeared at the arm of my chair.

"How's the patient?"

Significantly better now that you're here and smiling at me instead of looking at me as if I'm a creature from outer space.

"Fine. I still don't know what all of the fuss is about," I said.

"The fuss is that you got yourself injured and, while you seem to think of yourself as either invincible or disposable, you are neither. We kinda like having you around." He reached to push back a strand of my hair, remembered we had an audience, and settled for a chaste pat on the hand.

"That's what I've been trying to tell her all day. Maybe she'll listen to you." Ginger threw her hands up in the air then hobbled off to the kitchen.

But I wasn't listening to what Ginger was saying. *Luke liked having me around?*

"Since when?" My voice came out way huskier than I had intended, and I felt the hot crimson flood my cheeks.

"I don't know. You tend to grow on people. An acquired taste, I guess." Those blue eyes twinkled.

"Like caviar?" I grinned at him like an idiot.

"I was thinking something sweeter."

Tiffany dropped a glass, and it shattered on the floor just inside the kitchen. "I wondered what you wanted to drink," she mumbled as she bent to pick up the broken glass.

"Let me help you with that." Luke jumped up from the chair arm and bent over to gather the shards. I wasn't above admiring the view. It was nice to have someone around to help pick up the pieces.

And I wasn't the only one to notice.

After our pizza, Luke went home and Ginger went to bed. Tiffany decided to stay up with me for a while. I wasn't sleepy for a couple of reasons. First, I was used to staying up until the wee hours of the morning, thanks to working at The Fountain. Second, I'd slept too much during the day and was suffering from that hazy over-rested yet under-rested feeling.

"Beulah, do you like Reverend Daniels?"

I thought of his lips pressed against my forehead and then against my lips, his callused hand in mine. *Like* didn't begin to tell the half of it.

I looked over to where Tiffany leaned against the armrest, her chin in her hand as she watched an infomercial for some kind of miracle dicer. She was trying hard not to betray any sort of emotion, a surefire indicator she was feeling strong emotions and lots of them. I needed to tread with more care than I had during the discussion about her father.

"Of course I like him."

"No, I mean do you *like* him, like him?"

"Tiff, what is this? Fifth grade?"

She turned those big, brown Bambi eyes on me. "Do you think there'd ever be a chance someone like him would want to go out with a girl like me?"

I wanted to laugh. There was no chance a preacher would ever want to go out with a girl like either of us. Otherwise he surely would've said something to me before he left, wouldn't he? Any feelings I had for Luke had to be a sad example of how opposites attract. "Well, there's always a chance, but you're eighteen, and he's closer to my age."

"Four or five years isn't that much." She sat up straight and crossed her arms. The action reminded me of a toddler—not exactly the maturity level she was going for.

"You're a sweetheart, but try seven or eight." I needed to proceed with caution. "Tiffany, you might want to look for someone your own age."

"You're only saying that because you *do* like him."

She toyed with the edges of an afghan Ginger had finished right after I moved in. "I think I'll wait until you're feeling a little better. Then, maybe I'll ask him out if he doesn't ask me out first."

She stared into space, oblivious to the fact I was still listening to her. "Imagine, being the preacher's wife. I would always have a parsonage—no more musty trailers for me or my baby. The ladies in town wouldn't be able to look down their noses at me anymore. Or we could move to a new church. I could start all over again far away from here."

I wasn't about to remind her that ministers typically did not date young, unwed mothers to be. Obviously, this was Tiffany's pipe dream. After my run-in with Carl, I couldn't fault her for having dreams that involved a kind and handsome husband with a secure job and a nice home. And didn't we all want to start over?

Normally, I was one of the first people to pop someone's bubble, to point out the pitfalls of any undertaking in the name of being realistic. For some reason, I couldn't bring myself to tell Tiffany she was reaching, but I *could* tell her she didn't need Luke Daniels to get all of those things she wanted. She could move to another town, get a job, buy a house, settle down with a nice man who wasn't Luke.

Then why didn't I do all those things?

Because Ginger needs me.

And what traitorous part of me wanted to live out Tiffany's dream, too?

The same idiotic part that can't stop thinking about a certain vegetarian minister who shall remain nameless.

"I think I'm going to go to bed, if that's okay with you." Tiffany patted her belly even though she was barely showing.

"That's fine. My sleep schedule is still off so I'll watch TV for a while."

Tiffany paused at the bottom of the stairs and yawned as she looked back at me with a mischievous smirk. "Wake yourself up every two to three hours, now, you hear?"

"Every three hours. I don't see the need for this two-hour business."

"Fine, every three hours." Tiffany rolled her eyes. "Promise?"

"I promise." I made an imaginary cross over my heart, and she grinned as she climbed the stairs.

I listened to her footsteps go up the staircase and down the hall to her room. I should have told her she didn't need a man to change her life. I should have told her she could move out and start over on her own. But those were all things I could tell her later.

Her footsteps disappeared, but the door to the nursery creaked open, and my heart skipped a beat as the tip of a beam of light from the door shone at the top of the stairs. Funny how the one room I avoided was the one to draw her in. Her room full of promise was my room of tragedy.

The rings holding the curtains scraped the curtain rod, and I imagined Tiffany holding out the fabric and studying it. She didn't know I had picked out airplanes because I wanted my little boy to be able to touch heaven.

"The sky's the limit for this little dude," I would tell Ginger as I patted my stomach.

"You know it," she would say as she reached over to give my stomach her own little pat. I hadn't seen the sadness in her eyes or the tight set of her mouth back then, but I could see it in my mind's eye now that I knew her story.

I wondered if Tiffany was still going through her dreams of marrying Luke and moving far away. Was she, as the old saying went, picking out curtains? Maybe I didn't know if I wanted to pick out curtains with Luke, but the thought of Tiffany picking them out disturbed me more than I cared to admit.

He'd called me an acquired taste. While there was the promise of something more in our talk of caviar and something sweeter, I couldn't help but wonder if I'd made the whole thing up. In my own desperation had I invented the flirting, the protectiveness, the kiss? Or had he simply not been alone with me long enough for us to sort out the emotions that had come bubbling to the surface?

Chapter 13

By Wednesday I needed to get out of the house. Bill had called to let us know that Luke's boxing skills were now the stuff of legend all around town. After coming home to a cleaned-out trailer, Carl went to The Fountain and created such a scene that he became only the second person to incur a lifelong ban. It had only been a couple of days, but I still hadn't heard from Luke, which meant I still didn't know how he really felt about me.

Did he regret the kiss? Hell, did he regret the hospital bill?

Either way, I wanted to know, I needed to know, and I was pissed at Ginger for having Tiffany take her to the church to get Luke's sermon for me to read.

"Ginger, I'm fine. I need to get out of this house before I lose my mind!" I huffed.

"Enough to get the groceries?"

I whistled low. Ginger knew how I felt about going to the store. I might even run into my mother at the store. She and I would choose opposite ends of the store like we always did, but my heart would still race and my stomach pitch. I always forgot something on the days I ran into her because I was in such a hurry to get away.

But the cabin fever would be the end of me if I didn't get out of the house.

"Yes, I will get the groceries." And possibly drive by the parsonage even though it's several miles out of the way.

"Beulah, I can go do that," Tiffany said as she reached into the pantry for the Cheerios. She wore a red paisley bandana over her hair because she'd been on a dusting and vacuuming frenzy. A damp strip on her shirt over her belly suggested she'd cleaned out the tub, too.

"I'll go. I need some fresh air."

"This is crazy. You need rest."

"Says the pregnant woman who's been cleaning the entire house!"

"I like having an actual house to clean," she said, pouting. "And I can grocery shop, too!"

"Let her go, Tiffany. You go on to work, now. Beulah's a big girl." Ginger panted as she tried to raise the footrest on the recliner. I reached down to give her a hand, and she nodded her thanks.

"If you're sure." Tiffany shrugged her shoulders and stuck her hand into the box of Cheerios to take out another large handful. *Buy more Cheerios.*

"I'm sure." I reached for the Toyota keys where they hung on the hook inside the kitchen. "Just a little stir-crazy, I think."

Tiffany closed the cereal box and put it on the counter. She shuffled to the fridge and took out the strainer of grapes she had washed earlier that morning. She two-fisted the grapes, eating one from the left hand then one from the right. *Buy Cheerios . . . and grapes.*

"Take the Caddy, Beulah Lou. I know how you are when you start buying groceries, acting like there's going to be some blizzard and you'll never be able to get home." Ginger's eyes fluttered but remained closed as she leaned back into the recliner.

I looked down at the Toyota keys incredulously. "I thought old ladies couldn't hear."

"I'd know your keys anywhere with all that crap jangling

around," she mumbled. "They're going to tear the hook off the wall one of these days."

I looked down at my key ring complete with house key, tavern key, two sets of car keys—even though one of the cars was long gone—a metal B, a whistle, and an old Opryland key chain. I put them back on the hook and took down the keys to the Caddy with their sedate leather patch of a key chain. "Thanks, Ginger."

She mumbled something that sounded a lot like "You're welcome," and opened her eyes long enough to watch the ladies on *The View* gesticulate wildly.

I leaned down to kiss her cheek. "I'll be back before you know it."

"Take your time," she said, her eyes closed. "Oh, but I think I'd like some Dr Pepper."

"Okay." I frowned. Never had I known Ginger to drink Dr Pepper.

Settling into the Cadillac, I inhaled and exhaled with my hands squarely at ten and two. I always had to steel myself before driving into Ellery. Going to the Piggly Wiggly meant I would run into at least ten people I knew. At least eight of them would want to chitchat, and at least four of those would look down their noses at me the whole time. The Piggly Wiggly was, after all, the domain of Miss Lottie and Miss Georgette and many other ladies of both high moral standards and substantial girth.

Turning the key in the ignition, I couldn't help but think of what Luke would do. He would drive into town with a pleasant smile and go about his business calmly even if everyone knew he'd punched Carl twice. Better yet, Tiffany had no qualms about driving into town. She went about her errands with chin held high despite the rumors already swirling. For all of my bluster, I had always been an imposter, secretly hurt by all of the snubs and snide comments.

But not today.

Today, I was going to do my grocery shopping, and I was going to enjoy the summer sun and fresh air. Today, I was going to take my time and take the high road if anyone ran into me. Today, I was going to enjoy being alive and no longer concussed. I backed slowly down the drive and eased Ginger's land barge onto Crook Avenue.

Oddly, I saw Ellery with new eyes. Massive oaks and elms canopied Crook with overripe leaves in a shade of green that would soon fade to yellows and browns. Clapboard Victorians and squat bungalows lined either end of the street for the blocks that took me to Main, and the residential area suddenly gave way to the heart of town with the post office on the right and the fire station on the left. Next to the post office sat the old grocery store that had been converted into government offices, but I was basically looking at the butt of the town. Ellery's courthouse showed me her rear end to the left, and the first row of main street buildings showed me their posteriors on the right. Those shops reminded me of a movie façade—the storefronts that faced Main Street were old but well maintained, but the backs of the buildings were dirty and run-down with ancient air-conditioning units and boards nailed up in strategic places.

I passed both and eased up to the stop sign on Main Street. Looking left, I saw the stately entrance to the courthouse and less than a block of businesses. To my right, two blocks of businesses clung to Main Street with only parallel parking in front.

At this point I realized I hadn't been looking at the scenery. No, I'd been looking for Carl. If he couldn't raise hell in The Fountain anymore, then where would he go? Tiffany thought Carl would go back to his trailer to lick his wounds, but still. The crazy bastard might show up when we least expected it.

The person behind me honked to remind me to go. I turned right to head to the Piggly Wiggly on the outskirts of town. I wanted to flip her the bird, but I didn't want to hear about it from Ginger as I most assuredly would. Besides, a casual glance in the rearview mirror showed a lady who reminded me of Ginger with her curly grayish blond hair and expression of extreme annoyance.

As I drove over the bridge that crossed the railroad tracks just beyond the two blocks of two-story buildings, at least four people waved at me. For once in my life, I waved back, wondering if they thought I was Ginger. Only two stop signs stood between me and the grocery store, and it took less than five minutes to pass them. By that time, I was breathing deeply, confident that I could handle whatever town had to throw at me. Then I reached the parking lot to see a profusion of Cadillacs, Lincolns, Buicks, and other sensible-yet-aged sedans. Senior Citizen Discount Wednesday.

That horrifying realization explained why I was still sitting in the car when Luke tapped on the window.

"Beulah, are you going to get out or are you casing the joint?"

I sighed in relief. There he was. I didn't have enough claim on him to ask him where he'd been, but he also hadn't received a mail-order bride in the meantime. That I knew of.

I motioned for him to move out of the way and grabbed my purse and Ginger's list before sliding out of the car. We stood there in the middle of the parking lot staring at each other. Were we finally going to talk about what had happened at the hospital?

He frowned. "Are you supposed to be driving yet?"

Apparently not.

"Of course," I said a little too quickly. "Today is the first day, and I needed to get out of the house and get some fresh air."

He arched an eyebrow. "At the grocery store on a Wednesday?"

I crossed my arms and levied my best indignant look. "Well, you're here."

He winced. "Out of milk. And bread. And peanut butter." He put his hands in his front pockets and leaned forward ever so slightly. "That does not explain why you, with all of your helpers, are here today."

I slumped. "I was desperate, okay? And I've been conked on the head and had no clue what day it was."

"Fair enough. What say I treat each of us to a Coke once we're done?"

Not quite what I had in mind, but I summoned a smile anyway. "Good idea."

We made it through a third of the store before we came across Lottie Miller gossiping with Georgette Lane. Their buggies sat side by side as the two women blocked coffee on one side and cereal on the other to discuss in whispers all of the goings-on of Ellery. Blissfully unaware of the traffic jam they were causing, they gesticulated wildly over something that had happened at the Baptist Church, then about the Potter boy, who had wrapped his car around a tree the previous weekend.

Miss Georgette could have been a clone of Miss Lottie, only she wore knit tops with matching pants where Miss Lottie preferred Alfred Dunner polyester pantsuits. Miss Georgette also dyed her hair Lucille Ball red while Miss Lottie preferred an auburn shade to clash with all of her earth-tone clothing. Since Miss Georgette was wearing bright blue, I thought of a Rhode Island Red clucking to a peacock.

"Excuse me, ladies, but I need to get to the coffee over there." Luke had taken the lead, and I was grateful.

"Why, Reverend Daniels, I didn't see you there," Miss Lottie said as she backed her cart behind Miss Georgette. "Have you heard any more about the handbells?"

"They are supposed to arrive this afternoon," he said.

"Then I will have to come over and—"

As Luke leaned forward to get the lone bag of free-trade organic coffee, Miss Lottie spotted me. "Beulah, good to see you."

She and Miss Georgette looked from Luke to me and back to Luke, trying to gauge if we were together and, if so, in what capacity.

"How's Ginger doing these days?" Miss Georgette asked.

"She's doing all right," I lied. If I told Miss Georgette the truth, there would be a candlelight vigil that evening. And Ginger would kill me.

Miss Georgette shifted from one impossibly small foot to the other, and her thigh muscles jiggled. "And how are you? My niece told me you were in the ER with a concussion the other night."

Out of the corner of my eye, I saw Luke's eyes widen. He had no concept of the intricacy and depth of Miss Georgette's network of informants. Compared to Miss Georgette, Miss Lottie was a piker.

"I'm feeling much better," I said. "In fact, I decided to shop for groceries today just to get out of the house for a little while."

"That's good to hear," Miss Georgette said as she patted my hand. "You need to get away from that tavern before you get hurt, because I do not know what Ginger would do without you. She was telling me the other day all the things you do for her. Oh, tell me you are not going to keep playing there after you were *assaulted*."

"That's so sweet of you to be concerned, Miss Georgette, but I'll be back in business tomorrow night. Gotta pay the bills, you know."

"Actually, we'll be having Bible study there this evening," Luke said in a calm voice. "Both of you are more than welcome to join us."

That wiped the smiles off their faces.

"I-I think tonight is our knitting circle over at the American Legion," Miss Lottie said. "Doesn't that sound right to you, Georgette?"

"Yes, I do believe you are right. I would love to come, but I simply couldn't cancel on Lola and the other girls. We have to meet our quota of blankets for that charity, you see."

"Well, that's too bad," Luke said blandly. "You ladies have fun tonight, then."

He reached around for some unbleached coffee filters and moved his cart forward. Both Miss Georgette and Miss Lottie looked ready to burst with the need to spread the news that the new minister was having a Bible study in a bar. And that he had had the audacity to invite two upstanding citizens such as themselves to said study. I stifled my giggle until we got to the next aisle.

"Well played, Mr. Daniels." I had to stand on tiptoe to whisper over his shoulder into his ear.

"I gotta do what I gotta do, Miss Land," he whispered back

with a grin. Our eyes locked. For a minute I thought he might kiss me there in the middle of the Piggly Wiggly, but he came to his senses and set off down the condiments aisle in search of dressings for his fifteen bajillion salads.

As it turned out, shopping with Luke was good for my health for a variety of reasons. Not only did he save me from a sudden spike in blood pressure at the Miss Lottie-Miss Georgette blockade, but it was very difficult to justify Twinkies and Ho Hos when he was buying dried beans, cheese, tofu, and frozen vegetables to steam. Inevitably, we landed in the produce section.

"Hey, have you ever tried clementines?" Luke asked.

"No, but I do love melons," I said, waiting patiently for him to look up and see the two melons I was holding in front of my chest.

"Very funny," he said before taking each of the honeydews and putting them back gently on the appropriate stack.

"Do I need to put red lace on them instead?" I said just loud enough for him to hear me.

"You," he said, pointing a finger at me. "You are incorrigible."

"Shush!" I held a finger to his lips.

A tall, lanky man unloading watermelons sang lightly, "*There's a land that is fairer than day. . . .*"

I stepped closer to the deep, deep voice. His rich bass voice sounded too world-weary to belong to such a young man. He couldn't be much over twenty.

When he hit the chorus, I jumped in. His head snapped up, but he quickly switched from the call to the response. By the time we reached the end of the chorus, people had started to gather behind Luke.

"*In the sweet . . .*"

"*In the sweet . . .*"

"*By and by . . .*"

"*By and by . . .*"

We looked at each other, and harmonized, "*We shall meet on that beautiful shore.*"

Four or five people stood around the periphery of the little produce section, including Miss Lottie and Miss Georgette. Miss Lottie crossed her arms over her chest with a "Hmph," but Miss Georgette started to clap.

"That was absolutely wonderful," she said as her flabby underarms flopped double time. "I had no idea you could sing like that, Beulah. I knew all about the piano playing, but I had no idea you could sing, too. And who is this young man you are singing with? I don't know that I recognize him—"

"Have you ever tried clementines, Miss Georgette?"

I didn't have to turn to see Luke was distracting her for me. And she jumped on the bait like a pond-fed catfish who'd never met a worm. While they chatted up citrus, I extended a hand to the tall farmer. He stood Green Giant tall with sandy blond hair and a plethora of freckles. His blush couldn't hide how his fair skin had repeatedly burned in the hot sun, making him an honest-to-goodness redneck.

"Hi, I'm Beulah Land," I finally said.

He cleared his throat. "Sam Ford."

I gauged his accent. Like Luke, he didn't hang on his r's quite like us West Tennesseans. There was something different, but still Southern. "Where you from, Sam?"

"Just moved up from south Georgia to help my uncle out on the farm," he said as he pointed to some of the biggest, prettiest watermelons I'd ever seen.

"So, you're going to be here for a while?" Out of the corner of my eye, I saw Luke hesitate in the middle of his conversation with Miss Georgette. From the set of his lips, I would have almost said he was . . . jealous? A tingle began at my toes and worked its way up.

Sam Ford grinned to show a slight overbite. "I may stay on forever. Uncle Dancy has a huge spread, but he and Aunt Nona never had any kids. He said he might very well leave the farm to me if I'd help him keep it running."

Dancy and Nona Rockwell were good people, and I already

liked this Sam guy, too. "As it happens, I need someone to sing bass in my choir out at County Line Methodist. Think you might be interested?"

His face paled and he ran a hand over his head absently as though searching for a ball cap he'd left in his truck. "I don't know. Never been much on church."

"Funny you should mention that," I said with my most persuasive grin. "I never have been, either. Why don't you come out to The Fountain to try it out? I'll buy you a beer."

That rendered him speechless.

I left him slack-jawed in the middle of the produce section trying to put together all of the incongruent puzzle pieces I'd handed him.

As we wheeled to the checkout, Luke leaned over to whisper in my ear. "It's not nice to use your feminine wiles on hapless young men, you know."

"I did not use my feminine wiles!" I sputtered. "I smiled and offered to buy him a beer! That's all. I showed *you* my melons."

He stared fiery holes through me until I blushed.

"Is there a particular reason you might be concerned about my feminine wiles, Mr. Preacher Man?"

"I don't play games, and I'm not having this discussion in the grocery store."

"Then where and when are we going to have it?" *Because I want to talk about our kiss. And I don't want an audience.*

"My place. After Bible study."

His answer, so quick and fierce, took me aback. But I'd never really been one to back down. "Done."

Chapter 14

When I walked into The Fountain that night, Bill grabbed me into a bear hug. "Where you been? You okay? I thought I told you never to go out there by yourself."

"Bill, I'm fine except for the fact that you're squeezing me too hard."

He let go. "Sorry. We've all been so worried about you. And it's been so quiet around here. Ol' Pete and Greg played a little 'Heart and Soul,' but there's really only so many times you want to go through that."

"I've only been gone for two days!"

Tiffany burst through the door, singing along to Taylor Swift in her headphones. I grinned at Bill. "No chance of it being quiet for long. She's been on a tear ever since she got over her morning sickness."

"Tell me about it," Bill said. He grabbed hold of his suspenders and sighed. "But we're losing her, did you hear?"

"No, she hasn't said word one to me about it." Which was odd because there wasn't a whole heckuva lot she hadn't commented on as of late.

"Kari down at the flower shop—heck, she's your cousin, isn't she? She hired Tiffany. Said she could use a driver."

Kari Vandiver and I didn't speak anymore, but I flirted with the idea of rescinding my promise never to set foot in her establishment to thank her for taking a chance on Tiffany. Then I decided a thank-you note would suffice. I tried to imagine a pregnant Tiffany hauling flowers around. Surely flowers wouldn't be too heavy for a pregnant woman.

"Said she'd teach her about flower arranging, too." Bill reached over to the narrow wall shelf where he'd set his beer.

"Does Kari know she's pregnant?"

"Oh, yeah," he said. "Tiffany told her that, first thing. Said she didn't want to misrepresent herself."

I looked at my feet. I had told Tiffany to lie. Well, to omit the truth. I wanted to be mad at her for both being right and for making me feel like a heel. Instead I was proud of her for listening to Ginger instead of me and for being true to herself.

"That's really great. If you see Kari before I do, tell her I said thanks."

He frowned and shook his head as if to say he would never understand the complexities of women. "Yep. Sure will."

"Thanks," I said, ignoring how he was muttering, "She's *your* cousin" under his breath. There was more to the story than Bill knew, and that's the way I wanted it.

Sam Ford chose that moment to duck inside the door, a welcome distraction if I'd ever seen one. His eyes scanned the room until they landed on me, and he grinned. Maybe I had led him on. A little.

"Sam! I'm so glad you could make it." I put my arm in Bill's and dragged him a few feet forward to meet our newest member. "This is Sam Ford, our new bass. Sam, this is Bill. He runs The Fountain."

The two men shook hands and sized each other up. For a minute I thought they might circle each other and sniff their respective behinds like a couple of coonhounds, but they blessedly stood still.

"I promised this man a beer. Could you get him one while I warm up? Go ahead and put it on my tab, if you don't mind."

"Why, sure, I can do that," Bill said. "Come on over here and see what we've got," he added to Sam.

I left the two men to bond over beer and climbed the risers to get ready for choir practice. By the time I'd settled into the piano seat and found a hymnal, Bill and Sam were laughing in a corner. Sam's voice was so low I couldn't make out what he was saying, but I thought I caught a snippet of "A priest and a take-your-pick enter a bar" type joke. Yep, Sam Ford was going to fit in just fine.

And, as it turned out, Sam could sing circles around Carl Davis—probably because his vocal cords hadn't suffered from thousands of cigarettes and who knew what else. Even better, twice I caught him sneaking a glance at Tiffany then looking back to me as though reminding himself he was here to see me, not the buxom soprano with the ethereal voice.

After practice, Luke wandered in to set up his materials. He refused to let his eyes meet mine. I caught Sam's arm before he could wander off. "So, do you think you'd like to join the Happy Hour Choir?"

Sam looked at me then looked at Luke and back to me again. "You only wanted me for the choir, didn't you?"

I blushed to the roots of my red hair. I liked his honesty, and I could stand to learn more on the subject myself. "Yeah. You really do sing well."

He nodded twice to the affirmative, although his brain was still working through my question. Then he fixed me with a stare that said he wasn't ready to give up on me quite yet. "I reckon I like to sing, and I need to meet some new people, so I'll do it. Aunt Nona'll be glad to see me going to church again, anyway."

I exhaled with a whoosh of breath I hadn't realized I'd been holding. "Thank you! Thank you! Thank you!"

I gave him a quick squeeze and jumped on the riser to grab my purse. I gently laid my song suggestions on Luke's Bible study notes while he was in the corner talking with Bill.

"Hey, where are you going?" Sam asked.

"Oh," I said. "This is the Bible study portion of the evening. I usually don't stay for that."

"Why not?"

What to tell him, what to tell him. Should I tell him I wasn't too friendly with God? That I was only playing the piano as a favor to a little old lady riddled with cancer? That I didn't think I could sit still while I waited for Luke to finish whatever he was going to do so we could finally have a much-needed heart-to-heart? I decided on something simple and true. "I really need to check on my . . . Ginger."

"Don't you want to show me the ropes here?" he said with a wide smile.

I felt Luke's glare and looked in his direction before I could stop myself. His beer was suspended in midair again. If Luke didn't want me to stay and sit next to Sam, then maybe that was the very thing I ought to do. "You know what? I think I might. Here, let's sit down next to Tiffany."

What was wrong with me? What was I doing in Bible study? And why was I leading on one man in the hopes of making another jealous? I had already learned that the only person I could truly count on was myself. And Ginger. And maybe Luke. And most likely Tiffany. Okay, so there were a few people I could trust—that didn't mean I was ready to include God in that exclusive little group.

Each member of the Happy Hour Choir was there as well as Goat Cheese, who was no doubt gathering intel. I smiled and nodded through Bible study, thinking of anything else but what was going on. For one, there was a crack on the wall beyond the piano—that would need to be fixed before it got cold. I'd forgotten to fill some of Ginger's prescriptions, but I could do that the next day. And then there was the hint of hair at the collar of Luke's shirt and how he rolled up his sleeves like a benevolent politician on the campaign trail.

As everyone concluded a spirited discussion about jealousy, Saul, and several other things I didn't care about, Luke pulled out his phone and frowned down at the number, placing it on the table beside him. When it was time to pray, I bowed my head with everyone else then waited a few sentences before I looked up to watch Luke pray.

I had watched him many times before, but I had only seen the back of his head; the perfectly squared line of his hair where the barber had shaven the locks with precision. Looking at his face, though, was revelatory. He didn't furrow his brow or squint his eyes as some preachers did. He didn't keep his eyes open and consult a list of requests like others. No, he bowed his head slightly, his face perfectly serene as his ridiculously long and dark eyelashes hardly fluttered. No smile, only a calm I envied.

"Amen."

"Hey, Beulah, Sam's going to take me home," Tiffany said.

Sam nodded to me, and I saw purpose. He figured if I could use him to make Luke jealous, he could use Tiffany to make me jealous. I shot him a return look that hopefully said, "This ain't *All My Children*, and you had best not hurt my friend."

He frowned, but who knew if he could read my mind. I wasn't going to count on it. I did, however, curse under my breath as Tiffany locked arms with him and looked up with blatant admiration.

"Stick around for me, if you will." I turned to see Luke walking toward the door with his cell phone at his ear. As if I was going anywhere. Instead, I sat and fiddled with my purse strap while I watched everyone else file out.

"Yo, Beulah, can you lock 'er up for me?" Bill pulled out his suspenders and let them fly back at his belly with a satisfying slap.

"I'll do it for a Stella," I said.

He waved away my request as he waddled to the door. "Take two if you need to. Marsha hates it when I'm not back in time to watch her shows with her."

I grinned at him and walked back to the bar to get a beer. When I saw Luke put his phone in his pocket and reach for the door, I took out a Heineken for him. He took two steps in, his face serious.

"What's wrong, Preacher Man? Looks like you can use one of these." I slid the Heineken his way.

"Nothing's wrong." He took a swig and put the bottle back down with a frown. Then his eyes brightened. "Something good for you, maybe."

"Oh?" I put the bottle to my lips and drank.

He frowned. "You're never going to believe who just called."

"Clem Kadiddlehopper."

"Who?"

"Never mind." Living with an old lady meant your pop culture references were often outdated.

"Remember that day in the cemetery when I had something to tell you? I forgot all about it, thanks to the trip to the hospital, but Tom Dartmouth told me he has a nephew who's interning as a talent scout for a little Christian label in Nashville. He wants his nephew to hear your choir."

That sucked the air right out of me. A *talent scout?* As in a record company? As in a golden ticket out of Ellery? I grabbed Luke and hugged him before I even registered what I was doing. "I can't believe it!"

My heart pounded. I was already thinking of studios and limos and crowds full of people. Wouldn't that show everyone? For once in my life I had the chance to be *someone*. Well, my Happy Hour Choir and I had the chance to be a bunch of someones.

Luke put a hand on my shoulder, effectively dissolving my daydreams. "Look, this is only one meeting with an intern. Please tell me you're not going to get your hopes up."

"No, *Ginger*, I'm not going to do anything as silly as that. When is he coming?"

"Next week. After Sinners to Saints. I told him you sounded great live, but Tom has Sunday appointments and can only come on a Wednesday."

"I can't believe it. Nothing like this ever happens to folks around here. I've got to go call Ginger."

I was already taking my cell out of my pocket when Luke grabbed my arm. "Beulah, about our kiss—"

"What about our kiss?" My pulse was officially out of control.

"I'm hoping you don't think I was out of line."

"Out of line? Are you crazy?"

"The more I thought about it, the more I thought—"

I put a finger to his lips to silence him. "Preacher Man, you think entirely too much."

"You have no idea how happy I am to hear that," he murmured as he took a step closer. My body leaned forward without consulting my brain. All of a sudden, oxygen was in short supply. The Fountain's silence shouted. My heart beat a million times a minute, reminding me of a day almost ten years ago when I'd breathlessly waited for a kiss in a hand-me-down ragtop, the last time I'd breathlessly waited for anything.

His lips glanced mine, and I almost blacked out before they made another gentle, grazing pass. He hesitated for a second then kissed me full-on, a hungry kiss that left us both clinging to each other as tightly as we could. One of his hands knotted in my hair and the other palmed the small of my back to pull me closer. My hand traced his spine as I stood on tiptoe to reach him while my fingers flicked through his precisely cut hair.

And this is why people have sex, I thought, as he set me up on the counter and leaned into me. It was beyond a need to procreate. No, we each needed to be needed, a need interrupted by the slam of the screen door.

We broke apart to see Mac frozen just inside the door. His eyes immediately shifted to the floor. "Forgot my wallet," he muttered.

Leaning over by his chair with a grunt, he raised his trophy high with a cheery "Found it!" and beat the hastiest retreat I'd ever seen.

The spell broken, Luke rested his forehead on mine. "This is not a good idea."

Forget picking out curtains, I didn't even merit a third kiss.

"You're right," I said, leaping from the counter. "Because I'm me, and you're you. You could lose your job over this."

"You have no idea," he muttered, jamming his hands into his pockets.

I took a step back, willing any tears I had to stay unshed. "I mean, this relationship, or whatever it is, could never go anywhere. Obviously, we were just caught up in the moment."

Two of them, to be precise.

"Yes. I mean, no."

"I agree." I wrenched The Fountain key off my ring and tossed it at him. "Lock up when you're done, you hear?"

He grabbed my wrist instead. "I meant we weren't just caught up in the moment. At least I wasn't."

He stared down at me looking for something, some sign he could kiss me again.

My pride still stung. "Well, maybe I was."

And I'd hauled off and hurt the Preacher Man again.

The hurt in his eyes flickered to understanding, and he kissed me once more, another feathery kiss teasing promise. "Sure about that?"

Hell, no. I'm not sure of anything. "Still just a kiss."

"I don't think so," he said. "I think you're afraid of something."

Snakes? Zombies? Falling in love with a man who couldn't possibly ever love me? Getting that man fired? Oh, there were plenty of things that scared me—not that I planned to admit any of them.

"Not even the dark," I lied as I slid from his embrace. "I meant it when I said to lock up."

When I got to the door, I turned to see if he would follow me. I wanted him to barge over, slam the door shut, and then tell me I wasn't going anywhere. I wanted him to say to hell with his job and to hell with what everyone else thought. Instead he leaned against the counter with a calculating look.

I walked out the door, catching the screen door to keep it from slamming, holding back tears and willing my throat to stay open. And I wished with every bit of my aching heart that he wouldn't be able to sleep for other things that ached. Just like me.

Chapter 15

Everything was up-tempo the next night at The Fountain. Somewhat reconciled to the idea that Luke and I weren't going anywhere, I couldn't help but feel hope about the scout's visit. I mean, karma may be a bitch, but I'd done a good turn by leaving Luke alone. Surely that had to count for something in the scheme of the universe.

Bill was trying out a new waitress, a brunette version of Tiffany, who hefted trays with a similar beefy-armed ease. Tiffany, for her part, was excited about her job at the florist, and Ginger had even treated us to a New Orleans sing-along earlier that afternoon. It was one of those rare moments when the world made some semblance of sense. I sighed and leaned a little deeper into the Beatles' "All You Need Is Love," complete with the Gates brothers drunkenly blaring the "bum-ba-dum-da-dum" in all the right places.

Luke pushed through the door, and my first thought was that he had recognized the song and wanted to join in. The set of his jaw, however, told me that something was very wrong.

"*All you need is—*"

"Beulah, you gotta come now. It's Ginger."

"*—love.*" I stopped, leaving the chord progression unresolved. He offered his hand, and I jumped to the floor.

Bill picked up his Co-op cap and put it back down on his head. "What's going on?"

"Miss Ginger's in the hospital," Luke answered for me.

"What's wrong?"

"We'll find out when we get there," he said, holding open the door for me.

"We'll be sure to say a prayer for her," Bill said.

"She'd appreciate that," I ground out. As if a moment of silence in a bar would amount to anything.

And then I was in Luke's ridiculous roadster racing for the hospital. "That's all you know?"

He sighed. "Tiffany called 911 for an ambulance. Then she called me. She said Miss Ginger grabbed around her heart." His lips pressed together, and he sped up. I should have been amused by the vision of Reverend Luke Daniels breaking the law, but I was too busy picturing Ginger clutching her heart.

"A heart attack?" I whispered. *Not yet. Please, not yet.* We only had a little bit of time left, and I wasn't ready to give her up.

I crossed my arms and fumed for a good ten minutes before Luke spoke up again. "Good thing Tiffany was there to catch Ginger when she fell and to call for an ambulance."

"Yeah, but not as lucky as I would be if Ginger were still sitting in her recliner watching *CSI*," I snapped, even though he had a point.

I closed my eyes and rubbed my temples. It was all Luke's fault. And Ginger's. I wouldn't have been trying to figure out the mysteries of the universe if I hadn't been forced to play all of those religious songs or to sit through Luke's sermons.

Or if I hadn't tasted heaven only to have it wrenched away.

"Beulah, are you praying?"

My eyes snapped open. I'd had enough prayer for a lifetime. "No, I'm not praying. Why does everyone seem to think I'm either praying or ought to be? I've never seen anything to tell me a prayer could amount to a hill of beans."

Luke nodded, unruffled by my outburst. "You're living proof prayers come true."

I snorted. "I'm living proof prayers *don't* come true. Just ask my momma what she prayed for all her life. I'm not it."

Luke took a corner way too sharply and had to jerk to the right to avoid a one-eyed car trying to take his half down the middle. "Yes, but I prayed you would be okay after Carl threw you into that cinder-block wall. Miss Ginger prays for you every day, and here you are."

"If prayer is so potent, why did I lose my baby? Why did Ginger get cancer? Why did my daddy have to die, and why, in heaven's name, did my momma have to yell at me all the time and beat me with her damned wooden spoon?"

Luke sighed and pinched the bridge of his nose. His eyes never left the road. "It's a world of good and evil."

I tuned him out, thinking only of all those wasted prayers that I would somehow be a half-decent mother and that my baby boy would grow up to be healthy and happy. I prayed and prayed for that child—right up until the day I walked into the nursery and couldn't hear him breathing anymore.

Hot tears slid down my cheeks. "I loved my baby boy so much." My throat ached, and my words stuck there. "I didn't mean to love him. I didn't want to love him, but I could believe—I could see—as long as I cradled him in my arms. When he died, I saw what a fool I had been to think I could make myself someone different just for him."

The good Reverend Daniels didn't have anything to say about that.

Of course, he wouldn't. The night before, I'd convinced myself not to get involved with him for his sake, but here was a potent reminder of why *I* needed to stay away from *him*. I couldn't spend the rest of my life listening to religious mumbo jumbo. I was the last person who needed to be the preacher's girlfriend, much less the preacher's wife.

I swiped away my tears. Time to put on my game face for Ginger. "Anyway, that's why I'm done praying."

He pulled into the hospital parking lot, sliding into the first available parking space with a squeal of tires. He didn't say anything at first, letting the hot engine click and fizz. Finally, he turned to look at me with more compassion than I deserved. "Then I guess I'll have to pray enough for both of us."

I sat with Ginger through the night and well into the next day. It was as though I hadn't realized how much she had gone downhill over the past few months until I saw her lying there in the hospital bed with her skin gray against the white linens of the hospital bed. They still didn't know what was wrong with her, but they had ruled out a heart attack. For the moment, she had a morphine drip to help with the pain.

She slept, but her body still tensed against the pain. She hadn't penciled in her eyebrows nor put on lipstick, and she looked oddly naked without her clip-on earrings. I couldn't bear to look at her, but I couldn't bear to look away.

"Miss Belmont?" A doctor leaned into the room.

"Miss Belmont?" he repeated before I realized he was talking to me.

"Yes." I didn't bother to correct him. Sometimes organizations underestimated the family we had created, somehow thinking it inferior to those defined by shared blood. In my experience, many of the strongest bonds came from those who *chose* to be together.

"Thanks to some of the tests we ran last night, I think we've narrowed it down to a clot in the spleen."

"What does that mean?" *And what the hell is a spleen?*

He smiled at me then pushed his glasses back up his nose. "That means a little blood thinner should take care of the clot, and we should have Miss Ginger back to her old self in no time."

I released a shaky breath. "How long?"

"It's hard to say, but it should be a little less than a week."

He turned to go, but I touched his shoulder. "No, I meant the cancer?"

He shrugged. "You'll have to ask the oncologist about that, but such clots are not uncommon among patients with cancer."

"But, has the cancer spread?"

His formerly friendly face went blank. He didn't want to get anywhere near cancer or any predictions of what such an unpredictable disease might do next. "You'll have to ask the oncologist."

I nodded, and he turned to go. My throat was too closed up to speak any more. I glanced at Ginger, but she slept on. Someone rustled behind me, and I knew it was Tiffany because she carried the overwhelming, cloying odor of the florist with her.

"I can sit here with Miss Ginger," Tiffany said quietly as she slid her arrangement of flowers onto the windowsill. Now three vases of her practice arrangements sat on the sill, each a riot of color.

"I think I'll stay."

"Go. You haven't eaten anything since lunch yesterday." Tiffany laid a gentle hand on my arm and bumped me with her belly by accident.

Showing? Already?

Tamping down an irrational panic, I looked at Tiffany, and she raised her eyebrow and lifted one hand as if to spank me. Motherhood had come naturally to that one. I backed out of the room, but I didn't really know what to do with myself.

Luke would tell you to pray.

Luke can kiss my grits.

I frowned. Where was Luke anyway? Had I permanently offended him? And why did that thought twist my insides into a bunch when I had no intentions of taking back a word of what I'd said?

And there I stood in front of the elevator. I pushed the "down" button just as I saw a sign to the chapel. No way was I going to that chapel. Not after what I'd told Luke. But I also had a deep, aching need to keep Ginger close.

The bell dinged.

The door opened, but I was on my way down the hall to find the chapel.

At the end of the hall, I found the tiny, dark room with plain chairs and only one stained glass window. A six-foot rail stretched across the tiny room, and Luke knelt at that rail.

Dammit. He used to make his hospital visits on Thursdays. He must've stopped for a prayer before making his way over to Ginger's room.

He took up almost the entire room, and I sucked in a breath. Need, desire, and desperation mixed together.

Hearing my gasp, he stood.

"What are you doing?" he asked, his voice low but optimistic.

"I, uh, wondered if you wanted to go down and get some lunch." My shoes were fascinating. The carpet was fascinating. Anything that kept Luke from asking me what I was doing in the chapel was fascinating. But I looked up at him anyway.

"That sounds like a great idea," he said with a sad, tired smile. In that smile I saw yet another person in a long line of people I had disappointed. He had hoped I had come there to pray, to redeem myself after all the awful, sacrilegious things I'd said.

My feet stayed bolted to the floor.

"I hear they have an extra-salty cream of tomato," he said. He smiled to rid his face of any remaining disappointment and laid a hand on my shoulder.

Tears ran down my cheeks hot and fast.

"Okay, we'll find something other than cream of tomato. . . ." Luke was no stranger to crying women, but he clearly didn't like it any more than any other man.

"Not the soup," I croaked over the lump in my throat. No, it was the roller coaster of emotions, the belief that I had finally figured out what life was all about—the whys and the hows—only to be slapped down by the reality that I would lose Ginger sooner rather than later.

"I know." He folded me into his embrace, and I burrowed into his crisply ironed shirt, drinking in his scent of sandalwood and soap. I had wanted the comfort of his arms from the beginning so I let myself have a really good cry.

As my sobs subsided, he held me tighter before planting a kiss on the top of my head. I reached up to touch one of the dimples I liked so much, and his smile faded. His eyes lost their twinkle.

He leaned forward, but I met him halfway. We were desperate for fingers to touch, for lips to meet. His lips were every bit as soft as his hands were callused, and I leaned into him, into the memory of him from the night before. But something had changed. He tore his mouth from mine before either of us could deepen the kiss. He leaned his forehead against mine, his eyes closed. Another woman might think he didn't want to kiss her, but I could feel, almost touch, how badly he wanted to kiss me.

"Good to see that the two of you are so concerned about Miss Ginger's health," someone said as I touched my fingers to my swollen lips.

"Miss Lottie." Luke nodded dismissively, his eyes never leaving mine. "What a pleasant surprise."

His tone suggested it was anything but.

Miss Lottie carried on, oblivious to the steel in his tone of voice. "Bill's wife told Miss Georgette, who told me that Ginger was in the hospital. I thought I'd stop by for a moment of prayer. That is what this room is for, right? Prayer?"

And who was to say a heartfelt kiss wasn't a prayer?

"It is a place of prayer as well as a place to reflect on minding one's own business." He took my arm and led me out of the small chapel. Lottie Miller's mouth hung open.

"Beulah, I'm so sorry," Luke said.

"You're sorry?" I hissed. "What are you apologizing for?"

"For letting my emotions get the best of me in a place like this," he said. "There's something about you. I can't stand to see you hurting."

I jerked my arm from his embrace. "So you were kissing me because you felt sorry for me?"

"That's not what I said."

"That's what it sounded like. Am I an embarrassment to you?"

"No, of course not." But there was Luke the minister again,

carefully choosing the words he would say next. "With my job, though, I have a certain obligation to be beyond reproach. I can't think only of myself. I have to—"

"You know what? You're a horrible liar." I turned on my heel to head back to Ginger's room. My stomach growled in protest, but I didn't want to share a hallway with Luke in that moment, much less a table.

He grabbed my wrist and twirled me back in front of him. Gone was Luke the minister, and back was Luke, the mortal of the flashing eyes. "Don't put words in my mouth, Beulah. And don't project emotions on me that aren't my own. No, I didn't want one of my church members to find me kissing you in a chapel, but I did it, and I would do it all over again."

"That's not how you felt before. Do it." I dared him. "Here. In front of God and everybody."

The elevator dinged to announce its arrival, and he let my arm drop.

"That's what I thought," I said softly.

Fire snapped in those blue eyes, and his hand reached the small of my back before I could gasp. "There's more to it than you think. Come downstairs and let me explain."

I shook my head no and wriggled away from him. He thrust his arm between the elevator doors to keep them from closing.

"Beulah?" he asked from the elevator, his hand holding the door open as an invitation for me.

"I've heard enough explanations," I muttered before walking back in the direction of Ginger's room.

Chapter 16

Ginger was awake, but pain pinched her face into new wrinkles. I sat on the side of the bed and held her hand. I resisted the urge to bring my fingers to my lips, and, if she had deduced my latest little scandal, she wasn't saying anything. She had *Jerry Springer* on, but the TV was muted as always. She had long maintained that the best way to watch daytime TV was without sound. Unfortunately, I was beginning to feel I was better suited to appearing on an episode of *Springer* than to real life.

"Beulah, we need to talk."

No French toast to soften the blow this time.

I didn't say anything, and she squeezed my hand. "I'm serious. The more I think about it, the more there is to tell you. Especially now that we've inherited Tiffany."

I took a deep breath. "If I listen to what you have to say, promise me that you won't up and die because you've told me everything you think you need to?"

Ginger chuckled. "I never get tired of telling you what to do, Beulah. It's one of my greatest joys in life. I'm not going anywhere yet, but I thought a heart attack was taking me home."

Home. Ginger considers heaven to be home.

"First, I had to spend a little bit of your inheritance—"

"What inheritance? What are you talking about, Ginger?"

"Your inheritance, Beulah. It's not like I have a bunch of cats and need to establish a trust fund for them—the house and all of my money is going to you."

What money? I thought of all of the bills and tanks of gas I'd paid for during Ginger's first round of chemo—not that she was with-it enough to know what I was doing.

It took a couple of tries before I could get out the words. "Ginger, I don't need your money. You need to spend your money on you."

"Beulah, I'm too old and sick to go gallivanting around the world or to buy fancy cars. I've had everything I've ever wanted and then some. There are some bank accounts I didn't tell you about before, but I cleaned out one of them to pay Luke back for your little trip to the emergency room."

My heart landed at my toes. I had been waiting for them to send the bill in the mail before officially worrying. "Ginger, I'm so sorry about that."

Ginger waved away my concern then winced at the pain such motion caused. "Don't worry about that, but can't you see you need a real job? One with health insurance? The time for playing around is over. I made you graduate from high school for a reason, you know. And that's where my life insurance policy comes in."

"Your what?"

"When I thought I might have a baby of my own, I bought a life insurance policy, one of those that you keep. I kept paying into it because I didn't need that much money, I guess. I got a statement that I'd paid up right after you started living with me and thought it'd be a good way for you to go to college. It seems I underestimated both your stubbornness and my longevity," she sniffed.

"But—"

"There's over a hundred thousand in there. I've already spoken with Mr. Cohen over at the Farm Bureau. The policy's in the lock box. He'll tell you what to do when the time comes."

"Okay, but—"

"There should be enough for both you and Tiffany to get started at the community college. She won't be able to play softball, but I think she'll be okay with that, don't you?"

"Ye-yes." This was a surreal conversation, one that brought tears. Some were tears of sadness at the thought of losing Ginger; others were tears of gratitude.

Ginger pointed to the box of tissues on the table by her bed. "Oh, quit blubbering, Beulah. You're going to get me started, and it's just plain silly. I've lived a long, long life. And if I haven't taught you how to make it in the world by now, then it can't be done."

I grabbed a tissue, blew my nose, and nodded to show I was on board.

"All right. I already told you I don't want an open casket visitation. You remember that. Everything should be paid for because I went to see Mr. Anderson a few weeks ago and prepaid. There may be shysters in the mortuary business, but Declan Anderson is not one of them."

"But, Ginger—"

"It's done. And paid for. There are some advantages to living alone frugally for most of your life. Now, the house." Ginger yawned. "When I'm gone, you can do with it as you please, but you're going to have to do something about the nursery."

I closed my eyes to the memory of my recent disastrous attempt to reconcile with the nursery.

"Tiffany wants to redecorate a little, and you're not going to let her lift anything heavy, are you?"

"No, ma'am."

"And if she decides she wants to paint the room, you're not going to let a pregnant woman paint and breathe in all those fumes, are you?"

"But—"

"I know you painted that room, but we didn't know any better. Now, are you going to let Tiffany paint?"

"No, ma'am."

"Good." Ginger took one of my hands into two of hers. "It's a room, Beulah, just a room. Sooner or later, you have to go into that room and make peace with what happened there."

I nodded my head affirmatively, even though I had no intentions of doing what Ginger suggested.

"That's enough for now," she said. She lay back on her bed and waved one hand at me as though dismissing me from her royal presence. "Everything else I'm going to write out for you, but I wanted to lay out the important stuff. Especially about your hospital bill, because I knew it would eat at you once it came in the mail."

She settled into the pillow and closed her eyes. I didn't want her to go to sleep. I had the oddest urge to shake her by the shoulders until she woke up and stayed awake, because if she went to sleep she might die. And I wasn't ready for that, no matter how much money Ginger had stashed away.

She opened one eye. "Beulah, it's creepy having someone watch you while you're sleeping. Go downstairs and get yourself a Coke. Read the paper. Do something."

I backed out of the door against my will. Why couldn't I do *something?* For that matter, why couldn't I take the cancer instead of Ginger? I was younger, stronger, almost as stubborn. If anyone deserved cancer, it was me. I was the bad person here, the person who got pregnant at sixteen, the person who refused to pray, and the person who played hymns in a honky-tonk. Ginger didn't deserve cancer; she deserved a cabana boy who looked like a young Tom Selleck to feed her grapes by the pool while he massaged her feet. She gave and gave. And she got cancer in return? It wasn't fair.

I tamped down that familiar feeling of injustice and took the elevator downstairs to find a Coke and a paper. I knew Ginger would get a kick out of the celebrity magazines, so I picked up a couple of those, too. On impulse, I picked up a Milky Way, her favorite candy bar.

At the register, my fingers reached out to touch a necklace with a cardinal pendant. I turned it over to see it was still twenty dollars, even on sale.

Ginger does love her cardinals.

"Do you want the necklace, too?" the cashier asked, but I jerked my fingers away and quickly shook my head. Jewelry was frivolous, and old habits died hard.

"I'll take it, though."

His familiar voice rumbled through me. I couldn't decide if I wanted to throw myself into his arms or run like hell. Another Coke appeared on the counter beside mine. "In fact, this purchase is on me."

"Luke, you don't have to do that." I wheeled around. *After all, I'm freaking rich, apparently. Rich enough to go to college just as soon as the nicest old lady in the history of man dies of a ridiculously horrible disease.*

"Beulah, you've got the frantic eyes again. Let me get this one."

"Frantic eyes?" He reached around me, and my traitorous body almost swayed into him.

"Come on," he said as he grabbed the paper and the little white bag with one hand then guided my shoulder with the other. He led me to a sunny seating area just inside the hospital's main entrance and took a seat across from me.

We each took a Coke and popped the top.

"I wanted to apologize for earlier today. And for last night," he said. "I shouldn't have kissed you. Either time." He studied the Coke can as though he'd taken a sip only to discover it wasn't what he wanted after all.

Apologize?

"So, you *are* embarrassed to be seen with me." It should have been anger bubbling up, but instead despair pulled me down. Not that I was about to let him see that.

He slammed the Coke down too hard, and some fizzed over the top. "No, I was not embarrassed. I was taking advantage of you, and that isn't right."

"Taking advantage of me?" *I* wish *that was how being taken advantage of felt. Luke had no idea.*

He ran a hand through that glossy black hair, and it all fell right back where it was supposed to be. What I would give to see it mussed just once. "Look, you turned to me for comfort, and I knew you were hurting. And I took advantage of that. And I'm sorry. And it won't happen again."

I had walked away. And now that he had taken the hint, I realized I had wanted him to follow me. No way to fix that now. "Apology accepted. I'm sorry I taunted you."

He nodded his acceptance. "I'm glad that's settled."

He handed me the paper, then held up the necklace. "Need help with the clasp?"

"I was getting it for Ginger," I said with a smile I didn't feel.

"Of course," he said with a tight smile as he let the necklace spill into my cupped hand. I wondered if he wanted to stand behind me and fasten the necklace as badly as I wanted him to. Maybe so, but he quickly drew his hand back instead.

"Well, I still need to see Miss Ginger," he said. I had already run into him by accident twice. He was giving me the chance to avoid him this time.

"Thanks for the necklace . . . and everything else."

"You're welcome." He stood reluctantly, but collected himself and walked briskly down the hall. In his odd Dr. Jekyll and Mr. Hyde routine, Luke the minister had squelched Luke the man. Only, Luke the man was certainly not the monster he seemed to think he was.

I stretched out the chain of the necklace. Both chain and pendant were nothing special—some type of cheap gold plating. Still, the extra-fat cardinal reminded me of the one outside our window, and I wondered if Ginger would remember him.

He bought it for you.

So he had, but I couldn't put on a necklace I'd intended for Ginger, not even for the brush of his fingertips against the nape of my neck.

They released Ginger a couple of days after they admitted her. We all knew it was too soon, but Ginger was ready to escape the hospital, so I pulled the car around and waited while Tiffany and a nurse eased Ginger into the front seat. I noticed her new necklace had left a yellowish-green stain around her neck, but she refused to take it off.

"You know," Ginger said with a twinkle in her eye, "I believe I'm actually hungry. Beulah, you think we can swing by Burger Paradise on the way home, maybe give Tiffany something to check off her list?"

I chanced a look in the rearview mirror just in time to see Tiffany grinning from ear to ear. She held a flower arrangement with each arm and propped the third between her feet, looking like an animal sticking its head out of exotic foliage. "Please, please, please. I'll have my burger with extra pickles."

Ginger's hand flew to her mouth. Even before cancer and her first round of chemo, she'd hated pickles, refusing to put them in potato salad or chicken salad, which was fine by me. "Life's too short for something so sour," she would tell me.

"Yes, Miss Momma to Be." I shifted my voice to a whisper. "Just don't say the p-word again."

Tiffany nodded, her face solemn with no smile in those huge brown eyes. She looked like little more than a child, yet she was going to be a mother. That had been me once upon a time. Only I wouldn't have shut up. I would have shouted "Pickles! Pickles! Pickles, how I love their sour flavor and the green slime they leave behind on the bun!" It took me a long time to feel remorse for hurting Ginger's feelings, a lot longer than it'd taken Tiffany.

"Beulah, can you get me a plain burger?" Ginger turned to the window.

"And—"

"Tiffany, baby, I know you want a double burger with cheese, no lettuce, no tomato, but extra . . . *you know*."

She nodded with a grin. "And a chocolate-banana milk shake."

As I smiled at her, I felt love even if I couldn't articulate it. A chocolate-banana milk shake. I was becoming such a softie. If she'd asked me, I probably would've had them put pickles in her milk shake, too.

Instead I eased out of the car and walked up to the outside window to place my order. Burger Paradise might be the best restaurant in town, an institution for far longer than I had been alive, but they had their own way of doing things. Some folks went inside to eat, but I knew Ginger didn't want to wait that long or to be seen in public while still green around the edges.

I sneaked a glance at her and Tiffany in the car as I finished giving the waitress my order. Then I slipped her an extra twenty. "Could you kinda push this one to the top of the pile? I have a couple of ladies who need to get home."

The teenager tried not to grin at me, but she nodded as she slipped the extra twenty into the back pocket of her jeans. Ten minutes later I walked back to the car with a Styrofoam cup and a white grease-stained sack in hand.

"Well, that was the fastest service I've ever seen here," Ginger said as I handed her the sack and passed the cup back to Tiffany.

"Guess it's your lucky day." I shrugged my shoulders.

"Guess it is," she mumbled to herself as she lay back in the seat and took a nap during the short ride home.

Burger Paradise claimed they had the "Best Burgers This Side of Paradise." Normally, I would have said they were exaggerating, but sharing burgers with Ginger and Tiffany at the little kitchen table could almost make me forget about Luke. Almost. Their burgers had never tasted as divine as they did that night because Ginger was ready to eat something other than hospital food, Tiffany thought everything tasted great, and I was happy to be sitting at the table with both ladies happy and healthy.

"Beulah, what did you tell these folks?" Tiffany asked.

Her burger looked to be half beef and half pickles. Ginger looked out the breakfast room window in disgust.

"Ith tho good," Tiffany intoned through a full mouth. If I had known $20 would have softened up the staff at Burger Paradise, we would have been eating like queens a long time ago. Of course, back then I didn't know I stood to inherit a lot of money.

"Greasing palms at a greasy spoon?" muttered Ginger.

"Is there a problem with that?" I felt my own eyebrow arch. Apparently, I had learned a few things from Ginger.

She fixed me with a stare, and her bleary eyes were angry, not like herself. "We could have waited like everyone else, you know. There might have been other people who needed their food more than we needed ours. Did you ever think of that?"

My appetite abandoned me. "Ginger, I'm sorry. I was thinking about getting you and Tiffany home, I didn't mean to upset you. . . ."

But Ginger was shaking her head as though trying to get rid of mental cobwebs. Then she massaged her temples. "No, I'm sorry. I don't know where that came from."

Her eyes met mine again. Now they were lost, a little confused.

But I forgot all about how weird Ginger was acting because that's when the brick crashed through the living room window.

Chapter 17

"What in the blue blazes?" Ginger was saying for the third time by the time I got the loaded shotgun out of the coat closet.

I crept to the door. In my peripheral vision, I saw Tiffany help Ginger to her feet. I pulled back the curtain. Carl Davis stood on the lawn, his hair fading into the hazy gray of twilight. He staggered to one side and bent to pick up another of the bricks that circled our oak tree out front.

"Tiffany, call the police and tell them your daddy's throwing bricks at us." I didn't hear movement, and I turned to face her. She was frozen in one spot, but I couldn't tell if it was fear or anger.

"I told you to call the police. Now do it before he does something really stupid!" I took the shotgun and then fiddled with the dead bolt with the other hand.

"Beulah, what are you doing?" Ginger was supporting herself by leaning on the table just outside the kitchen.

"I'm going to try to talk some sense into Carl. If that doesn't work maybe I can scare him off." I opened the door a crack, and held the gun up in what I hoped was an I-mean-business pose.

Ginger took a step toward me, but tripped a little and clutched at her chest, a spot I now recognized as more spleenward than heartward. "You couldn't hit a bull in the ass with a bass fiddle. Hand me that shotgun."

"And you need to sit down," I said calmly. "I don't have to hit him with this bad boy; I only have to get close. Besides, he doesn't know if I'm a good shot or not."

Ginger muttered something about how he could tell by the way I was holding the gun like a sissy, but she sat down in the chair closest to the kitchen. I turned to Tiffany. "When I get out on this porch, lock the door behind me."

Tiffany was wringing her hands again. "But—"

"I'm not kidding. Lock the door and don't open it until the police get here."

Finally, she nodded that she would.

I opened the door with my foot and edged out on the porch with the gun up to my shoulder and my eye looking down what I hoped was the sight. "Carl, you need to go home and not come back."

Carl staggered right then left, but he dropped the brick and held up his hands. "Beulah, I want my girl back. You can't keep her. You just can't."

He took a step forward.

"Stop right where you are, or I will shoot."

He stopped. "I'm lonely without her. I need my little Tiff-Tiff."

A disgustingly awful realization formed in my mind as Carl began to weep.

"You should have thought about that before you beat her up. And if I shoot you now, I don't think anyone's going to have trouble thinking it's self-defense."

"Aw, Beulah, don't shoot." He fell to his knees.

"Daddy?"

"Tiff-Tiff." Carl's face lit up. "Look at you, so pretty like your momma."

Tiffany took another step forward, and I could've strangled her for coming out on the porch. "He's fine. Go back inside."

She started forward, and I had to balance the gun with one hand to hold her back with the other. "If not for you, go back in the house for the baby."

She took one step backward then another. The dead bolt locked behind me.

Carl fell face forward into the lawn and beat his fists on the ground. "I need my little girl!"

As I lowered the shotgun, he said, "You took her away from me."

Something behind his eyes flashed from sad to mad. He grabbed a brick and leaped to his feet like a cat. "I will bash your head in if you don't move away from that door."

I lifted the gun. "Carl, don't get any closer or I will shoot."

He took another step, and my finger itched to squeeze the trigger, but I couldn't make myself do it. Just as he reached the barrel of the gun, the wail of sirens drowned out the cicadas. Flashing blue lights lit up the night as a cruiser pulled up the drive.

"Freeze!"

To this day, I have never been so happy to see Len Rogers. I even promised myself not to sarcastically call him "One of Ellery's Finest" anymore.

"Carl Davis, I told you to freeze." Len's voice cracked.

Carl dropped the brick. "This ain't going to be the last of me."

"When I get done you're not going to be able to come within a mile of me or Tiffany." I shifted the shotgun back into a safer position. I really was going to have to learn to shoot one of these things.

Carl's eyes had taken on the wild expression of the night he had thrown me into the wall. He sneered. "Nothing's going to keep me from my girl. You just wait."

Len cuffed Carl and read him his rights before his deputy took Carl away. He sauntered over to me, a gangly young Barney Fife without the steadying influence of Andy Griffith. "I'm going to need to ask you a few questions."

* * *

An hour later, we had each given Len a statement of what happened. As I studied Tiffany, I noticed she didn't make eye contact with Len or with anyone else for that matter.

"Young man, I told you I didn't see a thing!" Ginger's lip quivered a little, and the hand she held up shook.

"Really, Len. Ginger didn't see much of anything, and she's had a really hard few days of it. Don't you think that's enough?"

Len looked at Ginger and back at me before flipping his notepad closed. "I suppose so. I'm guessing you want a restraining order?"

Since I'm not keen on a chain-link fence and a pit bull, yeah. "I think that'd be best, don't you?" I crossed my arms over my chest and raised my eyebrow in my best impersonation of Ginger.

"Yeah," Len said. His shoulders slumped. "I heard about what happened between you and ol' Carl earlier. You should have called the police and got one then."

My eyes cut to the landscape over the fireplace. "I didn't want to drag Bill into it."

Len nodded. He had been known to happen over to The Fountain on occasion when he wasn't on duty. And when it wasn't an election year for sheriff.

"Go on down to the courthouse tomorrow and they'll give you all the paperwork you need to file." Len stood and adjusted his hat with an antiquated "ma'am."

I showed him to the door and tried not to roll my eyes at his Old West sheriff impersonation because I had just turned over a new leaf as far as he was concerned. When I closed the door, I immediately turned to Tiffany.

"Tiffany Davis, I think there are some things you aren't telling us. I would love to help you, but I'm going to need to know the whole story here. Who's the father of your baby and why is your daddy so riled up?"

"It's nothing, Beulah. Maybe he's been mixing his meds with beer, pot, and who knows what." She was wringing those hands like a regular Lady Macbeth, and she refused to meet my eyes.

I walked over to Tiffany and took her chin in my palm so her eyes had to meet mine. "Tiffany, who is the father of your baby?"

Tears made her brown eyes go glassy, but she made no move to tell me.

"I think I already know," I said.

"Daddy." Her voice came out in a horrible whisper, and she immediately looked at the carpet.

Ginger gasped and clamped a hand over her mouth to hold her dentures in. "Child, why didn't you say so?"

Tears rolled hot and fast down Tiffany's cheeks. "I didn't tell anyone because it ain't right."

Nothing we could say to that.

Ginger and I looked at each other. Would the baby have two heads? Would this be another baby that didn't make it to term due to severe in-breeding?

"He isn't my real daddy, you know. Momma and me showed up on his doorstep when I was three."

I tried to keep my expression level when I looked back at Tiffany. I tried not to let her see my immense relief that at least her baby might not be born with three heads. I thought, maybe, if I didn't say anything at all, she would keep talking.

"But it still ain't right."

My eyes bugged out.

I need my Tiff-Tiff.

You're so pretty. Like your momma.

I wouldn't have felt bad about shooting him.

Dammit, was there a woman alive who hadn't been abused at some time in some way by some man? And Tiffany had been going to make it out of Ellery and off to college, and now this? It was one thing to accidentally get pregnant—quite another to have the only father you'd ever known rape you.

Just dammit.

I cleared my throat because I didn't want to ask the question I was about to ask. "Do you want to go back to him, Tiffany?"

"No!" Her brown eyes widened with sufficient horror for me to believe her. *Thank God.*

Ginger closed her eyes and nodded slowly, a touch of relief on her pale face.

"Tiffany, do you want to tell me what happened?"

She shook her head fiercely. "No."

"I think you need to call the police."

"What kind of good is that going to do? It's my word against his. Besides, *you* didn't press charges against him."

"That was different. I was trying to protect Bill."

She stared through me stubbornly. It was a case of her word against his. At this point, he'd even squeaked past statutory.

"Okay," I said with a sigh of defeat. "I think I speak for Ginger, too, when I say you are welcome to stay here as long as you want to. Anytime you want to talk, you know where to find me."

And we have more in common than you think.

Tiffany raced up the stairs with the same speed she'd once used to steal bases. I stood and walked to the kitchen. I needed a drink. I looked forlornly through each cabinet before I remembered that Ginger was a teetotaller. When I'd told her about my new job at The Fountain, she'd made sure I knew she wasn't happy about it but that she didn't feel like she could make decisions for me. She mainly told me I wasn't bringing any of that mess into her house.

I heard Tiffany tromping around upstairs. Down the hall and into the nursery she went, no doubt to cry.

"Beulah." Ginger's voice was so low I almost didn't hear it.

"Ma'am?"

"There's a bottle of Jack in the laundry room on the top shelf underneath the old dishpan. I'll take mine with that Dr Pepper you bought, thank you."

Ginger had been hiding booze from me all of these years? I didn't know if I could handle any more secrets.

I looked at Ginger, and her beady eyes met mine. "Before you came along, I was lonely. I used to take a few too many nips. I decided I was going to have to quit that behavior if I was going to help you turn out all right."

She shifted in her seat. "I put Gentleman Jack underneath

that old pan and didn't touch him again, but I think whiskey ages just fine. I think we could both use one about now."

I nodded and went out to the laundry room, a place Ginger knew I hated to linger. Sure enough, Jack was hiding underneath the pan on the top shelf.

I took out the bottle and went about the business of fixing our drinks, putting a little Dr Pepper in the Jack. It felt weird making a drink for Ginger, especially now knowing she had stopped touching the stuff for me. Sure enough, as I thought about it, I had *assumed* she was a teetotaller; she had simply said she didn't want me to bring any alcohol into her house. Red-hot shame burned my cheeks. She had been protecting herself more than me back then, and I had never once seen her do that, so I assumed—

"Beulah, what are you doing in there? Grinding and fermenting the corn yourself?"

"I'm coming, Ginger, but this doesn't feel right." I handed her one drink.

"Can you put the footrest up on the recliner?"

I bent to comply, holding my own drink steady in the other hand, but I stumbled on my first step to the couch.

"You okay? I thought the doctor said to avoid alcohol." Ginger was already reaching for my drink.

"Not so fast," I said. "He was referring to the first twenty-four hours, and he hadn't just found out a friend of his had been raped and impregnated by her stepfather. Nor had he discovered that his straightlaced piano teacher had a love affair with Tennessee whiskey." I tossed back half my drink before she could take it away.

Ginger was still studying her glass, her eyes glazed over as though Jack himself were enchanting her.

Whiskey burned down my throat. "Maybe you're the one who shouldn't be drinking."

Her eyes snapped up and narrowed. "Beulah Lou, I only have a few more months. I might as well go out in style, especially since there's no fear of my becoming a hopeless alcoholic. I simply don't have the time." And with that prim declaration, she took a dainty sip of her Jack.

She licked her lips and cocked her head to one side, then she tossed hers back and drank half of it. "Yep. Still good."

I could almost see her relax in the first throes of intoxication. "Gentleman Jack was my one friend and constant companion before you came to live with me."

I tried to picture the piano teacher going home and fixing herself a drink, but I couldn't. "Aren't we all full of secrets this evening," I murmured.

Ginger jerked her head ever so slightly toward the stairs. "And who knows what else there is to come?"

Chapter 18

The more I thought about it, the madder I got.

"Luke, I know it's not Wednesday, but I need to talk to you." I barged into his office without knocking, and he took off his reading glasses as he looked up at me.

I was almost used to the sight of him in his undershirt sweating like a Calvin Klein underwear model at a French Riviera photo shoot. Not that I'd contemplated what that might look like. At least not too often.

"And good morning to you, too, Beulah. How's your day been so far? Mine has been fantastic! Thanks for asking."

"I get it, I get it," I said with a sigh. "I'm very sorry for being rude, but I can't take it anymore. You have to explain all of this, this mess to me."

"I'm listening," he said. His tone was inviting, but his posture suggested he wasn't that far along on his sermon. Either that or he wanted me to leave him alone after our "indiscretions" in The Fountain then later in the hospital chapel. I shifted from one foot to the other, suddenly uncomfortable being in his presence. Ironically, only a few moments before, he had been the first person I wanted to tell about everything I had learned in the past twenty-four hours. Now I didn't know where to start.

"Tiffany's father, who's really her stepfather, has been molesting her. He's the father of the baby."

Luke winced and leaned back in his chair, his attention now riveted on me.

"He also came by last night, drunk as a skunk, to throw bricks at my house."

"Is everyone okay? Are you okay?" Luke's hands clenched the arms of his desk chair, ready to leap from his seat and right some wrongs. "Did you call the police?"

"Yes, I called the police this time. We're fine," I said, watching him relax back into his chair before adding, "But then I found out Ginger had a miscarriage when she was younger and an alcohol problem before I came along."

His smile turned into a frown by fractions of an inch. Finally, he said, "And what about you, Beulah? What's the rest of your story?"

"What does my story have to do with anything?"

He rubbed his temples and wiped a sheen of sweat from his brow. I sat back a little farther because I knew my deodorant couldn't keep up with the oppressive heat in the non-air-conditioned building. "That's why you're here, right?"

"No. I know why bad things have happened to me," I blurted. *The same reason you'll kiss me once or twice but not seriously consider dating me.*

"Oh?"

"Because I'm a bad person."

He stared at me forever, and it was so quiet in that church that the only thing I heard was the incessant whir of the box fan and the refrigerator across the building humming to life.

"You can't be serious." Gone were any traces of irritation or sarcasm. "You can't really believe—no, I can't ask you. I'm already too close to you to be able to counsel you."

"Counsel?" I wasn't there for counseling. Was I?

He was already fishing through his top desk drawer for a business card. "Here. This is the info for the Reverend Grace McDonald. She's a very, very good Christian counselor."

I knocked the card from his hand. "I'm not seeing a shrink—Christian or otherwise."

He opened his mouth to speak. "I want to help you, but the lines between us have already been blurred. I don't think it's—"

"There was a boy. And a backseat. Then I did something stupid, and I got pregnant and broke my daddy's heart. Which caused him to have a heart attack. And my mother disowned me. Then, after all that, the baby died. That's what happened."

He opened his mouth and then clamped his lips back together. I couldn't tell if he wanted to ask me more questions, if he wanted to try to push me off on the counselor again, or what. He was torn. I could see the anguish in his eyes.

"Have a seat," he said. "I suppose this is the part where I tell you that it rains on the just and the unjust. I guess I should remind you of free will or that what God does may not make sense to us because we mortals aren't privy to God's divine plan. I could tell you one of a million things, but the truth is . . . I don't know."

"You don't know?"

"I don't know why bad things happen to good people. I live each day on faith that there are forces at work beyond my ken. I do my best, I say my prayers, and I try to listen to what God tells me to do. But I can't tell you why Miss Ginger, of all people, had to get cancer. I can't tell you why Tiffany's father did such horrible things to her, or why your baby had to die. I can't even tell you why my mother had to be in the path of that drunk driver, or why I . . ." He paused, and I realized I wasn't the only one with secrets.

". . . I've done some of the things I've done," he finally finished.

Like kissing me? Or something worse? I swallowed hard. Why had I come here? Why did I *have* to talk to Luke?

He leaned back in his chair. "The longer I live and pray, I learn the truth of 'Ask and it shall be given.' The problem is we usually don't have a clue what to ask for."

How could I feel better and confused all at the same time? I got up to go.

"And, Beulah?" When I turned at the doorway he stood by his desk with his hands in his pockets. "You're not a bad person. You're one of the best people I know."

"You know it's really hard to believe you, based on what happened between us. If I'm such a good person, then you wouldn't have been ashamed to kiss me."

His eyes flashed. For a moment I thought he might take the bait. "I held the doors open for you. You're the one who walked away."

Pain slashed between my ribs, and again I walked away, this time before he could see the tears stinging my eyes.

I wasn't thinking straight when I left Luke's office. I couldn't have been thinking straight because I did something I hadn't done in a long time, if ever.

I went to the Dollar General and picked out the prettiest fake flowers I could find, then I drove over to Grace Baptist Church before I could stop myself. The cemetery where my daddy rested lay beside the church, but far enough away that I took the gravel road that ran along the outer edge of the graveyard.

I had already stepped out of the car when I realized a dusty red Ford Explorer was parked on the other end closest to the church. And that Explorer belonged to my mother.

I wanted to turn and drive away, but she had already seen me. She stood by my daddy's grave with her hands on her hips. She had put on another ten or fifteen pounds, all of which had landed in her belly. Even from a distance I could see her hair was now entirely gray. She was beginning to stoop, too. For the first time I thought of how life had been steamrolling over her all these years with one tragedy right after another.

My feet moved me forward just as they had driven me to the Dollar General then here without consulting my brain. I clutched the two bunches of fake daisies to my chest like a shield, wondering if God had a whacked sense of humor. Of all the days for me to decide to visit my father's grave, why did it have to be the day my mother was there?

"Beulah." My mother's eyes ran up and down me in appraisal.

"Mother." I nodded. My heart hammered against my chest, and bile crept up my throat.

"You're looking good," she said, but she was staring at the marker.

"Thanks. You are, too."

She waved away the thought, and I was surprised to discover I was only half lying. She did look good to me.

"I hear you're playing piano for County Line now." Her hands traveled back to her hips, her position of superiority when I was a child and she could tower over me. Now she had to look up a few inches, thanks to osteoporosis.

"Yes, ma'am." I winced, ready for the ten-minute diatribe about hypocrisy.

"Good. I'm glad to hear it. Maybe I'll see you around." With a curt nod, she turned to go.

"Maybe," I murmured under my breath as I watched her pick her way around the graves and back to her car. I had the inexplicable urge to check all over for bruises or for scratches, but there were, of course, no physical wounds. Emotional wounds maybe, but, for the first time, I saw her emotional scars, too. Maybe her heart had pounded at the thought of seeing me. Maybe she had wondered what sort of cruel joke would send her daughter to the cemetery on the one day she decided to visit her husband's grave.

She drove off, and I turned my attention to Daddy's grave. The front of the double marker contained his name and dates on one side and already had my mother's name and birth date on the other side. The little *d* was already underneath, as though waiting for her to keel over so someone could chisel in that last date for the stone to be whole.

Even the position of my father's grave at the outer fringe made me wonder if I'd pushed him to the outskirts of the cemetery just as I had pushed him into an early grave. As a former pastor, shouldn't he have been closer to the church where the lots were spaced out more? Or were pastors with pregnant teenage daughters pushed to the side?

"Daddy, I'm sorry," I said as I took the daisies and stuck them firmly in the ground behind the marker. "I'm so sorry I disappointed you like I did."

If I expected the heavens to open and a loud voice to boom, "Beulah, your father and I forgive you," then I was destined to be sorely disappointed. Nothing happened. A car in need of a new muffler passed behind me. Two bobwhites called to each other from one thicket to another. A lizard skittered over the marker to my right.

The wind caught the branches of the trees around the cemetery, whipping them in another direction as I walked up the hill to another grave along the fringe. I stopped cold. Flowers sat just behind the smaller marker with the engraved lamb. I hadn't been here in years because I couldn't bear it, so who had left flowers? It wasn't Ginger—she would have told me.

The crisp, white, fabric lilies danced in the breeze, perfectly pristine without a hint of dirt. I jerked around. There, several markers behind me, an identical bunch of lilies bobbed behind my father's tall headstone. I fought back tears. I tried to swallow the lump in my throat at the realization that my mother had been putting flowers on the grave of the grandbaby she'd never met.

Chapter 19

I have always hated handbells.

Some say they're the tongues of angels, but I see them as expensive and impossible to keep clean. Playing them requires such concentration and precision that they aren't *fun*. People ringing those bells are so focused on studying the music that they can't look up and smile.

Also, handbells reminded me of the music they play in funeral homes. Old Mr. Anderson had music piped through the entire funeral home, chime-like music played at half speed.

And then there was the fact that Lottie Miller loved her new handbells.

Luke gave the Happy Hour Choir the day off, but I still had to play the piano for introductions and things like the doxology. Supposedly, he wanted to let Miss Lottie show off her new toys, but I figured it had more to do with the fact that I didn't show up on Wednesday to give him any song numbers. Ginger insisted on going to church anyway, even though Tiffany and I tried to convince her otherwise. Tiffany sat with Ginger while I played piano, but Lottie took over the rest of the service. She guided her bell ringers through the prelude, through the anthem, and through the offertory. She also had a postlude picked out, as she was only too happy to inform me.

Luke cleared his throat a lot that Sunday, and he didn't give his best sermon. From my perch in the choir loft I counted over forty heads. An improvement or friends of Miss Lottie? Only time would tell. Despite the lackluster sermon, Miss Lottie was tickled pink after church.

"Why, today has been an inspiration, a revelation, wouldn't you say? I think we should have the handbells every Sunday, don't you?" Miss Lottie batted her eyelashes furiously, but her Ship of Flirtation had sailed many, many years ago. Probably met a fate similar to the *Titanic*, too.

Luke cleared his throat. "I think we can easily open up one Sunday a month for the handbells. That okay with you, Beulah?"

Before I could say fine by me, Lottie's face gathered color. "Oh. I should've known you'd be looking to her for approval."

"I don't need her approval," Luke said, his voice growing dangerously low. "I thought, however, it would be polite to ask."

"Ask *her?*" Lottie sneered. "I've been singing in this church for the past forty years or more and I've never once been asked my opinion. I should have known she would end up cozying up to you."

"Enough!" His voice reverberated off the walls, and we were all taken aback. "Miss Lottie, I have tried to be nice, but I've had enough. You *will* stop insinuating there is some kind of inappropriate relationship going on between me and Beulah. Futhermore—"

Miss Lottie's eyes bugged out of her head as she pointed a finger in his face. "We could have you defrocked. I will call Tom Dartmouth the minute I get home!"

"You go ahead," Luke challenged. "See how far it gets you."

I had no clue what *defrocked* meant, but I didn't like the sound of it. "Don't cast aspersions on this man. I did kiss him, but he was smart enough to turn me down."

Miss Lottie's bosom heaved up and down, her face now a dangerous shade of purple. Fortunately, almost everyone had left, but there were a few stragglers just in front of the door who had turned to watch the fireworks. She pointed one fat finger at me, the undersides of her wrinkled arms wiggling, her double chin jiggling. "You, you. Yes, you brought all that riffraff in here. You threw yourself at this fine young man while playing piano in your den of iniquity. You have no business telling me when I should or shouldn't play my handbells. You shouldn't even be here until you get your head screwed on straight."

"And that's enough from you." Ginger stood at Lottie's elbow with her hand on the end of one pew and Tiffany's hand under her other arm. Her bottom lip trembled with rage, and Tiffany's face was an ashen white. At that moment my heart squeezed with pain. I could handle being called riffraff, but Tiffany deserved better.

"Look at this one here," Lottie said, unable to stop now that she was on a roll. "You been teaching her how to act, Beulah?"

"Miss Lottie, it isn't your place to pass judgment. If you can't be civil, I'm going to have to ask you to leave," Luke said. He gently took the older lady by the arm and escorted her down the aisle.

"I have to put up the handbells," she said. "Don't let any of them touch them. They'll get their nasty, oily fingerprints all over them—"

"They'll be taken care of," Luke said through his teeth. From the tone of his voice, I could only hope he meant melting them down and selling them for scrap metal.

"If I leave, I am *not* coming back!"

How I wished that were true.

The last of the crowd reluctantly dispersed at the sight of the minister and the church's self-proclaimed music star coming down the aisle. I thought I caught a glimpse of Goat Cheese Ledbetter out there and wondered what he could possibly be up to. He studied Luke and Miss Lottie, and I wondered if he could hear what they were saying. Luke's voice came to me as a measured murmur, but Miss Lottie squawked like an enraged parrot.

I don't know what made me do it, but I planted a thumb on the biggest of the handbells, satisfied by the perfect whorls it left behind. Then I tried my index finger on another bell. I planted pinkie fingerprints all in a row on the smallest one.

"Beulah Louise, you stop touching those handbells!" Ginger yelled so loudly I was afraid she might burst a blood vessel.

"But she is so mean! And she was mean to Tiffany! And Luke, too!" I touched another bell three or four times, my eyes never leaving Ginger's. She reached across and slapped my hand. I was acting like a toddler, so it was a fitting punishment.

"The time for an eye for an eye has passed," Ginger said.

"Oh, no. We're not doing the turn-the-other-cheek routine," I said, shaking my head. "She made Tiffany cry. She doesn't have any idea what it's like to be Tiffany or to be me. And she threatened to defrock Luke, whatever that means!"

Ginger gave me an arched non-eyebrow that suggested she had heard about our not-so-clandestine chapel kiss. "And just what *is* going on between you and Luke?"

I scanned the sanctuary to see that everyone but Tiffany had finally filed out. Probably to get a better view of the fireworks outside. "He kissed me in the hospital chapel." *And the emergency room. And in The Fountain, but who was counting?*

Ginger's eyes lit up. "Good!"

Tiffany quit sniffling and looked up. That was the end of another dream for her.

"No, Ginger, not good," I said. "He apologized for kissing me, so his charity only extends so far."

"Now, Beulah—" Ginger's mouth had pulled back to one side, the expression that said I was being melodramatic. Luke chose that moment to interrupt her.

"Beulah, Tiffany, I'm very sorry I didn't get Miss Lottie out of here before she said those hurtful things. She and I have had a discussion, and she has something she would like to say to you."

Tiffany and I looked back at Miss Lottie, who, bless her heart, had tears in her eyes. Her "I'm sorry" came out breathy because she was about to lose her voice to sobs.

My eyes went to Tiffany, but she shook her head back and

forth, so I apologized for the both of us. Even if she didn't deserve it. "I'm sorry, too, Miss Lottie."

Miss Lottie waddled off. Luke stalked up the aisle. One glance at the handbells, and he looked back at me with fire in his eyes. "Couldn't leave well enough alone, could you?"

"Not my strong suit," I said.

He exhaled sharply, pinching the bridge of his nose. "I'm going to have to ask you to clean those after lunch."

"Why don't y'all go ahead to lunch, and I'll clean them now," I said as I sat back in the first pew and crossed my legs.

"If that's the way you'd like it," he said. "Ladies?"

Tiffany helped Ginger start down the aisle. My stomach growled, and I clamped a hand over the traitorous organ. Luke paused where he was opening the cases for the handbells. He had heard my stomach. "You are the most stubborn woman I have ever met."

"Then you haven't met a whole lot of women."

He handed me a pair of gloves and showed me how to wipe away my fingerprints with a special polishing cloth. "When you finish, why don't you come join us at Las Palmas."

"I'll think about it," I said as I grimaced at the task before me.

Suddenly, he leaned over and whispered, "And for the record, it was you who turned me down."

Chapter 20

Sam Ford was an excellent addition to the Happy Hour Choir and just what I needed to get my mind off the debacle that was the Sunday before. He'd seemed so shy, but now that he knew everyone he would kid around by singing the bass line in a ridiculous falsetto or hiding all of the hymnals under the bar before practice. On that particular Wednesday he surprised even me by playing an impassioned and impromptu kazoo solo in the middle of a particularly sedate piece. Ginger would've loved that, but at the last minute she'd declared she didn't feel like coming. I'd hated to leave her at home alone, but she assured me she needed some peace and quiet most of all.

"That's a wrap, folks," I said as I wiped a tear of laughter from my eyes.

The choir scattered, and I noticed almost all of them had brought Bibles for the bar Bible study to follow. I frowned. Apparently, Luke wanted to turn my singers into a bunch of Vacation Bible School students. Next Bill was going to start serving Kool-Aid and Nutter Butters.

I stacked the hymnals on top of the piano. No need to return them since Luke had caught me with them weeks ago. I put the cover over the keys and let my fingers linger. Tonight was the night. Tonight the intern, Tom Dartmouth's nephew, was coming to hear my Happy Hour Choir.

I took a deep breath and wondered if Luke felt the same anxiety since the superintendent was coming for his Bible study, too. We were both going to perform tonight.

Newcomers broke my reverie. Goat Cheese, Hank Satterfield, and the hairdresser I recognized as Delilah walked up to the bar. Goat Cheese was acting like he owned the place, but Delilah looked around with those sharp eyes of hers as if not sure why she'd agreed to come. Hank looked like a man who'd lost a bad bet and was having to pay up. Well, good for Luke, then. A straggler or two had come and gone from Bible study, but three extra people would help. He sure wouldn't need me. I almost made it to the door before Luke caught my arm. "Could you please stay tonight?"

I closed my eyes at the thought and took a deep breath before I turned around to face him. If I looked into his eyes, I was a goner, and I was beginning to think he knew that. Counted on it, even.

"Luke, you know how I feel about all this. I really—"

"For once, I'm not asking you to do this for you. I'm asking you to do it for me."

His eyes didn't waver. "Besides, where are you going to go for the hour, hour and a half? You need to be here ready to play when Tom and his nephew arrive."

I nodded. Any hope of not staying went out the window when I turned around and saw Tiffany's eyes pleading. And darn Luke for always being so logical, too! "I don't have a Bible."

Luke reached behind him to hand me a book with a soft gray cover. "Now you do."

I took his gift, and he walked back to the risers where he'd spread out his notes on the floor. The Bible felt heavy in my hands, and I didn't like how the soft cover flopped to one side, shifting the balance and almost causing me to drop the book. I steadied it with both hands and took a seat behind Sam and Tiffany.

Tom Dartmouth entered in khakis and Rockports, and I wondered if there was a ministerial dress code that required pressed chinos. His nephew walked through the door seemingly with every hair on his head that Tom Dartmouth had shed and then some. A study in contrasts, the superintendent was just as I remembered him: short and stooped with dark, bright eyes. His nephew, the talent scout, was tall and blond with tanned skin and super-white teeth. And, of course, blue eyes. I prepared to sigh, but, for some reason, I wasn't at all susceptible to his eyes. Maybe he was too pretty for me. Or maybe too young with his frat-boy vibe.

The talent scout surveyed the room, his eyes immediately finding the youngest people in the room and then narrowing it down farther to young women. He dismissed Tiffany at the sight of her baby bump and sat next to me. I shifted in my seat.

"Name's Derek. What's yours?" He gave me an excellent view of those pearly whites and extended a hand, a very smooth hand.

"I'm Beulah," I said.

His eyes widened. "So, you're Beulah. I've heard so much about you. I have to confess, from the sound of your name, I was expecting someone a little older."

I gently took my hand from his. "I get that a lot."

"Well, I—"

"Okay, folks, we're still discussing David, so let's take a look at Second Samuel. Sam, that's all you, right?"

Sam's deep voice carried no humor as he read of how David dressed himself in sackcloth and fasted and lay on the ground as he prayed for the life of his first son with Bathsheba.

I fidgeted in my seat.

In the story, the child died, and David got up, took a bath, went to the temple, then came back and ate a hearty meal. His reasoning was that he couldn't change anything at that point, so why mourn? David and I were never going to see eye to eye on that one.

I studied the cracks on the opposing cinder-block wall, and the Happy Hour Choir/Sinners to Saints Bible Study began a lively discussion of whether or not it was fair for the innocent baby to die because David had sinned. Pete Gates was silent for most of this, then he spoke up: "But maybe the baby's death was *for* the sake of the child."

Tiffany splayed a protective hand over her belly. "What are you talking about?"

"Well," Pete continued, "that baby would always remind Bathsheba of why her first husband had been killed. And don't you think his brothers and sisters would be after him all the time? What about his daddy's family? They might try to hurt him to get revenge against David."

"I really don't think those are good reasons for an innocent baby to die." Tiffany's nostrils flared. Her baby would be a living reminder of her stepfather's treachery and of her dashed dreams of going to college, but she fiercely protected the child, wanting better for her baby. She was a helluva lot stronger than I'd first thought.

"Maybe not," Pete said. "But it ain't easy being the kid who broke up your parents' marriage, and it ain't easy being living proof of how your momma cheated on your daddy. Going up to heaven sure sounds better than being made fun of or beaten up on the playground after school. Or having your brothers and sisters hating you because you're the reason Daddy left."

Up until this point I'd taken the Gates brothers for who they were. I'd never really thought about how Pete's caramel complexion didn't match with Greg's pale freckles or what that might mean in a family full of kids vying for attention. No wonder he and Greg ended up in a fight when one or both had been drinking too much. The real miracle was that they ever got along at all.

Come to think of it, the Gates brothers hadn't had a good knock-down drag-out in at least a month. Just as Mac was cleaning up his act, they'd made great strides in cleaning up theirs.

I might have been having a revelation, but my new friend Derek was shifting uncomfortably in his seat. Apparently, he hadn't been prepared for such a gritty prelude to my audition. I looked over at the superintendent, though, and he nodded appreciatively. I breathed an inward sigh of relief for Luke; if he was bringing out these emotions every Wednesday night, then someone needed to give him some kudos for what he was doing.

"Okay, so let's read the next few verses. Beulah, why don't you take verse twenty-four."

If looks could kill, Luke would have been a goner. I stared down at my Bible, and it almost slid off my crossed legs because my hands were shaking. Still, I read, "Then David consoled his wife Bathsheba, and went to her, and lay with her; and she bore him a son, and he named him Solomon."

Unless all of my years of Vacation Bible School were failing me now, Bathsheba lost a baby then gave birth to the wisest king of Israel.

Nope. Do not get sucked in again.

Oh, I'd already been had once, thanks to Ginger and New Orleans jazz. I was not going to fall for this mess again. Even Luke wouldn't meet my gaze as though he hadn't necessarily meant for me to read that particular verse but might've lost track of where we were in the lesson.

In spite of my best efforts, though, hope bubbled to the top. Just because I'd lost one baby didn't mean I could never have another child.

Everyone looked at me. I had snorted at my own memories.

So much for stellar first impressions.

Luke glared at me for disrupting his closing prayer. I shrugged my shoulders. No way would I admit to him what I'd been thinking.

"How about I listen to your Happy Hour Choir after a little break?" Derek was all teeth and confidence.

"Go grab a beer and we'll get started in a few."

"Really?"

He had to be fresh out of college. "Yep. See Bill over there. We'll get started in a minute."

When I moved toward the piano, Luke stepped in front of me. He whispered, "I'm sorry about giving you that passage. I wanted you to read, but I should've had you read a different one."

"Or not at all."

"No, I wanted you to read." He opened his mouth to add something. If he told me a higher power wanted me to read that verse I would punch him.

"Is that all you wanted?"

"That and to tell you good luck. Not that you need it."

Who knew what I needed anymore? I sure as hell didn't.

Derek came to stand beside the piano. I caught a whiff of his cologne, something spicy and exotic. "I hope you don't mind if I stand here."

"Not a lot makes me nervous," I said with a grin.

"Pretty intense little Bible study we had there," he said as he leaned against the old upright.

"I've only been twice," I said, immediately regretting the words. What if Derek told the superintendent on the way home?

"I'm sure you had your reasons." He showed off even more of his supernaturally white teeth.

"Prior commitment," I said as I played a little "As Time Goes By" to warm up. "What would you like to hear?"

"Uncle Tom has been raving about the group's 'rough-around-the-edges sound.' You pick whatever you'd like."

I shuffled through several upbeat classic gospel songs while I was waiting for everyone to settle in. Then I called Tiffany up for a duet. She was pink with embarrassment at first, but we harmonized so well on the chorus of "Ivory Palaces," I decided we would sing the song together for the offertory the next Sunday.

"So this is the infamous Happy Hour Choir?" Derek asked as he swept his hand in the direction of our audience. I looked out and saw everyone had cleared out except Tiffany, Sam, Pete and Greg Gates, and Mac. "It's everyone but Ginger, but I sing alto, too, if you'd like to hear us."

"Please do, then we'll see what else you can play."

We went through a couple of classics, a spiritual, and Mac's request, "In the Sweet By and By." The last note hung in the bar the way smoke usually congregated at the ceiling. Derek Martin, hotshot intern, was speechless for a few seconds. "That's amazing! And you put together this choir from some random folks in a bar?"

"Yeah," I said softly, even though they didn't seem so random to me. "I guess I did."

He continued raving about the premise of the Happy Hour Choir, something about niche markets for gospel music. I wasn't listening. I was looking at my choir and wishing I'd brought Ginger that night.

"Beulah?"

"What? Oh, sorry." I looked up at him, blinking a few times to bring myself back to reality.

"Luke says you play the Beatles and Scott Joplin."

"She does a mean Patsy Cline, too," Bill shouted from the back.

Derek made me play all of them, segueing from classical music to "When I'm Sixty-Four" and back to "The Tennessee Waltz." I played for almost three hours and the Sinners to Saints slowly slipped away one by one. Even Tom Dartmouth went over to the parsonage to talk business with Luke.

Bill caught me between songs and yawned. "Beulah, lock up on your way out, will ya?"

I nodded, and Derek sat down on the bench beside me. "You know, Beulah, you're really good."

My throat went dry. This could be the moment that changed my life.

"I learned from the best," I said with a grin. "So what do you think? Is there a place for the Happy Hour Choir in Nashville?"

"I don't think so." His smile never faded, so it took me a minute to realize he wasn't kidding.

"What do you mean?"

"Oh, you're all fantastic—especially for a group of amateurs, but, come on, a group of beer-swilling gospel singers? Who's going to sign that group?"

"What about that niche market stuff?"

"I'm not saying the audience isn't there. I'm saying you might need to rent a studio and make your own recordings to find them."

My heart pumped double time, causing my hopes to flood out even faster. "Then why'd you even bother coming out here?"

"Between Uncle Tom and my mom, it was easier to take the drive than to argue. Besides"—he shrugged—"you never really know, do you?"

"You got some hopes up." *Mainly mine.*

"The trip doesn't have to be a total loss."

Was he giving me the smolder? He was not seriously giving me the smolder.

"That so?"

"Yeah. Now, you? You've got what it takes. With someone to guide you, you could make some good money playing as a studio musician. Especially if you branched out into country, too."

There'd been a time I would've jumped at the chance to go to Nashville.

He sat on the piano bench, his nose hovering only inches from mine. Even as young as he was, he knew it would be completely unprofessional to make a pass at me. I, on the other hand, could always kiss him.

There'd been a time I would've kissed a man for the chance to leave town.

That time had passed. I looked straight ahead. "That's certainly something to think about."

He sighed. "Do you have a business card on you?"

A business card? What would it say? Beulah Land, Prodigal Daughter and Honky-Tonk Piano Player? "Um, no."

He reached for his wallet and took out two business cards. "Keep this one. Put your info on the other. I'll give you a call if anything pans out."

"I'd appreciate that," I said, even though I didn't expect anything to "pan out."

He slipped out the door, and I helped myself to a beer from the cooler before flopping down in one of the café chairs to study his business card and think.

Ginger said I needed to go to college and get a real job, but that didn't appeal to me for many reasons. This Derek dude said I could work as a studio musician, but did I want to do that right now with Ginger feeling as poorly as she did? If I told her, she would insist I needed to strike while the iron was hot—as if I would even think about leaving her at a time like this.

Then there was the question of Luke, Mr. You're-the-One-Who-Turned-Me-Down. Did I dare walk across that parking lot and try one more time?

I almost made it to the door, but I chickened out and went for another beer instead.

Chapter 21

Two beers led to four. I heard lots of voices in my head. On the one hand, I heard Luke saying, "For the record, it was you who turned me down." Then I heard the cocky intern's "Now, you? You've got what it takes." I laughed. I cried. It was *not* better than *Cats*.

Sometime around two in the morning I got the bright idea to call Tiffany.

"Hey, Tiffany. 'S me, Beulah."

"It's almost three. Are you drunk?"

"No." The Fountain dipped and spun around me like a Tilt-A-Whirl. "Maybe."

She yawned. "Do you need me to come get you?"

"No. If Ginger asks, tell her I'm going to be later than usual."

Tiffany paused. "Are you sure you don't want me to come get you?"

I shook my head then remembered that phones didn't yet allow head shaking to come through. "I won't drive till I'm okay."

"That should be about noon tomorrow," Tiffany muttered.

"Then I'll sleep on the risers. Sorry I woke you up."

"God, Beulah. Be careful."

"I always am." *Not.*

After she hung up I stood there until the phone made that annoying you-left-me-off-the-hook sound. Then I looked down at the phones in each hand, unable to remember if I'd been talking to her on my cell phone or on the old rotary phone that hung on the wall. Finally, my brain cells remembered only the landline made that obnoxious sound, so I hung up the wall phone and put the cell in my pocket.

The phone confusion should've been the first clue I wasn't doing my best thinking.

I had taken five steps across the parking lot when I remembered Bill had asked me to lock up. I pivoted and staggered back, tripping over a large piece of gravel.

That should have been the second clue.

Once I'd locked up, I took the stairs of the parsonage at a slow clip, shuffled the two steps to the door, then knocked loudly, wincing at how the sound reverberated oddly. The world spun around me. We had moved from the Tilt-A-Whirl to the Gravitron, only I had my forehead against the clapboard to the side of the door instead of having my back plastered against a wall.

Luke opened the door with a scowl on his face. "Beulah, what are you up to at this time of night?"

I answered him with a kiss, a sloppy, drunken kiss. Then the scent of his skin and the scratch of his not-quite beard stirred something I had forgotten or had maybe never known, and I kissed him for real.

My memory's a little shaky, but I still say he kissed me back. When I trailed my hands down his bare chest, though, he grabbed my wrists.

"What are you doing?" he panted.

"What does it look like I'm doing?" I tried to pull my hands free, but he wouldn't let me.

"Why?"

"I'm not turning you down." This time when I kissed him I had enough wits about me to make it tender, framing his face with my hands before letting them wander. He refused to give in. My hands wrapped around him and traveled down his back to his ass. Boxer briefs, not tighty whities. I giggled, but he growled.

He pulled me inside and slammed the door hard enough that somewhere a picture fell off the wall. Pushing me against the door, he gave in completely, kissing his way from my neck back up to my lips and across my other jawline.

"Be my David," I whispered.

"What?"

"I'll be Bathsheba, and you . . . you can be my David."

His eyes shone intensely. I sucked in a deep breath while he weighed his options. He muttered something under his breath, but I drew him close again. Finally, his lips found mine and his hand started a steady climb from my waist. My heart did a somersault at being wanted, at being chosen after all.

His hands roamed all over my body, while mine remained fascinated by his arms, his chest, and his powerful shoulders. He backed us in the direction of the living room, and I let him pull me. When we reached the couch, he pulled me down on top of him. What few brain cells I had snapped and popped until I thought my brain might explode from the sheer bliss of my body resting on top of his.

And then he ripped his lips from mine with a ragged sigh.

Before I could fully process what was going on, he stood at the end of the couch looking down. "If Eve was anything like you, no wonder Adam was a goner."

"Then why don't you come down here and take a bite?"

He leaned forward, but stepped back with a "Dammit, no!" then muttered what I thought was "Not again. Not this time." He ran a hand through his hair, and this time a few strands didn't make it back into place. I would've cheered if my head hadn't been spinning and I hadn't been so afraid I'd done something wrong yet again.

"Beulah, I can't be your David."

"Luke, that was me flirting. I want you for you." My response startled me. Apparently, I'd had more than enough beer to tell the whole truth and nothing but the truth.

His eyes looked gray in the dim kitchen light shining over his shoulder. "But for how long?"

Forever.

My quick answer scared me. What was I saying? Hell, I was too drunk to know what I was saying. *Or drunk enough to tell the truth.*

If I gave him the answer he was looking for, I would probably get exactly what I wanted—even more, if his response to my kiss was any indication. If I gave him the wrong answer, though, I knew he was going to send me packing. My brain swam.

To my credit, I stuck with the truth. "I don't know."

His strong shoulders slumped. "The intern said no, didn't he?"

"Yes, but—"

He released my wrists. "And you've had too much to drink, haven't you?"

"Probably, but—"

"Then your heart's not in the right place. I'll get my keys and drive you home." He walked down a short hallway and returned shrugging into a T-shirt.

He pulled me to my feet, and I stood there in his living room, mouth agape. The world had slowed down considerably, almost enough for the embarrassment to creep in.

We didn't say anything on the way home. He never once chastised me nor did he tease me. He killed the engine in the driveway, and he turned to look at me. "Beulah, I'm not the saint you seem to think I am. I don't know what's between us, but I think it'd be best to forget tonight happened for now."

Fat chance. But I swallowed hard and nodded affirmatively.

"And don't drink so much. Not when you're sad—especially not when you're sad."

I nodded again. He had reverted to preacher mode, a stilted, authoritarian tone far different from his whisper of "And for the record, it was you who turned me down."

I suppose we're even now.

"I care a lot about you." He reached for my cheek, but his hand landed on my shoulder instead. "We all do."

My eyes met his but quickly looked away. He hadn't been willing to give me the help I needed—at least not the help I thought I needed.

"Thanks for the ride." I scooted out of his car before he could tell me anything else that might make me want to cry.

Ever the gentleman, he waited until I made it inside before starting his car and backing down the drive. I closed the door behind me and leaned against its solidity. I had kissed a minister. I had had every intention of fornicating with a minister. No fewer than twelve of my Baptist ancestors were rotating in their graves like pigs on spits while demons readied my room in hell.

I tiptoed across the foyer and made it as far as the bottom step before I heard Ginger's voice.

"Beulah Lou," she said softly. "I think you need to come in here and have a seat with me."

My head whipped around, but it took me a few seconds to adjust enough to the dark to see her. She sat in the recliner, with her hands splayed at the end of the armrests and her fingers digging into their cushioning.

"Are you okay? What are you still doing up?"

"I'm fine." She grimaced, and the pain etched in lines above her would-be eyebrows proved her a liar.

"You are not okay. Let me take you to the doctor."

"Nothing they can do. It's this damn itching. I itch all over, but there's not a scratch in this world that will fix it."

I had some idea of what that was like. Well, but there was a cure for me. I just couldn't seem to get my hands on him. "Can't we do something?"

"Oh, baby, it'll pass. It always does." Ginger shifted in her seat. "Celebrating too much?"

"No. The intern didn't think our little group was marketable. He said we might be able to rent a studio and do it ourselves, maybe sell copies out of the trunk of our car."

"Well, then. Do that!"

"Now, Ginger. Can you imagine me loading everyone up for a trip to Nashville?"

"Then do a recording at the church or the bar or something. There's no rule that says it has to be fancy."

"That's not the worst idea. I'll think about it." I didn't tell her about his studio musician suggestion. I wasn't sure how I felt about that yet.

She grunted as she shifted again. "His loss. Who drove you home?"

I opened my mouth to ask her how she knew that, but Ginger never missed a beat. She had heard the car pull up, kill its engine, then start up again. "Luke."

She nodded, her eyes closed. She had known the answer before she asked the question.

"That was nice of him," she said. Her grip eased on the arms of the chair, and the creases in her brow lessened as her eyes remained closed.

"Yes," I said softly. "Yes, it was."

"Turned you down, huh?"

I plopped on the end of the couch closest to her chair. "He turned me down flat. I don't know what I was thinking."

"You weren't, but that's not entirely a bad thing. Luke's too much of a gentleman to sleep with you while you're drunk," Ginger's words were slurred. She turned to shine her bleary eyes on me for a moment before looking back at the ceiling and letting her eyelids droop.

"He's too much of a gentleman in general." *Your heart's not in the right place.*

"Take off the 'gentle,' and you'll have what Luke is, and there are damn precious few of those running around." A few of the lines in her brow disappeared. Whatever had caused the itch was receding.

"Ginger, do you think Luke could ever fall in love with a girl like me?"

But she didn't answer because she'd fallen asleep.

That night I sat on the couch to be near her. I had no desire to sleep, but I needed to be close to her, to hear the sound of her breathing. She would inhale, hold her breath, then let it go with a snore. Each time she held her breath I held mine.

I wanted to tell her more. I wanted to tell her about knocking on a preacher's door for a booty call. I wanted to ask her what she thought about Luke's conversation in the driveway. Did she think we could forget what happened? Did she think we should?

In the end, I couldn't bear to wake her up once she was peaceful. And I couldn't bear the thought of disappointing her, of showing her how I hadn't learned from my mistakes. She would've understood me, though. She would have told me I staggered across that parking lot due to a primal need I'd never had the chance to figure out on my own. She would have pointed out that Bathsheba's tale of losing one baby but gaining another had given me hope.

But Ginger wasn't awake to counsel me through my feelings.

Nor was she at the parsonage to assure Luke my intentions had been purer than even I had intended.

Tears coursed silently down my cheeks because life without Ginger was going to be a life without someone to champion me, without someone to explain to me why I did the things I did.

I reached over to squeeze her hand, but I couldn't bring myself to possibly interrupt her hard-won sleep. Instead I whispered, "Ginger Belmont, I love you more than you'll ever know."

Chapter 22

The next Sunday I considered faking my own death to get out of playing piano at the church. How in heaven's name was I supposed to pretend that things were okay between me and Luke?

I'd chickened out of telling the Happy Hour Choir what happened with Derek the intern. I'd told Tiffany, though, certain that she would tell anyone else who would listen because she was so indignant on my behalf.

"Beulah Lou, time to go!"

I plodded down the stairs in the lowest-cut sundress I had, halfheartedly hoping Ginger would send me back upstairs and not let me come back down.

She didn't say a word.

At the church, we had to park on the outer edges of the parking lot. "Hey, Tiff, what's this all about?"

She offered me a hand, and I helped her slide out of the backseat. She tried to hide her blush by walking around the car to help Ginger. "I don't know."

"Well, I know you're a horrible liar."

Once we had Ginger in the choir loft, Tiffany turned me toward the congregation and faced the wall while she spoke softly in my ear. "The flower shop is next door to the beauty parlor, and I heard that Goat Cheese has been talking about the choir, telling everyone they need to come see us. Then Miss Lottie has been telling anyone who will listen that you and Luke are an item."

My stomach bottomed out around my toes.

"I don't think her rumors have done what she intended," Tiffany continued before I could stop her. "Kari, for one, said she thought the two of you would make a handsome couple."

My heart knocked around in my chest. *Maybe we would've made a handsome couple if I weren't so screwed up.* As I stood there willing my body to continue with the basic function of breathing, I realized there were more people than I could count.

"Tiffany," I whispered. "All those people are here to see the choir?"

She bit her lip as she nodded yes.

I took a deep breath and forced myself to smile. "Then let's give them something to remember."

She took her seat, and I laid the jazz thickly to "The Battle Hymn of the Republic." Half the congregation sang softly along with the glory, glory, hallelujahs. If Luke minded I had just called an audible with the prelude, he didn't say anything.

Sam provided the perfect touch to "The Church in the Wildwood" and, blessedly, kept the kazoo out of it. Tiffany and I sang an even better version of "Ivory Palaces" for the offertory than we had in practice. Then Luke started to read from the same passage about David and Bathsheba that the Bible study had covered that week.

It was all I could do to school my face into indifference. I couldn't hear his words for analyzing that night six ways from Sunday. Had he been repulsed? Had I given the wrong answer? What was the right answer? If my heart hadn't been in the right place, then where could I put it? My mind went around and around in circles, and I tried not to blush too fiercely when Jason Utley caught me daydreaming instead of starting the invitation.

Stupid, stupid, stupid.

As the church sang about being weary and heavyhearted, I led them through their paces. I refused to turn around to watch Luke shaking hands at the door, but I could hear a crowd—it had to be more than fifty people. And was that the giggle of a child? There were children at County Line?

Well, Luke had what he wanted, what he needed.

I slipped out the back door trying not to be so sad that what he needed hadn't included me. I didn't need him, either. I'd made it just fine before he came along, and I would have my hands full with Tiffany and Ginger.

The next month passed in a flurry of taking care of Ginger and playing at The Fountain. Luke and I managed to be cordial with each other, but he didn't request that I stay for Bible study anymore. Even though staying after choir was the last thing I wanted, I irrationally wanted him to ask me to stay. He'd finally realized he was better off without me, the very thing I'd tried to tell him at the beginning.

Most days Ginger felt okay, but there were bad days, too. I had the feeling the only thing really keeping her with us was her desire to see Tiffany through her pregnancy. Well, that and her innate stubbornness. If the doctor said she only had six months to live, then she was going to live seven just to spite him.

Then somewhere at the beginning of August she had to go back to the hospital because the blood thinner that had cleared the clot from her spleen then caused her spleen to rupture. She joked with the doctor, saying, "Can't you folks fix one problem without causing another?" She was less forgiving of the hospital food, though, and threatened to launch a campaign for caffeinated coffee on all morning trays.

She came home mid-August and had a few days where she went on a ridiculous cleaning spree. Tiffany and I had to practically tie her down to keep her from hurting herself. We couldn't stop her as she worked in the little planter boxes on the front porch or started freezing meals for when she was gone. One day, I even caught her putting labels on the backs of pictures, plates, and other household items. I didn't let her see me, but when I came back later to find she was dividing up her possessions and marking to whom they should go, I ran upstairs and cried yet again. I sobbed into my pillow so no one could hear me because I didn't want to be the one that sent that first domino of sorrow toppling over.

At the end of August, she started to walk with a limp. The doctors determined she had developed a tumor on her spine, a tumor that was pinching the nerves of her right leg. I begged her to take treatment to ease the pain. She refused. Her only request? She wanted to go to choir practice then stick around for the Sinners to Saints Bible study.

I couldn't tell her no for a couple of reasons. First, she was getting so thin I was beginning to fear I might lose her at any moment. I wanted to keep her in my sight at all times even if it meant facing Luke at Bible study. Also, I couldn't tell her no without admitting that Luke and I weren't on the best of terms. Despite my best efforts, I only held her off until early September just after Labor Day.

She used her cane to enter The Fountain. "Never thought I'd see the day I came in here," she said.

"That makes two of us," I muttered under my breath.

"Quit holding my arm. That's what I've got this cane for."

I let go, and she trudged across the room, her leg obviously hurting her. She sat down behind Tiffany. Sam sat down on her left. "Hey, there, tall boy!"

"Hey, Miss Ginger," he said. "Can I get you a beer?"

"Yes, you can. I don't believe I've ever had a beer, and I think I'll try one before, well, you know. Not getting any younger here. What do you suggest?"

"Uh, Heineken?"

"Would you mind getting me one of those?" Ginger batted her eyelashes, and Sam jumped to his feet as if Scarlett O'Hara herself had sent him on a sacred mission. He procured a Heineken longneck and popped off the cap before handing it to her.

Ginger looked at the bottle, smelled its contents, then held it out with her face scrunched up in disgust. She yelled up to me at the piano. "Do you really drink this stuff?"

"Hey, you gotta do what you gotta do. Go ahead and taste it. If you don't like it, I'll drink it."

"I wish I could have a beer." Tiffany sighed mournfully.

"Oh, you're underage anyway, so quit your bitching," Ginger said to a collective gasp.

Sam spewed his beer.

"It's only a few more months." She studied the label of her beer.

"But then there'll be breast-feeding and—" Tiffany began.

Sam almost spewed again, but Ginger didn't miss a beat as she switched from battle-ax to grandmother and gave Tiffany a gentle pat on the knee. "But it will all be worth it. That much I promise you."

Tiffany struggled to turn sideways and placed a hand on Ginger's arm. She teared up for no reason, as she'd been doing often the past few weeks. "Miss Ginger, then you drink and enjoy that beer for me."

"Cheers!" Ginger turned the bottle up and chugged more than she should have. As a result she belched loudly and, instead of apologizing, said, "That tastes like shit."

The entire Happy Hour Choir hooted and hollered, really rolling in the aisles. Old Mac laughed so hard he had to wipe away tears, and the Gates brothers were both about to bust a gut. Ginger's eyes twinkled, and she took another swig. "Hey, Beulah, I think I should have been coming to these practices. These folks are fun."

I grinned. "I told you they weren't so bad."

"No, but the beer is." Ginger took another drink, then looked at the label and up at Bill. "Maybe I'm not a beer drinker. Bill?"

"Yes, ma'am." Bill waddled over so quickly he lost his breath.

"Think you might be able to get liquor in here? I've heard it's quicker."

Bill's eyes opened the widest I'd ever seen them. When he recovered, he shook his head ruefully. "My permit only allows beer and wine."

"Then for heaven's sake, you need to get some wine. That would make more sense for the Happy Hour Choir anyway. Wasn't Jesus's first miracle turning water into wine?"

Bill took off his Co-op cap and started opening and closing the plastic adjustable band at the back. "What kind of wine would you like, Miss Ginger?"

"I don't know, Bill. I used to drink the hard stuff, personally. But that was only until Beulah came along. All I know is there has to be a wine out there somewhere that would taste better than this beer."

"Maybe you need to try another brand," Bill said. He brought her a Bud Light, a Coors, a Miller Light, and finally a Corona.

"I guess this'll have to do," Ginger said after the swig of Corona, not realizing she was too buzzed to tell the difference among the beers by that point. "But next week you need to have some wine for me to try." She wagged her finger at him, and he took a step back.

"Yes, ma'am."

I desperately needed to regain order. "All right, y'all, now we're running behind schedule. Open your hymnals to 'Yield Not to Temptation.' "

"Do we have to sing this again?" Tiffany's objection surprised me.

"What?"

"We've already sung this song three times this month, Beulah. What's the deal?"

Apparently, I was trying to remind myself not to ever yield to temptation again. That and I obviously had some "dark passions" to subdue. "Okay, okay. Let me think for a minute."

I closed my eyes, but all I could think of was Luke. At the thought of him, all I could think of was temptation. And the need to not yield.

"How about 'What a Friend'?" Ginger belched but remembered to excuse herself that time.

"Thank Go—thank goodness." Pete Gates looked relieved, too. Apparently, no one liked "Yield Not to Temptation"—

probably because we were all bona fide experts at yielding and not so good at the not.

We played through Ginger's suggestion then we practiced a couple of other numbers. We still needed an invitation, though, and Sinners to Saints was set to start in five minutes.

"Okay, now all we need is an invitation. Let me think. Let me think . . ."

" 'Pass Me Not'?" I looked up to see Luke in the doorway with his Bible tucked under his arm. I sucked in a breath. I could have asked him the same.

Everyone turned to look at Luke. He hadn't made a song suggestion in months. My heart did a little dip. Not only did Luke not want to have anything to do with me, but he had also proven he didn't need me. He'd just picked the perfect invitation.

"You heard the man." I cleared my throat and choked back tears I was determined not to let fall. "A quick run-through and y'all can get to Bible study."

And a quick run-through was all they needed. The Happy Hour Choir kept getting better and better. I had taught all of them the basics of reading music by then, and I caught myself thinking about what equipment it would take to make a CD. I shook those thoughts off. I didn't know where to begin with such things.

Sometimes I would catch Tiffany sitting at the piano with the Gates brothers as they picked through their parts. Sam usually watched from the sidelines. I liked to think he was gathering his courage to take a turn at the piano beside her, but sometimes he would still gaze at me. Increasingly, that gaze grew puzzled instead of interested. After all, Miss Georgette and Miss Lottie had made sure everyone knew about my and Luke's "torrid love affair." Fortunately for Luke, such gossip had led to a new record attendance at County Line, not the opposite.

When I quit playing piano, my choir members shifted from singing to talking. They laughed at jokes and teased each other raucously. From the risers I had that awful outside-looking-in feeling again, especially as others wandered in. Goat Cheese had become a regular, and Bill's wife, Marsha, sometimes came to knit while she listened.

"Going to stay tonight?" Luke asked without looking up from where he had laid his Bible. I glanced up in surprise. He looked thinner, gaunter. Or was it just my imagination hoping he was pining for me?

"Yeah, Ginger and Tiffany need a ride." I immediately regretted the words because my tone suggested I was mad at him when I was really still mad at myself.

"I've been hoping you'd come back."

His eyes met mine. I felt a little flutter of hope but didn't dare let it free.

"Beulah, come sit down here with me and help me drink some of these extra beers. No sense in letting them go to waste."

At that moment, for one split second, Ginger Belmont was not my favorite person, but the sensation passed. I picked up the Bud Light and made a note to pay for our beer as well as put a generous tip in the jar on Bill's counter.

When I sat down, she leaned in close. "Have you noticed how that Sam fellow makes goo-goo eyes at Tiffany?"

"No." That would've required me to think about something other than Luke. I looked up, and sure enough, Sam was contemplating Tiffany with what could only be described as a soul-searching gaze. Or, by its scientific name, goo-goo eyes.

"Wake up and smell the coffee, Beulah." Ginger snorted, her eyes watching as Sam joined Tiffany by the bar. "I think she might need a date with him."

"Ginger, she's pregnant."

"And?" There went the eyebrow, this time delicately penciled in.

I sighed. "So now you want me to play Cupid?"

She grinned. "Now you're getting the idea. What do you think it's going to take to get the two of them to go on a date?"

"One of them—probably him—asking the other—probably her—to go to the movies. If it's meant to be, I'm sure they'll figure it out." I chugged half my Bud and eyed her other discarded beer because I didn't want to be having this conversation. Well, that and waste not, want not.

"But what if they need a little nudge in the right direction?" Ginger stared at the two of them, not a trace of a smile on her face. An invisible fist clutched my heart. She didn't think she had time for romance to take its natural course, and she wanted to make sure Tiffany was taken care of.

"Fine. I'll see what I can do, but I thought you only had one last request of me?"

Ginger patted my cheek. "I only had one last *formal* request of you. I may start making requests from the great beyond someday."

Her hand trembled, and I leaned into it. Her face was so pale and wrinkled, her eyes so bleary. And I loved her so much. "I wouldn't expect anything less."

"Now you need to pay attention to Luke, dear."

But if I look at him I might not look away.

He stood front and center in his jeans and cowboy boots with his black T-shirt. He hadn't needed my input to fit in; in some ways he was starting to fit in better than I ever had.

"Tonight, I'm afraid we have to have a serious discussion."

Pete Gates and Mac booed. My last session aside, serious discussions were apparently not the norm for the Sinners to Saints.

"My superintendent has requested I stop leading this group."

"What? Why?" Tiffany's face crumpled. She grabbed her stomach as the baby gave a seemingly indignant kick. I agreed with the baby. The superintendent had seemed so pleased that night.

Luke must have been upset and possibly disappointed that night, too. But he hadn't drunk too much or made a pass at me. I looked down at my shoes. I really was a lost cause and had no business obsessing over a preacher.

He leaned against the risers and crossed his arms. "The Methodist Church has always supported abstinence from—"

"You can't have sex if you're a Methodist? I'm outta here." Greg Gates was already on his feet.

"No, no. Abstinence from alcohol," Luke said. "It's not a hard-and-fast rule, but sobriety is preferred."

"But I was finally learning something," Mac interrupted.

And he had. He had been shaving, showering, and dressing better. I couldn't remember the last time I had actually seen Mac drunk at The Fountain. And, thank goodness, I hadn't seen or heard of him waiting around the side of the building to flash anyone.

"I thought you said the Bible only said we shouldn't drink to excess, that too much of anything was bad." Pete Gates stood beside his brother. After several weeks of keeping their fists under control, the Gates brothers were itching for a fight—and this time not with each other.

"Look, you're all right." Luke held out a steady hand. "*We're* right."

"So what's the problem?" Sam's deep voice echoed off the walls.

"The superintendent made it very clear. It's either this or the church."

And I'm sure the church's rise in attendance had nothing to do with having a minister who was willing to lead a Bible study in a bar.

"So, now we're chopped liver," Greg Gates muttered.

"No, not at all," Luke said. "But I made a promise when I took the church, and I have to honor it."

Bill stepped forward. "Well, now what do we do?"

"I was hoping someone else would like to lead the group and keep it going because I believe we've done good work here. And I think we could do more good work, but that's going to be up to you guys. Sometimes I think I'm preaching to the converted."

Indeed, he was. Each member of the Happy Hour Choir now went to church every Sunday because they were expected to sing. They also formed the core group of the Sinners to Saints Bible study, although every week a new person or two dropped in to check things out.

Luke stood with his hands on his hips. "Is there anyone who would like to lead?"

Silence reigned. No one wanted to step into Luke's cowboy boots. Knowing the powers that be had condemned the group, or at the very least weren't supportive of it, made everyone nervous. I felt somewhat condemned myself. What had ever possessed me to think I could take a group of tavern-goers and make a choir out of them?

"Luke, dear," Ginger said. "Maybe it's too much to ask someone to lead the group permanently. Why don't you pass around a sheet and everyone can take turns? And I'm sure there's a book, isn't there? Something to guide us?"

Luke's wide grin caused my heart to skip a beat.

"You're right as always, Miss Ginger," he said. "Taking turns is a wonderful idea, and I can always recommend a course of study."

"That's what I thought," Ginger said. "Now, you can write me down for next week and people can sign up after that."

Tiffany opened her notebook and wrote Ginger's name then hers in painstaking cursive at the top of a page. She tore out the sheet and handed it to Luke.

Bill took the sheet and wrote his name, then Mac grabbed the sheet. Then the Gates brothers and Sam got into a mock fight. One corner of the paper was ripped, but it was all in good-natured fun. Marsha stopped knitting long enough to consider the sheet, but she passed it on to Goat Cheese, who passed it to Tiffany with a wink.

"I'm so glad you decided to continue," Luke said. "I wanted to read you one more verse before I go: 'You shall love the Lord your God with all your heart, and with all your soul, and with all your strength, and with all your mind; and your neighbor as yourself.' Such simple words, so difficult to follow."

We all stared.

"That's it," he said softly. "I would say I'm going to miss you all, but I'm across the parking lot if you need me. Thank you for letting me speak with you about God's word." He closed his Bible gently, and he stood.

Mac rose and started clapping, the sound reverberating off the cinder-block walls. Bill stood and joined him, then Pete Gates, then Greg. Sam stood, and Tiffany pushed herself to her feet with some effort. Even Goat Cheese and Marsha stood. Finally, Ginger leaned heavily on her cane, and that left me.

Luke's eyes now bored through me, his lips not even twitching up into a smile. Not until I stood and clapped as loudly as I could because I had seen change in others I could only hope to find for myself. I clapped because he wasn't the stick-in-the-mud I had first thought him to be and because he had been willing to bend the rules—well, some of the rules, anyway.

And when I clapped, he finally gave me the gift of those dimples.

He gave a curt, old-fashioned bow and ducked out the door. The applause faded, but the dull buzz of people talking over one another became a raucous roar.

Ginger put her two fingers to her mouth and gave a sharp whistle, something she had never been able to teach me. "I don't think we can top that, do you?"

Tiffany and all the guys around her murmured a lot of no's and shook their heads.

"Then I say we head home early, and I'll find something for next week." Ginger tried to take a step with her cane, but she knocked over her half-full bottle of Heineken and her third-full bottle of Corona. Then she tried to bend to pick them up, but only succeeded in bending a quarter of the way down and panting a lot.

"For heaven's sake, let us get that, Miss Ginger," Tiffany said as she moved her chair and bent to get the bottles. She lightly bounced bellies with Bill, and they laughed.

"I'm due any day now," Bill said as he rubbed a towel across the rough-hewn wooden floor. "How about you?"

"Not until the end of December, I'm afraid," Tiffany said with a grin as she picked up the two bottles and stood with a grunt.

Ginger shook her head at the two of them. "Thank you. I hate not doing for myself."

Tiffany looked her straight in the eye and said something I wish I'd said: "Ginger Belmont, I've been living with you for three months now, and I've seen you do for everyone but yourself. Now, let us do something for you for a change."

Ginger nodded, too choked up to say anything as Bill and Tiffany giggled all the way to the trash can and the big utility sink behind the bar.

Almost no one knew she was dying.

I kept thinking people were stupid if they couldn't see it, but most folks are really good at seeing only what they want to see.

Chapter 23

Ginger made me promise to talk to Luke on Sunday about a possible "double date" to help Sam and Tiffany get together. I had spent the previous three days making every argument I could think of against meddling. Ginger wasn't going for any of them, and when I asked her why she was so gung ho to see the two of them together, she said, "Because I'm a crotchety old battle-ax, that's why!"

And what could I say about how pregnant women shouldn't date? I'd jumped a minister's bones just because he'd been talking about Bathsheba. I could see the twisted logic that had caused my drunken mind to draw important parallels with my life, but I wasn't sure anyone else would.

No, Ginger was having none of it. She had even decided to take Tiffany to lunch somewhere else so Luke and I would have an excuse to sit together and discuss our impending date. I could almost see Ginger riding along as chaperone. Instead of holding people apart with her cane, she would use the curved end to pull them together.

Just the thought of it made me smile, and I almost added a verse to the doxology.

I stood to hear the reading of the word and marveled at how it felt as though I spent more time in church than at The Fountain. Rationally, I knew I racked up more time at The Fountain, but I spent more time thinking at church. It didn't hurt that Sundays were the only days I got to spend with Luke. Sure, he was in the pulpit, and I was above him in the loft—an irony not lost on me—but we were close on Sundays, in proximity if not in spirit.

Luke read from Hebrews that morning. "Now faith is the assurance of all things hoped for, the conviction of things not seen. . . ."

Luke kept reading about the merits of faith, his steady baritone guiding his lambs, a record-breaking eighty-two of them in the fold that day. I was still stuck on that part about "all things hoped for."

I had wanted.

I had hoped.

I had not received.

And before then I had received what I didn't want. Then, just as I wanted what I had received, it was taken away. I rubbed my temples as my mind worked through hope, want, and receipt. Had I given up faith because I'd lost Hunter, or had I lost my faith because I'd stopped wanting and hoping?

And did I dare hope for something, or someone, else?

I'd never been happier to play the final chords of the postlude.

Because there were only two of us, Luke and I had to share a cozy booth at Las Palmas.

"I'm so glad you invited me to lunch, Beulah." Luke dipped a chip into his salsa. "I've been worried about you."

"Worried about me?" My heart thudded against my rib cage. I had to sit on my hands to keep them from pulling me to the end of the booth so I could run away. It'd been so long since it was just him and me. My mind played a never-ending loop of each one of our kisses.

"Yeah, Miss Ginger doesn't have much longer, does she?"

Hope did another nose-dive. He wasn't worried about *me.*

"No, I don't think so. Well, I don't know. The oncologist has no idea for sure."

Tears stung my eyes. Commiserating with Luke might help me feel better, but it also felt as though I was violating Ginger's sacred trust.

He considered me as he ate. His eyes took on a world-weary sadness. "I've seen a lot of sick people, Beulah. I've seen a lot of people die. I've also seen a lot of people worry themselves sick trying to take care of those people, especially fielding outlandish requests."

My chip froze in midair. Did he know about Ginger's plan?

"That's not a criticism," he added. "Just be sure you don't forget how to take care of yourself."

I cleared my throat. "It's good that you don't think honoring final wishes is a bad thing, because I have one for you."

"Oh?"

I took a deep breath, letting him wonder what the wish was. "Ginger thinks that Sam and Tiffany should lighten up and go on a date instead of"—here I paused for air quotes—"making 'goo-goo eyes' at each other."

"Me too!" Luke's eyes lit up. "Well, let me back up. I'm not in the business of telling couples who should date and/or get married, but they seem to really like each other."

I decided to test his ministerial super-mind-reading powers by simply looking through him calmly.

"What?"

I kept looking at him.

"Uh-uh," he said with his mouth still full. It was cute the way he forgot his manners in that moment of epiphany. "I'm not going to set them up on a date."

Close, but no cigar. "No, Ginger wants us to go on a double date with them."

Luke leaned back as the waiter slid a bean burrito in front of him, then it was my turn to lean back for my chimichanga. "A double date?"

"I know, I know." That damn blush only he was able to cause crept up my neck and into my cheeks. "I'll tell her you refused. I promised her I'd ask, but I didn't promise anything else—"

"I'll do it." His expression couldn't be read.

I couldn't look away. "You'll what?"

"I'll do it," he said as his fork sawed into the burrito. "It is a final wish, after all."

"Luke, I hate to tell you, but she's already made about two hundred final requests, so I'm not feeling bad about blowing this one off." I shifted uncomfortably, but that brought my knees against his, reminding me of our very first lunch together.

"Still, how are you going to feel if there is one thing left you didn't do for her?" The sun from the window caught a hint of stubble on his stubbornly set jaw. "We'll go, and they can take it from there. Easy as that."

"Easy as that?" I echoed. "No, not easy as that. The minute we go out, a lot of things are going to happen. Folks are going to start talking again and—"

"I don't care what people say. I never did." He was already a third of the way through his meal, and I hadn't started. "Besides, we're here having lunch. Alone. Right now."

"But you didn't . . . you wouldn't—"

He leaned forward to whisper, "Take advantage of you while you were drunk?"

I blushed. "When you put it that way."

"I thought," he started, then gauged how much of himself he wanted to give away. Finally, his eyes met mine with an unexpected vulnerability. "I thought you only wanted that one night. And that's not good enough for me."

My heart got stuck in my throat, and tears stung my eyes. "That's not what I meant. Even drunk that's not what I meant."

"Then maybe we do need to try this again. From the beginning."

My heart kept time with the Tejano music.

"From the beginning." I swallowed hard and willed those

tears back. Somehow we were going to try this all from the beginning. "But what are people going to say? You're lucky no one saw me on your porch that night. Or my car in the parking lot."

"Oh, they did." He took another bite, completely nonchalant. My stomach was too knotted to even consider my lunch. "Miss Lottie finally called Tom up."

"Are you still frocked or whatever?"

Luke chuckled, "Still a man of the frock, yes. Tom told her to mind her own business and to think and pray on the possibility that she might need to find a home in another congregation."

I sucked in a deep breath. That would explain why I seemed to feel additional invisible daggers of Christian love and fellowship each Sunday morning. "But still."

He gave me a full smile, the one with the dimples. "Beulah. I. Don't. Care."

My heart squeezed in on itself, and my fork stopped in midair. All of the color and warmth drained from my face then rushed back all at once.

"Beulah Land, are you blushing?" He smiled enough for me to see both dimples again.

"Shut up."

"Oh, that was a classy comeback," Luke said. "I don't know if I can go out on a date with such a quick-witted woman."

"Can I get you anything else?"

Neither of us looked up at the waiter, but we both said, "No, thank you" at the same time.

"Okay, then, here's your bill." He laid the bill on the table. My hand hit the bill first, but that left Luke's hand on top of mine. He let it rest there for an inordinate amount of time, his thumb stroking the top of my hand. Finally, he slid the bill out from under my fingers, his eyes never leaving mine.

"Lunch is on me," he declared.

"Then thank you." I took another bite in my bid to catch up with him. "I was only trying to be an independent woman."

"No man—or woman—is an island," he said as he put the check out of reach and returned to his burrito.

"So, we're really going to go out on a date. Do you think that will work?"

"Of course," Luke said. "You can tell Tiffany that you're nervous and would feel better if she came along just in case—"

"Why do I have to be the nervous one?"

"Because Sam's not going to come along with a nervous man. That's not what men do. My approach has to be that I really like you—obviously—but you'll only double date since we've had some ups and downs."

I rolled my eyes at him. "And you really think this junior high plan is going to work?"

He studied me as I took a couple bites more. "Yeah, I think it will because they *want* to go out. We're merely lending them an excuse."

"Aren't you supposed to be against devious machinations since you're a minister?"

"Still human," he said with a shrug as he slid to the edge of the booth. "Besides, it's for a good cause."

Too true, I thought as he took the bill to the cashier. The thought of going out on a date with him—even a fake date—did make me nervous. And taking Tiffany along would make me feel better about the whole thing. Of course, her presence would make me feel better because I would know I was doing something good for Ginger, not because I needed her to help me overcome a case of nerves.

"Don't rush," Luke said as he slipped back into the booth. He slid two Andes mints across the table. "I don't have anywhere to be this afternoon."

I stared at the mints. He'd noticed I always bought one on the way out the door. And he'd remembered. I was about to shed a few tears over Andes-mint thoughtfulness. I cleared my throat. "I think I'm full."

I handed one of the mints back to him, and we ate them slowly as we left the restaurant. We took a seat on the bench where Ginger had lectured us on how we were going to have to learn to work together.

"So, when are we going on this first date?" Luke asked.

I frowned. I worked every night but Wednesday when I had choir practice, and Sam and Tiffany were both going to Bible study. That only left Sunday, the other night The Fountain closed.

"Next Sunday night?"

Luke nodded. "Any preference for where we go?"

"I thought all first dates took place at the movies," I said.

"True, but I usually go for something a little different."

Usually? The thought of Luke with another woman made me want to take up cat fighting. But then curiosity got the better of me. "Such as?"

"Wouldn't you like to know," he said with a cryptic smile. "Since Tiffany's pregnant, I think a movie would be best."

I thought of how her bladder had to have shrunk to the size of an acorn. "A short movie would be even better."

Luke shrugged. "I came up with the backstory. You pick out the movie." He extended his hand. "Deal?"

"Deal," I said as we shook hands.

It would be hard to say who held whose hand a little too long.

"I guess I should be going," he said as he slowly withdrew his hand.

"Yeah, I need to check on Ginger and to quietly tell her the good news," I said.

He walked along the side of the building a couple of steps. "I'll see you on Wednesday to talk about the hymns for the bulletin?"

"I'll drop by around noon."

He squinted against the sun to study me. "Sounds good," he said, looking like he really didn't want to go.

Funny, I didn't want him to go, either.

He turned for the parking lot, and I gathered my purse in front of me. My emotions swirled around, excitement mingling with apprehension. I knew my way around men, or at least I'd always thought I did. Truth be told, though, I'd been on precisely two "dates" in the past ten years. I didn't know how to act or what to wear.

I didn't even know if he would still want to date me if I told him the whole truth, but, if we were going to start at the beginning, I would have to tell him everything eventually.

Chapter 24

In my mind, I would tell Tiffany about the double date and she would squeal with delight and clap her hands together. In reality, she looked me straight in the eye and said, "No."

I stared at her where she sat on the edge of my bed playing with the fringe on my Raggedy Ann, one of the few things I'd salvaged years ago when I sneaked back into my parents' house to get some of my things.

I closed my eyes at the memory of holding on to that doll after I lost Hunter. When I couldn't drift off to sleep, the weight of the doll helped me, but I had to stare into the darkness until the doll warmed from being near my body because Raggedy Ann was cold where Hunter had been warm. She was limp and lifeless where he had been plump and wiggly.

"Gosh, I guess I can go if it means that much to you," Tiffany said.

"Why wouldn't you want to go?" I asked as I sniffed and hastily wiped away a rogue tear. She didn't have to know I'd been crying for Hunter instead of myself.

Now who's being devious, Beulah?

Tiffany looked down at her belly. I noticed for the first time her shirt was held together with a safety pin. The pants probably were, too. Tiffany had bought nothing maternity other than underwear; everything else she wore had been mine. And it had been secondhand when I wore it.

"He's not going to think I'm pretty while I'm so fat!" Tiffany bellowed before going into a sob-fest that made my lone tear amateurish.

I sat down beside her, started to put my arm around her, but hesitated. When I realized I had paused because I was afraid I would jinx her baby, I forced my arms around her.

"Know what? I think it's time we went to the mall and got you a pretty new outfit, something you could wear on your date and to work at the florist."

She wanted to quit crying but kept making that hiccuping sound that you do when you can't stop. "Do-do-do you think so?"

"I know so."

"Oh, the baby!" Before I could stop her, she put my hand on her hard, rounded stomach, and I felt the baby kick. For a moment, I felt that same despair, the feeling that my insides were hollow and rotten, but then, like the Grinch, my heart expanded. The baby kept kicking my hand as if to say, "Lady, you're cramping my style down here."

Tiffany giggled then sighed. "Isn't it amazing?"

"Yes, yes it is," I murmured. Hollow and rotten? *Lord, I hope not.*

"Do you want to get married again?"

I frowned at the thought that Tiffany might be reading my mind.

"I never married the first time," I said slowly.

"Why not?"

"I wouldn't have married him even if I could," I said with a shiver.

"But I thought it was the Vandiver boy. That's what I heard." Tiffany sat up straight, her hands splayed protectively over her belly.

"That's what Roy Vandiver's daddy wanted everyone to think," I said softly.

"But? How did you? I don't understand."

I didn't understand, either. And I didn't want to tell her my sordid story because I hadn't even told Ginger what had happened. She had never once asked. I clamped my mouth shut, but a nagging voice in the back of my mind said, *Tell her.*

I shrugged. "I was in the wrong place at the wrong time."

Tiffany cocked her head to one side, obviously not pleased with the explanation.

Tell her.

"But, Beulah, how did you end up with Roy's daddy?" Her brown eyes pleaded. She was no stranger to sex with a much older man. She was no stranger to sex with a man who *was*, at least on paper, a father.

Tell her, Beulah. She'll understand.

I exhaled, knowing I had lost the battle. "Remember those purity pledges at First Baptist?"

Tiffany snorted. "A purity pledge? What's that?"

"They drew up this sheet of paper, said it was a covenant with God that you would save yourself for marriage." I hesitated. "When we were all thirteen, everyone signed it. Even Amanda Powell, and everyone knew she already wasn't a virgin."

"And what does this have to do with how you ended up with Roy's daddy?" Tiffany put both hands on her stomach as though she could somehow rearrange it into a more comfortable position.

"Roy Vandiver asked me out on a date a couple of years after I signed the purity pledge," I said. "Then he decided he didn't want to go for dinner and a movie. Instead he took me to some Civil War cemetery to show me some general's grave."

"But that's not why he really took you there." Tiffany's eyes narrowed.

"No, of course not. And I should have known that." I ran a hand through my hair. It flipped into my face, an ironic reminder of how Luke's hair always flipped back into place. I shook my head to clear it of the image of Luke. He didn't belong in this memory. "But I was young and stupid. I did like that first kiss, at least until Roy's hands really started wandering and tried to relieve me of my pants."

Tiffany grimaced and nodded her head. She had been in that situation before.

"So, I made him take me home."

Tiffany's brow furrowed, and her brown eyes widened in confusion. "But I don't understand. How did you . . . ?"

"I did something really stupid at that point."

And as I told the story, I began to relive it.

I let Roy drop me off at my house, even flipped him the bird as I climbed the front stoop.

But I stopped shy of the front door.

When I walked into the living room, my mother was going to ask me how my date with the "nice Vandiver boy" went. If I told her what happened, it would immediately become my fault for leading him on or for being stupid enough to go with him somewhere deserted. And then I would have to hear her question me because she wouldn't be able to believe Roy Vandiver had done such a thing. After all, his daddy was in charge of the purity pledge program!

The hypocrisy pushed my blood to boiling.

I was a teenager and thus not the brightest crayon in the box, so I got it into my head to march on over to Mr. Vandiver's house to give him a piece of my mind. I would tell him he would have better luck keeping the girls of Ellery virginal if he had a little chat with his own son about how "no means no."

I walked the four blocks to the Vandiver house. It was a brick ranch just like ours, only the Vandivers had a porch shaded by overgrown crepe myrtles. I picked my way up the flagstones in the yard and hopped up the steps.

All of the lights were out except for the flashing light of the television, which I could see faintly through the dining room window. I knocked on the door.

Mr. Vandiver came to the door, but he didn't look like the Mr. Vandiver I knew. He hadn't showered, nor had he dressed in anything other than a bathrobe. Stubble covered his cheeks, and his gray-streaked hair stood up in awkward, oily angles. "What do you want?"

The smart answer would have been nothing, but I was almost sixteen. I wouldn't have known "smart" if it had hit me upside the head.

"Sir, I wanted to tell you that your son was trying to get into my pants. And it's a little difficult to keep my pledge to purity that way."

I stood there with my hands on my hips in righteous indignation.

Roy, Sr., stepped out on the porch and closed the door behind him. "So, did you let him into your pants?"

He towered over me, swayed over me. That's when I realized he'd been drinking. A lot.

"No, no sir," I stuttered. I knew I needed to run home as fast as my little legs could carry me, but I couldn't seem to move. I instinctively stepped backward, but that only got me deeper behind the shade of the crepe myrtles.

"My wife hasn't let me into her pants in two years," Roy, Sr., growled as he reached for the belt on his robe. "I guess I haven't been setting the proper example for my son."

And he threw me down on the porch. He pinned my wrists above my head and jerked at my jeans. I opened my mouth to scream but only a squeak came out. Tangled crepe myrtle branches poked at me through the porch railing and swayed in the wind, mesmerizing me and taking me away for the moment. The branches scratched against the porch posts for what seemed an eternity as Roy, Sr., drove into me, scooting my bare back against the concrete, the same concrete that ripped at my hair and scratched the backs of my hands as his palms ground them into the porch. It took only a matter of minutes for Roy, Sr., to take what he had told me to guard until marriage, but that handful of minutes would haunt me for years.

He finished and slumped down on top of me. My insides burned like he'd used a pine cone, and I whimpered. He sat up, his eyes wide with fear, dilated from who knows what drugs he'd mixed with his alcohol.

Then those eyes narrowed with the realization of what he'd done.

He leaned down, intentionally crushing the breath out of me when he half slurred and half whispered into my ear, "If you tell anyone, I'll kill you."

He staggered to his feet, and I put myself back together—on the outside, at least. I trudged home like a zombie and tiptoed past both

Momma and Daddy softly snoring in their chairs. Then, I went upstairs and had the first of many, many good cries.

And even though all of that had happened over ten years ago, another good cry loomed on the horizon.

"But what happened after that?" Tiffany asked.

"Well, when Momma found out I was pregnant, she kicked me out of the house. She assumed it was Roy, Jr., and I let her. Ginger happened along that day to find out why I'd missed so many piano lessons. She rescued me."

Why had Ginger come that day? Why had I never thought to question that?

"But what happened to Roy, Sr.? And the baby?"

I took a deep breath. "Roy, Sr., had a nervous breakdown and spent some quality time at the mental institute up at Bowenville. While he was there he came to Jesus. Again. Then he came to me and begged my forgiveness, told me he wasn't right in the head that night and he wasn't ever going to be able to forgive himself for what he'd done. Then he gave me a check for ten thousand dollars for the baby."

Tiffany gasped.

"He didn't say it was hush money," I said. "But that's what I took it to mean. And it was hard to hate him quite as much after all of the apologies. Don't get me wrong, it was hard to forgive him, too. I'm not sure I'll ever be able to forgive him, but it did make me feel better about the baby. That's when I finally started to look forward to having Hunter."

Tiffany smiled at what should have been the bittersweet ending of the story. "And the baby?"

"Hunter . . ." But I couldn't say the word *died*. Instead I crumpled into tears, and it was her turn to hold me as I cried.

"What happened?" she soothed as she stroked my hair. My head rested on her belly, and her baby gave me a kick to the temple for encroaching on his territory.

"SIDS."

Tiffany drew in another sharp breath, and I pulled myself

away and took both of her hands. "I don't want you to worry. It was something weird, and it doesn't happen that often. Everything is going to be okay with your baby, I just know it."

Because it has to be.

"I know that," Tiffany said with a huge smile as she rubbed her belly. "I've prayed a lot about this baby, and it's going to be A-OK."

She stood. "But one thing still confuses me."

"What's that?" I grabbed a Kleenex and blew my nose. I hated crying. If I never shed another tear it would be fine with me.

"What happened to the money?"

"Remember how Ginger had cancer? The insurance companies don't pay every dime for chemo and radiation treatments," I said. I bit my tongue before I could add that I was sure money was one of the reasons Ginger had refused treatment this time around.

"That's a shame," Tiffany said. "You could've started college with that money."

I never thought of college back then. I wouldn't have finished high school if Ginger hadn't made me. Then I went straight from high school graduation to driving Ginger all the way to Memphis for her treatments. That's where a lot of the money had gone: gas money and living expenses while I watched Ginger instead of playing at The Fountain.

And all this time, she'd had money squirreled away. I hadn't had to spend mine, but she'd been too weak and out of it to ask where the money had come from. Or gone.

"Quid pro quo, Miss Davis," I said with a sad smile, thinking of my discussion with Luke in the cemetery.

"What?"

"What's your story?" I asked softly.

She turned to face me, her brown eyes flat with knowledge she should have never learned. "My momma doesn't know who my real daddy is. She took up with Carl when I was so young, I didn't even know he wasn't my real dad until I was ten. That's when *he* decided to play house with me. I was too young to know better. I knew something was wrong and I told my momma, but she ignored me because she was always strung-out and too weak to live without a man. He left me alone for a long while after I told her, but then she took off with a truck driver. I avoided Da—*him* whenever I could. Sometimes I wasn't so lucky. He told me no one would want to have anything to do with me if they ever found out."

Tears streamed down her cheeks.

"Tiffany—"

"Don't 'Tiffany' me! I let him, and I have to live with that disgust in myself for the rest of my life. And you know no decent man is ever going to want to marry me when he finds out." She spat out the words, her tone flat. "Especially not when they find out I also slept with some other guys trying to figure out what was so special about sex or me or both."

"I might have slept with a few folks around town," I said, averting my eyes to a cobweb in the corner of the room. "I think sometimes you look for something better, or you try to figure out what TV and movies and all the romance novels are raving about because you sure didn't have that experience."

"Figured it out yet?" Her eyes searched mine. She wanted to know. She desperately needed to know that sex could be something other than sex.

I swallowed hard as I forced my eyes to meet hers. "Not yet, but I've had some ideas."

She looked at her shoes—or what she could see of them. "Do you think any decent man is ever really going to want to be with me when he finds out?"

"Tiffany, you'll know he's decent when he accepts you for who you are."

"At least you don't have to live with the guilt of going along with it." Her voice was so low she could have sung bass.

"Stop. Your situation is the same as mine," I said. "No, it's worse. Someone you loved and trusted took advantage of you. It's going to take a decent man to understand that, and you will find one. Sam could be that one."

She held her head high. "I've got to go . . . do something." She slammed the door, and a piece of paper fluttered from the vanity mirror to the floor. I bent to pick it up and wondered if I should go after her.

No, she needed to be alone for her cry. Her pain was still too sharp around the edges to be shared, especially with her pregnancy hormones making her bawl at everything including Hallmark and coffee commercials. Hopefully, I hadn't made anything worse. Hopefully, she'd come around.

I looked at the sheet I held in my hand: Luke's drawing. I could see myself as the girl who had been a disappointment to her parents, an instigator to a crazed, grieving drunk, or a woman who had been a crazed griever. Or, somehow, I could be the beautiful woman in the picture, the woman who smiled back at me.

I didn't feel better right then. In fact, I wondered if I would ever feel better, if I would ever figure out what kind of messed-up world we lived in. Later, however, Tiffany would tell me our conversation changed her life. It changed mine, too, because for the first time in a long while, I considered the choices life offers us about who we're going to be. I could be the person I had always been, the woman who trusted no one. Or, I could be the person Luke saw when he drew me, the beautiful woman with a smile on her lips and the wind in her hair.

Most important, confessing to Tiffany what I had never confessed before changed my life because I listened to the quiet, persistent voice inside me. I don't know if it was the voice of God. Maybe it was self-reliance or becoming one with my chi, but I believe God spoke to me that day. Only, when I heard His voice, it sounded an awful lot like mine.

Chapter 25

Wednesday rolled around, and I had something to look forward to for once. John O'Brien—or as I liked to call him, John the Baptist—had finally returned from his mission trip and could tune both pianos. Thanks to going with Tiffany to an OB appointment that morning, I'd missed him when he came by to tune the house piano. I wasn't about to miss him at the church for a couple of reasons. One, John was my favorite Baptist, and, two, I needed him to tune the piano over at The Fountain, too.

"Beulah! Long time, no see!"

I jumped up from my seat on the first pew and ran down the aisle to smother him in a hug. "Glad you're back from Guatemala. Are you going to stay put for a while?"

"I might," he said with a grin.

A throat cleared behind us, and I turned to see Luke in the doorway beside the piano. "Luke, meet John O'Brien, best piano tuner in town. John, this is Luke Daniels, the new minister here at County Line."

Luke walked down the aisle stiffly, and it took me a minute to realize he was . . . jealous? Over John?

I glanced from my future date to my old friend as they shook hands. John was a few inches shorter than Luke, but square-jawed with blond hair pulled back in a ponytail. He didn't appear older than me until you looked carefully at his hazel eyes with the lines at their corners.

"Nice to meet you," Luke managed.

"Same here," John said, clearly amused by the once-over the preacher was giving him. "Mind if I get to the piano?"

Luke stepped aside, and John picked up his little black case of tools. I noticed he was wearing a pair of ripped jeans, his knees sticking out. John had to be the anti-Luke.

"I'll be in my office if you need me," Luke said before turning and walking away. I took a moment to admire the view and relish the smattering of jealousy he'd shown.

John liked to chat as he worked, wielding tuning hammer and mutes with an easy grace. He'd check his auto-tuner, but he had the best ear of anyone I'd ever known, so it was usually a passing glance.

When he finished working on the church piano, he played a few bars of Bach then yielded the seat to me. As the notes washed over me, tension melted from my shoulders. An in-tune piano was better than a massage. I didn't wait more than two beats before asking, "Think you can work on the one over at The Fountain, too?"

"I got a few minutes," he said with an easy grin. "Why not?"

As we walked across the street, I marveled at how easy it was to hang around with John. He never drank—not since his days as a roadie for some hair band—but he had no hesitation walking into The Fountain. At least not anymore.

A roadie. Wait.

"Hey, John, know anyone who could make a recording for me?"

"Like a demo?" he asked as I opened the door.

"Ho, Beulah. Hey, there, John! Wanna beer?"

"No thanks, Bill," he said easily. "I'll take a water if you've got it."

Bill looked around the counter, but we all knew he didn't have bottled water. "Maybe from the tap?" he asked sheepishly.

"That would be fine." John hopped up on the risers and looked back at me. "Now, what's this about a demo?"

I hesitated only for a minute before I told him most of what had happened with Derek, leaving out only a few key parts.

Bill handed up a water and gestured back to the bar in place of asking me if I wanted a beer. I shook my head no as I finished my tale. "Something about making them myself and selling them?"

John chuckled. "Making a recording and burning a few to CD wouldn't be too hard. I've got a mixing board and a few mikes if you wanted to do it here—as long as you aren't looking for anything fancy."

"No . . . that'd be perfect!"

We worked out a plan for John to come record at practice one night, and I walked over to the bar to have that beer after all.

Goat Cheese sat in his usual spot, grizzled as ever and still chain-smoking.

"Been enjoying church and Bible study, Mr. Ledbetter?"

He squinted at me, pausing long enough to make me uncomfortable and meaning to. "Thought I might ought to look into salvation. Can't live forever, you know."

More likely he was enjoying having dirt on the Happy Hour Choir and Luke's Bible study since his rival gossip, Miss Georgette, wouldn't be caught dead in The Fountain.

"Say, if you make a recording, I'd like one."

His request took me aback, and I almost choked on my beer. "Really?"

"Yeah. Y'all do some pretty singing. Good old songs, too."

"Well, thank you," I whispered. Compliments from Goat Cheese Ledbetter were few and far between. He nodded in acknowledgment as he exhaled another plume from his cigarette.

"That does it," John said from the risers as he put the piano back to rights. "This one wasn't bad at all. You must love it more."

I grinned. I was used to the piano at the church now, but The Fountain's old upright just felt better. "Maybe I do. Thanks, John."

I walked him back to his car and gave him the check from the church and the cash from me. As I waved good-bye, I noticed Luke sitting on the porch looking wistfully at The Fountain.

"Miss us already, Preacher Man?" I hollered across the parking lot.

"More than you know," he said.

None of us knew what to expect on the first day of the Sinners to Saints Bible Study sans Luke. I hadn't wanted to stay, but I had to wait for Ginger and Tiffany anyway. Neither wanted me to catch a ride with someone after choir practice. Both of them made a big show of how much they needed me. Ginger's back hurt, and she needed me to help her walk. Tiffany couldn't drive very well because of her baby bump—never mind how she managed the florist's van just fine. In the end, I gave in. Living with them had made me a big softie, I guess.

Bill was super-proud of himself. He'd spent the entire week reading up on wines, how to serve them, what to eat with them. He'd made a cheese tray that did not include Kraft Singles and had bought who knew how many bottles of wine.

"This here's a Mos-cato," he said to Ginger as he took the bottle of a pinkish-yellow wine out of the cooler where he normally kept the beer. "It's supposed to be sweet."

She nodded. "Sweet sounds good. Let's start with that."

"All right," Bill said. "Then you can try this merlot." He pronounced it "mer-*lot*." I would have laughed, but I didn't know any better back then, either. "This one's supposed to be served at room temperature, though. It's a . . ." He squinted as he tried to read the label. ". . . dry, full-bodied wine."

"Maybe I should go with that. I don't have my full body anymore," she muttered.

"What was that, Miss Ginger?"

"Oh, nothing. Pour me some Moscato, and I'll try your mer—, your other one later."

Bill poured her wine into a red plastic cup. "Sorry, forgot to buy any wineglasses."

"Now, Bill, this is fine." Ginger took a sip of the Moscato, swirled it around, and took another sip. "Just fine—kinda like Kool-Aid. Much better than beer."

She handed her wine to Tiffany and guided her walker to the stage. Tiffany sneaked one sip then another as she trailed after Ginger. Behind their backs, Bill made a sour face to let me know what he thought of the Moscato.

"How much do I owe you?" I asked as I sidled up to the bar.

"It's on the house tonight," Bill said as he gazed at Ginger. I hadn't been giving folks enough credit. Bill could see she wasn't doing well at all.

"Bill, that's awful nice of you," I said.

"Well, there's something I've been meaning to talk to you about." Bill dipped his chin to his chest and started fiddling with his suspenders.

"Okay, folks, it's time to get started if we're going to finish on time for Bible study," Ginger said. "That, and if I drink any more of Bill's Mos-ca-to, I'll be too tipsy to read the notes on the page."

I turned to Bill.

He waved away his thoughts. "It ain't that important. Go on and play. We'll talk about it later."

I took two steps toward the piano before I remembered I wasn't well lubricated. Bill was already pouring as I turned around. He handed me the red plastic cup, and I held it up to my nose. He'd given me the Moscato, which smelled like fruity vinegar. I took a sip as I walked. I'd had worse.

The Happy Hour Choir sat up straight, all drinks on the floor and hymnals in hand. They reminded me of the one time I went to see the Jefferson Symphony Orchestra, of that moment of silence when all of the members sat with their instruments at the ready.

"Y'all are too serious. I think we need to fly away."

Ginger clapped her hands together. "I like that one!"

"I know," I said as they turned to "I'll Fly Away." "Sam, I'm going to need you to belt it. Think you can?"

"Absolutely," he said. I gauged his expression to see if Luke had done a better job of selling the double date than I had. Based on the flush in his cheeks, I was going to guess yes.

"I know this one," Greg Gates said as he punched Pete on the arm. "Grandma Gates used to sing this one while she was putting the laundry on the line."

"Yeah, this is a good one, Beulah." From his chipped-tooth grin, I don't think Pete would have been happier with "Sweet Home Alabama." And he routinely put an Andy Jackson in the tip jar to get me to play that one. Come to think of it, I might need to go up to fifty—Tennessee inflation, you know.

"Let's jump in then." I played the last part of the chorus to get them started, and the Happy Hour Choir began:

"*Some glad morning when this life is over. . . .*"

Mac's tenor warbled up with Tiffany's soprano, and I decided then they would make a nice duet come Sunday morning. One Gates brother took tenor and the other took bass, their voices blending with Ginger's well-worn alto.

Sam's rich voice naturally pushed to the forefront. "*When I die—*"

Carl Davis crashed through the door and stumbled into the room with a drunken slur:

"*Hallelujah, by and by.* Why ain't y'all still singing?"

Tiffany leaned into Sam, clenching his plaid shirt with one hand and holding her belly with the other. "You're not supposed to be here."

"Aw, baby," Carl said. He staggered two steps in her direction, and she stood to lean into Sam. "Look at you. You're as big as the side of a barn."

Sam pushed Tiffany behind him, and I jumped down into Carl's path. "We will call the police this time, Carl. You are way too close."

He took another step and stood nose to nose with me. "Government can't keep me from what's mine."

I nodded to Ginger, who had already fished through my purse

for my cell phone, but her hands were shaking too badly to actually hit the numbers. Mac calmly took the phone from her and stealthily dialed as he shifted to face the piano and edged carefully behind Carl.

Carl didn't turn to look at him. "Take another step toward that door, MacGregor, and I'll kill you."

His bloodshot eyes were entirely too close to mine. My eyes itched and watered, but I refused to look away. Not even the sour beer stench of his breath could sway me from our staring match.

Finally, he looked at Mac, and I blinked furiously to put my eyes back to rights.

"Nine-one-one, what's your emergency?" The voice was faint because my phone hung limp at Mac's side. Carl had a knife.

"Carl Davis has lost his mind and has a knife on Beulah. Over at Bill's place on County Line Road," Ginger yelled. "Come quick."

Carl turned on Ginger with a snarl, but her beady eyes bored through him. Her hands clenched the walker in front of her until the swollen knuckles turned white. "Go on, Carl. I've lived a long life. You gonna stab an old lady?"

His nostrils flared. Twice he leaned toward her. Twice I leaned toward him. He held the hunting knife extended in front of him, and the blade caught the light.

"This isn't the last you'll hear of me," he snarled at the first hint of a siren. He stumbled out the door and disappeared. No one dared move until they heard him rev his truck.

"I woulda never thought Carl was that crazy," Mac muttered.

"My cousin Mike said he's started using meth," Greg said. Pete jabbed his brother as if he'd said too much.

"What?"

"Yeah, and Mike said not to talk to anyone about that," Pete added with a pointed stare.

So much for the good influence of the Happy Hour Choir.

I sat down beside Ginger and tried not to think of the Gates brothers covering for their cousin, Mike the meth cooker. Even

Mac looked dejected, emasculated, since he hadn't had the courage to do what Ginger did. Of course, Ginger didn't have much to lose—not that he knew that.

At the sound of a muffled sob, I looked to see Tiffany had buried her face in Sam's chest. They swayed in their own world, and he rubbed a hand protectively over her back. The thin set of his mouth suggested he would have preferred to have been a bigger hero, but I don't know how he could have convinced Tiffany to let him loose long enough to face Carl.

"Well, Bill. I believe we could all use a round before Len gets here, party pooper that he is." Ginger drained her glass and held it up. Somehow her hand held the glass steady, and her steadiness set the room in motion.

"Lotta good that restraining order did," Pete Gates muttered to Greg. "Maybe we oughta amble over to Crook Avenue from time to time. See if shotguns work a little better than paper."

Ginger either didn't hear them or was pretending not to. I didn't see the need to contradict them. Best I could tell, Carl Davis had gone from bad to worse, and the Gates brothers had always been better friends than enemies.

"Want me to take you home?" Sam's eyes crinkled with concern.

Tiffany vigorously shook her head no. "I don't want to go home to be by myself."

"We'll all go as soon as we can," I said. "You know Len's going to be here soon, and he's not about to let anyone go anywhere until he's done questioning everyone about everything."

As if summoned by my thoughts, Len Rogers walked through the door. He spread his arms wide, looking like a gangly Alfred E. Newman scarecrow with Don Knotts's bulging eyes. "Bill, we're gonna have to shut you down until we can resolve this."

"Len, it's Wednesday. I am shut down," Bill said as he ran nervous fingers up and down his suspenders.

"Then what in heaven's name is going on here?" Len had his notepad open and had already licked his finger to turn a page.

"Bible study," said Ginger.

"And choir practice," added Mac.

Len surveyed the crowd for a moment then he laughed. "No, really, what are y'all up to? Don't pull my leg. Y'all have to be here for some reason."

"For choir practice and Bible study," Tiffany said with a mighty sniffle. She held up her Bible as proof. Slowly, each and every member of the Happy Hour Choir held up a hymnal in one hand and a Bible in the other.

"Man, y'all are freaking me out. I thought this was all some crazy rumor the ladies had cooked up," Len said as he tried to turn the page of his notepad only to realize his saliva had long ago dried. "Beulah, you'll always tell me straight. What's this all about?"

So I told him the whole story. I told him about Luke's Bible study and about the choir. I told him how Carl Davis had originally been in the choir and about how he'd thrown me against the wall when I kicked him out. Len shook his head as he took notes at a furious pace. I left out the part about how Carl was Tiffany's baby daddy, and she slumped into Sam with relief as I said, "And that's pretty much the whole story, Len."

Len took off his hat and scratched at his reddish-brown hair. "That's about the craziest thing I've ever heard."

Ginger raised her glass to him. "Truth is stranger than fiction."

She hiccuped, and Len looked from her to me. I shrugged.

"I reckon I'm gonna have to interview all y'all," he said.

I retrieved my glass from the top of the piano and plopped down on the risers while Len moved around the room.

That's when I saw Luke at the door motioning for me.

Chapter 26

I followed him across the parking lot to his house. The lone deputy outside admonished us not to go far, so we sat on the porch in an ancient swing. Luke's feet easily reached the floor, and he pushed off for both of us, but the swing swayed a little too fast on his side and lagged behind on mine because my feet didn't touch the floor.

I clasped my hands in my lap to keep from reaching for him. When I looked over, he had his hands clasped, too.

"So," he said.

"So."

I wondered if he remembered the last time I had been on his porch. At the memory of flinging myself at him, I felt a blush start at my hairline and move across my face.

"What happened? I've been worried since the cars pulled in, but they wouldn't let me go in to make sure you were all right."

I looked at his face, but he gazed at the blue lights flashing in the parking lot. "Oh, Carl stopped by. With a hunting knife and a bad attitude."

The swing jerked to a halt. He turned to face me, his eyes wide as he searched for wounds. "Are you okay?"

"Fine," I said.

"And Tiffany?"

"Everyone's fine. I don't imagine Carl got too far, and there were several witnesses who saw him threaten Mac and Ginger. Well, all of us really."

Luke shook his head. "I don't like it. They'd better catch him this time. He needs to be locked up somewhere before he hurts someone."

I opened my mouth to tell him about the Gates brothers and Carl's latest habit, but I quickly closed it. No need to worry him with information that might or might not be true. "He got a decent head start. I don't know if they'll get him or not."

"Is he going to have to hurt someone before they do anything about it?"

The preacher man was riled up. I tried for a little levity. "Shouldn't you be advocating a little 'turn the other cheek' about now?"

He cupped my face so quickly I flinched, but his touch was gentle. "Beulah Land, if he hurts you again, I—well, I don't know what I'll do. So, be careful. And don't get hurt."

My eyes widened. "I won't. I promise."

He closed his eyes and exhaled sharply. When his eyes found mine, Luke the man was gone. Luke, the rather resigned preacher, was in his place. "You don't have to promise to not get hurt. I know you too well for that. Just promise you'll be careful."

"I'll be careful, Luke." I swallowed hard. For the first time I let myself see a future with the two of us together. Up until this point, I hadn't let myself think past a couple of dates, but Luke wasn't a man who played the field. He was opening himself to me totally, and that thought both exhilarated and chilled me to the bone. And when he cupped my face like this, he looked for all the world like he wanted to kiss me just as much as I wanted to kiss him.

"Beulah!" Tiffany's voice cracked, and I broke away from Luke.

"I've got to go," I said.

"I know."

Was he disappointed, relieved, or a mixture of both?

"Right here!" I yelled across the parking lot. I stopped on the front step and turned to face the enigmatic preacher man. "Still on for Sunday?"

"Still on," he said, his eyes meeting mine with an emotion I couldn't read.

"Good," I exhaled unexpectedly. "I'll see you then."

I dashed across the gravel lot, arriving at The Fountain's screen door just in time to hold it open for Ginger. Tiffany and I eased her into the front seat of the Corolla.

"I believe it may be time for this car to retire," she muttered as Tiffany slid into the backseat with a grunt. "Next time we take the Caddy."

"Thank God," Tiffany breathed from the backseat where she was scrunched up like a contortionist.

"You know the doctor said you couldn't drive anymore with the meds, right?" I chanced a glance at the passenger seat, and Ginger looked almost skeletal under the beam of the security light.

"I think I've done enough driving for a few lifetimes," she said as she lay against the seat.

I cranked the car and got us headed back to town. Ginger's comment wasn't sitting well with me. I knew she was talking about driving, but the oncologist had said that it could be tomorrow or it could be several months. He did fear the cancer had spread even though the test results didn't back up his hypothesis.

Be on the lookout for strange behavior, he had said. A few short months ago cursing and drinking would have been strange behaviors for Ginger. Willingly giving up driving privileges wouldn't have happened, either. Permanently handing over the keys to the Cadillac was worse. I decided then and there that if Ginger tried to make French toast the next morning, I wouldn't let her.

Tiffany helped me get Ginger into the house and to the bathroom. We stumbled over each other like the Three Stooges, but we finally got Ginger situated in her favorite recliner.

Then she dismissed us. "Go upstairs. I don't feel like company tonight."

Tiffany and I looked at each other, and I'm sure she was thinking what I was thinking: *Please, please don't let Ginger die yet, even if she is acting weird.*

"Go on," Ginger said, waving her hand in the direction of the stairs.

I took the steps at a gallop, and Tiffany puffed behind me. I sat down on my bed and cradled Raggedy Ann. No way was I going to sleep yet—not with the image of Carl and his hunting knife alternating with the one of Luke cupping my face with his hands.

"Beulah?" Tiffany leaned in the doorway, one hand under her belly, supporting it.

"Yeah?"

"Can I ask you a question?"

I patted a spot on the bed beside me. "Sure."

She plopped down, still trying to catch her breath from climbing the stairs. "If something happens to me, will you raise my baby?"

My lungs froze. My heart stopped beating.

"Seriously. I'm scared Da—he's going to do something to me one day. If that happens, would you take care of him? Or her?"

"Yes, of course. But nothing's going to happen to you. We won't let anything happen to you. You know Len's out there looking for Carl right now. He's going to jail."

Her hands reached over Raggedy Ann to clasp mine. "That's only if they catch him, but I would feel much better knowing you would raise my baby."

Baby. I immediately pictured a son, my son, but Tiffany refused to find out if she was having a boy or girl.

"But are you sure you want me?"

Tiffany smiled, the sweet, glowing smile of a pregnant woman. "You're the only one who could ever understand me, so you're the only one I want to raise my baby. You're going to be such a good mother someday."

My womb, that part of me I had believed rotten, clenched and reminded me of what those first baby kicks had been like, and I blushed. "Then I would be honored. Just take care of yourself, though, because this is an emergency situation only."

"Of course," Tiffany said as she squeezed my hand. She pushed herself up from the bed with a grunt. "I'm going to bed."

When she reached the doorway she froze. "Did we lock all the doors?"

"I'll go down and double-check in a few minutes," I said.

Her shoulders relaxed, and she leaned on the door frame. "Of course, you know this means you're going to have to go into the nursery."

My stomach flip-flopped, but I kept the smile on my face. "No, I'm not, because you're going to be fine. I'm only plan B. Besides, Mac agreed to do all of the painting and the heavy lifting."

She went to bed, and I trudged downstairs to check all the locks once more—not that I thought they could possibly keep Carl out if he had a mind to get in. Our best hope was that Len's deputies had caught up with him and taken care of him at least for the night. Or that the Gates Brothers Militia would find him while on unofficial patrol.

Once upstairs, I paused in front of the nursery. I pushed the door open and turned on the light. Gone were my airplanes. In fact, everything was gone or covered up because Mac had been in the process of painting the nursery under Tiffany's direction. The crib, changing table, and rocker all hid underneath a plastic tarp in the middle of the room. My buttercream walls had given way to a bright yellow, a neutral color, since Tiffany insisted on being surprised. Blue painter's tape still lined the baseboards, windows, and ceiling.

I should have been able to step into the new room, but I couldn't. The memories were faded around the edges, but my heart rate still spiked. I slammed the door and ran to the sanctuary of my bedroom.

But this time I didn't cry.

Chapter 27

There we were, two damaged women in our cutest outfits, ready to conquer the dating world. Ginger leaned heavily on her walker and looked us over. "Beulah, you need some mascara."

I scowled. "I don't like mascara."

"Do you like having eyelashes?"

"Well, yeah."

"Then run upstairs and put on some mascara."

I huffed, reminded myself I wasn't sixteen or anywhere close to it, then ran upstairs to put on the least amount of mascara I could. I heard the murmur of voices. Ginger needed to tell Tiffany something.

I ducked into the bathroom and started to put on some Dial A Lash when I realized the stuff had to be germ central because they didn't even make it anymore. I fished through the makeup drawer until I found a sample of a different brand, a tube that hadn't been opened. I took my time. Sure, I wanted to know what Ginger was saying to Tiffany, but I knew better than to get into Ginger's business. Besides, a perverse part of me wondered what was going to be "wrong" with Tiffany so Ginger could then have a chat with me.

Sure enough, my feet had hardly hit the last step when Ginger turned on the pregnant lady.

"Tiffany, I really think you need a different pair of shoes," Ginger said with a frown. "Why don't you go back upstairs and get those slip-on Dr. Scholl's. They aren't much to look at, but you don't want varicose veins, now, do you?"

That was all Tiffany had to hear. She was scared to death of stretch marks, varicose veins, and any other physical deformities associated with pregnancy. I didn't have the heart to tell her they couldn't be avoided no matter how much magic cream she slathered on.

"Okay, Ginger, so what's your super-secret message to me?"

Her lips twisted into a smile. "Can't get much of anything past you, now, can I?"

"No, ma'am."

"Just that if ol' Sam seems like a stand-up guy on this date, I think you ought to let him drive her home."

I frowned. "I thought us girls should stick together."

"Beulah," she whispered in exasperation. "Tiffany is seven months pregnant. She's about to get really big. Let her have a little fun while she can."

And then Ginger winked at me. My mouth hung open. Was she suggesting what I thought she was suggesting? I was still trying to wrap my mind around that when Ginger pressed a stack of crinkly packets into my palm. "You're not too old to have fun, either. You have my permission to make a sinner out of that saint."

My eyes widened to match my mouth. "Ginger Belmont!"

At the sound of Tiffany's sensible shoes clunking on the stairs, Ginger pointed upward, and I stuffed my "gift" into my purse.

The doorbell rang. Ginger hugged Tiffany then pulled me into an embrace.

"Life is short," she whispered. "Life is awful damn short."

Tiffany opened the door to find Sam standing there on the stoop. I might've developed a fondness for chinos, but there's still nothing like a country boy dressed up for a trip into town. Sam Ford played the part well in his nicer denim jeans and freshly ironed button-down shirt. He wore a cowboy hat and boots, and smelled of something Western. Stetson?

He and Tiffany made goo-goo eyes at each other with the door wide-open, letting in the last mosquitoes of the year. But there was someone missing. My heart plummeted to my stomach or somewhere below.

"Um, where's Luke?"

"Luke's coming in a minute, since neither of us has a car that will hold all of us," Sam said sheepishly. That made sense, I supposed. Sam drove an older model pickup, and Luke drove his little two-seater.

"Go on to town, then," Ginger said. "You're letting all the cold air out."

Sam tipped his hat, reminding me of an old-time cowboy, and Tiffany gave us the widest grin I'd ever seen. Peering past the gauzy curtain on the door, I watched Sam escort Tiffany to his pickup then help her up into the cab. Beyond them, dark gray clouds hung on the horizon.

"Don't worry. He'll be here."

I looked at my twinkly-eyed fairy godmother of sorts.

"I don't know what to say to you." I shook my head and tried not to think of the handful of condoms that weighed down my purse.

"I may be old, but I'm not dead," she said. "He's a good-looking man. I should have taken advantage of a few more good-looking men in my time. Before I got too old for that mess."

"You planned this for me just as much as for Tiffany." I wanted to smack myself for being so stupid as not to see it from the get-go. I sucked in a breath. But Luke had seen it. First, my adrenaline soared at the thought that he saw the ruse and went along with it, then those same emotions dipped faster than a determined kamikaze because he wasn't there. Maybe he had changed his mind after our discussion on the porch. Maybe he'd decided he didn't want to be manipulated by a little old lady.

Ginger shrugged. "I gotta do what I gotta do. How many dates have you been on in your life?"

Well, the ill-fated date with Roy, Jr., had been my first date. Then there were a few hookups after hours at The Fountain after Hunter died. As to formal "dates," I could count them all on one hand.

She reached up and pinched my cheek. "I'm not saying you have to marry the man, but I've seen a whole heckuva lot worse. Besides, I have to get you in the habit of dating. No one's going to hand you condoms and push you out the door when I'm gone, and you don't want to end up an old cat lady, do you?"

"I like cats," I sniffed. I couldn't cry or it would ruin my mascara. No doubt that had been part of Ginger's devious plot as well.

Fifteen minutes later, Luke still hadn't shown. I paced the floor as though I'd actually wanted to go on the date. Ginger had wilted into her chair—she hadn't planned on this possibility. The phone rang, and I jumped for it.

"Hello?" My voice was entirely too breathless.

"Beulah, thank goodness. I got a flat tire in Harlowe Bottom where there is no cell reception to speak of. I think I've walked halfway to town trying to get a signal. It'll take me a few minutes longer because I have to walk back to the car and I can't find my tire iron, either."

A flat tire. Of course. Relief washed over me, and I couldn't believe I had even for one minute thought Luke might not show. How could I have doubted him?

"You want me to bring you a tire iron?" I wondered if he could hear the relief in my voice.

"Would you?"

"Of course. I'll be right there."

I had just hung up the phone and grabbed my purse when he called for me again. "Hey, Beulah, why don't you call Tiffany and tell them where we are and to go ahead without us?"

They'd done just that, but my heart warmed at his thoughtfulness. "Okay, I'll text her and be right there."

Luke hung up, and I texted Tiffany. When I looked up, Ginger was smiling at me, the prettiest smile I'd seen in months. "See?"

"Did you arrange for the flat tire, too?"

"No, dear. I can't bend over like I used to, and I'm fresh out of thumbtacks. Now, you go and have fun doing whatever you end up doing. You look beautiful, and I couldn't be prouder of you."

I held out my skirt. Ginger and Tiffany had picked out the sour-apple-green sundress with the Queen Anne neckline. Ginger said it went well with my red hair and green eyes. Tiffany had loaned me her platform sandals to give me some height, and I noticed Ginger wasn't suggesting I exchange them for Dr. Scholl's.

Thunder rumbled in the distance.

"Go, go, Cinderella, before the clock strikes midnight!"

Ginger pulled me down to her height so she could kiss my cheek. I instinctively reached up to rub away the lipstick but noticed she wasn't wearing any and frowned. No eyebrows today, either.

"Go on, quit worrying about me," she said as she sank carefully into her chair. "I'm going to watch some old movies, I think. Maybe something with Cary Grant."

By the time I reached Harlowe Bottom, it was misting. The road stretched flat and straight through the swamp, so I quickly saw Luke's car.

Luke leaned against his little roadster, oblivious to the precipitation. He had jacked the car up, but that was as far as he could get without the tire iron.

I stepped out of the car, and he gave a low whistle. "I had intended to say you were a sight for sore eyes, but that was even before I saw how pretty you're looking tonight."

I blushed to my core. His compliments were far different from the lewd remarks I usually got in The Fountain. Come to think of it, I hadn't heard as much whistling and carrying on in the past few nights. It'd been really, really quiet in there. Almost too quiet.

I handed him the tire iron and he set to work. He was wearing khakis and a polo, a look that had really grown on me. Unfortunately, it was raining harder, and he was destined to ruin the knees of his pants by kneeling on the soft mud of the road's shoulder. "Why don't you get into the car so you don't ruin your dress?"

"I'm not so sweet I'm in danger of melting," I said. "You might need my help."

He wrenched off the flat tire and rustled in his trunk for the spare. The rain pelted us relentlessly, steady enough to make me blink and for drops to roll down my nose.

And then Luke Daniels let loose with a couple of four-letter words that made me giggle.

"Reverend Daniels," I said in my best Southern belle impersonation as I stepped to the trunk to see what had caused such a string of curse words. "I cannot believe such filth would come out of your mouth."

"My spare is flat." He ran his fingers through his hair, and it lay limp on his forehead this time. "What are the odds of that?"

I dangled my keys in front of him. "You can use mine."

Luke headed for my car just as a pickup with only one working headlight eased toward us. I shielded my eyes against the bright light and the rain. It was Mac.

His brakes squealed as he eased to a stop beside me then had to reach over to manually roll down the window. "Hey, there, Beulah. You need any help?"

"I think we've almost got it," I said.

"No, wait!" Luke ran up to the side of the truck. Rain pelted us now. "Got a spare, Mac?"

"Nope, sure don't. Why don't you lock her up and head on home until this mess quits so you don't catch a cold. You can put on a new tire tomorrow."

"Probably a good idea," Luke conceded. I had to agree, since the fall rain was chilling me to the bone.

Mac went on his way, and Luke locked his roadster and put everything in order.

"What's wrong with my spare?" I asked once we were both safe in my car. I shivered from being wet. The Toyota's heater had given up the ghost some time ago so the fan was blowing cool air on me. I reached over to turn it off.

"I think the more appropriate question would be *where* is your spare?" Luke showed only a hint of irritation and waited patiently for the question to register.

Then it was my turn for a string of four-letter words. I have to confess, Luke was quite the amateur on that score, too. I had put the spare on the Caddy last spring, but I had forgotten to transfer it from the Caddy's trunk to mine when we got a new tire.

Luke grinned. "I'd say we're even now."

I guided the car on the road with a squeal of tires. "But I'm not the preacher."

He frowned, and I wished I could take back those words.

When we got to the parsonage, we sat there for a moment. He could send me home, or he could ask me in, but we both knew what had happened the last time he let me through the door.

"Why don't you come in and dry off?" he said.

I started to speak, but I couldn't find the particular words I needed.

"I know it's not what we had in mind, but we can watch a movie and pretend it's a date. I don't know about you, but I've been really looking forward to tonight."

I smiled.

"Unless you're so miserable you need to go home."

"No, I'm not miserable." Which was funny because, although I had always liked piña coladas, I had never much cared for getting caught in the rain. Especially not a cold fall rain. "I think I was looking forward to tonight, too."

"Well, let's go build a fire even if it's not yet October. I'll see if I can find some clothes for you to borrow."

He bolted out of the car before I could contradict him. I stepped out then sat back down in the driver's seat to reach behind and grab my purse.

Even though Ginger's gift couldn't weigh more than a few ounces, my bag still felt weighed down.

Chapter 28

For all of my drunken bravado on a certain night that would live on in infamy, stepping into Luke's house this time scared me. We would be alone, and *things* could happen. To give myself to a man while sober would be new and intentional. To give myself to a man I actually had feelings for would be different still.

Not that Luke tackled me at the door.

No, his eyes held a patient, calculating look.

He offered me some of his old sweats and then closed the door to give me privacy. When I came out of his bedroom, practically swallowed by his Vandy sweatshirt and matching pants rolled up five times, he'd already made a fire. He changed quickly and bustled around the kitchen making a tray of cheese and crackers, veggies and hummus.

"It's not much, but I'd planned to let someone else do the cooking tonight." Ah, there were the dimples.

"Looks like a feast to me." I was mainly glad to have something to do with my hands. I dragged a baby carrot through hummus and wondered what was going through Luke's mind. So he'd been looking forward to the date. What did that mean? He wanted to see the movie or he wanted to see me?

We ate in silence, and I wanted a glass of wine or a beer almost as much as I needed oxygen. I didn't have to look into his fridge to know it was bare. Then I felt guilty for needing such a crutch.

"Trivial Pursuit?" he asked.

I nodded, even though that wasn't the pursuit I'd had in mind.

We played in front of the fire and finally found some small talk about church, the choir, and folks around town. I thought he would cream me at the game, but I won the first round and he won the next. He might have history and sports, but I had entertainment and literature. We split the difference on science and geography.

"Well, I wonder how Tiffany and Sam are doing on their date?" he finally asked while we stared into the fire. I wanted to move to the couch since his sweatshirt was getting warm and I didn't have a T-shirt on underneath, but I didn't want to ruin the moment. It was a moment I'd always envisioned since my relationships with men had been quick and frenzied and never in the least domestic.

"I'd imagine they're getting along just fine," I said.

"And what about you, Beulah? How's your night going?"

I felt his stare on me but kept looking into the fire. My heart hammered. "I'd say it's been close to perfect."

When I forced my eyes to lock with his, I saw hunger. He upended the board as he reached for me, and game pieces rattled across the room. "Not quite perfect."

I expected his lips to crush mine, but he surprised me with a soft-yet-insistent attack. Then he deepened the kiss, which sent my arms around his neck to draw him closer. He pulled me underneath him, and I almost passed out from the unexpected bliss even as my heart raced with that old apprehension. I'd never wanted a man like I wanted him.

I've never really *wanted a man at all.*

The realization skittered down my spine just as his hand reached under my sweatshirt and cupped my breast. I arched into him with a gasp. He yanked his sweatshirt off my body, and it was his turn to gasp at the white lacy confection I'd chosen for a bra.

Turnabout was fair play, so I yanked off his shirt and reveled in the planes of his chest. He picked me up to sit on his lap so we could kiss while skin to skin, and we both groaned at the delicious feel of it. Finally finding my confidence, I pushed him back and straddled him, pinning his hands above his head so I could better explore his jawline. In the past I'd always taken this position, one of control. I had given up my body, but always under my terms.

He flipped me over to return the favor.

My breath caught when his hands clamped down gently over my wrists, but he must have thought it was surprise rather than the first stab of panic.

Kissing me thoroughly, he tested each breast but somehow missed the hammering of my heart underneath. His leg found a particularly sensitive spot at the juncture of my thighs. Pleasure and pain, past and present intermingled, and I couldn't catch my breath. I fought and clawed until I found myself huddled on the couch gasping for breath.

"Beulah?" His beautiful blue eyes widened. Tears coursed down my cheeks, but I only squeaked when I tried to talk.

He sat down at the other end of the couch and tentatively opened his arms, crushing them around me when I crawled over to his side.

"Who hurt you?" The tone of his voice said "Thou shalt not kill" was a commandment he was willing to break.

"I need to go." I tried to scramble out of his embrace, but he held me tighter.

"No. You're not running away from me this time."

"I've got to go. I need to check on Ginger. I—"

"What you mean is you need to run away because I've discovered some kind of deep, dark secret."

You knew at some point you would have to tell him everything. You knew it.

I wrestled against him again, but this time he was expecting it and he held me close for an entirely different reason. I slumped against him. "I was stupid to think for even a minute I had a chance with you."

He had the gall to snort at me. "You're being stupid to think for even a second that you don't. Tell me."

I lay back into his arms, and I told him the whole story from beginning to end. I told him about my parents, about the Vandivers, and about losing Hunter. Almost choking on the words, I told him about my quest for what was so special about sex and how rumors of my sluttiness were greatly exaggerated.

I sat up and looked him in the eye. "And the sad thing is I want to have sex with you right now—just not like that."

He cupped my cheek. "You really know how to stroke a guy's ego, you know that?"

"I know how to stroke something else," I said, planting a hand on his crotch. My words sounded hollow, not my own.

His hand grabbed my wrist, and his eyes turned harsh and dark. "No. Not with me."

The world flickered black. He was going to kick me out now that he knew the full story. He was going to be a goody two-shoes and kick me out. All of the cheese and crackers threatened to come right back up as I scooted to the edge of the sofa. "I'll get my purse."

"Stop running!" His arm held me like a vise. He lifted my chin, forcing me to look into his eyes as he thumbed away the damned tears I couldn't seem to stop. "That's not what I meant. When, if we have sex, it's going to be because you want to and because you're sharing all of yourself, not just your body."

The *when* gave me hope.

"You would still . . . ?"

"What kind of man do you think I am?"

A good one. One who's way too good for me. I swallowed hard. "Right now. I'll give you all of me right now."

"No, no you won't," he said with a sad smile that still managed to show his dimples. I couldn't help but touch them, marvel at them. "Not yet, anyway."

"But someday?"

"Someday," he agreed as he pulled me tighter and planted a

warm kiss on my scalp. The warm feelings cascaded down my head and over my body, a baptism of fire instead of water.

"Hey, you did me a favor," he said with a chuckle after we'd been staring into the fire for quite some time.

"I did?"

"You sorely tempt me. That's twice now I've come close to breaking my vow of chastity."

"What?"

"Fidelity in marriage and chastity while single—that's what we Methodist ministers vow to do. But you make me forget myself."

I blushed. At least I thought that was a compliment, and he still didn't know about the wad of condoms in my purse, red foil, if I remembered correctly. I giggled.

"What's so funny, Miss Land?" he asked while lazily stroking my arm.

"Check my purse."

He reached over to the little table on his side of the couch and came back with my purse.

"Go ahead, look through there and find the little giftie Ginger gave me on my way out the door."

He pulled out the line of condoms and let them dangle in front of us. "Divinity school teaches spirituality, not stamina. I'm not Sting!"

I shrugged and giggled some more as he held up the foil packets even closer. "These don't expire for another two years. We could easily make that . . ."

I froze. Was he saying what I thought he was saying?

"Calm down, woman. We're going to take this one day at a time."

I snuggled deeper into his arms. It felt good to be with a man who knew what he wanted, and that that something was me. Exhausted from unloading my burdens, I fell asleep while he stroked my hair with a relentless tenderness.

Luke took me home at dawn with all of the foil packages intact, but I was happy nonetheless.

* * *

"That was some flat tire," Ginger said as I tried to tiptoe into the house. She had made it as far as her favorite metal chair and was looking wistfully at the coffeepot.

"Need coffee?" I leaned against the counter and tried to figure out by looking at her if it was going to be a good day or a bad one.

"Does a fat baby fart?"

Definitely a good day. Just as long as I got the coffee brewing quickly.

"Those are some nice duds you have there." Ginger sat up a little to read my sweats, winced, and sat back down gently.

"It's not what you think." I already had the coffee brewing and butter sizzling in the skillet. I started cracking eggs.

"Well, that's a shame," Ginger said. "I had such high hopes."

"I'll have to keep your gift for *much* later." I gave her a kiss on the cheek and put a cup of coffee, black with two sugars, in front of her.

"Well, well," Tiffany said with a yawn as she waddled into the kitchen scratching her belly. "Look who's sneaking in early this morning. In a conspicuously large sweatsuit."

"It's *not* what you think," I repeated as I flipped the eggs.

"Mmm-hmmm."

"I'll tell you all about it over breakfast," I said as I opened the loaf of bread and started putting slices in the toaster.

"Bow-chicka-bow-bow," sang Tiffany as she took her seat.

"That's enough."

"Give the girl some details," Ginger said. "She only got a chaste kiss at the door."

My eyes cut to Tiffany, but she looked away. A chaste kiss was all she needed for now, and, despite what I'd said the night before, Luke had given me no more than I needed. Tiffany and I both had a lot to figure out.

"Yeah, Beulah, spill," Tiffany murmured.

"What has gotten into you two?" I slid eggs and toast on plates and placed them in front of my so-called friends. I rustled up butter, jelly, and calcium-fortified orange juice for the pregnant lady.

"We're sitting over breakfast. *Now* tell me all about your date." Tiffany couldn't even wait for me to sit down. She waggled her eyebrows for effect, but her smile didn't quite reach her eyes.

I told them about the flat tire, the Trivial Pursuit, even the long conversations. I didn't get into all of the details since there were parts that Tiffany knew that Ginger didn't and vice versa, but they got the idea. They expressed the proper amount of incredulous indignation at the idea of a celibacy vow, but then Tiffany started mooning about how it was so romantic.

"Uh-oh, they've both got the glow, and it's *not* because they got some." Ginger shook her head.

Tiffany went to the coffeemaker to hide her blush.

"Hey, momma to be, you're not supposed to have that," I said.

Tiffany leveled me with a glare that told me she would eat and drink whatever she damn well pleased. I backed down. It was only half a cup; if she wanted to have that big ol' baby tap dancing on her bladder because he'd been fed caffeine, then so be it.

"What about your date?"

"It was great," she said with a dreamy look before yanking herself back down to earth. "It's a shame."

"What's a shame?" Ginger and I asked in unison before turning to look at each other.

"It's a shame I had to meet him now. Maybe if I'd met him before . . ."

Before would've been a lot easier. I had to give her that.

"I mean, he probably only asked me out as a favor to Luke," she said. "I wouldn't want to date a pregnant woman if I were him."

"But you're not him," I said.

"And he doesn't know the real me, now, does he? How could he, when I'm not even sure who I am?"

I couldn't say anything to that.

"Give him a little time," Ginger said. "You never know what a man's going to do."

Chapter 29

Despite Ginger's warning, both Sam and Luke were very predictable. Sam called Tiffany later that afternoon, and Luke called me that evening. We finally did have a real double date, a trip to the fair, where I learned the good reverend wasn't fond of Ferris wheels—at least not until I gave him a peck on the cheek while we were sitting up top.

October came and went. We did our recording for John the Baptist not long afterward and had to redo an entire song when we realized Sam had been singing while wearing Dracula teeth. I was in love, so dangerously in love I didn't notice what was happening around me. Sure, Tiffany's belly got bigger and Sam got even more protective. Luke brought me flowers and even made me a mix CD that was heavy on the Beatles. But there were other things. Things I should have noticed. The Fountain wasn't as crowded as it used to be, and Ginger stooped a little lower and walked a little slower each day. Sometimes she would wake up from a nap, and it would take her a minute to remember who I was. Then she would make a smart-aleck comment, and I would forget my apprehension.

Then I got two pieces of news on the first of November: one good and the other bad.

My cell phone rang with an unfamiliar number as I was

headed out the door for The Fountain. "Hey, Beulah, this is Derek."

"Who?"

"Derek, from Nashville."

Oops. I should've known that.

"Listen, I have a guy who's looking to do something with a real honky-tonk feel, and he needs a pianist. I immediately thought of you. Think you could come in the first weekend of December?"

"I-I think I can," I said, glad Derek wasn't holding it against me that I'd turned him down.

"We're talking about thirty dollars an hour."

"What?"

"You can start charging more once you have some experience under your belt."

I could make more than that?

I didn't hear the rest of the conversation because I had dollar signs dancing in my head. Derek yammered on about sending me some music to look at. Strictly hush-hush. Then he tacked on a sentence that grabbed my attention. "But I'm sorry about the Happy Hour Choir."

"Oh?"

"Yeah, I tried my best to pitch it, but no one was going for it. If you could show everyone had honestly reformed, you'd probably have the story of the year, but I saw that crew. They're still cussing and drinking. None of the gospel labels want to touch them." He paused for a minute. "You know, you could probably make a fortune, though, if you did your own recording. Make some CDs and sell 'em out of the trunk of your car. That's what you have to do sometimes. To get started, you know."

"Well, thanks for the advice," I said.

"No problem. You've got some things you need to muddle through before you can make a career of it, but I want to be able to say I knew you when."

Muddle through. You have no idea.

And with a distracted good-bye he was gone.

I pulled into The Fountain's parking lot about to bust a seam. How was I supposed to keep such good news to myself?

"Hey, Beulah, can I have a word with you?"

Bill didn't look like himself at all. His face was drawn into a deep frown that accentuated his Droopy Dog jowls. I resisted the urge to manually pull the corners of his mouth up into a smile to match my mood. "What's up?"

He gestured to a stool along the wall. I took one in the corner, and he carefully lowered himself onto the next closest one. "You know I care about you, don't you?"

I stopped fidgeting with the stack of cocktail napkins I was straightening. "Uh-oh. Are you trying to dump me, Bill?"

He picked up his hat, scratched his balding head, and slammed the cap back down. "Dang it! It's not your fault, it's—"

"I know, I know, the old 'it's not you; it's me' speech. Very clever."

"This ain't a joke," Bill bellowed, and I leaned back. I had never heard him lose his temper once.

"Remember a while back when I needed to talk to you? I'm going to have to let you go or close the place down. You and Reverend Daniels have driven all my best customers away."

"What?"

"Well, half the folks in here don't drink like they used to because they go to church, sing in the choir, even go to Bible study, for God's sake. The other half won't come in here because they see your crowd as goody two-shoes."

My happiness faded. I looked out over the bar. Sure, Monday nights were usually slow, but there couldn't be more than five people. Mac couldn't even get a decent poker game going.

"I'm sorry. I never saw this coming, and I doubt Luke set out to run you out of business, either."

"Aw, hell, Beulah, I was getting too old for the honky-tonk business anyway. Marsha tells me she's sick and tired of my long hours. Says she wants to move to Florida."

I shook away the mental image of Bill in Bermuda shorts and sandals with black socks. "What do you think about that?"

He took off his cap again and flattened what was left of his hair before he shoved it back down on his head. "I was born here in Yessum County, and I reckon I'm going to die here. When I die she can find her a new geezer and make *him* move to Florida."

I smiled. "You're a good egg, Bill."

He slugged me lightly on the shoulder. "You're something special, Beulah."

"So this is it?" I stood and played with a loose thread at the bottom of my shirt so I would have something to do with my hands.

"This is it," Bill said. I could have sworn I saw tears in his eyes, but I'm sure he would deny it.

I made it halfway to the piano before I remembered to ask one last question. "How are you going to convince your wife to stay here?"

Bill grinned so wide I could see his silver-capped molars. "Oh, I told her we didn't have enough money. Told her we'd have to open one of them nudey bars right off the Interstate just to make a living."

I grinned back at him but rubbed one pointer finger over the other in the traditional "shame, shame" gesture. He laughed.

When it came time to play "Dwelling in Beulah Land," I stopped to address the crowd. Only a few more folks had shown up. I noticed Bill was running beers from the counter to the patrons, which meant he'd let go of the waitress before me. I hadn't noticed because I'd been so busy being in love.

About twelve or so faces stared at me blankly, and it was the quietest I had ever seen The Fountain on a regular business day. "Folks, this is my last night at The Fountain."

A few people booed.

"Now, now. It's time for me to move on, I suppose." I took a deep breath. "But before I do, I'm going to sing this song one last time. And I'm going to sing it right. And I would appreciate it if you would help me out."

A couple of people actually cleared their throats as I poised my hands over the keys and steeled myself to play my song.

No beer bottles clinked together that night.

The minute Bill decided to close up I gave him a big hug before running across the parking lot to tell Luke my news.

I rapped lightly at first, but he didn't answer the door. I rapped a little harder and heard some stirring. The oddest sense of déjà vu pricked me as Luke came to the door, shirtless once again.

"Beulah, it's three in the morning."

I kissed him and pushed my way in. "I'm sorry, but I had to tell you my good news." I frowned. "And my bad news. Which do you want first?"

"Bad news?" Luke yawned.

"Well, the bad news is that Bill fired me from The Fountain."

"That's great," Luke said. My eyes narrowed, and he took a step back. "I mean, that must be very disappointing for you."

I folded my arms over my chest. "We'll come back to that. The good news is that Derek, the talent scout, has found a gig for me in Nashville on the first of December."

"Oh, Beulah, that's awesome." He picked me up in a bear hug and spun me around.

"It's only a studio musician job," I told him, laughing. "It's not that big a deal."

He stopped spinning me and held on tight to both shoulders. "No, it's a huge deal. When God closes a door—"

"Enough with the preacher mode for now." I kissed him to shut him up. I grinned at him then kissed him then grinned at him some more. Everything with him was the beginning of something great. I couldn't believe I had been lucky enough to finally find a man like Luke.

Then emotions deep within shifted from happiness to need. Luke's hand knotted the hair at the nape of my neck, and suddenly there was no place on earth that was close enough to him.

"Beulah," he murmured.

"Mmm-hmm?"

His hand hesitated just below my bra, and his breath was ragged. "Is it time?"

Was it? Was I ready? Was it a sin? Did I care?

My love for him washed through me, a tsunami to match the tornado of emotions under my rib cage. "Yes, I think so. No. Wait."

I put my hands on his shoulders and pushed him to arm's length. "No. I'm going to walk out that door."

He pulled me close and kissed me again.

"In a minute, I'm going to walk out that door," I murmured as he traced kisses down my neck. My fingers trailed down his muscular arms and wrapped around his waist. And to think, I still had a handful of condoms burning a hole through my purse, too.

"I'm going to leave before we do something *you* regret." I slapped his behind. "But I thought I'd leave you with something to think about."

I slipped out the door with a grin on my face, and I could've sworn I saw the ghost of his smile in the dim kitchen light.

Chapter 30

I still had a grin on my face when I walked through the front door. Light from the TV flashed on the wall behind me, and I tiptoed into the living room to see what Ginger was pretending to watch while she slept. Rick was telling Ilsa maybe not that day, maybe not tomorrow, but someday she would regret not going with Lazlo if she stayed with him.

Fat chance, I thought with all the self-assurance of a woman who had found a noble, self-sacrificing man.

"Ginger." I nudged her shoulder, noticing she'd finally taken off the cheap cardinal necklace and laid it on the end table. "Hey, you need to go to bed."

We had been through this scenario a million times over the years. I would walk in late. She would be asleep in the chair. I would wake her up and help her to her room.

But that night, Ginger didn't stir. She didn't give me a groggy "Wha—?" and pop her dentures back into place. In fact, she wasn't asleep at all. Instead, she stared blankly beyond the television, her eyes not focused.

"Ginger!"

She tried to say something, but I couldn't understand a word. Something wasn't right; something wasn't right at all. Ginger tried to reach for me with both hands but only her right hand came up. And she couldn't talk.

"Tiffany!" I yelled. "We gotta go now!"

She came down the steps so fast I was afraid she would trip and become my second patient for the hospital. As though reading my thoughts, she gripped the handrail and took her steps slower before helping me get Ginger into the Caddy.

As I started the car, I racked my brain, going through the list of possible maladies that could occur to cancer patients or to old people. Only one possibility seemed likely.

"Stroke?" I asked Ginger as I took a corner entirely too sharply. Tiffany reached around the passenger side seat to gently hold Ginger's shoulders in place.

My heart hammered all the way there. Was this it? Was I going to lose Ginger here? Like this? What could I say? What did I want to say? I told myself to say something to make her feel better, to make Tiffany feel better, anything. But I couldn't think of a blessed thing.

We rolled under the ER pavilion on two wheels. Tiffany helped me get Ginger into a wheelchair then took the keys to move the car.

I soon discovered that Medicare and a stroke were a magic combination to get you to the head of triage—well, that and we'd been there so many times it wouldn't surprise me if we hadn't maxed out some kind of secret rewards program.

I followed Ginger back as she went through a series of tests that made me dizzy just to watch. I walked with her from room to room. I squeezed one arm as they took blood from the other. By the time they wheeled her to her own room she had come in and out of consciousness several times. I wouldn't leave her side, but I finally sent Tiffany out to get burgers because she was way too pregnant to pace in a hospital room and hungry enough she was starting to growl. Like a bear.

By morning, Ginger had become more and more lucid, lucid enough to get thoroughly annoyed with her doctor when he came in to check on her. Dr. Perkins, a tall, blond man with a deep cleft in his chin, didn't deserve her rancor but also didn't have any problems ignoring it.

"She appears to have had a transient ischemic attack, but—"

"What's that?" My heart pounded. Anything I would have difficulty pronouncing could not possibly be good.

He winced. "I hesitate to say a small stroke because the prognosis for recovery from a TIA is much better, but that's the general idea. The MRI didn't show anything, but we'll know more when we get some of the other test results back," Dr. Perkins said in his best soap-opera-narrator voice. "Symptoms shouldn't last much longer, but she is at increased risk for another stroke."

"I am sitting right here, you two," Ginger tried to say. I winced at her garbled speech, but I didn't have any trouble understanding her.

"And the tests suggest the cancer may have spread to her brain, although you would need the oncologist to verify that. Has Ms. Belmont exhibited any odd behavior lately? Maybe something uncharacteristic or uninhibited?"

You mean like handing me a wad of condoms and commanding me to sleep with a preacher? "Nothing too weird."

"Hey, hey . . ." Her slurred speech sounded a great deal like Harry Caray, but I knew better than to mention it. Ginger Belmont was a lifelong Cardinals fan.

"Obviously, we'll need to keep an eye on her. Try to get some rest for now."

I put a hand on his jacketed arm before he could leave. "What are her chances for recovery?"

"Oh, she should recover fully from this episode, but she's at greater risk for a bigger stroke or other complications from her cancer."

I swallowed hard and closed my eyes. This wasn't it, but the end was near whether I liked it or not. "Thanks, doc."

He nodded and left to make his rounds.

Ginger mumbled something, but I couldn't understand it. She tried again and I made out, "Should buy stock in this place."

I patted her hand and bit back both my lip and my tears.

"No. Pity."

Those words came out loud and clear, and I looked her straight in the eye. Her beady eyes shone fierce. I nodded, but I had no hope of speaking without breaking down.

Luke poked his head in the door early the next morning and motioned for me to join him in the hall. I tiptoed out and saw he came bearing two large Dunkin' Donuts coffees.

"I love you," I said breathlessly as I took the warm Styrofoam cup in both hands.

He stiffened, and I blushed. "It's an expression?"

"Don't try to explain it." His small smile suggested he wished I'd left it at my first comment.

"Really, thank you for the coffee. The only thing better might be a masseuse, because I'm pretty sure my neck has been permanently damaged by the chair in Ginger's room."

"Maybe we could look into massage later," he said with a twinkle in his eye that caused me to blush all over again. I punched his arm lightly.

"Ouch!"

I punched him again. Harder.

"Now I need a massage," he said as he rolled back the offended shoulder.

"Exactly."

Then it was his turn to blush.

"If you two are done flirting, I thought I might check on Miss Ginger." Tiffany's voice shouldn't have surprised me, but I jumped through the ceiling anyway.

"She's still sleeping, Miss Grumpy-Pants," I said.

"Well, I wouldn't know since *someone* sent me home." Tiffany tried to cross her arms, but she didn't have anywhere to put them but on top of her belly.

"Yes, I wouldn't let the pregnant lady sleep in the hospital chair. I'm an awful human being." I chugged the coffee, ignoring how it burned my tongue. Something else was bothering Tiffany, but I would have to wait to find out what it was because Dr. Perkins came out of the neighboring room. We had to move aside for him to take the chart from the plastic bin outside Ginger's room.

"Is the patient awake yet?" he asked. He had shadows under his eyes. I started to ask him if it'd been a rough night, but I probably didn't want to know the answer.

"Not as of a few minutes ago," I said.

"Well, let's see." He pushed through the door, and I followed him. Ginger's eyes fluttered open. Once again I was struck by how thin she looked underneath the hospital blanket.

"Ms. Belmont." Dr. Perkins turned to her with a small bow. "How are you feeling this morning?"

"Like shit."

That one came out loud and clear. Dr. Perkins didn't miss a beat. "We'll see if we can get you feeling better by lunch then, maybe let you go this afternoon?"

"This afternoon?" My voice echoed off the concrete walls, and the good Dr. Perkins shot me a lethal look.

"I know this has been a traumatic event, but you are going to have to be calm for her sake. She's already doing much better, and the symptoms should abate in less than twenty-four hours. You need to conserve your energy and be more concerned about trying to prevent any future strokes that could be more serious."

I looked at Luke then Tiffany as Dr. Perkins spoke with Ginger, murmuring to her as he checked her vitals. He brushed past us with an admonition to have a good day, and Tiffany plopped down in my chair and took knitting out of her purse.

I shook my head as I watched her labor over what appeared to be a baby bootie.

"What?" Her brows scrunched over her eyes in a "Wanna make something of it?" expression. She was holding knitting needles, so make something of it I did not.

"Nothing," I said with a shrug. I should have been happy a

tavern waitress had taken up knitting. I shouldn't have felt as though another part of my past life was missing. I looked over to where Luke leaned against the wall nursing his coffee, and, suddenly, I didn't miss anything at all.

"You know, I didn't think to bring something for you ladies—want me to walk back across the street and get a coffee and—" Luke looked at Tiffany. "A hot chocolate?"

"That would be wonderful," she said.

We didn't have to look at Ginger to know how she felt about the hospital's decaf.

"I'll be right back," he said.

Ginger struggled to sit up and said something I couldn't understand.

"I'm sorry, Ginger, try that one again?"

I couldn't make out everything, but I picked out "saint" and "sinner," and the twinkle in Ginger's eyes helped me figure out the rest. I felt the heat of my blush start somewhere around my collarbone and rise all the way up to my ears and across my cheeks.

Ginger half laughed and half gurgled.

"What?" Tiffany put down her needles with a definitive clack and stood to see what the fuss was about. Ginger used her good hand to form an O with her bad hand, then with her good hand she pointed to me then put her finger into the half-formed O.

"You did not!" Tiffany gasped as she looked me over with wide brown eyes.

At the rate I was blushing, I was in danger of turning purple. "Not yet."

"Not yet means someday!" Tiffany squealed and clobbered me with a full body hug. The baby kicked me for good measure, creating an echo of longing in my own womb.

I looked over Tiffany's shoulder to where more than half of Ginger's mouth smiled. Even when it should be all about her, it became about others. I would be lucky if I could ever figure out how to be more like Ginger Belmont.

"I forgot to ask how Miss Ginger likes her contraband coffee."

All of us turned to see Luke standing in the doorway. "Why are you all grinning?"

It was the good reverend's turn to blush, although his eyes caught mine. "Do you women have to share everything?"

I held up my hands in surrender. "I didn't say a word."

He nodded with a smile. "Sure you didn't."

Ginger used her good hand to point to herself. I prayed she wouldn't use the crude gesture again.

"Oh, so you're the troublemaker, eh?"

She nodded slowly.

"Then I suppose I shouldn't go get you any coffee, huh?"

Her eyes widened, and she used her good hand to draw half a halo over her head.

"Black with two packets of sugar," I said with a grin.

"Done," Luke said before pointing two fingers at his eyes and then at Ginger. "But I'm watching you."

That afternoon Luke helped us get Ginger home since I didn't want the massively pregnant lady lifting people, even if the person in question was as light as a feather.

Ginger, unfortunately, was a little loopy and kept asking Luke if he'd finally got laid.

"Is she asking what I think she's asking?" Luke handled her with care, and I couldn't look at his hands without thinking of other places they had been.

"Mmm-hmm." I didn't want to make eye contact with him, either.

Tiffany went ahead to unlock the door, and the rest of us crossed the threshold, an awkward threesome. Luke and I panted as much from trying to maneuver three people through the door as from the exertion of carrying Ginger.

"Hey, Tiffany, could you be a sweetheart and start a pot of coffee?" I asked as I read a text from John the Baptist saying he'd mixed the Happy Hour Choir CD for us and that I could pick it up whenever. It took me a minute to realize the house was too quiet. And smoky.

Tiffany stood stock-still at the edge of the kitchen, not hearing or, at the very least, not acknowledging.

Luke helped me ease Ginger into the chair.

"Tiffany?"

I tasted panic—the bitter, metallic taste of anticipation gone wrong. Did her water break? Was she going into premature labor? Had she hurt herself helping me with Ginger?

Then I saw Carl Davis sitting at the breakfast room table. He was smoking a cigarette and dumping the ashes into one of the dainty saucers from Ginger's fine china. An ornate collector's pistol sat beside the saucer. His knobby fingers hesitated nearby.

"You're looking good, Tiff-Tiff." His stone-cold demeanor repulsed me more than his drunken delirium had.

I touched Tiffany's arm to get her attention. "Why don't you run upstairs?"

"Hey, I got something to say to you, girl."

She stopped at the bottom stair and turned around. I wanted to stand between her and her stepdaddy. I wanted to tell her to run upstairs and never listen to another thing that came out of his mouth. But I couldn't. This was her fight. I could support her, but I couldn't fight it for her.

Something crashed to the ground out of Carl's line of sight, and he picked up the pistol and pulled the hammer back. I looked behind me to see Luke in the living room with the phone in his hand. "Knocked over some books. That's all."

I nodded slightly before I turned back to Carl. I gauged the distance between him and me then between me and the closet where the shotgun sat, fully loaded and ready.

"It's time to come home." He took another drag of his cigarette, exhaling a plume of smoke in Ginger's smoke-free house.

Tiffany couldn't speak.

"She is home, Carl." Ginger's voice came out clear as a bell. "Now, you need to go."

He narrowed his eyes at Ginger, and I stepped between the two of them. "You heard the lady. You're in violation of our restraining order as well as having broken and entered—"

"Just entered. I ain't broke nothing. Yet." Carl pointed the gun at me. His finger curled around the trigger.

"Is that a threat?" Luke stepped in front of me. He was stalling, but he was also ready to take a bullet if he needed to. "Four witnesses. I'd leave if I were you."

Carl stood. "Well, you aren't me, now, are you, pretty boy? I ain't gonna let you or anyone else take what's mine."

"I'm not your property."

We all turned to Tiffany. Her knuckles shone white against the newel ball. She lost her balance, and it came off in her hand. Carl swung the gun to face her, and Luke backed me out of the way. Carl took one step toward Tiffany, but she took the newel ball and wound her arm in a flash of movement to give a quick, hard, underhanded pitch. The ball whizzed past me and smacked into Carl's forehead. As he fell backward, he hit the back of his skull on the table with a sickening thud before crumpling to the floor. His glassy eyes stared up at the ceiling, his mouth agape in an eerie way.

Sirens wailed in the distance.

Tiffany grabbed her side and sat down on the stairs and cried.

The police report later said that no one else—well, maybe Roger Clemens—could have thrown that newel ball with the same amount of force. The ball to the forehead felled him, but the blow to the back of the head on the table killed him. In the official report, Len left out the part where I described Tiffany's pitch as a thing of beauty, but she had hurled that newel ball with ferocious grace. One would expect no less from a highly ranked fastpitch softball prospect even if she was eight months pregnant.

While Declan Anderson put the body on a gurney and took Carl off to a more respectful burial than he deserved, Tiffany spilled her entire story to them, and I held her hand as she did. Luke, Ginger, and I also gave our statements. In the end, they decided Tiffany had acted in self-defense—especially since Carl had brought a gun. I bit my tongue to keep from saying I only wished she could have acted in self-defense a lot sooner.

Tiffany was officially cleared of all wrongdoing not long before Thanksgiving, so we were all looking forward to the holidays. Luke and Sam were going to join us, and Ginger joked about finding a man who liked women with really short Brillo pad hair so she could have a date, too.

She tried to pretend she was fine, but I had a lot of time to watch over her that November, since I only worked at the church on Sundays and picked up just enough weddings and funerals to keep us afloat. She wouldn't do anything when she knew I was looking, but I came home from the grocery store early one day to see Declan Anderson in the living room going over funeral arrangements with her yet again. The man had the patience of Job.

Another day I caught Ginger with more masking tape, putting little stickers on the backs of books, dishes, even pieces of furniture. I asked her if I could help, but she smiled and said, "No, thank you." No explanation, no nothing.

And then there were the letters each morning. She would write as long as her arthritis allowed her. Her handwriting bobbled all over the place, and she stuck her tongue out a little as she wrote, reminding me of a second grader learning to write in cursive.

"So," I finally said one day. "When are you going to let me read this letter you've been working so hard on?"

She looked up from the letter, her nonexistent eyebrow raised. "When are you going to get a full-time job?"

We both knew the answer to that question, but neither of us wanted to say it, so we kept up our game of her hiding things and me spying on her all the way to Thanksgiving. Of course, if I'd known then what was in her letter, I might not have waited so long to read it.

Might have saved us all a lot of trouble.

Chapter 31

The first person at the door on Thanksgiving morning was Luke. He took one step into the house, dipped me like Fred dipped Ginger, and kissed me the way Rhett kissed Scarlett.

"Well, I know what I'm thankful for today," I said once I was back in an upright position.

"You two really need to get a room," Tiffany groused on her way to the kitchen. I wanted to shout after her that she was just jealous, but I held my tongue. Then I marveled at how I had held my tongue. Then Luke decided to occupy my tongue a little while longer.

"Seriously," added Ginger, who was leaning on a walker but moving around like a pro. "Can a gal get some coffee first?"

"Someone's jealous," I whispered to Luke.

"As a minister, I know I'm supposed to feel sympathy for them," he whispered back. "But I don't."

"You know who you should feel sorry for?"

His eyes narrowed with concern. "Who?"

"The turkey." I grabbed his hand and led him into the kitchen. I had started getting the bird ready at six in the morning, but I still needed to check on him from time to time. Luke stood to the side as I opened the oven, inspected my handiwork, and decided to use the baster to add more moisture.

"How is ol' Bill?" Ginger took a dainty sip of her coffee.

Luke looked at her in confusion. "Bill?"

"Yeah, Bill ended up with two turkeys *somehow*," Tiffany said with a pointed look at me. "And he gave one to Beulah so she named the turkey after him."

"That was nice of him," Luke said. "Well, Bill the man, that is."

As I used the baster to suck up butter and turkey juice then squeeze it over Bill the turkey, I hoped Bill the man wasn't feeling the effects in some odd voodoo sort of way.

The toaster oven dinged, and I retrieved the previously canned cinnamon rolls. Luke looked at me as he slid Bill back into the oven.

"Yup, this is the sort of great cooking you could look forward to with me," I said as I spread the glaze over the hot rolls. I had meant it as a joke, but Luke's gaze grew intense.

"Something the matter?" I asked.

He shook it off. "Why is the Macy's Thanksgiving Day Parade not on? Unacceptable!"

He jogged to the living room to turn on the television then to open the door when the doorbell rang to announce Sam's arrival. Tiffany ran to Sam, but she had to hold an arm under her massively pregnant belly to do so. She leaned up for a kiss like mine but only got a chaste peck on the cheek.

"Go ahead and kiss her good," Ginger yelled from the table. "Luke and Beulah were making out in the foyer."

"We were not!" I narrowed my eyes at Ginger. I still loved her despite the effects of her brain tumor—in some ways I could only love her more. Sure, her uninhibited speech was at the bottom of the list, but at least I had a companion for my nightcap.

"Yeah, you were," Tiffany said over her shoulder before she turned and pulled Sam down for a kiss that gave us a run for our money. He blushed a new and exciting shade of red, one of the deepest shades of red I'd ever seen on a human being.

Tiffany took him by the hand and led him into the living room to watch the parade. They snuggled up to each other on the couch.

"You should make her get in here and help," Ginger grumbled under her breath.

I topped off her coffee. "She's going to have her hands full in a month or so. Let her rest while she can." I looked over my shoulder to yell, "Tiffany, get your feet up on that coffee table before they swell up!"

Ginger smiled and took my hand. "I always think I couldn't be any prouder of you, but you keep on surprising me."

Tears stung my eyes. What could I say to that? Not a damn thing, so I stood there in the kitchen and held her hand as long as she would let me.

"I love you, Beulah Lou." She squeezed my hand.

"I love you, too, Ginger." I choked out the words. "I love you so much more than you will ever know."

She squeezed my hand again and winked. "I think I have a pretty good idea. Now, I think I'm going to go into the living room and ignore those skinny-ass, knob-kneed Rockettes long enough to take a nap."

I pulled her walker in front of her. "But what about the dressing?"

"I think it's time for you to take over the dressing," she said with a yawn. My heart hammered against my chest. She was going to die during her nap; that's why she was being so sappy and was finally ready to give over the secret dressing recipe. "But, Ginger—"

"Oh, calm the heck down." She and the walker moved rhythmically across the kitchen floor toward the living room. "The recipe is in the pantry under the jar of pickles. Good luck deciphering it."

Under the pickles. There was a place Ginger knew I'd never look because I hated pickles almost as much as she did. I fished to the back of the pantry and picked up the lone dusty jar of most likely expired pickles. Sure enough, a ragged index card sat underneath. I took the card and scanned it.

"How am I supposed to make heads or tails out of this?"

She lay back in the recliner, her eyes already closed. "Sometimes you have to feel for what's right."

I took a deep breath. If I had known I was going to have to wing the Thanksgiving Day dressing, I would have practiced a week ago. I couldn't do this. I couldn't come up with the perfect combination on the very first try.

I muttered the ingredients to myself, a Southern woman's incantation: "cornbread, biscuits, eggs, chicken broth, diced onion, sage, Pepperidge Farm stuffing mix, cream of chicken, celery. Celery? I am *not* putting that in there."

The index card was full of notes on the side like, *Use cream of chicken to add more flavor* or *Some yuppies add thin slices of apple to add moisture.* The amount of eggs was five, which was marked out and a four added. Then the four was crossed out, and a three stood to the side next to a glob of something that looked suspiciously like cream of chicken.

I could do this. I could figure this out. I had the cornbread sitting on the stove from the night before. I had leftover biscuits in the freezer. I could do it. I would figure it out.

"Whatcha so tense about, Beulah?" Luke's voice caused me to jump.

"Oh, sorry." My hand traveled to my throat. "Ginger has informed me I will be making the dressing."

"And?"

"I've never made the dressing before."

"And?"

"It's the second most important part of Thanksgiving after the turkey!" I hissed. "No, I like the dressing better than the turkey. If I don't get the dressing right, I'll ruin Thanksgiving!"

He kissed me on the forehead. "No, the most important part of Thanksgiving is giving thanks. That would put the dressing at least second on the list. And you're going to do great."

"But what if I ruin it?" I shoved my hands into my jeans pockets to keep from wringing them.

Luke took me by the shoulders. "Do you like to eat dressing?"

"Yes, of course!"

"Then you can make dressing. You just have to have a little faith."

I chewed on my lip. "We're not talking about dressing anymore, are we?"

He kissed me on the lips. Gently. "Nope."

He went to check on Bill—the bird, not the man—and I thought about every time I'd watched Ginger make dressing. I got out the biggest bowl we had and started crumbling cornbread and biscuits then added what seemed to be the right amount of stuffing mix. I decided to leave out the onions as well as the celery. I left out the sage because the stuffing mix already had some in it. I added salt and pepper, four eggs instead of three, and kept adding chicken broth and cream of chicken soup until it looked right.

It looked about as sloppy as it did when Ginger poured it into the pan. It smelled right. I guessed it couldn't hurt to say a little prayer that it came out edible for everyone, then I poured the soupy concoction into the pan. I slid the pan into the oven, careful not to spill any over the sides.

Every now and then I would look into the living room to see what balloon was passing by or, later, to see if the Detroit Lions were going to pull out an unlikely victory. For the most part, however, I stayed in the kitchen, checking on green beans, peeling potatoes, and putting them on to cook. I made a corn soufflé and a sweet potato casserole. Then I had Luke put the marshmallows on top.

"Stop eating them! And put them closer together," I commanded.

He popped another marshmallow into his mouth while looking me dead in the eye, and I slugged him on the arm.

"Ow! You're going to be a tough momma. Tough, but fair!"

He turned back to the task at hand, and I wondered if I would ever get to be a momma. If Hunter had lived he would have been ten, going on eleven. I tried to picture an energetic boy jumping on the couch cushions in the living room while watching the parade with his aunt Tiffany and uncle Sam, but the picture wasn't there.

My Hunter would always be a baby to me, a sweet, sweet baby with intense blue eyes. He would always be a newborn who never got a chance to smile or to sit up. Luke slid up behind me and kissed me on the top of the head. "I'm sorry I said that. I didn't mean to make you think about what might have been."

"How do you do it?" I wheeled around on him.

"How do I do what?"

"How do you always know what I'm thinking? What I've been through? Are you psychic?"

"Beulah, you wear your heart on your sleeve. I don't know where you got the idea you were some kind of tough guy, because your emotions are always out there for anyone to read. It's one of the reasons I love you."

His eyes widened. He hadn't meant to say that, to put himself out there quite yet. My heart was a jackhammer on a particularly stubborn piece of concrete. What could I say?

"Luke Daniels, I have loved you from the moment you walked into The Fountain looking like a khaki fish out of water, even if I did try really hard not to at first."

"Hmm. Maybe I'm an acquired taste, too."

He kissed me again just in time for Tiffany to waddle into the kitchen in search of a snack. "Geez, would the two of you get a room? For real."

We sat down at the table, and Luke blessed the food. As we ate, we had to tell at least one thing we were thankful for—a Ginger Belmont house rule.

"I'm thankful I got transferred here to Ellery and that I met all of you," Luke said with a grin as he looked straight at me.

"I'm thankful I got to quit being a waitress even if I had to get pregnant to get out of it. And I'm really glad I met you, Sam." Tiffany took out a scoop of corn soufflé and passed him the casserole.

"Your turn," Ginger said to him.

He cleared his throat and loosened his already unbuttoned collar. "I think I'd like to go last," he said.

"Fine." Ginger shrugged. "Beulah, it's your turn."

I was sampling the dressing because I hadn't expected it to be my turn already. It was divine. "I am thankful for Luke, and for you, and for having Tiffany come into our lives. And I'm thankful the dressing came out right. And for you, too, Sam."

"Glad to see the dressing rates higher than me," he muttered. Then he took a bite of the dressing and nodded in my direction. "Okay, the dressing does rate better than me."

Tiffany slapped him lightly on the arm.

"I'm thankful for so many things," Ginger said. "I'm thankful for a long life and good friends. I'm thankful the good Lord sent me Beulah, even if I didn't like the way He did it. I'm thankful Tiffany's safe and sound and that we have two strapping young boys to improve the scenery around here. Most of all, I'm thankful to have made it this far, and I'm looking forward to seeing Tiffany's baby."

"Here, here," I said as I raised my glass of sweet tea. We all clinked our glasses around the table.

"Sam," Ginger said, "your turn."

I frowned. Maybe Sam was a little shy about such things; I knew I was when I first moved in with Ginger. Maybe—

"It's true I'm thankful for all of you," Sam said. "And I'm so happy I was singing in the Piggly Wiggly that day and that I got up the courage to go to Bible study at the bar and join the choir when Beulah asked me because if I hadn't then I would have never met you."

Then that tall, lanky boy dropped down to one knee. "Tiffany Davis, will you do me the honor of becoming this poor farmer's wife?"

Too much, too soon? I bit my tongue. They'd figure it out if it was.

Something bumped under the table, and we all gasped that Tiffany had hit her belly. "Yes, yes, a million times yes!"

She scanned our faces looking for happiness, then our concern over the bump registered. "It was my knee, y'all."

"Thank goodness," Ginger muttered, and we all clapped and cheered. Even better, Tiffany finally got her PG-13 kiss.

We ate happily until we could do nothing more but lay on the couch, chair, and floor like a group of beached whales. Tiffany held out her hand and watched her modest diamond twinkle while Sam dozed with a protective arm around her shoulders. Ginger snored softly in her recliner, holding her breath before each one in a way we'd all learned to live with. I cheered for the Cowboys, while everyone else napped. At halftime I looked up to see Luke's seat empty.

When I entered the kitchen, there he stood with his sleeves rolled up, rhythmically washing dishes.

A ping of desire shot through me, no longer an unwanted or alien feeling. "What are you doing?"

"The dishes."

"Obviously. I was going to get those in a while," I said.

"Yes, but you did the cooking, and you were watching the game."

I cocked my head to one side. To my father, football on Thanksgiving Day was a sacred tradition only to be interrupted by the large meal he ate between the two games. I had never seen him wash a dish. "But don't you want to watch the game, too?"

"I'll watch the fourth quarter, since that's the only part that counts," he said with a smile. "You go rest."

I dare any woman to say there's anything sexier than a smiling man with his sleeves rolled up and his hands in the sink. I thought that then, and it holds true today.

If only that Thanksgiving, one of the best days of my life, could've lasted a little longer.

Chapter 32

We put up the tree later that weekend, an artificial monstrosity from when Ginger had had chemo before and her immune system had been too compromised for a real one. Luke and Sam took turns helping to decorate the top of the tree or to string lights outside. By the end of November, all we needed were some gingerbread cookies, Santa, and December. Ginger was walking about, sometimes with a cane instead of the walker, and we were thankful for that early Christmas gift. Tiffany was due at the end of the month, and I couldn't remember a Christmas I had been happier. Not even Day-to-Night Barbie was going to top this one.

On the Friday before my recording session I sat down at the table with Ginger to chat about my trip to Nashville. She had me making French toast that morning. And she knew how I felt about the stuff, but at least I was making it instead of her—that made me feel much better. In fact, she was working the crossword puzzle in the paper and sipping her coffee like a lady of leisure.

"Beulah, what's his name? 'The Entertainer.' " Her face wrinkled even more as she screwed it up while her brain grasped for an answer she should have known.

"Scott Joplin." I turned back to the stove, frowning. Ginger had taught me about Scott Joplin, and now she couldn't remember his name? The tumor had to be getting worse.

"Are you sure you don't mind if I go? It should be an up-'n'-back if I leave early enough in the morning."

She looked up from the paper and peered over her reading glasses at me. "I'm fine. You're only a couple of hours away."

"Basically, three hours away, and—"

She waved away my concern. "You need a job and this is what you've always wanted to do. Besides, I have Tiffany here, and I was thinking about catching up on all of my favorite Christmas movies."

"*White Christmas*?" I flipped each piece of toast for what would be the last time.

She drew a hand over her heart. "Of course!"

"*Holiday Inn*?"

"You know I'm a sucker for old Bing."

"*Rudolph* and *Frosty*?" I slid the first piece onto a plate.

"Classics." She looked back at her crossword puzzle.

With a sly smile I slid pieces two and three onto separate plates and reached into the microwave for the bacon. "*It's a Wonderful Life*?"

That got her attention, and she looked up at me with a frown. "I just don't see what the big deal is on that one. Jimmy Stewart off stuttering around and complaining about his life. And we don't even know for sure if everything turns out all right in the end. Maybe the angel should've let him be."

"Hey, we all want to feel like we've made a difference in this world." I shrugged as I slid a plate of French toast in front of her.

"And you call me the sentimentalist," she said, her fork poised and her penciled-in eyebrow arched. I exhaled at the sight of Ginger with lipstick and eyebrows—even her clip-on faux-pearl earrings. Today was going to be a good day.

She took a bite. "This is not bad. Not bad at all. You can cook some French toast if you want to."

"Thanks," I said as I slipped some bacon onto a plate for Tiffany then some onto my own. "As I always say, I learned from the best."

"Tiffany!" I hollered upstairs before sliding into my spot and taking a bite of bacon.

Ginger studied me. "You need to give your momma a little more credit."

I almost choked. She had waited for me to take a bite to say that. "Aw, why do you have to ruin a pleasant morning by bringing up my mother?"

"I bet she's lonely without you and your daddy," she said as she took another bite. We heard the flutter of wings as birds squawked at the bird feeder outside the window. A lone blue jay was trying his darnedest to run off our cardinals.

I thought of the stoop-shouldered, gray-haired woman my mother had become. I thought of the identical lilies she had placed on both Hunter's grave and my father's. "Yeah, well, she should have thought about that before she got out her spoon without hearing my side of the story."

"You could tell her your side of the story," Ginger said.

My fork hit my plate. She didn't even know the whole story. Did she? I looked straight into her bleary, cataract-filmed eyes, and I said some words I regret to this day: "Making up with my momma is not a favor I will do for you, so don't even ask."

She shrugged and went about her breakfast as though I hadn't hurt her feelings, but, of course, I had.

Tiffany barged into the kitchen either not noticing our tense moment or not caring. She fixed herself a half cup of coffee then sat down at the table with us. "I LOVE French toast! Beulah, did you make this?"

I nodded.

She took a bite and closed her eyes, savoring her breakfast with an idiotic grin. "I think this is the closest thing to heaven on this earth."

Ginger sniffed. "Chocolate-chip pancakes would be closer."

The next day I had to leave for Nashville before five in the morning, so I tiptoed out the front door to avoid waking anyone else up. I didn't need coffee because I was so keyed up by the possibility of playing the piano in a real studio for a real song that was going to be on a real album or, even better, played on the radio.

My iPod was crammed with road songs, everything from "I Can't Drive 55" to "Route 66." I jammed along with each song, easily switching genres. I was singing a particularly spirited rendition of "Eastbound and Down" when the phone rang.

I recognized the number, and my heart soared. "Luke, I just made Nashville city limits while singing Jerry Reed! How cool is that!"

"Beulah—"

"I'm almost to the recording studio, and—" As usual, my mouth was about ten miles ahead of my brain. Halfway through that sentence, my brain registered the tone of his voice. "This isn't a social call, is it?"

"You might want to pull over."

"Spit it out. Is it Ginger? Did she fall or something? Oh, no, Tiffany. She's not due for another few weeks—she's not already in labor, is she?"

"Beulah, pull over."

"I'm on the freaking interstate doing sixty in six lanes of traffic. I can't exactly pull over right now, so you're going to have to tell me."

"Ginger passed away some time this morning."

Cars streaked past me on either side. People laid on their horns behind me, and I realized I had taken my foot off the gas. I eased the car to the shoulder in a zigzag pattern. And I didn't care.

She had been sleeping so peacefully when I left.

It was only going to be for a day.

"What . . . ?"

"Another stroke, a bad one. She'd passed by the time Tiffany found her, but the doctor said she didn't suffer. It was instantaneous."

That damn French toast. She made me make the French toast. I will never, ever make French toast again as long as I live, because she knew. She somehow knew, and she sent me off to Nashville anyway because she wouldn't know how to be selfish if she tried.

Because she really wanted chocolate-chip pancakes.

"I'm coming home."

"But," Luke hesitated, "what about your recording session?" His agony on my behalf would have comforted me if I had been capable of receiving comfort at that moment.

"I'll call them and tell them I can't come. Either they'll understand or they won't."

He paused on the other end. "Let me come get you. I don't think you need to be driving right now."

"I'm not a baby. And I couldn't stand to sit still and wait for you anyway. I'm driving home. Now."

"Beulah, be care—"

I hung up on him. My first instinct was to dive across those lanes of traffic straight into the concrete pylon, but I took several deep breaths. Then the sobs came. Deep, body-racking sobs. I slammed my head into the steering wheel, and my Toyota wailed, too. Drivers answered with short, angry beeps.

I had to make it home.

I forced myself to take long, deep breaths to keep panic's hyperventilation away.

I had to see to arrangements.

I had to take care of Tiffany.

Pulling back on to the interstate, I told myself to find an exit where I could turn around. Tears streamed down my face, but I swiped them away as fast as I could.

By the grace of God, I made it home.

Chapter 33

The next few days passed in a blur—an awful, terrible blur. A tornado touched down on the other side of town, but it didn't do too much damage. That night I didn't even bother going down to the cellar. I half thought it would be easier if the damned thing took me up to be with Ginger.

And Hunter.

Ginger had thought of everything. Declan Anderson had extensive notes of her final wishes, things she hadn't wanted to bother me about. She had picked out every song, every type of flower, what dress she was to wear. She had made arrangements for where she was to be buried and had paid for everything she could in advance. On one hand, it was one of the kindest gifts she could've given me. On the other, arrangements would have given me something to do other than sit around and stare at the sealed envelope she'd left for me.

At the very least I had plenty of time to call Derek back and explain why I hadn't shown up. He was more understanding than I deserved and said he'd keep me in mind for the future. I had a feeling that this second chance would be my last.

On the day of the funeral, I sat in one of the folding chairs to the side of the casket. Anderson's Funeral Home was older than Potter's, and a temporary partition separated the family section from the chapel proper. I had never been so glad for something to hide me from prying eyes.

Mournful chime music set at a glacial pace poured through the funeral home speakers. I gritted my teeth, glaring at the closed silver casket as Luke squeezed my hand. I looked at him and saw tears threatening to spill from his eyes, too.

At first it surprised me that Luke wasn't delivering the eulogy, but Ginger would have known I needed him beside me. Instead, she chose Walter Massengill, an ancient preacher who had been at County Line for the better part of thirty years. An octogenarian, Brother Walter stooped as he reached the podium, his white hair flying out from his head.

"We gather here to celebrate the life of Ginger Belmont, one of the finest ladies I've ever known." He cleared his throat, and the tears I'd been holding back spilled over in a flood. Luke drew me to him, and I sobbed quietly through the eulogy.

Brother Walter talked of highs and lows, things Ginger had done long before I knew her. He told stories of how she'd played rock and roll at the school dance and been banned from playing piano there. Just as a grin broke through my tears, he added a passage about rejoicing when our friends die, adding, "And I'm sure Ginger is in heaven and would want us to rejoice."

Anger choked me. How were we supposed to find these wonderful people then celebrate when we lost them? The more I thought about "celebrating" Hunter's death or "celebrating" Ginger's death, the greater that ball of anger became.

And then there was Luke. If some freak accident took him from me, would he want me to "celebrate" his passing? Maybe we'd both be better off if I didn't give us the chance to find out.

My entire chest burned as we walked outside to get into our cars, the cars that would follow immediately behind the black hearse.

"Beulah?" Luke asked as he slid behind the driver's seat of his ridiculous roadster. At least he was smart enough not to ask me if I was okay. No, I was not okay. I would never be okay.

I thought about letting my anger flow out like lava, but I

couldn't. I didn't want to lose Luke the man and have Luke the minister show up. My heart squeezed in my chest. Luke the man had been my constant companion for the past couple of months, and I loved him with all of my being.

But Luke the minister was always there, and he reminded me of who I was and who I had been.

If I blew my top, Luke the minister would show up. If I kept my rage inside, I would implode. I'd have to chance imploding.

I shook my head no, and he respected my wishes not to talk.

Luke held my hand as we walked from the parking lot to the corner spot of County Line Cemetery where Ginger's plot lay. The tent rustled in the cold breeze, and I drew my winter coat closer. He draped an arm around me as folks paid their last respects and the casket was placed into its protective lead casing then lowered into the ground. As if anything could protect us from what would inevitably happen. Nothing mortals did could protect a body from turning on itself.

Luke squeezed my hand as we turned to go. "Beulah, are you sure you feel up to this?"

I nodded affirmatively. Of course, I didn't want to play at Ginger's "going-away party," but doing so was a part of her explicit instructions. She wanted us to celebrate her passing, and she had even picked out a sound track.

Out of the corner of my eye I saw the wild salt-and-pepper hair of my mother only seconds before she was in front of me. "Beulah."

"Mother," I said. Luke put a reassuring hand on my shoulder.

"I'm sorry." She stared through me, leaving me to wonder if she was sorry about Ginger, about disowning me, or both. Ginger's words came back to me: *You could tell her your side of the story.*

Not today, Ginger.

"Thank you," I choked out. She hugged me fiercely then patted me on the shoulder before walking off. I was too stunned to call her back, and I still wasn't sure I wanted to.

Maybe tomorrow, Ginger.

Focusing on The Fountain, I crossed the street with Luke's

help. Asking me to play piano was one thing. Asking me to make up with my mother on the same day as Ginger's funeral would require more beer than Bill had on hand.

Ginger had known I wouldn't be able to think of songs to play, so she had provided a list. I took a deep breath and looked at the first item: *"Just a Closer Walk with Thee"—jazzy.*

Fortunately, my fingers knew the song far better than I did. People milled around The Fountain, a subdued crowd, but a larger one than I'd ever seen. Bill pulled at his suspenders when he wasn't pouring out libations.

From her first request I moved to "In the Sweet By and By," and Sam was kind enough to duet with me. Halfway through, the anger in my chest loosened. Ginger had wanted me to play because she knew. She knew I poured myself into what I played. She knew playing would ease the pain.

Or was she looking for a good excuse to get a bunch of teetotallers into The Fountain? For a minute I imagined Ginger looking down on our little party and cackling so hard she cried. Miss Lottie, Miss Lola, and Miss Georgette were all tipsy. They had opted for the punch in the corner, not knowing it had been liberally laced with Southern Comfort.

Miss Georgette stumbled over to where Bill stood right in front of me. "What is your punch recipe? I really must know."

He stifled a grin. "Aw, Miss Georgette, it's something Marsha cooked up."

And that part was true. Except for the part where Marsha *hadn't* added the Southern Comfort. That had been the Gates brothers. Bill had only looked the other way while they did it.

I played hymns about grace, hymns about our truth marching on, and hymns about laying our burdens down by the riverside. Then I delved into some of Ginger's favorites: "Moonlight Serenade," "St. James Infirmary," and a slew of Johnny Mercer.

While I rambled through an instrumental version of "Accentuate the Positive," John the Baptist came over with a friendly smile. "I got your CD made."

"Thank you! I do appreciate it even if I forgot to come by."

"I know," he said, his eyes kind as ever. "I would've waited for you, but I thought you might want it now."

Of course. It was the only link to Ginger's voice that I had. My eyes filled with tears as I whispered thank you again. Despite my sorrow, the tavern-goers reached a raucous happiness thanks to both the punch and the liberal amounts of wine and beer I had yet to sample. More people arrived than had even been at the funeral: Goat Cheese, the Satterfields, and all sorts of people I didn't recognize, people who'd no doubt taken lessons from Ginger over the years. My numb fingers hit the keys clumsily, but I had no intention of quitting.

Then the cuckoo clock sounded in the corner.

The chorus of "All You Need Is Love" once again hung in the air unresolved as my head snapped toward Bill.

No one spoke.

"I promise I unplugged it just like you asked." Bill shrugged and went back to fiddling with his suspenders.

I hopped down from the risers and pushed my way through the crowd to the wall where the cuckoo clock hung.

The cord dangled to the ground, clearly not plugged in. "Who did this? Who plugged it in then unplugged it?"

Pete leaned on his pool cue. "Ain't no one touched it, I promise. I've been standing here this whole time waiting for this jackass to take his shot."

Greg elbowed Pete, and I stepped closer to look deep into his eyes. Pete's wide brown eyes suggested he was telling the truth.

"All right, Ginger," I bellowed to the heavens. "You want to hear the song? We'll give you the song."

My fingers froze above the keys.

I couldn't do it.

I squeezed my fingers together into fists and tried again.

My fingers hovered over the piano, but they refused to strike. Instead I closed the cover over the keys and stood. I jumped down from the risers, and the eerily quiet crowd parted like the

Red Sea before Moses. I only made it as far as the door before my Happy Hour Choir started the singing for me.

"Far away the noise of strife upon my ear is falling."

I turned. Mac and the Gates brothers had stepped up on the risers. Sam and Tiffany stood in front, his arm draped around her shoulders.

"Then I know the sins of earth beset on every hand."

To my side, Luke joined in with an even baritone. John the Baptist sang from somewhere in the corner.

"Doubt and fear and things of earth in vain to me are calling."

Miss Lottie's abrasive soprano rose above the other voices, but seemed to be what the crowd needed to join in, a reminder that what's in our hearts is more important than the perfection with which we sing.

"None of these shall move me from Beulah Land."

I paused and nodded to the crowd around me, tears blurring my vision and my throat too closed up to join them.

"I'm living on the mountain, underneath a cloudless sky."

"Praise God," whispered Mac.

"I'm drinking at the fountain . . ."

A silent wave of red plastic cups lifted to the ceiling.

". . . That never shall run dry. Oh, yes, I'm feasting . . ."

Luke's arms slipped around me, and I leaned into him.

". . . On the manna from a bountiful supply."

The crowd turned to look at us, and my Happy Hour Choir finished almost at a whisper.

"For I am dwelling in Beulah Land."

I turned and buried my face in Luke's chest, inhaling his scent and memorizing the feel of his arms around me. Ginger had always said one reason why it was so important to be a member of a church was that community picked up where you had to leave off, holding you up when you felt like lying down. I felt like crumpling up in the corner, but they weren't going to let me. Luke would never let me.

"I think I need to be alone for a while," I managed to choke out.

Luke nodded.

I meant to give him an innocent peck on the cheek, but that wasn't enough for good-bye. Instead, I put a hand on either side of his face, running my thumbs against his smooth cheeks. I pulled his face down to mine and pressed my lips against his, a light touch but enough. Then I slipped out the door, wondering if I would ever be back.

Chapter 34

Only one sealed envelope remained: mine. Tiffany had opened hers immediately; so had Sam and Bill. I didn't know if Luke had opened his because I had been studiously avoiding him since the funeral and wake. I hadn't left the house. I hadn't showered. And Tiffany had learned very quickly not to question me on any of those points.

Seven days after Ginger's funeral, smack-dab in the middle of December, Luke Daniels knocked on my door. Tiffany had already gone to work so I ignored him.

"I know you're in there," he said.

"Go away."

"We've missed you at church." His shadow shifted from one side to the other. "I've missed you."

I got up and walked to the door. There was no easy way to have the conversation we were about to have, so it was best to go ahead and get it over with. I opened the door, and he came in. He crushed me to his body and planted kisses on the top of my greasy head. "I've missed you so much, and I've been so worried about you. Why won't you answer any of my calls?"

I couldn't meet his eyes. "I don't want to see you."

"Beulah Land, didn't you say less than a month ago that you loved me?"

"Yes." *In a moment of weakness.*

"Didn't I tell you that I love you?"

"Yes." *But only your God knows why.*

Something behind his eyes shifted from Luke the man to Luke the minister. "We need to support each other. We need to pray for strength and understanding."

My rage boiled over. "And that's why I haven't called you."

Later, my therapist would tell me this episode demonstrated how denial had moved to anger and that my rage was a perfectly natural part of the grieving process. I told her I didn't care much about process. I was pissed off, and it had been a long time coming.

"I love you, Luke, but I can't do this preacher's girlfriend thing. I played piano for the church. I went to Bible study. I even started praying, sometimes about big stuff like Tiffany or Ginger, and sometimes about small stuff like making sure that the dressing came out right on Thanksgiving."

"Stop." Luke held out one of his carpenter's hands. I wanted to take that hand in mine, to lace my fingers through his. Instead, I put my hands against my sides and let them curl into fists.

"No, I will not stop! God hates me, so I don't see why I shouldn't hate Him back."

And those, ladies and gentlemen, are fighting words for a preacher.

"Beulah, you sit down and you listen for a minute," he said. He tried to lead me to Ginger's chair, but at the sight of her empty chair, I wrenched my wrists from his grasp.

"No! No more listening. I don't want to hear another sermon. I don't want to sing another song. I want to know why all the people I love have to die. And I want to know why I had to be raped and why Tiffany had to play house with her stepdaddy. I want to know why doing something supposedly good, like a Bible study, had to run Bill out of business. And I want to know why pregnant mommas lose their babies and why in the hell something as ugly and painful as cancer has to exist."

I panted. I was hoarse.

"Beulah—"

"It's not fair. I did the right thing. I kept that baby even though I didn't want him, even though it wasn't really my mistake. And just when I learned to love him and to want him, he was taken away from me. You tell me how that could possibly be fair."

Luke tried to pull me into his embrace, but I pushed him away.

"And I came to this house because my momma kicked me out. I learned to love and respect Ginger, and what happened to her? She got cancer. I helped her through that as best I could even though I was still hurting over losing Hunter. You ever been a caregiver to someone with cancer, Luke? You ever shuttled someone back and forth on two-and-a-half-hour trips to the hospital with every muscle in your body stiff because you're straining to make sure they're still breathing? You ever cleaned vomit out of places you didn't know could get vomit in them? You ever seen a chemo port, how nasty it looks? You ever been with someone when they get a mastectomy? Looked at flatness and scars and skin that stretched flat over ribs? I was with the world's sweetest lady while she experienced pain and nausea and lost her hair and did it all without one single, solitary complaint. And I wished every day I could take her place because the pain of the treatment would have to be better than sitting beside her and holding her hand and knowing it was the only damn thing I could do for her."

"Are you about done?"

"What kind of cruel joke was it to have me get all the way to Nashville, to get so close, only to have to drive back? She wanted to live to see Tiffany's baby. She was *supposed* to live long enough to see Tiffany's baby! And I didn't even get to tell her good-bye or that I loved her one last time."

"Stop!" He took me in his arms. I tried to beat him away with my fists because he was the enemy. He was a man of the church, a representative of how I was supposed to meekly accept the skewed injustices of my life. But he grabbed my wrists and he pulled me tight and let me cry.

When I had no more energy to scream or cry, I looked up at him and said the stupidest thing I have ever said in my entire life: "Luke, I think you need to go now."

"I'm not leaving," he murmured into my hair.

"No. I'm done. I thank you for everything you've done for me, for Ginger, for Tiffany. And I love you, but I can't be with you. It's not fair to you, and it's not fair to me."

Ever the preacher, he added, "I know you feel this way now, but—"

"No, there is no but. Not this time. Because right now I hate your God."

He kissed me on the forehead, on one cheek then the other. "Your God still loves you. And I do, too."

"Get out before I start hating you, too!"

He stiffened at that, but he kissed me on top of the head once more and walked out the door.

Chapter 35

I couldn't sit in Ginger's chair, so I took the box of Kleenex and sat on the floor using one after another until the box was empty. Then I threw the empty box against the wall and went to the kitchen pantry to get more.

But I stopped by the oven.

I could put my head in an oven.

My eyes traveled to the knife drawer. Ginger had always sharpened her knives until the old blades were razor thin.

Then my gaze settled on the basket full of prescription drugs. There had to be enough pain pills left to kill a horse.

No heat, no blood, just blessed oblivion.

And what would go well with blessed oblivion? I took Ginger's whiskey from its new hiding spot in the pantry and poured a couple of fingers into a coffee mug printed with cardinals. I lifted the mug in salute and took my first swig before rummaging in the pill basket for the best chaser.

Then Tiffany slammed the front door so hard two of the panes of glass fell out and shattered on the front porch. Cold air whipped in behind her.

"Beulah Land!" she bellowed.

I waltzed into the living room with my drink.

"You're home early," I said with a sniff.

"Of course, I'm home early. I had to come home and deal with you." She stood with her hands on her hips, her nine-month-pregnant belly sticking straight out in front of her. Her brown eyes burned in narrow fury, and red splotches of rage covered her face and chest. I noticed, with some glee, that her blond roots were showing, since she couldn't keep dying her hair my shade of red while she was pregnant.

Good, you don't need to look like me.

"What have I ever done to you? Other than take you in and clothe and feed you?" I regretted the words as soon as I said them. Ginger had never said words like those to me, and I'd deserved far worse than Tiffany.

"It's not about what you've done to me. It's about what you've done to Luke."

"What? The favor of telling him to find a girlfriend who actually believes in God?" I gulped down the rest of my drink, thankful for the fire in my throat and the dizzy, queasy sensation in my head and belly.

"And to think I wanted to be just like you."

My blood ran cold even as my gullet burned hot.

She shifted her weight from one foot to the other, grimaced, and placed a hand on her belly. "I thought you were smart, smart enough to take care of me and Ginger. Frickin' brilliant on the piano and kind to people, especially the ones folks ignore. Then you find someone like Luke, and you have the gall to spit in his face."

"Maybe I told him to get away from me because I'm a magnet for disaster. Maybe bad things always happen to the people I love, so if I were you, I'd get to packing. Maybe I need to declare that I hate you just to keep you alive." I threw my mug against the front door, and it shattered. "There, I hate you, Tiffany Davis, now get out of here before something happens to you or—or—or—or . . . to the baby."

Tiffany looked at the mess behind her then back at me, the mess in front of her. "*You* are a drunken idiot. Get yourself together. Read the damn letter."

"I don't want to read the letter. Who knows what Ginger's going to ask me to do in that damn letter. And there is nothing I can do to bring her back."

"Did you ever stop to think for one single, solitary minute that Miss Ginger didn't want to come back? Did you ever think that Miss Ginger might be happier where she is? Well, you would know the answer if you read the letter. Of course, you're too busy being a chicken to do that."

Then Tiffany folded her arms and clucked like a chicken. I was about to laugh at the ridiculous sight of a pregnant woman clucking and flapping her wings like a chicken, but her water broke.

"Oh," she said as she looked down at the reddish clear liquid trickling down her legs.

"We've got to get you to the hospital," I said. I reached for the car keys from where they hung on the hook inside the kitchen.

She took the keys. "*You* aren't driving anyone anywhere. I'll drive myself to the hospital, and *you* will sit here until you sober up. This conversation isn't over yet, by the way. Read your letter while you wait."

"I'm not reading that damn letter."

She looked up from the drawer where she'd gathered an armload of kitchen towels. "Miss Ginger was right. You are the most stubborn person on the face of the planet."

Clutching her stack of kitchen towels with as much dignity as she could muster, she crunched her way over a sea of broken glass in front of the door then another on the other side of the door. Her calmness in the face of our argument and her broken water was surreal, but she slammed the front door behind her, which caused me to jump and sent another pane of glass tinkling to the porch to shatter.

I took a shower, drank a half a pot of coffee, then called Mac to ask for a ride to the hospital. Tiffany had taken the Caddy, and the Toyota wouldn't crank. He agreed to give me a ride, but he gave me the cold shoulder all the way there. He wasn't pleased with me, either. I couldn't tell if it was for leaving the Happy Hour Choir, my meltdown at Ginger's wake, leaving Luke, or all of the above.

I wondered how Mac and Tiffany had found out so quickly that Luke and I had split. But, of course, Luke would have gone to The Fountain to calmly tell everyone I'd quit the choir. He had a good poker face, but they could have easily deduced the rest or even asked him point-blank questions he wouldn't have lied about.

Mac's pickup sputtered in the drop-off lane of the Women's Center portion of the hospital. "Sure hope you know what you're doing."

"Don't have a clue. Thanks for the ride."

He nodded and drove off. His truck backfired then belched exhaust.

I kept expecting someone to stop me on the way to the waiting room, but they didn't. The first person I saw when I walked through the door was, of course, Luke.

I swallowed hard and sat down a few seats away from him.

"That should be you in there with her, you know."

"I know." I picked up a magazine. "She's not real happy with me at the moment."

"I don't think many people are," he said with a sigh.

We both looked up to see *It's a Wonderful Life* on television. I smiled.

"You like *It's a Wonderful Life*?"

My smile twisted bittersweet. "I loved it, but Ginger hated it."

Luke couldn't resist. "Why?"

"She said it might've been better if Jimmy Stewart had jumped off the bridge already."

"Better or easier?"

"Whatever."

"That doesn't sound like Miss Ginger at all," Luke said. Realization dawned in his blue eyes. "You haven't read your letter."

I scowled and said several words better suited to the delivery room than the waiting room. Fortunately, there were no children there at eight o'clock at night. "What is it with you and Tiffany and this letter business? What could Ginger possibly have to say that I haven't already heard?"

"Maybe some things you still need to hear."

Before I could respond to that, Sam burst through the doors into the waiting area, his eyes wide with panic. "Beulah, thank goodness you're here. Tiffany kicked me out, said she'd do it alone if she had to."

"No need for that." I didn't tell either of the two men I had done it alone because I'd been too stupid and too stubborn to let Ginger come with me. Knowing now what I didn't know back then, I would hold my worst enemy's hand through labor rather than let anyone else birth a baby by herself.

Sam grabbed my hands as I went to pass him. "Thank you, thank you."

I looked away. He had too much trust in his eyes, and I knew only too well how thin and fragile life felt in those moments when you hung in the balance for the audacity of trying to create a new life all your own. I barreled through the double doors down the imposing hall lined with tall doorways and stopped the first nurse I saw. "Excuse me, I'm looking for Tiffany Davis?"

"I want an epidural. *Now*." Her voice was an unearthly growl, but I still knew Tiffany when I heard her.

"Never mind," I said with a smile. The voice had come from two doors down, and I walked with purpose, pausing for a moment before I stepped into the small birthing room. As my eyes blinked to adjust, I took in the lower lighting, the comfortable décor. The hospital had come a long way since my stint there.

"Beulah, thank God. Tell this woman to—" Tiffany's face screwed up in agony, and she held her breath as the contraction gripped her. Obviously, she hadn't paid any attention in Lamaze class, either. Pain washed away, and she panted for a second as she reached for the thought the contraction had displaced. "—get me a damned epidural."

The woman at the foot of Tiffany's bed looked as though she could stand serenely through a hurricane. I could picture her in hemp clothing with a flower in her hair, a true earth mother. "Tiffany, you're already four centimeters dilated, which is really good for a first-time mother, and the epidural could slow your labor. Are you—"

"Get. Her. The epidural. Now."

I like to think I channeled Ginger Belmont to get Earth Mother moving.

"Beulah, thank God." Tiffany grunted and clamped down on my hand as another contraction rippled through her. She panted in its wake. "She's the nurse midwife. If I'd known she was all about natural birth, I would have waited for the doctor on call to get out of his emergency C-section. Hell, at this point, I would take an emergency C-section."

Regret washed over me. I should have gone with Tiffany to her classes. I should have made sure she knew all of the doctors and what they favored. But I had been selfish because I hadn't wanted to relive any of this. I tamped down my panic. I had done this part just fine, so I could help Tiffany get the baby into the world. After that, she was on her own.

I stood beside her for another few minutes, holding her hand and mentally coaching her to breathe deeply and evenly.

"Beulah!"

She was going to break every bone in my hand if the anesthesiologist didn't get there soon. I gritted my teeth. Giving up piano was the least I could do, considering some of the things I'd said to her.

"How did you do this?" Tears streamed down her cheeks. "I don't want to do this."

"Darlin', you don't have a choice at this point," I said as I pushed a strand of hair away from her face. "Truth be told, that's how most of us get through childbirth: There comes a point where you don't have any choice."

She nodded bravely.

"Hello, ladies!" The anesthesiologist breezed into the room. He explained the procedure to Tiffany then pushed me to the side. When Tiffany gave me a questioning look, I nodded that it was just as I had done before. She hunched over the side of the bed, her profile noble with teeth gritted and eyes determined. I couldn't bear watching the needle, so I watched Tiffany's knuckles turn white instead.

"You did a fabulous job," the anesthesiologist murmured. "Now it will be a lot easier for your sister to take care of you," he added with a wink.

I stepped tentatively over to Tiffany's side.

"Now, I can be mad at you again," she said with a sigh. "Sis."

I shrugged off the "Sis," but it secretly pleased me. "You have every right to be mad at me," I said. "But what say we have a baby now, and you can be mad at me later?"

She turned those wide brown eyes on me, and I saw fear for the first time. "Please?"

"Of course," I said, forcing a smile to my face. "But I want to know how Sam got kicked out."

She shook her head from side to side. "That midwife heifer was carrying on about all of my pain-relief options, and she finished up talking about the miracle of natural childbirth. She had Sam scared to death of complications and groggy babies, and he had the gall to agree with her. He thought I should 'give it a try.' He had to go."

I chuckled.

"It's not funny. Besides, he was white as a sheet and looked like he was about to toss his cookies."

"Well, do you want me to go get him now that you've had the epidural?"

"No!"

I took a step back.

"I mean, no, please don't." Tiffany sighed and shifted, struggling with the lack of feeling in her lower body. "I don't want him to see me like, well, you know."

I nodded. I knew. I had given birth to Hunter all by myself because I hadn't wanted anyone to see me splayed up on a table, not even Ginger. If I could have done it without the doctor and three nurses between my legs, I would have given that a try.

"Maybe if we really do get married," she said. "When he's already promised for better or worse." Her brown eyes locked with mine, and her mouth twisted into a little smile.

"I think that's a great idea," I said, heartened by her "if." I loved Sam dearly, but my baggage had a similar pattern to Tiffany's, and I didn't want her to be in too big a hurry. "Do you want me to at least let him know that you're doing okay now that you have the epidural?"

"Oh!" She sat up on her arms before she thought about what she was doing. "I suppose he might be worried about me, huh?"

"D'ya think?"

"Yeah, go tell him I'm fine," she said as she gently lay back. "I think I'll take a catnap."

"That's a good idea," I said as I patted her shoulder.

"Beulah?" she said when I reached the door.

"Yeah?"

"Could you send in Luke for a second? To say a prayer, you know?"

"Sure. Anything else you need?"

"Hurry back?"

I smiled. "You know I will."

She lay back and closed her eyes, happy to let her body do all the work while she was oblivious to everything happening below her waist.

Chapter 36

Sure enough, Sam was trying his best to pace a hole in the floor, and Luke frowned at him, not quite sure how to comfort him.

"Sam, have a seat and calm down," I said as I pushed through the double doors.

He sat down then popped back up. "Is the baby here?"

"No, the baby is not here, but Tiffany did get her epidural. She wanted me to let you know she's fine now."

He sat down slowly but popped up again. "And not in so much pain?"

Define pain.

"No, she's going to be fine now that she's got the epidural." I walked over and reached up to put a hand on his shoulder, pushing him back down to the seat.

"And I told her not to get the epidural." Agony twisted his features. "I was so confused, and the midwife was talking about the baby being groggy and what was best for the mother and—"

I put a hand on his other shoulder. "It's okay. Everything is going to be okay."

"Is she still mad at me?"

"Honey, she was mad at the whole world there for a while. She's not in pain anymore, and I'm going to go hold her hand through the rest. It's all going to be fine."

He reached up and put a strong hand over mine. “Thank you. She was afraid you wouldn’t come, you know.”

His words cut me to the core, but I wasn’t about to show it. “You need to cut a woman a lot of slack while she’s having a baby. How many more times do I have to tell you it’s all going to be fine?”

Now, if only I could believe my own words.

He nodded, and I felt Luke’s eyes boring through me. I released Sam’s shoulders and stood up straight. “Hey,” I said, willing my eyes not to seek his. “Tiffany wants you to come say a prayer, if you don’t mind.”

I told myself not to look at him, but I did. His eyes were windows to an old, tired soul. His lips twisted into an expression that said he didn’t necessarily believe everything was going to be okay. “I can do that.”

I plopped down beside Sam and watched Luke go. I had disillusioned a preacher and pissed off a pregnant lady to the point of sending her into labor. It really was a banner day.

The epidural did, indeed, slow Tiffany’s labor—not that we were about to tell Earth Mother she was right. Still, she managed to make nine centimeters in another six hours, far quicker than any previous record.

“Okay, Tiffany, it’s time to push.” Earth Mother had everyone arranged to her liking and was seated at Tiffany’s feet looking at a fully crowned head. I looked away. There was a reason I had requested *not* to have a mirror for me to witness the miracle of birth. It was a miracle I had just as soon leave a mystery.

“How do I do that? I can’t feel anything.” Tiffany’s frantic eyes locked with mine, and I felt rather than saw Earth Mother’s mouth open to give a “gentle” I-told-you-so. My head turned so I was speaking to her instead of to Tiffany. “Close your eyes and do your best. After a couple of tries, you’ll get the hang of it.”

Earth Mother closed her mouth.

Tiffany grunted, a good sign, even if Earth Mother’s mouth was still pressed into a thin line that indicated a lack of progress.

I gently put my hand at the top of Tiffany's pregnant belly. "In your mind, push from here. Then the baby's gotta go down, right?"

Earth Mother glared at my lack of understanding of the birthing process, but Tiffany closed her eyes and started pushing.

I glanced between Tiffany's legs in spite of myself and saw some progress.

"There we go," Earth Mother soothed. Nurses moved in a flurry around her, taking towels and replacing them. "Keep doing what you're doing."

Tiffany's eyes popped open with wonder. "I can feel it!"

"Good, good," Earth Mother said. "Now push harder."

"Harder?" Tiffany looked to me for confirmation.

"The harder you push, the sooner this is over."

She tilted her chin and put on her game face. Twenty minutes later, she'd given birth to a bright pink, screaming baby girl. The nurses shifted from mother to baby as they placed the newborn under a lamp and suctioned, bathed, and poked her for their tests. Finally, they gently swaddled the child and brought her to Tiffany.

Relief washed over me as I watched her cradle the blond-tufted baby with dark blue eyes. My own eyes filled with tears. This was the magic moment, the moment you started to forget about the pains of labor. I closed my eyes, and I remembered looking down into Hunter's serious little old man face. He might have been grunting like a Pekingese, but his eyes showed such trust. I hadn't deserved such trust. I hadn't been able to keep him safe.

"So, they say I need to try to nurse her," Tiffany said. She couldn't take her eyes off her baby, but a blush crept up her cheeks nonetheless.

I snapped back to reality. "It's just me. I have boobs." I looked around at a room full of women. "Hey, we all have boobs in here. Get to nursing or I'll start singing the Ruth Wallis song."

She stared through me, so I sang, "You need boobs to hold out a sweater. . . ."

"That's enough."

I helped her pull the gown to the side and to get the baby situated. The baby girl struggled at her mother's breast, her little arms flailing. Her mouth rooted around, but she couldn't quite get the concept.

"Why won't—"

"Like all things, it takes time," I said. I forced my eyes to hold hers. I wouldn't think of the irony that was having sore, engorged breasts at Hunter's funeral. He had finally started to nurse well when—

No, I would not think of death at a time like this.

Earth Mother said nothing. She had been taking care of the afterbirth and the stitches. Tiffany didn't really want to know how many, best I could tell. "You can try again in a little while," she said, and, for the first time that night, I was grateful for her calm, soothing nature.

Tiffany nodded and looked down at her baby and back up at me. "Wanna hold her?"

My arms ached to hold her. "Sure."

A nurse darted around the side and took the baby, smiling down at her, before handing her to me. Tiffany shuffled to get her gown straight.

"What are you going to name your beautiful baby girl?" Earth Mother asked.

I looked at the bright, alert, surreal blue eyes of the beautiful baby with Tiffany's pointed chin. It didn't matter what her name was because she was beautiful. *Lord, please take care of this one. I don't care what else you do to me, but please, please take care of this little one.*

She got one tiny arm free from the blanket and waved it around with grunts and a yawn.

"I'm going to call her Beulah Ginger," Tiffany said with a voice that dared me to argue with her.

"Oh, that's . . . an unusual name," Earth Mother said. I snorted because I'd already envisioned Earth Mother's children as Timberline, Moonbeam, and Ragweed.

"Well, congratulations, Miss Davis, you did well," Earth Mother said before floating from the room.

I turned to the window to hide my tears as I lightly bounced the baby. "I can't tell you how touched I am you want to name her after me, but don't saddle her with the name Beulah."

Tiffany sat up as though she was going to reclaim her baby. "That's going to be her name, and that's—"

"You know how Ginger always called me Beulah Lou? How about Ginger Louise?"

Tiffany's eyes misted over. "My grandmother's name was Louise. Ginger Louise. I like that."

I didn't tell Tiffany that Louise wasn't my real middle name; it was my middle name as far as Ginger was concerned and that was enough for me.

Tiffany half laughed and half cried as I handed the baby back to her. "I think she looks like a Ginger Lou."

"Oh, let's hope for your sake she doesn't act like one."

Tiffany extended her other arm to give me a hug. "If she turns out anything like you and Miss Ginger, she's going to be A-OK. Especially with her aunt Beulah to keep her straight."

It was my turn to wipe away a few tears.

She grasped my hand. "Now would you please go home and read that letter?"

"I don't know." I squeezed her hand. "Maybe."

"I need you to get my overnight bag, anyway. I forgot it."

"I will definitely get your bag. How about that?"

"It's in the nursery," she said with an apologetic smile.

I gritted my teeth. "I will get your bag out of the nursery."

"Thanks—the keys to the Caddy are in my jacket over there. Will you go tell Sam I'm ready to see him now?"

"As soon as you try to go to the bathroom," said the only nurse left in the room as she took little Ginger Lou and put her in the clear bassinet under the heat lamp. I resisted the urge to snatch the baby and yell, "She's not an order of fries!"

"So, tell him to give me a few minutes then," said Tiffany as she heaved herself to sitting and let the nurse help her to the bathroom. "That'll give him enough time to get me a hamburger."

I grinned at her retreating back and turned to little Ginger. My heart melted for the blond, red-faced little girl with her mother's determined chin. "You're one lucky little girl, Ginger Lou, did you know that?"

Sam had resumed his pacing routine, but Luke was gone. My heart pitched at the thought that I'd scared him off.

"Ginger Louise is here. She weighs seven pounds, five ounces, and her mother would like to see you just as soon as you go get her a hamburger."

He collapsed into a chair with a goofy grin. "A girl, huh?"

I nodded. "Yep, another troublemaking girl."

He grabbed me into a bear hug before I could protest. "Thank you, Beulah. Thank you so much for being with her. I know she was scared. She didn't want anyone to know, but she was scared."

I wriggled free. "I know, but she's fine now, and you'd better scoot and get that hamburger or she'll have both of our hides."

He jumped to his feet. "I'll get her two hamburgers. And fries! And a sweet tea!"

I watched the lanky guy with the bounce in his step and felt the letter burning a hole in my back pocket. I don't know why I had put it in my back pocket to go to the hospital, but I had been keeping it close because it was the last thing I had of Ginger's. Maybe that's why I was so hesitant to read it, too. Once I read her letter, there would be nothing left of her.

But there would be another Ginger. She wouldn't take the place of my Ginger, but she would grow up with an aunt Beulah. I would see to it. As long as Tiffany would still have me, once the exhausted euphoria of giving birth had worn off.

Maybe I felt ready to conquer the world now that I'd seen Ginger Lou, now that I had seen she was healthy and hearty and going to be fine. A darker part of me whispered I didn't know for sure she was going to be fine, but I tamped that part down. If I allowed myself to think of the worst possibilities, I'd certainly finish going crazy.

Better to open the letter and read it than to think about Ginger Lou in a little pink coffin. I took the letter from my pocket and sat down in the waiting room to read.

Chapter 37

Dear Beulah,

How long did it take you to get around to reading this letter? A couple of days? A couple of months? I'm hoping sooner rather than later because you have been known to fly off the handle and do some spectacularly stupid things.

First, I want you to know I'm fine. I promise you I have gone to be with my Lord and Maker. I can't explain to you how I know these things, but a peace has come over me, and I just know that's how it's going to be.

We've never been so good at expressing our emotions with each other. We've joked, we've yelled, but usually we putter around and hope for the best. I've always regretted I couldn't do a better job of taking care of you after Hunter died because it didn't take long before I was in no condition to take care of myself. But that beautiful baby boy got me through more chemo treatments than you will ever know. I thought of him on many, many scared and lonely nights.

I kept telling myself that, if I did die, at least I

would get to see Hunter again. Knowing I would be with the baby I've missed so much has helped me find my peace. I could never bear to tell you because I knew it would hurt you. You've been hurt too much already in this lifetime, and I've always wanted to spare you any extra.

Beulah, another reason why I had to write this letter is because you would argue with me if I tried to tell you what I'm about to write. So, I want you to behave for once and read the next few lines.

Shit happens.

I don't mean it in a glib way, I mean no matter what we believe, there is evil in this world. Some bad things come from evil. Some bad things come from chance. Some we bring on ourselves through bad decisions. But you know what else?

Good happens.

I've been on this earth longer than you, and I still believe the good outweighs the bad. I still believe there are more good people than bad people—it's just the bad people get all the press. And you? You're a good person. Don't let a few bitter old biddies make you think less of yourself when I've watched you help others the way you do.

This old lady would like for you to think on something: Everything happens for a reason. I can't tell you exactly why or how I know, but when you've lived as long as I have you have a whole life to dissect and think about. Maybe there's a whole pattern there that we mere mortals can't decipher.

Here's what I think. You can take it or leave it, but I hope you'll take it. God sent you to me because you needed someone to take care of you, and I needed someone to keep me from becoming a bitter old drunk. God sent Tiffany to you because you wouldn't judge her, and she could teach you not to be scared anymore.

God sent Luke to all of us to straighten us up even as we taught him to let loose.

But he mainly sent Luke to you so you would finally see how lovable you are and so he would see it's okay to be the man he wants to be. Don't do something stupid to mess that up because he makes you so very happy. You should see his eyes when he's looking at you like you're the only woman in the world.

Now, Beulah Lou, you're going to have to let go of your pain. You can look to God as I always have or you can become a Buddhist monk, but pain and anger will eat you up inside. You're still young, baby doll. I don't care if you listen to your heart, the Holy Spirit, or the rain as long as you keep loving and start living.

Now to do that, you are going to have to set foot into that nursery. You're going to have to step in there and make peace with God. If not for me, then do it for Tiffany. You remember how hard it is to have a little one. She's going to need your help with diaper changes and nighttime feedings. She's going to need you to pace the floors with her those nights the baby's crying and she can't figure out why. You can't help her if you won't walk into the nursery.

Remember how we always fought over It's a Wonderful Life*? Well, life is wonderful. I wouldn't trade one second I had with you or Tiffany. And you, like George Bailey, have touched a bunch of lives for the better. Think of all the other folks you can still touch! I'm only sorry I held you back as long as I did. You're free now to work in Nashville and sing your songs. You're free to get married and go make beautiful babies with Luke.*

To tell you the truth, sometimes I think I have to die just to give you the proper shove out of the nest.

Otherwise, you would've stayed with me out of loyalty, and I would've let you because I'm too lonely and weak to let you go.

Baby girl, I love you. You go out there and be the best Beulah Land you can be. I'll be cheering you on from heaven. And you can bet your bottom dollar, I'll be holding baby Hunter if that's at all the way they do things up there.

Love always,

Ginger

P.S. I meant it when I said I would send rain when you misbehaved. I've got to do something to get your attention. Well, that and I'll get my jollies from watching you fuss over your hair.

Swiping at the silent tears that refused to stop, I folded the letter and put it back in my pocket. In death, Ginger could still chastise me with far more accurate precision than my mother ever had in life.

But pigs will fly before I set foot in that nursery.

Chapter 38

When I pulled into the driveway, the sun should've been up, but dark clouds blocked it out, bathing the world in gray. Not a light shone from the house, but Luke's roadster was parked to the left of the driveway behind my unresponsive Toyota. Thunder rumbled overhead.

I had parked too close to Luke's car, so I had to shimmy out of the Caddy to keep from hitting his car with the door. In the process I bumped my funny bone on something, and my keys went flying.

Letting out a stream of curse words that would have impressed any sailor, I set about finding my keys. No sun, and then the security light clicked off for the day, so I cursed some more.

The upstairs light came on, and a beam shone down to the ground in front of me. There, at the edge of darkness, sat my keys, just under the front fender of Luke's car.

I frowned at the light but snatched up the keys.

Luke had to be up there. Well, anyone could have been up there thanks to the broken panes of glass in the front door, but it had to be Luke. Ever since the Gates brothers had literally scared the pee out of two teenagers who'd tried to TP our yard, I'd seen no one loitering on our street.

I opened the front door with the key. The cardboard I'd thrown up over the missing panes was intact, so Luke must have used the spare key Ginger had given him. I dropped my purse and keys, gently closing the door behind me.

"Luke? Is that you?"

"Up here."

Obviously.

If he cared anything at all for me, he'd leave me alone and let me try to get over him.

Don't do something stupid to mess that up because he makes you so very happy.

Shut up, Ginger.

I climbed the stairs, but I froze when I saw that he had to be in the nursery. I raced to the doorway.

"Get out!" I didn't know I could make such primitive growling noises.

"I'm picking up Tiffany's bag," he said. "She sent me to get it."

You should see his eyes when he's looking at you like you're the only woman in the world.

Dammit, he was.

"But she sent me, too. . . ." Something behind him caught my eye, and I choked back a sob. Frilly curtains and new-to-us furniture rounded out the fully transformed nursery. There, on the border that ran around the center of the room, were pigs. Cartoon pigs dressed as angels flew around the room in a happy parade.

Pigs will fly before I set foot in that nursery.

Luke, handsome Luke, stood in the middle of that frou-frou nursery looking manlier than ever with his dress shirtsleeves rolled up. He took up most of the tiny room with his height and shifted his weight from one leg to the other, uncomfortable in the bright room with animated characters and an abundance of frilly flounces.

"Beulah, are you okay?"

I grabbed the door facing. I couldn't move my head to tell him one thing or another. "I can't make this shit up."

The spot under my breastbone grew warm. Somewhere under

there lay hope and faith, two muscles I hadn't exercised in quite some time, possibly ever. Those feelings swelled, and I could see clearly for the first time ever that chain of events Ginger had been trying to describe.

I couldn't explain why Roy, Sr., had done what he did, but if I hadn't gotten pregnant then I wouldn't have come to live with Ginger. Not only did Ginger help me, but who would have taken her to cancer treatments if I hadn't been there? And how would we have paid the bills the insurance didn't cover without the money from Roy, Sr.?

If I hadn't been playing at The Fountain, I wouldn't have met Tiffany. And she wouldn't have had anywhere to go when she got pregnant. Without Tiffany, I wouldn't have had anyone to help me take care of Ginger, and she wouldn't have had the perfect excuse to set me up on the date with Luke. We might never have given ourselves a second chance without the opportunity to do both Ginger and Tiffany a favor.

And if Ginger hadn't died and if Luke hadn't started his Bible study that half ran The Fountain out of business, I would still be playing piano in a bar instead of looking at the possibility of making a living through music. Ginger was right; I would have clung to her and she would have clung to me. One day I would have looked up to see my whole life had passed me by. It wouldn't have been unhappy, but it wouldn't have satisfied a different ache that lay next to hope and faith, the ache I had for love.

Lightning flashed through the room. The lights flickered and went out. Thunder boomed loud enough to shake the house, and I jumped out of my skin.

There were still painful questions, though. Why did my baby have to die? Why did Tiffany have to suffer and get pregnant? Couldn't I have found a better way to grow up other than to lose Ginger to cancer?

"Beulah, say something so I'll know you're okay." Luke's ragged voice broke me out of my reverie. "Ginger warned me you would need time, but it's killing me to wait for you to come back to me." He dropped Tiffany's bag and opened his arms to me.

And he still hasn't given up on me? Not after all of the nasty things I said?

He swallowed hard. I could barely see his Adam's apple bobbing up and down in the gray light of the nursery. The fine muscles of his jaw flexed as he prepared what he would say next. "I want to love you, Beulah. If you'll let me."

I blinked back tears.

I can't do it. They're all asking too much.

I ran down the stairs and out the door, crunching over the glass that still lay on the floor. I gasped for air as I reached my car, great gulping sobs because I had been holding my breath the whole time I ran through the house.

I couldn't do it. What if I got hurt? What if something happened to Luke? What if we got married and tried to have babies but couldn't? What if we had a baby but lost him as I'd lost Hunter? It was far better to live in practically painless solitude than to risk the deeper pain of giving myself to someone else.

A bolt of lightning hit the tree in the front yard, splitting the branches. Before I could recover from the shock of the maimed tree, thunder crashed and the heavens opened, dumping fat, cold drops that slapped my skin and pinged off the hoods of the cars.

I laughed out loud, a rich, throaty laugh that cleaned out my insides until they ached.

Ginger had met her God, and the two of them were already conspiring against me.

"Fine, I give up!" I yelled into the rain.

"Beulah?" Luke's voice came down from the open window above. I squinted into the rain to see wide eyes, suggesting he thought I might be having that nervous breakdown we had all feared.

"Luke Daniels, I don't know why you love me, but I'm glad you do because I can't seem to stop loving you no matter how hard I try."

He smiled down at me. "Stop trying."

I licked my lips. "I will."

"And get out of the rain."

I didn't have to be told twice. I jumped on the porch and ran through the door and up the stairs. I paused for a minute at the door to the nursery, but Luke stood in the middle of the room, tense but not moving toward me. He knew, maybe Ginger had even told him, that I needed to be able to walk into the nursery before he and I could have a chance.

I took a deep breath and ran into his arms. He kissed me hard, a longing kiss, a kiss that said he was afraid I would change my mind and run back out the door. Finally, I pulled away. "It's okay, Luke. I'm not going anywhere. I don't like it, hardly any of it, but I think maybe I can live with it."

"I don't have all the answers," he said, his eyes earnest. "I'm just a man."

Cupping his face with my hands, I said, "No, you're the best man I know. I don't need you to tell me the answers. I only need the space and time to find them for myself."

I pulled his face toward mine, but he drew away again. "I won't quit my job."

"I'm not asking you to."

We leaned until our foreheads touched and our lips grazed. "I can't promise I'm going back to playing piano at the church," I murmured.

"I won't make you." He drew me closer until our bodies touched. His ragged sigh told me everything I needed to know about his feelings for me. "This won't be easy."

"Nothing worth having ever is," I said as I nuzzled into his chest. "As long as I'm with you, it doesn't have to be."

"No more running off?"

"No more running off as long as you promise not to pontificate."

He chuckled, his chin resting on my head. "But I like to pontificate, and I'm very good at it."

I took a step back. "I'm serious. I've got to find my own way."

"No more pontificating." He smiled as his hands found my shoulders.

"Good. Glad that's settled. Now, kiss me, Preacher Man. A lady I once knew told me to make a sinner out of a saint, and I'm pretty sure she was talking about you."

A READING GROUP GUIDE

THE HAPPY HOUR CHOIR

Sally Kilpatrick

ABOUT THIS GUIDE

The following discussion questions are included to enhance your group's reading of *The Happy Hour Choir.*

Discussion Questions

1. How would *The Happy Hour Choir* change if it were written from Luke's point of view? Ginger's? Or if it included multiple points of view?

2. One of the themes of *The Happy Hour Choir* is family. At one point Beulah says, "Sometimes organizations underestimated the family we had created, somehow thinking it inferior to those defined by shared blood. In my experience, many of the strongest bonds came from those who *chose* to be together." Do you think Beulah, Tiffany, and Ginger make a "real" family? Why or why not?

3. Discuss the relationship between Ginger and Beulah. How does Beulah's relationship with Tiffany differ, and what are the parallels?

4. Is there a scene that made you laugh? Cry? Shake your fist?

5. Do you think Tiffany did the right thing by having the baby? Would you feel the same if Carl had been her actual father instead of her stepfather?

6. Why do you think Luke is attracted to Beulah and vice versa? Do you think their differing beliefs on faith will be a problem for them?

7. In *The Happy Hour Choir* we learn about abuse against female characters. Carl abuses both Tiffany and Beulah. Beulah was raped by Mr. Vandiver. How does that abuse color the story? How did it affect their characters?

8. An actual vow of ordained Methodist ministers is that they are to be faithful in marriage and celibate while single. Do you believe this should be a vow? Why or why not? Do you think Luke will abide by it?

9. What kind of parents do you think the Lands were? Do you think Beulah would've made the same choices if they had been different? Do you feel like Beulah should forgive her mother or try to mend their relationship?

10. Another theme of *The Happy Hour* Choir is to explore why bad things happen to good people. At the end, Beulah sees a series of connections between the good and the bad events in her life. Do you think that God had a hand in all of those events? Did free will play a part? Is life simply a series of events, some good and some bad?

11. Do you think *The Happy Hour Choir* will continue to sing together and finally go on to record their own music with the help of John the Baptist? Would you buy a CD of their work if they did?

12. What parts of *The Happy Hour Choir* are distinctly Southern? Do you think that some of the events could take place in any small town? In a city?

Dressing

(as dictated to my mother by her mother, Lucille Patterson)

Cornbread
Light bread or biscuits
Chicken and broth
Onion
Sage
Eggs
Salt
Celery

Make dressing thin.

Now, let me interpret that for you:

Cornbread (see page 310 for that recipe)

Light bread (about two slices of sandwich bread) and/or biscuits (about four from your own recipe made the night before or from the freezer where you've been collecting extras over the past few months. Thaw those first.)

Pepperidge Farm stuffing mix (about a third of a bag)

Chicken (traditionally a whole one, but we've used anything from chicken picked from the breast to boneless, skinless chicken. It depends on your preference. Mom prefers her dressing sans chicken. Oh, and cook the chicken first.)

Broth (At least two cans, plus a nice cream of chicken OR you can warm the broth with a stick of butter because . . . yes—but not too hot or else it scrambles the eggs.)

Onion (I skip this.)

Sage (I skip this, too, because there's more than enough sage in the Pepperidge Farm Mix.)

Eggs (anywhere from two to four)

Salt (and black pepper)

Celery (No. Just say no. Not in *my* dressing.)

Mix everything together in a bowl. Make dressing thin; the extra liquid will be absorbed. (Depends on how fast you want it to cook. The more liquid you add, the longer it's going to take. I prefer mine fluffier and thus don't make it as thin. Mom prefers hers sloppy and adds onions. These are the little things we squabble about on Thanksgiving Day.)

Other things you need to know that my Granny Patterson left out:

1. Crumble all the bread and stir in the stuffing mix before you start adding liquids. Apparently this was common sense to Granny.
2. Cook at 350 degrees for about 30 minutes, covered. Or longer. Often longer if it's especially sloppy.
3. Dressing cooks best in a well-seasoned cast-iron skillet of the Dutch oven variety. One of those disposable pans from the grocery store will do in a pinch.
4. This recipe is all about adding a little bit of each ingredient at a time and stirring until it "looks" or "feels" right so, um, good luck!

Cornbread, Rowlett Style

(aka the first recipe I learned)

Vegetable oil (a TBSPish)
1/2 cup corn meal
1/4 cup self-rising flour
1/2 cup buttermilk
1 egg

Put oil in a small cast-iron skillet and put the skillet in the oven while it preheats to 450 degrees. Mix all of the remaining ingredients and then pour into skillet once oil is hot. If the batter starts cooking as you pour it in, then you know you did it right. Bake for approximately 15 minutes or until brown—it will get brown on the bottom before it gets brown on the top. Dump bread on plate and serve. Smack the hands of those who pinch off the delectably crunchy crust around the circumference—unless, of course, it's your Daddy.

(When making cornbread for dressing, make it the night before.)